A CASE OF NEED

Michael Crichton was born in Chicago in 1942. His novels include *The Andromeda Strain*, *The Great Train Robbery*, *Congo*, *Jurassic Park*, *Rising Sun*, *Disclosure*, *The Lost World* and *Airframe*. He is also a film director and the creator of the hit television series *ER*.

Also by Michael Crichton

Fiction
The Andromeda Strain
The Great Train Robbery
Eaters of the Dead
The Terminal Man
Congo
Jurassic Park
Rising Sun
Disclosure
The Lost World
Airframe

Non-fiction
Five Patients
Jasper Johns
Electronic Life
Travels

A CASE OF NEED

Michael Crichton

writing as

Jeffery Hudson

ARROW

First published in Arrow in 1995

9 10 8

Copyright © 1968 Jeffery Hudson

The right of Jeffery Hudson to be identified as the
author of this work has been asserted by him in accordance
with the Copyright, Designs and Patents Act, 1988.

First published in the USA in 1969 by Signet,
a division of Penguin Books, USA

This edition published in 1997 by Arrow,
Random House UK Limited,
20 Vauxhall Bridge Road, London SW1V 2SA

Random House Australia (Pty) Limited
20 Alfred Street, Milsons Point, Sydney,
New South Wales 2061, Australia

Random House New Zealand Limited
18 Poland Road, Glenfield
Auckland 10, New Zealand

Random House South Africa (Pty) Limited
Endulini, 5a Jubilee Road, Parktown 2193, South Africa

Random House UK Limited Reg. No. 954009

Papers used by Random House UK Limited
are natural, recyclable products made from wood grown in
sustainable forests. The manufacturing processes conform to
the environmental regulations of the country of origin.

ISBN 0 09 960101 X

Printed and bound in Great Britain by
Cox & Wyman Ltd, Reading, Berkshire

I will prescribe regimen for the good of my patients, according to my judgment and ability, and never do harm to anyone. To please no one will I prescribe a deadly drug, nor give advice which may cause his death. Nor will I give a woman a pessary to procure abortion. But I will preserve the purity of my life and my art. . . .

—FROM THE HIPPOCRATIC OATH
DEMANDED OF THE YOUNG PHYSICIAN
ABOUT TO ENTER UPON THE PRACTICE
OF HIS PROFESSION.

There is no moral obligation to conserve DNA.
—GARRETT HARDIN

A CASE OF NEED: A new introduction

IN 1967, I WAS A SECOND-YEAR medical student at
Harvard Medical school, paying the cost of my
education by writing paperback thrillers under a
pseudonym. My method was to accumulate debts
until my next vacation. Then I would sit down, push
my textbooks aside, and write furiously eighteen
hours a day. I usually produced twenty-five pages of
typescript each day. By the end of the vacation, I sent
the finished manuscript to my publisher in New York
— hoping they would buy it at once, without asking
for revisions. In fact, it was essential that they buy it
immediately, because my term bills were always due;
and it was essential that they accept it without
revision, because the next day I would be back in
classes, and have no time to make any changes.

It was a frantic, rather desperate way to work. But
in retrospect, I have always been glad that my career
began this way, for I was freed from all the burdens
that new writers usually bear.

I didn't agonize over whether I was expressing
myself; I didn't worry about art; I was writing under a
pseudonym, at very high speed. And the usual
concerns about the quality or originality of one's
output were irrelevant since my explicit goal was to be
entirely unoriginal — to write something so perfectly
suited to the paperback market that my publishers

would buy my work without hesitation. I was engaged in a high-pressure exercise where the goal was absolute unoriginality.

My first paperbacks were standard variations on the 1960s cold-war spy story made popular by Ian Fleming. In my novels, the women were all beautiful; the men all drove Ferraris; and nearly everybody carried a gun. These books were great fun to do, in part because they had no connection to my everyday life as a medical student. I suppose it was inevitable that the pressure to produce new stories quickly would lead me to write a novel with a medical setting. The advantages were obvious — no research was required, and I had a great many experiences to draw upon. Some of these experiences troubled me very much: in my student days, I was often provoked to the high moral indignation that often characterizes young people in their twenties.

But it was also true that American medicine in the 1960s was very different from what it is today. Those were the days beore Medicare made physicians rich, and malpractice made them suspicious; before group practices made them interchangeable and proliferating lab tests made them technocrats. In those days, medicine was understood to be a calling. Doctors were revered. The public ranked physicians just below Supreme Court justices.

Perhaps not surprisingly, medicine in the 1960s was a distinctly self-satisfied profession. Problems and abuses often were not seriously addressed. There were only the faintest glimmerings of the ethical issues which would become so prominent in later years.

One issue ignored by medicine in my student days was the problem of abortion, which was then for the most part illegal in the United States. A million American women flew out of the country every year to have an elective abortion. Those who could not afford the plane fare often showed up, septic and bleeding, in hospital emergency rooms. There were abortionists in every city, back-room mills, and whispered addresses passed to frightened women in need — a tawdry, dangerous industry which the medical profession pretended did not exist.

I remember asking a senior physician why the profession did not address the inequities and health hazards of the present situation.

"Abortion is illegal," he replied.

"I know," I said. "It's also medically dangerous and unfair."

"But it's illegal," he said, as if that was all there was to say about it.

I felt there was more to say, and I devised a story that would talk about my concerns. I wrote *A Case of Need* in ten days during spring break. I sent it to my publisher, and received in reply the call I had been dreading for so long.

"We like it," my editor said, "but we want some revisions."

"Oh no," I groaned.

"You don't understand," he said. "This is good news. We want to publish this book in hard cover. But we think it needs some revision first."

"No," I said. "Let's just publish it in paperback, the way we always do."

There was a puzzled silence. "Usually authors *want* their book published in hard cover," he said.

"I don't," I said. "And I don't want to revise it. I'm in school. I have no time."

But in the end, he talked me into rewriting the novel during the summer, and *A Case of Need* was published the following year, in 1968. There was no photo of the author, Jeffery Hudson, identified only as "the pseudonym of an American scientist who was educated in Boston and currently lives in London." (I thought it wise to place the author far from potential interviewers.)

The book caused a small stir in Boston medical circles. All the students read it and asked, "Who is this Hudson guy that knows so much about the Medical School?"

I joined in the conversations. "Yes," I would say. "I wonder who he is?"

But I didn't want anybody to know. Medicine was serious business, and any student who was writing thrillers was obviously not showing proper seriousness.

And I was alarmed when I learned, some months later, that the book had been nominated for an Edgar by the Mystery Writers of America as the best mystery of the year. My agent, Lynn Nesbit, called to say that I would have to go to the banquet to New York and accept if I won. That prospect was horrifying, because it would reveal my identity. I consoled myself with the hope that I wouldn't win.

As luck would have it, I did win. Late one Friday afternoon, I slipped out of the hospital, flew down to

New York, and accepted my award. I was pleased to have an Edgar, but I made a very hasty acceptance speech. I didn't want to be photographed; every flashbulb filled me with dread. For the next few weeks, I lived in a state of panic that word of this honor would somehow get back to my professors in Boston.

But that never happened. Even when the book was sold to the movies, I somehow managed to keep my identity secret. At the same time, it was becoming more difficult for me to conceal what was happening to me — and how I was starting to feel. Now that I was having success as a writer, I found myself thinking seriously of leaving medicine, after I completed my degree. That is what finally happened.

So I feel, in retrospect, a good deal of affection for this little book, despite its all-too-evident shortcomings. It is the work of a young man, not yet twenty-five years old, writing with enthusiasm and considerable haste. Now that *A Case Of Need* is being reissued, I can only beg the reader's indulgence on behalf of this young man and his efforts, a quarter of a century ago.

Michael Crichton
Los Angeles
October 12, 1993

CONTENTS

MONDAY,
October 10
— 3 —

TUESDAY,
October 11
— 133 —

WEDNESDAY,
October 12
— 227 —

THURSDAY,
October 13
— 304 —

FRIDAY–SUNDAY,
October 14–16
— 380 —

POSTSCRIPT,
Monday, October 17
— 388 —

APPENDICES
— 394 —

BMW

CONTINUATION SHEET

best described as a plus four (4+) hypersensitivity reaction, with expiration at
4:23 am. Patient discharged at 4:34.

   Discharge diagnosis:

      1. hemorrhage 2° to spontaneous mis-
         carriage.
      2. systemic anaphylaxis following
         penicillin G administration i.m.

DISPOSITION-
DISCHARGE TO Ward A
date 11/15/—
sign John B Williamson, MD

John B. Williamson, M.D.

JB/ka

MONDAY
OCTOBER 10

ONE

ALL HEART SURGEONS ARE BASTARDS, and Conway is no exception. He came storming into the path lab at 8:30 in the morning, still wearing his green surgical gown and cap, and he was furious. When Conway is mad he clenches his teeth and speaks through them in a flat monotone. His face turns red, with purple blotches at the temples.

"Morons," Conway hissed, "goddamned morons." He pounded the wall with his fist; bottles in the cabinets rattled.

We all knew what was happening. Conway does two open-heart procedures a day, beginning the first at 6:30. When he shows up in the path lab two hours later, there's only one reason.

"Stupid clumsy bastard," Conway said. He kicked over a wastebasket. It rolled noisily across the floor.

"Beat his brains in, his goddamned brains," Conway said, grimacing and staring up at the ceiling as if addressing God. God, like the rest of us,

3

had heard it before. The same anger, the same clenched teeth and pounding and profanity. Conway always ran true to form, like the rerun of a movie.

Sometimes his anger was directed against the thoracic man, sometimes against the nurses, sometimes against the pump technicians. But oddly enough, never against Conway.

"If I live to be a hundred," Conway hissed through his teeth, "I'll never find a decent anes man. Never. They don't exist. Stupid, shit-eating bastards, all of them."

We glanced at each other: this time it was Herbie. About four times a year the blame fell on Herbie. The rest of the time he and Conway were good friends. Conway would praise him to the sky, call him the finest anesthesiologist in the country, better than Sonderick at the Brigham, better than Lewis at the Mayo, better than anyone.

But four times a year, Herbert Landsman was responsible for a DOT, the surgical slang for a death on the table. In cardiac surgery, it happened a lot: fifteen percent for most surgeons, eight percent for a man like Conway.

Because Frank Conway was good, because he was an eight-percenter, a man with lucky hands, a man with the touch, everyone put up with his temper tantrums, his moments of anger and destructiveness. Once he kicked over a path microscope and did a hundred dollars' worth of damage. Nobody blinked, because Conway was an eight-percenter.

Of course, there was scuttlebutt in Boston about how he kept his percentage, known privately among surgeons as the "Kill rate," down. They said Conway avoided cases with complications. They said Conway avoided jerry cases.[1] They said Conway never innovated, never tried a new and dangerous procedure. The arguments were, of course, wholly untrue. Conway kept his kill rate low because he was a superb surgeon. It was as simple as that.

The fact that he was also a miserable person was considered superfluous.

"Stupid, stinking bastard," Conway said. He looked angrily about the room. "Who's on today?"

"I am," I said. I was the senior pathology staff member in charge for the day. Everything had to be cleared through me. "You want a table?"

"Yeah. Shit."

"When?"

"Tonight."

It was a habit of Conway's. He always did his autopsies on the dead cases in the evening, often going long into the night. It was as if he wanted to punish himself. He never allowed anyone, not even his residents, to be present. Some said he cried while he did them. Others said he giggled. The fact was that nobody really knew. Except Conway.

[1] Geriatrics.

"I'll tell the desk," I said. "They'll hold a locker for you."

"Yeah. Shit." He pounded the table. "Mother of four, that's what she was."

"I'll tell the desk to arrange everything."

"Arrested before we got into the ventricle. Cold. We massaged for thirty-five minutes, but nothing. *Nothing.*"

"What's the name?" I said. The desk would need the name.

"McPherson," Conway said, "Mrs. McPherson."

He turned to go and paused by the door. He seemed to falter, his body sagging, his shoulders slumping.

"Jesus," he said, "a mother of four. What the hell am I going to tell him?"

He held his hands up, surgeon-style, palms facing him, and stared at his fingers accusingly, as if they had betrayed him. I suppose in a sense they had.

"Jesus," Conway said. "I should have been a dermatologist. Nobody ever dies on a dermatologist."

Then he kicked the door open and left the lab.

WHEN WE WERE ALONE, one of the first-year residents, looking very pale, said to me, "Is he always like that?"

"Yes," I said. "Always."

I turned away, looking out at the rush-hour traffic moving slowly through the October drizzle. It would have been easier to feel sympathy for Conway if I didn't know that his act was purely for himself, a kind of ritual angry deceleration that he went through every time he lost a patient. I guess he needed it, but still most of us in the lab wished he could be like Delong in Dallas, who did crossword puzzles in French, or Archer in Chicago, who went out and had a haircut whenever he lost someone.

Not only did Conway disrupt the lab, he put us behind. In the mornings, that was particularly bad, because we had to do the surgical specimens and we were usually behind schedule anyway.

I turned my back to the window and picked up the next specimen. We have a high-speed technique in the lab: the pathologists stand before waist-high benches and examine the biopsies. A microphone hangs from the ceiling before each of us, and it's controlled by a foot pedal. This leaves your hands free; whenever you have something to say, you step on the pedal and speak into the mike, recording your comments on tape. The secretaries type it up later for the charts.[2]

I've been trying to stop smoking for the past week, and this specimen helped me: it was a white lump imbedded in a slice of lung. The pink tag attached gave the name of the patient; he was down in the OR now with his chest cut open. The surgeons were waiting for the path dx[3] before proceed-

---

[2] The files containing the history of treatment of patients in the hospital. Called a "chart" because the bulk of the file consists of daily charts of temperature, blood pressure, pulse and respiration, the so-called "vital signs."
[3] Diagnosis.

ing further with the operation. If this was a benign
tumor, they'd simply remove one lobe of his lung. If
it was malignant, they'd take the whole lung and all
his lymph nodes.

I stepped on the floor pedal.

"Patient AO—four-five-two-three-three-six. Joseph Magnuson. The specimen is a section of right
lung, upper lobe, measuring"—I took my foot off
the pedal and measured it—"five centimeters by
seven point five centimeters. The lung tissue is pale
pink in color and crepitant.[4] The pleural surface is
smooth and glistening, with no evidence of fibrous
material or adhesions. There is some hemorrhage.
Within the parenchyma is an irregular mass, white
in color, measuring"—

I measured the lump—"approximately two centimeters in diameter. On cut surface, it appears whitish and hard. There is no apparent fibrous capsule,
and there is some distortion of surrounding tissue
structure. Gross impression . . . cancer of the lung,
suggestive of malignancy, question mark metastatic.
Period, signed, John Berry."

I cut a slice of the white lump and quick-froze it.
There was only one way to be certain if the mass
was benign or malignant, and that was to check it
under the microscope. Quick-freezing the tissue allowed a thin section to be rapidly prepared. Normally, to make a microscope slide, you had to dunk

---

[4] Crepitant means it is crackly and filled with air. This is normal.

your stuff into six or seven baths; it took at least six hours, sometimes days. The surgeons couldn't wait.

When the tissue was frozen hard, I cranked out a section with the microtome, stained the slice, and took it to the microscope. I didn't even need to go to high dry: under the low-power objective, I could see the lacy network of lung tissue formed into delicate alveolar sacs for exchange of gas between blood and air. The white mass was something else again.

I stepped on the floor button.

"Micro examination, frozen section. The whitish mass appears composed of undifferentiated parenchyma cells which have invaded the normal surrounding tissue. The cells show many irregular, hyperchromatic nuclei and large numbers of mitoses. There are some multinucleate giant cells. There is no clearly defined capsule. Impression is primary malignant cancer of the lung. Note marked degree of anthracosis in surrounding tissue."

Anthracosis is accumulation of carbon particles in the lung. Once you gulp carbon down, either as cigarette smoke or city dirt, your body never gets rid of it. It just stays in your lungs.

The telephone rang. I knew it would be Scanlon down in the OR, wetting his pants because we hadn't gotten back to him in thirty seconds flat. Scanlon is like all surgeons. If he's not cutting, he's not happy. He hates to stand around and look at the big hole he's chopped in the guy while he waits for the report. He never stops to think that after he takes a biopsy and drops it into a steel dish, an orderly has to bring it all the way from the surgical wing to the path labs before we can look at it. Scanlon also doesn't figure that there are eleven other operating rooms in the hospital, all going like hell between seven and eleven in the morning. We have four residents and pathologists at work during those hours, but biopsies get backed up. There's nothing we can do about it—unless they want to risk a misdiagnosis by us.

And they don't. They just want to bitch, like Conway. It gives them something to do. All surgeons have persecution complexes anyway. Ask the psychiatrists.

As I went to the phone, I stripped off one rubber glove. My hand was sweaty; I wiped it on the seat of my pants, then picked up the receiver. We are careful about the phone, but just to be safe it gets swabbed with alcohol and Formalin at the end of each day.

"Berry speaking."

"Berry, what's going on up there?"

After Conway, I felt like taking him on, but I didn't. I just said, "You've got a malignancy."

"I thought so," Scanlon said as if the whole path work-up had been a waste of time.

"Yeah," I said and hung up.

I wanted a cigarette badly. I'd only had one at breakfast, and I usually have two.

Returning to my table, I saw three specimens were waiting: a kidney, a gallbladder, and an appendix. I started to pull my glove back on when the intercom clicked.

"Dr. Berry?"

"Yes?"

The intercom has a high pickup. You can speak in a normal voice anywhere in the room, and the girl will hear you. They mount the microphone high up, near the ceiling, because the new residents usually rush over and shout into it, not knowing how sensitive it is. That blasts the ears off the girl at the other end.

"Dr. Berry, your wife is on the telephone."

I paused. Judith and I have an understanding: no calls in the morning. I'm always busy from seven to eleven, six days a week, sometimes seven if one of the staff gets sick. She's usually very good about it. She didn't even call when Johnny drove his tricycle into the back of a truck and had to have fifteen stitches in his forehead.

"All right," I said, "I'll take it." I looked down at my hand. The glove was half on. I stripped it off and went back to the phone.

"Hello?"

"John?" Her voice was trembling. I hadn't heard her sound that way in years. Not since her father died.

"What is it?"

"John, Arthur Lee just called."

Art Lee was an obstetrician friend of ours; he had been best man at our wedding.

"What's the problem?"

"He called here asking for you. He's in trouble."

"What kind of trouble?" As I spoke, I waved to a

resident to take my place at the table. We had to keep those surgical specimens moving.

"I don't know," Judith said, "but he's in jail."

My first thought was that it was some kind of mistake. "Are you sure?"

"Yes. He just called. John, is it something about——?"

"I don't know," I said. "I don't know any more than you do." I cradled the phone in my shoulder and stripped away my other glove. I threw them both in the vinyl-lined wastebasket. "I'll go see him now," I said. "You sit tight and don't worry. It's probably a minor thing. Maybe he was drinking again."

"All right," she said in a low voice.

"Don't worry," I repeated.

"All right."

"I'll speak to you soon."

I hung up, untied my apron, and placed it on the peg by the door. Then I went down the hall to Sanderson's office. Sanderson was chief of the path labs. He was very dignified looking; at forty-eight, his hair was just turning gray at the temples. He had a jowly, thoughtful face. He also had as much to fear as I did.

"Art's in jail," I said.

He was in the middle of reviewing an autopsy case. He shut the file. "Why?"

"I don't know. I'm going to see him."

"Do you want me to come with you?"

"No," I said. "It's better if I go alone."

"Call me," Sanderson said, peering over his half frames, "when you know."

"I will."

He nodded. When I left him, he had opened the file again, and was reading the case. If he had been upset by the news, he wasn't showing it. But then Sanderson never did.

In the hospital lobby I reached into my pocket for my car keys, then realized I didn't know where they were holding Art, so I went to the information desk to call Judith and ask her. The girl at the desk was Sally Planck, a good-natured blonde whose name was the subject of endless jokes among the residents. I phoned Judith and asked where Art was; she didn't know. It hadn't occurred to her to ask. So I called Arthur's wife, Betty, a beautiful and efficient girl with a Ph.D. in biochem from Stanford. Until a few years ago, Betty had done research at Harvard, but she stopped when she had her third child. She was usually very calm. The only time I had seen her upset was when George Kovacs had gotten drunk and urinated all over her patio.

Betty answered the phone in a state of stony shock. She told me they had Arthur downtown, on Charles Street. He had been arrested in his home that morning, just as he was leaving for the office. The kids were very upset, and she had kept them home from school that day, and now what did she do with them? What was she supposed to tell them, for Pete's sake?

I told her to say it was all a mistake and hung up.

* * *

I DROVE MY VOLKSWAGEN out of the doctors' parking lot, past all the shiny Cadillacs. The big cars are all owned by practicing physicians; pathologists are paid by the hospital and can't afford all those glistening horses.

It was 8:45, right in the middle of rush-hour traffic, which in Boston means a life-and-death proposition. Boston has the highest accident rate in the U.S., even higher than Los Angeles, as any EW[5] intern can tell you. Or pathologists: we see a lot of automobile trauma at autopsy. They drive like maniacs; like sitting in the EW as the bodies come in, you think there's a war going on. Judith says it's because they're repressed. Art has always said it was because they're Catholic and think God will look after them as they wander across the double stripe, but Art is a cynic. Once, at a medical party, a surgeon explained how many eye injuries occur from plastic dashboard figurines. People get into accidents, pitch forward, and have their eyes put out by the six-inch Madonna. It happens a lot; Art thought it was the funniest thing he had ever heard.

He laughed until he was crying. "Blinded by religion," he kept saying, doubled over in laughter. "Blinded by religion."

The surgeon did plastic stuff, and he didn't see the humor. I guess because he'd repaired too many punched-out eyesockets. But Art was convulsed.

[5] Emergency ward.

Most people at the party were surprised by his laughter; they thought it was excessive and in rather poor taste. I suppose of all the people there I was the only one who understood the significance of this joke to Art. I was also the only one who knew the great strains under which he worked.

Art is my friend, and he has been ever since we went to medical school together. He's a bright guy and a skilled doctor, and he believes in what he's doing. Like most practicing doctors, he tends to be a little too authoritarian, a little too autocratic. He thinks he knows what's best, and nobody can know that all the time. Maybe he goes overboard, but I can't really knock him. He serves a very important function. After all, somebody around here has to do the abortions.

I don't know exactly when he started. I guess it was right after he finished his gynecology residency. It's not a particularly difficult operation—a well-trained nurse can do it with no problem. There's only one small catch.

It's illegal.

I remember very well when I first found out about it. There was some talk among some of the path residents about Lee; they were getting a lot of D & C's that were positive. The D & C's had been ordered for a variety of complaints—menstrual irregularity, pain, mid-period bleeding—but quite a few were showing evidence of pregnancy in the scrapings. I got concerned because the residents were young and loose-mouthed. I told them right there in the lab that it wasn't funny, that they could seriously damage a doctor's reputation by such jokes. They sobered up quickly. Then I went to see Arthur. I found him in the hospital cafeteria.

"Art," I said, "something's bothering me."

He was in a jovial mood, eating a doughnut and coffee. "Not a gynecological problem, I hope." He laughed.

"Not exactly. I overheard some of the residents say that you had a half-dozen pregnancy-positive scrapings in the last month. Have you been notified?"

Immediately, the hearty manner was gone. "Yes," he said, "I have."

"I just wanted you to know. There might be trouble in the tissue committee when these things come up, and———"

He shook his head. "No trouble."

"Well, you know how it looks."

"Yes," he said. "It looks like I'm performing abortions."

His voice was low, almost dead calm. He was looking directly at me. It gave me a strange feeling.

"We'd better have a talk," he said. "Are you free for a drink about six tonight?"

"I guess so."

"Then meet me in the parking lot. And if you get some free time this afternoon, why don't you have a look at a case of mine?"

"All right," I said, frowning.

"The name is Suzanne Black. The number is AO—two-two-one-three-six-five."

I scribbled the number on a napkin, wondering why he should have remembered it. Doctors remember a lot about their patients, but rarely the hospital number.

"Take a good look at this case," Art said, "and don't mention it to anyone until you talk to me."

Puzzled, I went back to work in the lab. I was up for an autopsy that day, so I wasn't free until four in the afternoon. Then I went to the record room and pulled the chart for Suzanne Black. I read it right there—it wasn't very long. She was Dr. Lee's patient, first admitted at age twenty. She was a junior at a local Boston college. Her CC[6] was menstrual irregularity. Upon questioning, it was revealed that she had recently suffered a bout of German measles, had been very tired afterward, and had been examined by her college doctor for possible mononucleosis. She reported irregular spotting approximately every seven to ten days, but no normal flow. This had been going on for the last two months. She was still tired and lethargic.

Physical examination was essentially normal, except that she had a mild fever. Blood tests were normal, though hematocrit[7] was somewhat low.

Dr. Lee ordered a D & C to correct her irregularity. This was in 1956, before the advent of estrogen

[6] Chief complaint, the term for the medical disorder that brings the patient to seek treatment.
[7] A test of the amount of hemoglobin, or red cells, in the blood.

therapy. The D & C was normal; no evidence of tumors or pregnancy. The girl seemed to respond well to this treatment. She was followed for the next three months and had normal periods.

It looked like a straightforward case. Illness or emotional stress can disrupt a woman's biological clock, and throw off her menses; the D & C reset that clock. I couldn't understand why Art had wanted me to look at it. I checked the path report on the tissue. It had been done by Dr. Sanderson. The write-up was brief and simple: gross appearance normal, micro examination normal.

I returned the chart and went back to the lab. When I got there, I still couldn't imagine what the point of the case was. I wandered around, doing odds and ends, and finally began the work-up on my autopsy.

I don't know what made me think of the slide.

Like most hospitals, the Lincoln keeps path slides on file. We save them all; it is possible to go back twenty or thirty years and reexamine the microscopic slides from a patient. They're stored in long boxes arranged like card catalogs in a library. We had a whole room full of such boxes.

I went to the appropriate box and found slide 1365. The label gave the case number and Dr. Sanderson's initials. It also said in large letters, "D & C."

I took the slide back to the micro room, where we have ten microscopes in a long row. One was free; I slipped the slide onto the stage and had a look.

I saw it immediately.

The tissue was a uterine scraping, all right. It showed a rather normal endometrium in the proliferative phase, but the stain stopped me. This slide had been stained with Zenker-Formalin stain, giving everything a brilliant blue or green color. It was a rather unusual stain, employed for special diagnostic problems.

For routine work, the Hematoxylin-Eosin stain is used, producing pink and purple colors. Almost every tissue slice is stained with H & E, and if this is not the case, the reasons for the unusual stain are noted in the pathological summary.

But Dr. Sanderson had not mentioned that the slide was Zenker-Formalin.

The obvious conclusion was that the slides had been switched. I looked at the handwriting on the label. It was Sanderson's, no doubt about it. What had happened?

Almost immediately, other possibilities came to mind. Sanderson had forgotten to note in his report that an unusual stain was used. Or two sections were made, one H & E, the other Zenker-Formalin, and only the Zenker was saved. Or that there had been some legitimate mixup.

None of these alternatives was particularly convincing. I thought about it and waited impatiently until six that evening, when I met Art in the parking lot and got into his car. He wanted to go someplace away from the hospital to talk. As he drove, he said, "Read the case?"

"Yes," I said. "Very interesting."

"You checked the section?"

"Yes. Was it the original?"

"You mean, was it a scraping from Suzanne Black? No."

"You should have been more careful. The stain was different. That kind of thing can get you into trouble. Where did the slide come from?"

Art smiled thinly. "A biological supply house. 'Slide of normal endometrial scraping.'"

"And who made the switch?"

"Sanderson. We were new to the game, in those days. It was his idea to put in a phony slide and write it up as normal. Now, of course, we're much more refined. Every time Sanderson gets a normal scraping, he makes up a few extra slides and keeps them around."

"I don't understand," I said. "You mean Sanderson is in this with you?"

"Yes," Art said. "He has been for several years."

Sanderson was a very wise, very kind, and very proper man.

"You see," Art said, "that whole chart is a lie. The girl was twenty, all right. And she had German measles. And she had menstrual irregularity, too, but the reason was she was pregnant. She had been knocked up on a football weekend by a guy she said she loved and was going to marry, but she wanted to finish college first, and a baby would get in the way. Furthermore, she managed to get measles during the first trimester. She wasn't a terribly bright girl, but she was bright enough to know what it meant when you got measles. She was very worried when she came to see me. She hemmed and hawed for a while, and then blurted it all out and asked for an abortion.

"I was pretty horrified. I was fresh from my residency, and I still had a little starry idealism in me. She was in a terrible fix; she was a wreck and acted as if the world had collapsed around her. I guess in a way it had. All she could see was her problem as a college dropout, the unwed mother of a possibly deformed child. She was a nice enough girl, and I felt sorry for her, but I said no. I sympathized with her, feeling rotten inside, but I explained that my hands were tied.

"So then she asked me if it was a dangerous operation, to have an abortion. At first I thought she was planning to try it on herself, so I said it was. Then she said she knew of a man in the North End who would do it for two hundred dollars. He had been a medical orderly in the Marines, or something. And she said that if I wouldn't do it for her, she'd go to this man. And she walked out of my office."

He sighed and shook his head as he drove.

"I went home that night feeling like hell. I hated her: I hated her for intruding on my new practice, for intruding on my neatly planned life. I hated her for the pressure she was putting on me. I couldn't sleep; I kept thinking all night. I had a vision of her going to a smelly back room somewhere and meeting a leering little guy who would letch her and maybe even manage to kill her. I thought about my own wife and our year-old baby, and how happy it could all be. I thought about the amateur abortions I'd seen as an intern, when the girls came in bleeding and foaming at three in the morning. And let's face it, I thought about the sweats I'd had in college. Once with Betty, we sat around for six weeks waiting for her period. I knew perfectly well that anybody can get pregnant by accident. It's not hard, and it shouldn't be a crime."

I smoked a cigarette and said nothing.

"So I got up in the middle of the night and fought it out with six cups of coffee, staring at the kitchen wall. By morning I had decided that the law was unfair. I had decided that a doctor could play God in a lot of crappy ways, but this was a good way. I had seen a patient in trouble and I had refused to help her when it was within my power. That was what bothered me—I had denied her treatment. It was just as bad as denying penicillin to a sick man, just as cruel and just as foolish. The next morning, I went to see Sanderson. I knew he had liberal ideas about a lot of things. I explained the whole situation and told him I wanted to do a D & C. He said he would arrange to do the path examination himself, and he did. That was how it all started."

"And you've been doing abortions ever since?"

"Yes," Art said. "When I've felt that they were warranted."

After that, we went to a bar in the North End, a simple place, filled with Italian and German laborers. Art was in a talkative, almost confessional mood.

"I often wonder," he said, "about what medicine would be like if the predominant religious feeling in this country were Christian Scientist. For most of history, of course, it wouldn't have mattered; medicine was pretty primitive and ineffective. But supposing Christian Science was strong in the age of penicillin and antibiotics. Suppose there were pressure groups militating against the administration of these drugs. Suppose there were sick people in such a society who *knew* perfectly well that they didn't have to die from their illness, that a simple drug existed which would cure them. Wouldn't there be a roaring black market in these drugs? Wouldn't people die from home administration of overdoses, from impure, smuggled drugs? Wouldn't everything be an unholy mess?"

"I see your analogy," I said, "but I don't buy it."

"Listen," he said. "Morality must keep up with technology, because if a person is faced with the choice of being moral and dead or immoral and alive, they'll choose life every time. People today know that abortions are safe and easy. They know it isn't a long, tedious, dangerous operation. They know it's simple and they want the personal happiness it can give them. They demand it. And one way or another they get it. If they're rich, they go to Japan or Puerto Rico; if they're poor, they go to the Marine orderly. But one way or another, they get that abortion."

"Art," I said. "It's illegal."

He smiled. "I never thought you had so much respect for the law."

That was a reference to my career. After college, I entered law school and stuck it out for a year and a half. Then I decided I hated it and quit to try medicine. In between, I did some army time.

"But this is different," I said. "If they catch you, they'll toss you in the clink and take away your license. You know that."

"I'm doing what I have to do."

"Don't be an ass."

"I believe," he said, "that what I'm doing is right."

Looking at his face, I saw he meant it. And as time went on, I personally encountered several cases where an abortion was the obvious, humane answer. Art handled them. I joined Dr. Sanderson in covering up in the path department. We fixed things so that the tissue committee never knew. That was necessary because the tissue committee of the Lincoln was composed of all the chiefs of service, as well as a rotating group of six doctors. The average age of the men on the tissue committee was sixty-one, and, at any given time, at least a third were Catholic.

Of course it was not a well-kept secret. Many of the younger doctors knew what Art was doing, and most agreed with him, because he exercised careful judgment in deciding his cases. Most would have performed abortions too, if they had dared.

A few didn't agree with Art and would have been tempted to turn him in if they'd had the guts. Anal retentives like Whipple and Gluck, men whose religion precluded compassion and common sense.

For a long time, I worried about the Whipples and the Glucks. Later on I ignored them, turning away from their nasty knowing glances and pinched, disapproving faces. Perhaps that was a mistake.

Because now Art was down, and if his head rolled, so would Sanderson's. And so would mine.

THERE WAS NO PLACE TO PARK near the police station. Finally I came to a lot four blocks away and walked quickly back to find out why Arthur Lee was in jail.

TWO

WHEN I WAS IN THE ARMY a few years back, I served as an MP in Tokyo, and the experience taught me a lot. MP's were the most unpopular people in the city in those days, during the last phases of the occupation. In our white helmets and uniforms, we represented the final reminders of a tiresome military authority to the Japanese. To the Americans on the Ginza, drunk with sake or whiskey if they could afford it, we represented all that was frustrating or constricting about rigid military life. We were therefore a challenge to anyone who saw us, and more than one of my friends ran into trouble. One was blinded by a knife in the eye. Another was killed.

Of course, we were armed. I remember when we were first issued our guns, a hard-nosed captain said to us: "You have your weapons, now take my advice: never use the gun. You shoot a rowdy drunk, even in self-defense, and you'll find out later his uncle is a congressman or a general. Keep the gun in sight, but keep it in your holster. Period."

In effect we were ordered to bluff our way through everything. We learned to do it. All cops learn to do it.

I remembered this as I faced the surly police sergeant in the Charles Street Station. He looked up at me as if he'd enjoy breaking my skull.

"Yeah? What is it?"

"I'm here to see Dr. Lee," I said.

He smiled. "The little chink's uptight, is he? Too bad."

"I'm here to see him," I repeated.

"Can't."

He looked back at his desk and shuffled the papers on it in a busy, irritable dismissal.

"Would you care to explain that?"

"No," he said. "I wouldn't care to explain that."

I took out my pen and notebook. "I'd like your badge number, please."

"What are you, a funny guy? Beat it. You can't see him."

"You are required by law to give your badge number upon request."

"That's nice."

I looked at his shirt and pretended to write down the number. Then I started for the door.

He said casually, "Going somewhere?"

"There's a phone booth right outside."

"So?"

"It's a shame. I'll bet your wife spent hours sewing those stripes on your shoulder. It takes them ten seconds to get them off. They use a razor blade: doesn't even damage the uniform."

He stood up heavily behind the desk. "What's your business here?"

"I've come to see Dr. Lee."

He looked at me evenly. He didn't know if I could have him busted, but he knew it could be done.

"You his lawyer?"

"That's right."

"Well, for Christ's sake, you should have said so before." He took a set of keys from his desk drawer. "Come on." He smiled at me, but his eyes were still hostile.

I followed him back through the station. He said nothing, but grunted a couple of times. Finally he

said over his shoulder, "You can't blame me for being careful. Murder is murder, you know."

"Yes," I said.

ART WAS LOCKED IN A NICE CELL. It was tidy and
didn't smell much. Actually, Boston has some of the
nicest cells in America. They have to: lots of famous people have spent time in those cells. May-
ors, public officials, people like that. You can't
expect a man to run a decent campaign for reelec-
tion if he's in a lousy cell, can you?

It just wouldn't look right.

Art was sitting on his bed, staring at a cigarette
between his fingers. The stone floor was littered
with butts and ash. He looked up as we came down
the hallway.

"John!"

"You have him for ten minutes," the sergeant
said.

I entered the cell. The sergeant locked the door
behind me and stood there, leaning against the
bars.

"Thank you," I said. "You can go now."

He gave me a mean look and sauntered off, rat-
tling the keys.

When we were alone, I said to Art, "You all
right?"

"I think so."

Art is a small, precise man, a fastidious dresser.
Originally he's from San Francisco from a large
family of doctors and lawyers. Apparently his

mother was American: he doesn't look very Chinese. His skin is more olive than yellow, his eyes lack epicanthic folds, and his hair is light brown. He is very nervous, constantly moving his hands in fluttering movements, and the total effect is more Latin than anything else.

He was pale now and tense. When he got up to pace the cell, his movements were quick and abrupt.

"It was good of you to come."

"In case there's any question, I'm the representative of your lawyer. That's how I got in here." I took out my notebook. "Have you called your lawyer?"

"No, not yet."

"Why not?"

"I don't know." He rubbed his forehead and massaged his eyes with his fingers. "I'm not thinking straight. Nothing seems to make sense. . . ."

"Tell me your lawyer's name."

He told me, and I wrote it in the notebook. Art had a good lawyer. I guess he figured he'd need one, sometime.

"Okay," I said. "I'll call him when I leave. Now what's going on?"

"I've been arrested," Art said. "For murder."

"So I gathered. Why did you call me?"

"Because you know about these things."

"About murder? I don't know anything."

"You went to law school."

"For a year," I said. "That was ten years ago. I almost flunked out, and I don't remember a thing I learned."

"John," he said, "this is a medical problem and a legal problem. Both. I need your help."

"You'd better start from the beginning."

"John, I didn't do it. I swear I didn't. I never touched that girl."

He was pacing faster and faster. I gripped his arm and stopped him. "Sit down," I said, "and start from the beginning. Very slowly."

He shook his head and stubbed out his cigarette. Immediately he lit another, then said, "They picked me up at home this morning, about seven. Brought me in and started questioning me. At first they said it was routine, whatever that means. Then they turned nasty."

"How many were there?"

"Two. Sometimes three."

"Did they get rough? Slap you around? Bright lights?"

"No, nothing like that."

"Did they say you could call a lawyer?"

"Yes. But that was later. When they advised me of my constitutional rights." He smiled that sad, cynical smile of his. "At first, you see, it was just for routine questioning, so it never occurred to me to call one. I had done nothing wrong. They talked to me for an hour before they even mentioned the girl."

"What girl?"

"Karen Randall."

"You don't mean *the* Karen—"

He nodded. "J. D. Randall's daughter."

"Jesus."

"They began by asking me what I knew about her, and whether I'd ever seen her as a patient. Things like that. I said yes, that she had come to me a week ago for consultation. Chief complaint of amenorrhea."

"What duration?"

"Four months."

"Did you tell them the duration?"

"No, they didn't ask me."

"Good," I said.

"They wanted to know other details about her visit. They wanted to know if that was her only problem, they wanted to know how she had acted. I wouldn't tell them. I said that the patient had spoken in confidence. So then they switched tacks: they wanted to know where I was last night. I told them I had made evening rounds at the Lincoln and then taken a walk in the park. They asked me if I had gone back to my office. I said no. They asked me if anyone had seen me in the park that night. I said I couldn't remember anyone, certainly nobody I knew."

Art sucked deeply on his cigarette. His hands were trembling. "Then they started to hammer at me. Was I sure I hadn't returned to my office? What had I done after making rounds? Was I sure I hadn't seen Karen since last week? I didn't understand the point of the questions."

"And what was the point?"

"Karen Randall was brought to the Mem EW at four this morning by her mother. She was bleeding profusely—exsanguinating actually—and was in a state of hemorrhagic shock when she arrived. I don't know what treatment they gave her, but anyway she died. The police think I aborted her last night."

I frowned. It just didn't make sense. "How can they be so sure?"

"They wouldn't say. I kept asking. Maybe the kid was delirious and mentioned my name at the Mem. I don't know."

I shook my head. "Art, cops fear false arrest like they fear the plague. If they arrest you and can't make it stick, a lot of people are going to lose their jobs. You're a respected member of the professional community, not some drunken bum without a penny or a friend in the world. You have recourse to good legal advice, and they know you'll get it. They wouldn't dare charge you unless they had a strong case."

Art waved his hand irritably. "Maybe they're just stupid."

"Of course they're stupid, but not that stupid."

"Well," he said, "I don't know what they've got on me."

"You must know."

"I don't," he said, resuming his pacing. "I can't even begin to guess."

I watched him for a moment, wondering when to

ask the question, knowing that I would have to, sooner or later. He noticed I was staring.

"No," he said.

"No what?"

"No, I didn't do it. And stop looking at me that way." He sat down again and drummed his fingers on the bunk. "Christ, I wish I had a drink."

"You'd better forget that," I said.

"Oh, for Christ's sake—"

"You only drink socially," I said, "and in moderation."

"Am I on trial for my character and personal habits, or for—"

"You're not on trial at all," I said, "and you don't want to be."

He snorted.

"Tell me about Karen's visit," I said.

"There's nothing much to tell. She came asking for an abortion, but I wouldn't do it because she was four months' pregnant. I explained to her why I couldn't do it, that she was too far along, and that an abortion would now require abdominal section."

"And she accepted that?"

"She seemed to."

"What did you put in your records?"

"Nothing. I didn't open a file on her."

I sighed. "That," I said, "could be bad. Why didn't you?"

"Because she wasn't coming to me for treatment, she wasn't becoming my patient. I knew I'd never see her again, so I didn't open a file."

"How are you going to explain that to the police?"

"Look," he said, "if I'd known that she was going to get me arrested, I might have done lots of things differently."

I lit a cigarette and leaned back, feeling the cold stone against my neck. I could already see that it was a messy situation. And the small details, innocent in another context, could now assume great weight and importance.

"Who referred her to you?"

"Karen? I assumed Peter."

"Peter Randall?"

"Yes. He was her personal physician."

"You didn't ask her who referred her?" Art was usually careful about that.

"No. She arrived late in the day, and I was tired. Besides, she came right to the point; she was a very direct young lady, no foolishness about her. When I heard the story, I assumed Peter had sent her to me to explain the situation, since it was obviously too late to arrange an abortion."

"Why did you assume that?"

He shrugged. "I just did."

It wasn't making sense. I was sure he wasn't telling me everything. "Have other members of the Randall family been referred to you?"

"What do you mean?"

"Just what I said."

"I don't think it's relevant," he said.

"It might be."

"I assure you," he said, "it's not."

I sighed and smoked the cigarette. I knew Art could be stubborn when he wanted to. "O.K.," I said. "Then tell me more about the girl."

"What do you want to know?"

"Had you ever seen her before?"

"No."

"Ever met her socially?"

"No."

"Ever helped any of her friends?"

"No."

"How can you be sure?"

"Oh, hell," he said, "I can't be sure, but I doubt it very much. She was only eighteen."

"O.K.," I said. Art was probably right. I knew he usually aborted only married women, in their late twenties and thirties. He had often said he didn't want to get involved with the younger ones, though he did on occasion. Older women and married women were much safer, more closemouthed and realistic. But I also knew that he had recently been doing more young girls, calling them "teeny-bopper scrapes," because he said to do only married women was discrimination. He meant that partly as a joke, and partly not.

"How was she," I said, "when she came to your office? How would you describe her?"

"She seemed like a nice girl," Art said. "She's pretty and intelligent and well poised. Very direct, as I said before. She came into my office, sat down, folded her hands in her lap, and reeled it all off. She used medical terms too, like amenorrhea. I suppose that comes from being in a family of doctors."

"Was she nervous?"

"Yes," he said, "but they all are. That's why the differential is so hard."

The differential diagnosis of amenorrhea, particularly in young girls, must consider nervousness as a strong etiologic possibility. Women often delay or miss their menstrual periods for psychological reasons.

"But four months?"

"Well, not likely. And she'd also had a weight gain."

"How much?"

"Fifteen pounds."

"Not diagnostic," I said.

"No," he said, "but suggestive."

"Did you examine her?"

"No. I offered to, but she refused. She had come to me for an abortion, and when I said no, she left."

"Did she say what her plans were?"

"Yes," Art said. "She gave a little shrug and said, 'Well, I guess I'll just have to tell them and have the kid.'"

"So you thought she would not seek an abortion elsewhere?"

"Exactly. She seemed very intelligent and perceptive, and she seemed to follow my explanation of the situation. That's what I try to do in these cases—explain to a woman why it is impossible for her to have a safe abortion, and why she must reconcile herself to having the child."

"Obviously she changed her mind."

"Obviously."

"I wonder why."

He laughed. "Ever meet her parents?"

"No," I said, and then seeing my chance, "have you?"

But Art was quick. He gave me a slow, appreciative grin, a kind of subtle salute, and said, "No. Never. But I've heard about them."

"What have you heard?"

At that moment, the sergeant came back and began clanking the key into the lock.

"Time's up," he said.

"Five more minutes," I said.

"Time's up."

Art said, "Have you spoken to Betty?"

"Yes," I said. "She's fine. I'll call her when I leave here and tell her you're all right."

"She's going to be worried," Art said.

"Judith will stay with her. It'll be O.K."

Art grinned ruefully. "Sorry to cause all this trouble."

"No trouble." I glanced at the sergeant, standing with the door open, waiting. "The police can't hold you. You'll be out by the afternoon."

The sergeant spit on the floor.

I shook hands with Art. "By the way," I said, "where's the body now?"

"Perhaps at the 'Mem. But it's probably gone to the City by now."

"I'll check," I said. "Don't worry about a thing." I stepped out of the cell and the sergeant locked up behind me. He said nothing as he led me out, but when we reached the lobby, he said, "Captain wants to see you."

"All right."

"Captain's very interested in having a little talk."

"Just lead the way," I said.

THREE

THE SIGN ON THE FLAKING GREEN DOOR SAID HOMI-CIDE, and underneath, on a hand-printed name card, "Captain Peterson." He turned out to be a stiff, burly man with close-cropped gray hair and a terse manner. He came around the desk to shake hands with me, and I noticed he had a limp in his right leg. He made no effort to hide it; if anything, he exaggerated it, allowing his toe to scrape loudly over the floor. Cops, like soldiers, can be proud of their infirmities. You knew Peterson hadn't received his in an auto accident.

I was trying to determine the cause of Peterson's injury and had decided that it was probably a bullet wound—rarely does anyone get cut with a knife in the calf—when he stuck out his hand and said, "I'm Captain Peterson."

"John Berry."

His handshake was hearty, but his eyes were cold and inquiring. He waved me to a chair.

"The sergeant said he hadn't seen you around before and I thought I ought to meet you. We know most of the criminal lawyers in Boston."

"Don't you mean trial lawyers?"

"Of course," he said easily. "Trial lawyers." He looked at me expectantly.

I said nothing at all. A short silence passed, then Peterson said, "Which firm do you represent?"

"Firm?"

"Yes."

"I'm not a lawyer," I said, "and I don't know what makes you think I am."

He pretended to be surprised. "That's not the impression you gave the sergeant."

"No?"

"No. You told him you were a lawyer."

"I did?"

"Yes," Peterson said, placing his hands flat on his desk.

"Who says so?"

"He says so."

"Then he's wrong."

Peterson leaned back in his chair and smiled at me, a very pleasant, let's-not-get-all-excited smile.

"If we had known you weren't a lawyer, you'd never have been allowed to see Lee."

"That's possible. On the other hand, I was not asked for my name or my occupation. Nor was I asked to sign in as a visitor."

"The sergeant was probably confused."

"That's logical," I said, "considering the sergeant."

Peterson smiled blankly. I recognized his type: he was a successful cop, a guy who had learned when to take it and when to dish it out. A very diplomatic and polite cop, until he got the upper hand.

"Well?" he said at last.

"I'm a colleague of Dr. Lee."

If he was surprised, he didn't show it. "A doctor?"

"That's right."

"You doctors certainly stick together," he said, still smiling. He had probably smiled more in the last two minutes than he had in the last two years.

"Not really," I said.

The smile began to fall, probably from fatigue and unused muscles. "If you are a doctor," Peterson said, "my advice to you is to stay the hell away from Lee. The publicity could kill your practice."

"What publicity?"

"The publicity from the trial."

"There's going to be a trial?"

"Yes," Peterson said. "And the publicity could kill your practice."

"I don't have a practice," I said.

"You're in research?"

"No," I said. "I'm a pathologist."

He reacted to that. He started to sit forward,

caught himself, and leaned back again. "A pathologist," he repeated.

"That's right. I work in hospitals, doing autopsies and things."

Peterson was silent for some time. He frowned, scratched the back of his hand, and looked at his desk. Finally he said, "I don't know what you're trying to prove, Doctor. But we don't need your help, and Lee is too far gone to——"

"That remains to be seen."

Peterson shook his head. "You know better than that."

"I'm not sure I do."

"Do you know," Peterson said, "what a doctor could claim in a false-arrest suit?"

"A million dollars," I said.

"Well, let's say five hundred thousand. It doesn't matter much. The point is essentially the same."

"You think you have a case."

"We have a case." Peterson smiled again. "Oh, Dr. Lee can call you as a witness. We know that. And you can talk up a storm using the big words, trying to fool the jury, to impress them with your weighty scientific evidence. But you can't get past the central fact. You just can't get past it."

"And what fact is that?"

"A young girl bled to death in the Boston Memorial Hospital this morning, from an illegal abortion. That fact, straight and simple."

"And you allege Dr. Lee did it?"

"There is some evidence," Peterson said mildly.

"It had better be good," I said, "because Dr. Lee is an established and respected——"

"Listen," Peterson said, showing impatience for the first time, "what do you think this girl was, a ten-dollar doxy? This was a nice girl, a hell of a nice girl, from a good family. She was young and pretty and sweet, and she got butchered. But she didn't go to some Roxbury midwife or some North End quack. She had too much sense and too much money for that."

"What makes you think Dr. Lee did it?"

"That's none of your business."

I shrugged. "Dr. Lee's lawyer will ask the same question, and then it will be his business. And if you don't have an answer——"

"We have an answer."

I waited. In a sense, I was curious to see just how good, just how diplomatic Peterson was. He didn't have to tell me anything; he didn't have to say another word. If he did say more, it would be a mistake.

Peterson said, "We have a witness who heard the girl implicate Dr. Lee."

"The girl arrived at the hospital in a state of shock, delirious and precomatose. Anything she said will constitute weak evidence."

"At the time she said it, she wasn't in a state of shock. She said it much earlier."

"To whom?"

"To her mother," Peterson said, with a grin of satisfaction. "She told her mother that Lee did it. As

they were leaving for the hospital. And her mother
will swear to that."

FOUR

I TRIED TO PLAY IT PETERSON'S WAY. I tried to keep my
face blank. Fortunately you have a lot of practice at
that in medicine; you are trained to show no surprise if a patient tells you they make love ten times
a night, or have dreams of stabbing their children,
or drink a gallon of vodka daily. It is part of the
mystique of the doctor that nothing surprises him.

"I see," I said.

Peterson nodded. "'A reliable witness," he said.
"A mature woman, stable, careful in her judgments. And very attractive. She will make an excellent impression on the jury."

"Perhaps."

"And now that I have been so frank," Peterson
said, "perhaps you would tell me your special interest in Dr. Lee."

"I have no special interest. He is my friend."

"He called you before he called his lawyer."

"He is allowed two telephone calls."

"Yes," Peterson said, "but most people use them
to call their lawyer and their wife."

"He wanted to talk to me."

"Yes," he said. "But the question is why."

"I have had some legal training," I said, "as well as my medical experience."

"You have an L.L.B.?"

"No," I said.

Peterson ran his fingers across the edge of his desk. "I don't think I understand."

"I'm not convinced," I said, "that it is important that you do."

"Could it be you are involved in this business in some way?"

"Anything is possible," I said.

"Does that mean yes?"

"That means anything is possible."

He regarded me for a moment. "You take a very tough line, Dr. Berry."

"Skeptical."

"If you are so skeptical, why are you convinced Dr. Lee didn't do it?"

"I'm not the defense attorney."

"You know," Peterson said, "anyone can make a mistake. Even a doctor."

WHEN I GOT OUTSIDE into the October drizzle, I decided this was a hell of a time to quit smoking. Peterson had unnerved me; I smoked two cigarettes as I walked to the drugstore to buy another pack. I had expected him to be stupid and pointlessly tough. He was neither of those things. If what he had said was true, then he had a case. It might not work, but it was strong enough to protect his job.

Peterson was caught in a quandary. On the one hand, it was dangerous to arrest Dr. Lee; on the other, it was dangerous not to arrest him, if the case seemed strong enough. Peterson was forced into a decision, and he had made it. Now he would stick by it as long as he could. And he had an escape: if things began to go bad, he could blame it all on Mrs. Randall. He could use the familiar line so famous among surgeons and internists that it was abbreviated DHJ: doing his job. That meant that if the evidence was strong enough, you acted and did not care whether you were right or not; you were justified in acting on the evidence.[1] In that sense, Peterson's position was strengthened. He was taking no gambles: if Art was convicted, Peterson would receive no accolades. But if Art was acquitted, Peterson was covered. Because he was doing his job.

I went into the drugstore, bought two packs of cigarettes, and made some phone calls from a pay phone. First I called my lab and told them I'd be gone the rest of the day. Then I called Judith and asked her to go over to the Lees' house and stay with Betty. She wanted to know if I'd seen Art, and I said I had. She asked if he was all right, and I said

[1] This happens a lot in medicine. For example, a patient presents with fever, leukocytosis—increased numbers of white cells—and pain in the right-lower quadrant of the abdomen. The obvious diagnosis is appendicitis. The surgeon may perform an appendectomy only to find that the appendix is normal. But he is vindicated, so long as he is not overhasty, because the evidence is consistent with appendicitis, and delay may be fatal.

everything was fine, that he'd be out in an hour or so.

I don't usually keep things from my wife. Just one or two small things, like what Cameron Jackson did at the conference of the American Society of Surgeons a few years back. I knew she'd be upset for Cameron's wife, as she was when they got divorced last spring. The divorce was what is known locally as an MD, a medical divorce, and it had nothing to do with conventions. Cameron is a busy and dedicated orthopedist, and he began missing meals at home, spending his life in the hospital. His wife couldn't take it after a while. She began by resenting orthopedics and ended by resenting Cameron. She got the two kids and three hundred dollars a week, but she's not happy. What she really wants is Cameron—without medicine.

Cameron's not very happy, either. I saw him last week and he spoke vaguely of marrying a nurse he'd met. He knew people would talk if he did, but you could see he was thinking, "At least this one will understand—"

I often think of Cameron Jackson and the dozen people I know like him. Usually, I think of him late at night, when I've been held up at the lab or when I've been so busy I haven't had time to call home and say I'll be late.

Art Lee and I once talked about it, and he had the last word, in his own cynical way. "I'm beginning to understand," he said, "why priests don't marry."

Art's own marriage has an almost stifling sort of stability. I suppose it comes from his being Chinese, though that can't be the whole answer. Both Art and his wife are highly educated, and not visibly tied to tradition, but I think they have both found it difficult to shake off. Art is always guilt ridden about the little time he spends with his family, and lavishes gifts on his three children; they are all spoiled silly. He adores them, and it's often hard to stop him once he begins talking about them. His attitude toward his wife is more complex and ambiguous. At times he seems to expect her to revolve around him like a trusting dog, and at times she seems to want this as much as he does. At other times she is more independent.

Betty Lee is one of the most beautiful women I've ever seen. She is soft-spoken, gracious, and slender; next to her Judith seems big, loud, and almost masculine.

Judith and I have been married eight years. We met while I was in medical school and she was a senior at Smith. Judith was raised on a farm in Vermont, and is hardheaded, as pretty girls go.

I said, "Take care of Betty."

"I will."

"Keep her calm."

"All right."

"And keep the reporters away."

"Will there be reporters?"

"I don't know. But if there are, keep them away."

She said she would and hung up.

I then called George Bradford, Art's lawyer. Bradford was a solid lawyer and a man with the proper connections; he was senoir partner of Bradford, Stone and Whitlaw. He wasn't in the office when I called, so I left a message.

Finally I called Lewis Carr, who was clinical professor of medicine at the Boston Memorial Hospital. It took a while for the switchboard to page him, and as usual he came on briskly.

"Carr speaking."

"Lew, this is John Berry."

"Hi, John. What's on your mind?"

That was typical of Carr. Most doctors, when they receive calls from other doctors, follow a kind of ritual pattern: first they ask how you are, then how your work is, then how your family is. But Carr had broken this pattern, as he had broken other patterns.

I said, "I'm calling about Karen Randall."

"What about her?" His voice turned cautious. Obviously it was a hot potato at the Mem these days.

"Anything you can tell me. Anything you've heard."

"Listen, John," he said, "her father is a big man in this hospital. I've heard everything and I've heard nothing. Who wants to know?"

"I do."

"Personally?"

"That's right."

"Why?"

"I'm a friend of Art Lee."

"They got him on this? I heard that, but I didn't believe it. I always thought Lee was too smart—"

"Lew, what happened last night?"

Carr sighed. "Christ, it's a mess. A real stinking hell of a mess. They blew it in outpatient."

"What do you mean?"

"I can't talk about this now," Carr said. "You'd better come over and see me."

"All right," I said. "Where is the body now? Do your people have it?"

"No, it's gone to the City."

"Have they performed the post yet?"

"I haven't any idea."

"O.K.," I said. "I'll stop by in a few hours. Any chance of getting her chart?"

"I doubt it," Carr said. "The old man has it now."

"Can't spring it free?"

"I doubt it," he said.

"O.K.," I said. "I'll see you later."

I hung up, put in another dime, and called the morgue at the City. The secretary confirmed that they had received the body. The secretary, Alice, was a hypothyroid; she had a voice as if she had swallowed a bass fiddle.

"Done the post yet?" I said.

"They're just starting."

"Will they hold it? I'd like to be there."

"I don't think it's possible," Alice said, in her rumbling voice. "We have an eager beaver from the Mem."

She advised me to hurry down. I said I would.

FIVE

IT IS WIDELY BELIEVED IN BOSTON that the best medical care in the world is found here. It is so universally acknowledged among the citizens of the city
that there is hardly any debate.

The best hospital in Boston is, however, a question subject to hot and passionate debate. There are
three major contenders: the General, the Brigham,
and the Mem. Defenders of the Mem will tell you
that the General is too large and the Brigham too
small; and the General is too coldly clinical and the
Brigham too coldly scientific; that the General neglects surgery at the expense of medicine and the
Brigham the reverse. And finally, you will be told
solemnly that the house staffs of the General and
the Brigham are simply inferior in training and in-
telligence to those of the Mem.

But on anybody's list of hospitals, the Boston
City comes near the bottom. I drove toward it,
passing the Prudential Center, the proudest monu-
ment to what the politicians call the New Boston.
It is a vast complex of skyscrapers, hotels, shops,
and plazas, with lots of fountains and wasted
space, giving it a modern look. It stands within a
few minutes' lustful walk of the red-light district,

which is neither modern nor new, but like the Prudential Center, functional in its way.

The red-light district lies on the outskirts of the Negro slums of Roxbury, as does the Boston City. I bounced along from one pothole to another and thought that I was far from Randall territory.

It was natural that the Randalls would practice at the Mem. In Boston the Randalls were known as an old family, which meant that they could claim at least one seasick Pilgrim, straight off the Mayflower, contributing to the gene pool. They had been a family of doctors for hundreds of years: in 1776, Wilson Randall had died on Bunker Hill.

In more recent history, they had produced a long line of eminent physicians. Joshua Randall had been a famous brain surgeon early in the century, a man who had done as much as anyone, even Cushing, to advance neurosurgery in America. He was a stern, dogmatic man; a famous, though apocryphal, story had passed into medical tradition.

Joshua Randall, like many surgeons of his period, had a rule that no resident working under him could marry. One resident sneaked off and did; a few months later, Randall discovered what had happened and called a meeting of all his residents. He lined them up in a row and said, "Dr. Jones, please take one step forward."

The guilty doctor did, trembling slightly.

Randall said, "I understand you have gotten married." He made it sound like a disease.

"Yes, sir."

"Before I discharge you from the staff, do you have anything to say in your defense?"

The young doctor thought for a moment, then said, "Yes, sir. I promise I'll never do it again."

Randall, according to the story, was so amused by this reply that he kept the resident after all.

After Joshua Randall came Winthrop Randall, the thoracic surgeon. J. D. Randall, Karen's father, was a heart surgeon, specializing in valvular replacements. I had never met him, but I'd seen him once or twice—a fierce, patriarchal man, with thick white hair and a commanding manner. He was the terror of the surgical residents, who flocked to him for training, but hated him.

His brother, Peter, was an internist with his offices just off the Commons. He was very fashionable, very exclusive, and supposedly quite good, though I had no way of knowing.

J. D. had a son, Karen's brother, who was in medical school at Harvard. A year ago there was a rumor that the kid was practically flunking out, but nothing recently.

In another town, at another time, it might seem odd that a young boy with such a distinguished medical tradition would choose to try and live it down. But not Boston: in Boston the wealthy old families had long felt only two professions were worthy of one's attention. One was medicine and the other was law; exceptions were made for the academic life, which was honorable enough so long as one became a professor at Harvard.

But the Randalls were not an academic family, or
a legal family. They were a medical family, and any
Randall who could, contrived to get himself
through medical school and into a house officer-
ship[1] at the Mem. Both the medical school and the
Mem had, in the past, made allowances for poor
grades when it came to the Randalls, but over the
years, the family had more than repaid the trust. In
medicine, a Randall was a good gamble.

And that was about all I knew about the family,
except that they were very wealthy, firmly Episco-
pal, determinedly public spirited, widely respected,
and very powerful.

I would have to find out more.

THREE BLOCKS FROM THE HOSPITAL, I passed through
the Combat Zone at the corner of Mass and Co-
lumbus avenues. At night it teems with whores,
pimps, addicts, and pushers; it got its name because doctors at the City see so many stabbings
and shootings from this area they regard it as the
location of a limited war.[2]

The Boston City itself is an immense complex of
buildings sprawling over three city blocks. It has
more than 1,350 beds, mostly filled with alcoholics
and derelicts. Within the Boston medical establish-

---

[1] Position as an intern or resident, where one is an M.D. but not licensed
to practice, and still completing education.
[2] Formerly the most violent area in Boston was Scollay Square, but it was
demolished five years ago to make way for government buildings. Some
consider that an improvement; some a step backward.

ment, the City is known as the Boston Shitty because of its clientele. But it is considered a good
teaching hospital for residents and interns, because
one sees there many medical problems one would
never see in a more affluent hospital. A good example is scurvy. Few people in modern America contract scurvy. To do so requires general malnutrition
and a complete abstinence from fruit for five
months. This is so rare that most hospitals see a
case every three years; at the Boston City there are
a half-dozen each year, usually in the spring
months, the "scurvy season."

There are other examples: severe tuberculosis,
tertiary syphilis, gunshot wounds, stabbings, accidents, self-abuse, and personal misfortune. Whatever the category, the City sees more of it, in a
more advanced state, than any other hospital in
Boston.[3]

THE INTERIOR OF THE CITY HOSPITAL is a maze built
by a madman. Endless corridors, above ground and
below, connect the dozen separate buildings of the
hospital. At every corner, there are large green signs

[3] The frequently bizarre cases mean that every doctor and surgeon has a
backlog of strange stories. One surgeon is fond of telling how he was on
the Accident Floor—the City's EW—when two victims of an auto accident were brought in. One man had lost his leg at the knee. The other had
massive crush injury to the chest, so bad that the degree of damage could
not at first be ascertained from the heavy bleeding. On an X ray of the
chest, however, it was seen that one man's foot and lower leg had been
rammed into the second man's chest, where it was lodged at the time of
admission.

pointing directions, but they don't help much; it is still hopelessly confusing.

As I cut through the corridors and buildings, I remembered my rotation through the hospital as a resident. Small details came back. The soap: a strange, cheap, peculiar-smelling soap that was used everywhere. The paper bags hung by each sink, one for paper towels, the other for rectal gloves. As an economy, the hospital saved used gloves, cleaned them, and used them again. The little plastic name tags edged in black, blue, and red depending on your service. I had spent a year in this hospital, and during that time I had done several autopsies for the medical examiner.

THERE ARE FOUR MEDICAL SITUATIONS in which the coroner claims jurisdiction and an autopsy is required by law. Every pathology resident knows the list cold:

If the patient dies under violent or unusual circumstances.

If the patient is DOA.[4]

If he dies within twenty-four hours of admission.

If a patient dies outside the hospital while not under a doctor's care.

Under any of these circumstances, an autopsy is performed at the City. Like many cities, Boston has no separate police morgue. The second floor of the Mallory Building, the pathology section of the hos-

---

[4] Dead on arrival at hospital.

pital, is given over to the medical examiner's offices. In routine cases, most of the autopsies are performed by first-year residents from the hospital in which the patient died. For the residents, new to the game and still nervous, a coroner's autopsy can be a tense business.

You don't know what poisoning or electrocution looks like, for instance, and you're worried about missing something important. The solution, passed down from resident to resident, is to do a meticulous PM, to take lots of pictures and notes as you go, and to "save everything," meaning to keep pieces of tissue from all the gross organs in case there is a court action that requires reexamination of the autopsy findings. Saving everything is, of course, an expensive business. It requires extra jars, extra preservative, and more storage space in the freezers. But it is done without question in police cases.

Yet even with the precautions, you worry. As you do the post, there is always that fear, that dreadful thought at the back of your mind that the prosecution or the defense will demand some piece of information, some crucial bit of evidence either positive or negative, that you cannot supply because you did not consider all the possibilities, all the variables, all the differentials.

FOR SOME LONG-FORGOTTEN REASON, there are two small stone sphinxes just inside the doors of Mallory. Each time I see them, they bother me;

somehow sphinxes in a pathology building smack of Egyptian embalming chambers. Or something.

I went up to the second floor to talk to Alice. She was grumpy; the post hadn't been started because of some delay; everything was going to hell in a wheelbarrow these days; did I know that a flu epidemic was expected this winter?

I said I did, and then asked, "Who's doing the post on Karen Randall?"

Alice gave a disapproving frown. "They sent someone over from the Mem. His name, I believe, is Hendricks."

I was surprised. I had expected someone big to do this case.

"He inside?" I asked, nodding toward the end of the hall.

"Umm," Alice said.

I walked down toward the two swinging doors, past the freezers on the right which stored the bodies, and past the neatly labeled sign: AUTHORIZED PERSONNEL ONLY BEYOND THIS POINT. The doors were wood, without windows, marked IN and OUT. I pushed through into the autopsy room. Two men were talking in a far corner.

The room was large, painted a dull, institutional green. The ceiling was low, the floor was concrete, and the pipes overhead were exposed; they don't spend much on interior decoration here. In a neat row were five stainless-steel tables, each six feet long. They were tilted slightly and made with a lip. Water flowed constantly down the table in a thin sheet and emptied into a sink at the lower end. The water was kept running all during the autopsy, to carry away blood and bits of organic matter. The huge exhaust fan, three feet across and built into one frosted-glass window, was also kept on. So was the small chemical unit that blew scented ersatz air-freshener into the room, giving it a phony pine-woods odor.

Off to one side was a changing room where pathologists could remove their street clothes and put on surgical greens and an apron. There were four large sinks in a row, the farthest with a sign that said THIS SINK FOR WASHING HANDS ONLY. The others were used to clean instruments and specimens. Along one wall was a row of simple cabinets containing gloves, bottles for specimens, preservatives, reagents, and a camera. Unusual specimens were often photographed in place before removal.

As I entered the room, the two men looked over at me. They had been discussing a case, a body on the far table. I recognized one of the men, a resident named Gaffen. I knew him slightly. He was very clever and rather mean. The other man I did not know at all; I assumed he was Hendricks.

"Hello, John," Gaffen said. "What brings you here?"

"Post on Karen Randall."

"They'll start in a minute. Want to change?"

"No, thanks," I said. "I'll just watch."

Actually I would have liked to change, but it seemed like a bad idea. The only way I could be certain of preserving my observer's role would be to remain in street clothes. The last thing I wanted to do was to be considered an active participant in the autopsy, and therefore possibly influencing the findings.

I said to Hendricks, "I don't think we've met. I'm John Berry."

"Jack Hendricks." He smiled, but did not offer to shake hands. He was wearing gloves, and had been touching the autopsy body before them.

"I've just been showing Hendricks a few physical findings," Gaffen said, nodding to the body. He stepped back so I could see. It was a young Negro girl. She had been an attractive girl before somebody put three round holes in her chest and stomach.

"Hendricks here has been spending all his time at the Mem," Gaffen said. "He hasn't seen much of this sort of thing. For instance, we were just discussing what these little marks might represent."

Gaffen pointed to several flesh tears on the body. They were on the arms and lower legs.

Hendricks said, "I thought perhaps they were scratches from barbed wire."

Gaffen smiled sadly. "Barbed wire," he repeated.

I said nothing. I knew what they were, but I also knew that an inexperienced man would never be able to guess.

"When was she brought in?" I said.

Gaffen glanced at Hendricks, then said, "Five A.M. But the time of death seems to be around midnight." To Hendricks he said, "Does that suggest anything?"

Hendricks shook his head and bit his lip. Gaffen was giving him the business. I would have objected but this was standard procedure. Browbeating often passes for teaching in medicine. Hendricks knew it. I knew it. Gaffen knew it.

"Where," Gaffen said, "do you suppose she was for those five hours after death?"

"I don't know," Hendricks said miserably.

"Guess."

"Lying in bed."

"Impossible. Look at the lividity.[5] She wasn't lying *flat* anywhere. She was half seated, half rolled over on her side."

Hendricks looked at the body again, then shook his head again.

"They found her in the gutter," Gaffen said. "On Charleston Street, two blocks from the Combat Zone. In the gutter."

"Oh."

"So," Gaffen said, "what would you call those marks now?"

Hendricks shook his head. I knew this could go on forever; Gaffen could play it for all it was worth. I cleared my throat and said, "Actually, Hendricks, they're rat bites. Very characteristic: an initial puncture, and then a wedge-shaped tear."

---

[5] The seeping of blood to the lowest portions of the body after death. It often helps establish the position of the body.

"Rat bites," he said in a low voice.

"Live and learn," Gaffen said. He checked his watch. "I have a CPC now. Good to see you again, John." He stripped off his gloves and washed his hands, then came back to Hendricks.

Hendricks was still looking at the bullet holes and the bites.

"She was in the gutter for five hours?"

"Yes."

"Didn't the police find her?"

"Yes, eventually."

"Who did it to her?"

Gaffen snorted. "You tell me. She has a history of a primary luetic oral lesion, treated at this hospital, and five episodes of hot tubes, treated at this hospital."

"Hot tubes?"

"P.I.D."[6]

"When they found her," Gaffen said, "she had forty dollars in cash in her bra."

He looked at Hendricks, shook his head, and left the room. When we were alone, Hendricks said to me, "I still don't get it. Does that mean she was a prostitute?"

"Yes," I said. "She was shot to death and lay in the gutter for five hours, being chewed by sewer rats."

---

[6] Pelvic Inflammatory Disease, usually infection of the fallopian tubes by Neisseria gonococcus, the agent of gonorrhea. Gonorrhea is considered to be the most common infectious disease of mankind. Twenty percent of prostitutes are thought to be infected.

"Oh."

"It happens," I said. "A lot."

The swinging door opened, and a man wheeled in a white-shrouded body. He looked at us and said, "Randall?"

"Yes," Hendricks said.

"Which table you want?"

"The middle."

"All right." He moved the cart close, then swung the body over onto the stainless-steel table, shifting the head first, then the feet. It was already quite stiff. He removed the shroud quickly, folded it, and set it on the cart.

"You gotta sign," he said to Hendricks, holding out a form.

Hendricks signed.

"I'm not very good at this," Hendricks said to me. "This legal stuff. I've only done one before, and that was an industrial thing. Man hit on the head at work and killed. But nothing like this . . ."

I said, "How did you get chosen for this one?"

He said, "Just lucky, I guess. I heard that Weston was going to do it, but apparently not."

"Leland Weston?"

"Yes."

Weston was the chief pathologist of the City Hospital, a great old man and probably the best pathologist in Boston, bar none.

"Well," Hendricks said. "We might as well get started."

He went to the sink and began a long and thorough scrub. Pathologists who scrub for a post always annoy me. It makes them too much like parodies of surgeons: the idiotic reverse of the coin, a man dressed in a surgical uniform—baggy pants, V-neck short-sleeve blouse—cleaning his hands before operating on a patient who was past caring whether he received sterile treatment or not.

But in Hendricks' case, I knew he was just stalling.

AUTOPSIES ARE NEVER VERY PRETTY. They are particularly depressing when the deceased is as young and as attractive as Karen Randall was. She lay nude on her back, her blonde hair streaming down in the water. Her clear blue eyes stared up at the ceiling. While Hendricks finished scrubbing, I looked at the body and touched the skin. It was cold and smooth, the color gray-white. Just what you'd expect for a girl who had bled to death.

Hendricks checked to see that there was film in the camera, then waved me aside while he took three pictures from different angles.

I said, "Have you got her chart?"

"No. The old man has that. All I've got is a summary of the OPD discharge."

"Which was?"

"Clinical diagnosis of death secondary to vaginal hemorrhage complicated by systemic anaphylaxis."

"Systemic anaphylaxis? Why?"

"Beats me," Hendricks said. "Something happened in the OPD, but I couldn't find out."

"That's interesting," I said.

Hendricks finished with his pictures and went to the blackboard. Most labs have a blackboard, on which the pathologist can write his findings as he makes them—surface markings of the body, weight and appearance of organs, that sort of thing. He went to the board and wrote, "Randall, K." and the case number.

At that moment, another man entered the room. I recognized the bald, stooping figure of Leland Weston. He was in his sixties, about to retire, and despite his stoop he had a kind of energy and vigorousness. He shook hands with me briskly, then with Hendricks, who seemed very relieved to see him.

Weston took over the autopsy himself. He began, as I remembered he always did, by walking around the body a half-dozen times, staring at it intently, and muttering to himself. Finally he stopped and glanced at me.

"Observed her, John?"

"Yes."

"What do you make of it?"

"Recent weight gain," I said. "There are striation marks on her hips and breasts. She is also overweight."

"Good," Weston said. "Anything else?"

"Yes," I said. "She has an interesting hair distribution. She has blond hair, but there is a thin line of dark hair on her upper lip, and some more on her forearms. It looks sparse and fine to me, new looking."

"Good," Weston said, nodding. He gave me a slight, crooked grin, the grin of my old teacher. For that matter, Weston had trained most of the pathologists in Boston at one time or another. "But," he said, "you've missed the most important finding."

He pointed to the pubic area, which was cleanly shaven. "That," he said.

"But she's had an abortion," Hendricks said. "We all know that."

"Nobody," Weston said sternly, "knows anything until the post is completed. We can't afford to prediagnose." He smiled. "That is a recreation reserved for the clinicians." He pulled on a pair of gloves and said, "This autopsy report is going to be the best and most accurate we can make. Because J. D. Randall will be going over it with a fine comb. Now then." He examined the pubic area closely. "The differential of a shaved groin is difficult. It may imply an operation, but many patients do it for purely personal reasons. In this case, we might note that it was carefully done, with no nicks or small cuts at all. That is significant: there isn't a nurse in the world who can do a pre-op shave on a fleshy region like this without making at least one small slip. Nurses are in a hurry and small cuts don't matter. So . . ."

"She shaved herself," Hendricks said.

"Probably," Weston nodded. "Of course, that doesn't rule in or out an operation. But it should be kept in mind."

He proceeded with the autopsy, working smoothly and quickly. He measured the girl at five-four and weighed her at one-forty. Considering the fluid she had lost, that was pretty heavy. Weston wrote it on the blackboard and made his first cut.

The standard autopsy incision is a Y-shaped cut running down from each shoulder, meeting at the midline of the body at the bottom of the ribs, and then continuing as a single incision to the pubic bone. The skin and muscle is then peeled away in three flaps; the ribs are cut open, exposing the lungs and heart; the abdomen is widely incised. Then the carotid arteries are tied and cut, the colon is tied and cut, the trachea and pharynx are cut— and the entire viscera, heart, lungs, stomach, liver, spleen, kidneys, and intestine are removed in a single motion.

After that, the eviscerated body is sewn shut. The isolated organs can then be examined at leisure, and sections cut for microscopic examination. While the pathologist is doing this, the deaner cuts the scalp open, removes the skullcap, and takes out the brain if permission for brain removal has been obtained.

Then I realized: there was no deaner here.[7] I mentioned this to Weston.

"That's right," he said. "We're doing this one by ourselves. Completely."

I watched as Weston made his cut. His hands

[7] Deaner is a traditional term for the man who takes care of the dissecting room. It is an ancient term, dating back to the days when anatomy dissections were done by horse gelders and butchers. The deaner keeps the rooms clean, cares for the corpses, and aids in the dissection.

trembled slightly, but his touch was still remarkably swift and efficient. As he opened the abdomen, blood welled out.

"Quick," he said. "Suction."

Hendricks brought a bottle attached to a suction hose. The abdominal fluid—dark red-black, mostly blood—was removed and measured in the bottle. Altogether, nearly three liters were withdrawn.

"I wish we had the chart," Weston said. "I'd like to know how many units they gave her in the EW."

I nodded. The normal blood volume in an average person was only about five quarts. To have so much in the abdomen implied a perforation somewhere.

When the fluid was drained, Weston continued the dissection, removing the organs and placing them in a stainless-steel pan. He carried them to the sink and washed them, then examined them one by one, beginning at the top, with the thyroid.

"Peculiar," he said, holding it in his hands. "It feels like fifteen grams or so."

The normal thyroid weighed between twenty and thirty.

"But probably a normal variation," Weston said. He cut it open and examined the cut surface. We could see nothing unusual.

Then he incised the trachea, opening it down to the bifurcation into the lungs, which were expanded and pale white, instead of their normal pink-purple.

"Anaphylaxis," Weston said. "Systemic. Any idea what she was hypersensitive to?"

"No," I said.

Hendricks was taking notes. Weston deftly followed the bronchi down into the lungs, then opened the pulmonary arteries and veins.

He moved on to the heart, which he opened by making two looping incisions into the right and left sides, exposing all four chambers. "Perfectly normal." Then he opened the coronary arteries. They were normal too, patent with little atherosclerosis.

Everything else was normal until we got to the uterus. It was purplish with hemorrhagic blood, and not very large, about the size and shape of a light bulb, with the ovaries and fallopian tubes leading into it. As Weston turned it in his hands, we saw the slice through the endometrium and muscle. That explained the bleeding into the peritoneal cavity.

But I was bothered by the size. It just didn't look like a pregnant uterus to me, particularly if the girl was four months' pregnant. At four months, the fetus was six inches long, with a pumping heart, developing eyes and face, and forming bones. The uterus would be markedly enlarged.

Weston thought the same thing. "Of course," he said, "she probably got some oxytocin[8] at the EW, but still, it's damned peculiar."

[8] A drug to contract the uterus, useful for initiating birth and for stopping uterine bleeding.

He cut through the uterine wall and opened it up. The inside had been scraped quite well and carefully; the perforation was obviously a late development. Now, the inside of the uterus was filled with blood and numerous translucent, yellowish clots.

"Chicken-fat clots,"[9] Weston said. That meant it was postmortem.

He cleaned away the blood and clots and examined the scraped endometrial surface carefully.

"This wasn't done by a total amateur," Weston said. "Somebody knew at least the basic principles of curettage."

"Except for the perforation."

"Yes," he said. "Except for that."

"Well," he said, "at least we already know one thing. She didn't do it to herself."

That was an important point. A large proportion of acute vaginal hemorrhages are the result of women attempting self-abortion, with drugs, or salt solutions, or soaps, or knitting needles and other devices. But Karen couldn't have done this kind of scraping on herself. This required a general anesthetic for the patient.

I said, "Does this look like a pregnant uterus to you?"

"Questionable," Weston said. "Very questionable. Let's check the ovaries."

Weston incised the ovaries, looking for the cor-

[9] See Appendix I: Delicatessen Pathologists.

pus luteum, the yellow spot that persists after the ovum has been released. He didn't find one. In itself, that proved nothing; the corpus luteum began to degenerate after three months, and this girl was supposedly in her fourth month.

The deaner came in and said to Weston, "Shall I close up now?"

"Yes," Weston said. "You might as well."

The deaner began to suture the incision and wrap the body in a clean shroud. I turned to Weston. "Aren't you going to examine the brain?"

"No permission," Weston said.

The medical examiner, though he demanded an autopsy, usually did not insist on brain examination unless the situation suggested possible neuropathy.

"But I would have thought a family like the Randalls, medically oriented . . ."

"Oh, J. D. is all for it. It's Mrs. Randall. She just refuses to have the brain removed, absolutely refuses. Ever met her?"

I shook my head.

"Quite a woman," Weston said dryly.

He turned back to the organs, working down the GI tract from esophagus to anus. It was completely normal. I left before he finished everything; I had seen what I wanted to see and knew that the final report would be equivocal. At least on the basis of the gross organs, they would be unable to say that Karen Randall was definitely pregnant.

That was peculiar.

SIX

I HAVE TROUBLE BUYING LIFE INSURANCE. Most pathologists do: the companies take one look at you and shudder—constant exposure to tuberculosis, malignancies, and lethal infectious disease makes you a very poor risk. The only person I know who has more trouble getting insured is a biochemist named Jim Murphy.

When he was younger, Murphy played halfback for Yale and was named to the All-East team. That in itself is an accomplishment, but it is amazing if you know Murphy and have seen his eyes. Murphy is practically blind. He wears lenses an inch thick and walks with his head drooping, as if the weight of the glass burdened him down. His vision is barely adequate under most circumstances, but when he gets excited or tight, he walks into things.

On the surface it would not seem that Murphy had the makings of a halfback, even at Yale. To know his secret, you have to see him move. Murphy is fast. He also has the best balance of anyone I know. When he was playing football, his teammates devised a series of plays especially designed to allow the quarterback to point Murphy in the proper direction and send him on his way. This usually worked, though on several occasions Murphy made brilliant runs in the wrong direction, twice charging over the goal line for a safety.

He has always been drawn to unlikely sports. At the age of thirty, he decided to take up mountain climbing. He found it very agreeable, but he couldn't get insured. So he switched to sports-car racing and was doing very well until he drove a Lotus off the track, rolled it four times, and broke both clavicles in several places. After that, he decided he'd rather be insured than active, so he gave it all up.

Murphy is so fast he even speaks in a kind of shorthand, as if he can't be bothered putting all the articles and pronouns into his sentences. He drives his secretaries and technicians mad, not only because of his speech, but also because of the windows. Murphy keeps them wide open, even in winter, and he is an unrelenting opponent of what he calls "bad air."

When I walked into his lab in one wing of the BLI[1] I found it filled with apples. There were apples in the refrigerators, on the reagent benches, on desks as paperweights. His two technicians, wearing heavy sweaters under their lab coats, were both eating apples as I entered.

"Wife," Murphy said, shaking hands with me. "Makes a specialty. Want one? I have Delicious and Cortland today."

[1] Boston Lying-In Hospital.

"No, thanks," I said.

He took a bite from one after polishing it briskly on his sleeve. "Good. Really."

"I haven't got time," I said.

"Always in a rush," Murph said. "Jesus Christ, always in a rush. Haven't seen you or Judith for months. What've you been up to? Terry's playing guard on the Belmont first eleven."

He lifted a picture from his desk and held it under my nose. It showed his son in a football uniform, growling into the camera, looking like Murph: small, but tough.

"We'll have to get together soon," I said to him, "and talk about families."

"Ummmm." Murph devoured his apple with remarkable speed. "Let's do that. How's bridge game? Wife and I had an absolutely devastating time last weekend. Two weekends ago. Playing with——"

"Murph," I said. "I have a problem."

"Probably an ulcer," Murph said, selecting another apple from a row along his desk. "Nervous guy I know. Always in a rush."

"Actually," I said, "this is right up your alley."

He grinned in sudden interest. "Steroids? First time in history a pathologist's interested in steroids, I bet." He sat down behind his desk and propped his feet up. "Ready and waiting. Shoot."

Murphy's work concerned steroid production in pregnant women and fetuses. He was located in the BLI for a practical, if somewhat grisly, reason—he needed to be near the source of supply, which in his case was clinic mothers and the occasional still-births[2] assigned to him.

"Can you do a hormone test for pregnancy at autopsy?" I asked.

He scratched his head in swift, nervous, fluttery movements. "Hell. Suppose so. But who'd want to?"

"I want to."

"What I mean is, can't you tell at autopsy if she's pregnant or not?"

"Actually, no, in this case. It's very confused."

"Well. No accepted test, but I imagine it could be done. How far along?"

"Four months, supposedly."

"Four months? And you can't tell from the uterus?"

"Murph—"

"Yeah, sure, it could be done at four months," he said. "Won't stand up in a courtroom or anything, but yeah. Could be done."

"Can you do it?"

"That's all we got in this lab," he said. "Steroid assays. What've you got?"

I didn't understand; I shook my head.

"Blood or urine. Which?"

"Oh. Blood." I reached into my pocket and drew out a test tube of blood I had collected at the autopsy. I'd asked Weston if it was O.K., and he said he didn't care.

---

[2] Stillbirths, abortuses, and placentas are in hot demand at the BLI for the dozen or so groups doing hormone research. Sometimes rather bitter arguments break out over who needs the next dead baby most for their studies.

Murph took the tube and held it to the light. He flicked it with his finger. "Need two cc's," he said. "Plenty here. No problem."

"When will you let me know?"

"Two days. Assay takes forty-eight hours. This is post blood?"

"Yes. I was afraid the hormones might be denatured or something . . ."

Murph sighed. "How little we remember. Only proteins can be denatured, and steroids are not proteins, right? This'll be easy. See, the normal rabbit test is chorionic gonadotrophin in urine. But in this lab we're geared to measure that, or progesterone, or any of a number of other eleven-beta hydroxylated compounds. In pregnancy, progesterone levels increase ten times. Estriol levels increase a thousand times. We can measure a jump like that, no sweat." He glanced at his technicians. "Even in *this* lab."

One of the technicians took up the challenge. "I used to be accurate," she said, "before I got frostbite on my fingers."

"Excuses, excuses," Murphy grinned. He turned back to me and picked up the tube of blood. "This'll be easy. We'll just pop it onto the old fractionating column and let it perk through," he said. "Maybe we'll do two independent aliquots, just in case one gets fouled up. Who's it from?"

"What?"

He waved the test tube in front of me impatiently. "Whose blood?"

"Oh. Just a case," I said, shrugging.

"A four-month pregnancy and you can't be sure? John boy, not leveling with your old buddy, your old bridge opponent."

"It might be better," I said, "if I told you afterward."

"O.K., O.K. Far from me to pry. Your own way, but you *will* tell me?"

"Promise."

"A pathologist's promise," he said, standing up, "rings of the eternal."

SEVEN

THE LAST TIME ANYONE COUNTED, there were 25,000 named diseases of man, and cures for 5,000 of them. Yet it remains the dream of every young doctor to discover a new disease. That is the fastest and surest way to gain prominence within the medical profession. Practically speaking, it is much better to discover a new disease than to find a cure for an old one; your cure will be tested, disputed, and argued over for years, while a new disease is readily and rapidly accepted.

Lewis Carr, while still an intern, hit the jackpot: he found a new disease. It was pretty rare—a hereditary dysgammaglobulinemia affecting the beta-fraction which he found in a family of four—but that was not important. The important thing was that Lewis discovered it, described it, and published his results in the *New England Journal of Medicine*.

Six years later he was made clinical professor at the Mem. There was never any question he would be; simply a matter of waiting until somebody on the staff retired and vacated an office.

Carr had a good office in terms of status at the Mem; it was perfect for a young hotshot internist. For one thing, it was cramped and made even worse by the stacks of journals, texts, and research papers scattered all around. For another, it was dirty and old, tucked away in an obscure corner of the Calder Building, near the kidney research unit. And for the finishing touch, amid the squalor and mess sat a beautiful secretary, looking sexy, efficient, and wholly unapproachable: a nonfunctional beauty to contrast with the functional ugliness of the office.

"Dr. Carr is making rounds," she said without smiling. "He asked for you to wait inside."

I went in and took a seat, after removing a stack of back issues of the *American Journal of Experimental Biology* from the chair. A few moments later, Carr arrived. He wore a white lab coat, open at the front (a clinical professor would never button his lab coat) and a stethoscope around his neck. His shirt collar was frayed (clinical professors aren't paid much), but his black shoes gleamed (clinical professors are careful about things that really count). As usual, his manner was very cool, very collected, very political.

Unkind souls said Carr was more than political, that he shamelessly sucked up to the senior staff men. But many people resented his swift success and his confident manner. Carr had a round and childlike face; his cheeks were smooth and ruddy. He had an engaging boyish grin that went over very well with the female patients. He gave me that grin now.

"Hi, John." He shut the door to his outer office and sat down behind his desk. I could barely see him over the stacked journals. He removed the stethoscope from his neck, folded it, and slipped it into his pocket. Then he looked at me.

I guess it's inevitable. Any practicing doctor who faces you from behind a desk gets a certain manner, a thoughtful-probing-inquisitive air which is unsettling if there's nothing wrong with you. Lewis Carr got that way now.

"You want to know about Karen Randall," he said, as if reporting a serious finding.

"Right."

"For personal reasons."

"Right."

"And anything I tell you goes no further?"

"Right."

"O.K.," he said. "I'll tell you. I wasn't present, but I have followed things closely."

I knew that he would have. Lewis Carr followed

everything at the Mem closely; he knew more local gossip than any of the nurses. He gathered his knowledge reflexively, the way some other people breathed air.

"The girl presented in the outpatient ward at four this morning. She was moribund on arrival; when they sent a stretcher out to the car she was delirious. Her trouble was frank vaginal hemorrhage. She had a temperature of 102, dry skin with decreased turgor, shortness of breath, a racing pulse, and low blood pressure. She complained of thirst."[1]

Carr took a deep breath. "The intern looked at her and ordered a cross match so they could start a transfusion. He drew a syringe for a count and crit[2] and rapidly injected a liter of D 5.[3] He also attempted to locate the source of the hemorrhage but he could not, so he gave her oxytocin to clamp down the uterus and slow bleeding, and packed the vagina as a temporary measure. Then he found out who the girl was from the mother and shit in his pants. He panicked. He called in a resident. He started the blood. And he gave her a good dose of prophylactic penicillin. Unfortunately, he did this without consulting her chart or asking the mother about allergic reactions."

"She was hypersensitive."[4]

---

[1] Thirst is an important symptom in shock. For unknown reasons, it appears only in severe shock due to fluid loss, and is regarded as an ominous sign.
[2] White count and hematocrit.
[3] Five percent dextrose in water, used to replace lost fluid volume.
[4] Penicillin reactions occur in 9–10 percent of normal patients.

"Severely," Carr said. "Ten minutes after giving the penicillin i.m.[5] the girl went into choking spasms and appeared unable to breathe despite a patent airway. By now the chart was down from the record room, and the intern realized what he had done. So he administered a milligram of epinephrine i.m. When there was no response, he went to a slow IV, benadryl, cortisone, and aminophylline. They put her on positive pressure oxygen. But she became cyanotic,[6] convulsive, and died within twenty minutes."

I lit a cigarette and thought to myself that I wouldn't like to be that intern now.

"Probably," Carr said, "the girl would have died anyway. We don't know that for sure, but there's every reason to think that at admission her blood loss already approached fifty percent. That seems to be the cut-off, as you know—the shock is usually irreversible. So we probably couldn't have kept her. Of course, that doesn't change anything."

I said, "Why'd the intern give penicillin in the first place?"

"That's a peculiarity of hospital procedure," Carr said. "It's a kind of routine around here for certain presenting symptoms. Normally when we get a girl with evidence of a vaginal bleed and a high fever—possible infection—we give the girl a D & C, put her to bed, and stick her a shot of antibiotic. Send

[5] Intramuscularly.
[6] Blue.

her home the next day, usually. And it goes down on the charts as miscarriage."

"Is that the final diagnosis on Karen Randall's record? Miscarriage?"

Carr nodded. "Spontaneous. We always put it down that way, because if we do that, we don't have to fool with the police. We see quite a few self-induced or illegally induced abortions here. Sometimes the girls come in with so much vaginal soap they foam like overloaded dishwashers. Other times, it's bleeding. In every case, the girl is hysterical and full of wild lies. We just take care of it quietly and send her on her way."

"And never report it to the police?"[7]

"We're doctors, not law-enforcement officers. We see about a hundred girls a year this way. If we reported every one, we'd all spend our time in court testifying and not practicing medicine."

"But doesn't the law require——"

"Of course," Carr said quickly. "The law requires that we report it. The law also requires that we report assaults, but if we reported every drunk who got into a bar brawl, we'd never hear the end of it. No emergency ward reports everything it should. You just can't operate on that basis."

"But if there's been an abortion——"

"Look at it logically," Carr said. "A significant number of these cases are spontaneous miscarriages. A significant number aren't, but it doesn't

[7] See Appendix II: Cops and Doctors.

make sense for us to treat it any other way. Suppose you know that the butcher of Barcelona worked on a girl; suppose you call in the police. They show up the next day and the girl tells them it was spontaneous. Or she tells them she tried it on herself. But either way she won't talk, so the police are annoyed. Mostly, with you, because you called them in."

"Does this happen?"

"Yes," Carr said, "I've seen it happen twice myself. Both times, the girl showed up crazy with fear, convinced she was going to die. She wanted to nail the abortionist, so she demanded the police be called in. But by morning, she was feeling fine, she'd had a nice hospital D & C, and she realized her problems were over. She didn't want to fool with the police; she didn't want to get involved. So when the cops came, she pretended it was all a big mistake."

"Are you content to clean up after the abortionists and let it go?"

"We are trying to restore people to health. That's all. A doctor can't make value judgments. We clean up after a lot of bad drivers and mean drunks, too. But it isn't our job to slap anybody's hand and give them a lecture on driving or alcohol. We just try to make them well again."

I wasn't going to argue with him; I knew it wouldn't do any good. So I changed the subject.

"What about the charges against Lee? What happened there?"

"When the girl died," Carr said, "Mrs. Randall became hysterical. She started to scream, so they gave her a tranquilizer and sedative. After that, she settled down, but she continued to claim that her daughter had named Lee as the abortionist. So she called the police."

"Mrs. Randall did?"

"That's right."

"What about the hospital diagnosis?"

"It remains miscarriage. This is a legitimate medical interpretation. The change to illegal abortion is made on nonclinical grounds, so far as we are concerned. The autopsy will show whether an abortion was performed."

"The autopsy showed it," I said. "Quite a good abortion, too, except for a single laceration of the endometrium. It was done by someone with skill—but not quite enough skill."

"Have you talked with Lee?"

"This morning," I said. "He claims he didn't do it. On the basis of that autopsy, I believe him."

"A mistake—"

"I don't think so. Art's too good, too capable."

Carr removed the stethoscope from his pocket and played with it, looked uncomfortable. "This is a very messy thing," he said. "Very messy."

"It has to be cleared up," I said. "We can't hide our heads in the sand and let Lee go to hell."

"No, of course not," Carr said. "But J. D. was very upset."

"I imagine so."

"He practically killed that poor intern when he saw what treatment had been given. I was there, and I thought he was going to strangle the kid with his bare hands."

"Who was the intern?"

"Kid named Roger Whiting. Nice kid, even though he went to P & S."

"Where is he now?"

"At home, probably. He went off at eight this morning." Carr frowned and fiddled once more with his stethoscope. "John," he said, "are you sure you want to get involved in this?"

"I don't want anything to do with it," I said. "If I had my choice, I'd be back in my lab now. But I don't see any choice."

"The trouble is," Carr said slowly, "that this thing has gotten out of control. J. D. is very upset."

"You said that before."

"I'm just trying to help you understand how things are." Carr rearranged things on his desk and did not look at me. Finally he said, "The case is in the proper hands. And I understand Lee has a good lawyer."

"There are a lot of dangling questions. I want to be sure they're all cleaned up."

"It's in the proper hands," Carr said again.

"Whose hands? The Randalls? The goons I saw down at the police station?"

"We have an excellent police force in Boston," Carr said.

"Bullshit."

He sighed patiently and said, "What can you hope to prove?"

"That Lee didn't do it."

Carr shook his head. "That's not the point."

"It seems to me that's precisely the point."

"No," Carr said. "The point is that the daughter of J. D. Randall was killed by an abortionist, and somebody has to pay. Lee's an abortionist—that won't be hard to prove in court. In a Boston court, the jury is likely to be more than half Catholic. They'll convict him on general principles."

"On general principles?"

"You know what I mean," Carr said, shifting in his chair.

"You mean Lee's the goat."

"That's right. Lee's the goat."

"Is that the official word?"

"More or less," Carr said.

"And what are your feelings about it?"

"A man who performs abortions puts himself in danger. He's breaking the law. When he aborts the daughter of a famous Boston physician—"

"Lee says he didn't do it."

Carr gave a sad smile. "Does it matter?"

EIGHT

IT TAKES THIRTEEN YEARS from the time you leave college to the time you become a cardiac surgeon. You have four years of medical school, a year of internship, three of general surgery, two of thoracic surgery, two of cardiac surgery. Somewhere along the line, you spend two years working for Uncle Sam.[1]

It takes a certain kind of man to assume this burden, to set his sights on such a distant goal. By the time he is ready to begin surgery on his own, he has become another person, almost a new breed, estranged by his experience and his dedication from other men. In a sense, that is part of the training: surgeons are lonely men.

I thought of this as I looked down through the glass-overhead viewing booth into OR 9. The booth was built into the ceiling, allowing you a good view of the entire room, the staff, and the procedure. Students and residents often sat up here and watched. There was a microphone in the OR, so that you heard everything—the clink of instruments, the rhythmic hiss of the respirator, the quiet

[1] See Appendix III: Battlefields and Barberpoles.

voices—and there was a button you could press to talk to the people below. Otherwise they could not hear you.

I had come to this room after going to J. D. Randall's office. I had wanted to see the chart on Karen, but Randall's secretary said she didn't have it. J. D. had it, and J. D. was in surgery now. That had surprised me. I had thought he would have taken the day off, considering. But apparently it had not entered his mind.

The secretary said the operation was probably almost over, but one look through the glass told me it was not. The chest of the patient was still open and the heart was still incised; they had not even begun suturing. There I was not going to interrupt them; I'd have to come back later to try and get the chart.

But I stayed a moment to watch. There is something compelling about open-heart surgery, something fantastic and fabulous, a mixture of dream and nightmare, all come true. There were sixteen people in the room below me, including four surgeons. Everyone was moving, working, checking in smooth, coordinated movements, like a kind of ballet, like a surrealistic ballet. The patient, draped in green, was dwarfed by the heart-lung machine alongside him, a giant complex as large as an automobile, shining steel, with smoothly moving cylinders and wheels.

At the head of the patient was the anesthetist, surrounded by equipment. There were several

nurses, two pump technicians who monitored the
dials and gauges on the machine, nurses, orderlies,
and the surgeons. I tried to tell which was Randall,
but I could not; in their gowns and masks, they all
looked the same, impersonal, interchangeable. That
was not true, of course. One of those four men had
responsibility for everything, for the conduct of all
sixteen workers present. And responsibility for the
seventeenth person in that room, the man whose
heart was stopped.

In one corner, displayed on a television, was the
electrocardiogram. The normal EKG is a briskly
bouncing line, with spikes for every heartbeat, every
wave of electrical energy that fires the heart muscle. This one was flat: just a meaningless squiggle.
That meant that according to one major criterion of
medicine, the patient was dead. I looked at the
pink lungs through the open chest; they were not
moving. The patient was not breathing.

The machine did all that for him. It pumped his
blood, oxygenated it, removed the carbon dioxide.
In its present form, the machine had been in use
for about ten years.

The people below me did not seem in awe of the
machine or the surgical procedure. They worked
matter-of-factly at their jobs. I suppose that was
one reason why it all seemed so fantastic.

I watched for five minutes without realizing the
time. Then I left. Outside, in the corridor, two residents slouched in a doorway, still wearing their
caps with their masks hanging loosely around their

necks. They were eating doughnuts and coffee, and laughing about a blind date.

NINE

ROGER WHITING, M.D., lived near the hospital in a third-floor walk-up on the sleazy side of Beacon Hill, where they dump the garbage from Louisburg Square. His wife answered the door. She was a plain girl, about seven months' pregnant. She looked worried.

"What do you want?"

"I'd like to talk to your husband. My name's Berry. I'm a pathologist at the Lincoln."

She gave me a hard suspicious glance. "My husband is trying to sleep. He's been on call for the last two days, and he's tired. He's trying to sleep."

"It's very important."

A slim young man in white ducks appeared behind her. He looked more than tired; he looked exhausted and afraid. He said, "What is it?"

"I'd like to talk to you about Karen Randall."

"I've been over it," he said, "a dozen times. Talk to Dr. Carr about it."

"I did."

Whiting ran his hands through his hair, then said

to his wife, "It's O.K., honey. Get me some coffee, would you?" He turned to me. "Want some coffee?"

"Please," I said.

We sat in the living room. The apartment was small, the furniture cheap and rickety. But I felt at home: it had been only a few years since I had done my own internship. I knew all about the money problems, the stresses, the hellish hours, and the slop work you had to do. I knew about the irritating calls from nurses in the middle of the night, asking you to okay another aspirin for patient Jones. I knew how you could drag yourself out of bed to see a patient and how you could, in the small hours of the morning, make a mistake. I had nearly killed an old man with heart failure when I was an intern. With three hours of sleep during the last two days, you could do anything and not give a damn.

"I know you're tired," I said. "I won't stay long."

"No, no," he said very earnestly. "Anything I can do to help. I mean, now . . ."

The wife came in with two cups of coffee. She looked at me angrily. The coffee was weak.

"My questions," I said, "have to do with the girl when she first arrived. Were you in the ward?"

"No. I was trying to sleep. They called me."

"What time was this?"

"Almost exactly four."

"Describe what happened."

"I was sleeping in my clothes, in that little room just off the OPD. I wasn't asleep long when they called me; I'd just gotten through putting another IV into a lady who pulls them out. She says she doesn't, but she does." He sighed. "Anyway, when they called me, I was bleary as hell. I got up and dunked my head in cold water, then toweled off. When I got to the ward, they were bringing the girl in on a stretcher."

"Was she conscious?"

"Yes, but disoriented. She was pale, and she'd lost a lot of blood. She was feverish and delirious. We couldn't get a good temperature because she kept gnashing her teeth, so we figured it was about 102 and got to work on the cross-matching."

"What else was done?"

"The nurses got a blanket over her and propped her feet up with shock blocks.[1] Then I examined the lesion. It was very clearly vaginal hemorrhage and we diagnosed it as miscarriage."

"About the bleeding," I said, "was there any discharge accompanying it?"

He shook his head. "Just blood."

"No tissue? No signs of a placenta?"

"No. But she'd been bleeding for a long time. Her clothes . . ." He looked across the room, seeing it again in his mind. "Her clothes were very heavy. The nurses had trouble getting them off."

"During this time, did the girl say anything coherent?"

---

[1] Shock blocks are simply wooden blocks used to elevate the legs in cases of shock, helping to get blood to the head.

"Not really. She was mumbling every once in a while. Something about an old man, I think. Her old man, or an old man. But it wasn't clear, and nobody was really paying any attention."

"Did she say anything else?"

He shook his head. "Just when they were cutting her clothes off her. She would try to pull them back. Once she said 'You can't do this to me.' And then later she said, 'Where am I?' But that was just delirious talk. She wasn't really coherent."

"What did you do about the bleeding?"

"I tried to localize it. It was hard, and things were pretty rushed. And we couldn't angle the lights down properly. Finally I decided to pack it with gauze pads and concentrate on getting her blood volume back up."

"Where was Mrs. Randall during all this?"

"She waited by the door. She seemed all right until we had to tell her what had happened. Then she went to pieces. Just went to pieces."

"What about Karen's records? Had she ever been admitted to the hospital before?"

"I didn't see her chart," he said, "until . . . later. They had to be pulled from the record room. But she had been in before. Papp smears every year since she was fifteen. Usual blood tests from her twice-yearly physicals. She was well looked after medically, as you might expect."

"Was there anything unusual in her past history? Besides the hypersensitivity, I mean."

He gave a sad smile. "Isn't that enough?"

For a fleeting moment I was angry with him. He was soaking in self-pity, despite his natural fright. But I wanted to tell him he'd better get used to the idea of people dying in front of him, lots of people. And he'd better get used to the idea that he could make a mistake, because they happened. Sometimes the mistakes were balder than others, but it was just degree. I wanted to tell him if he'd asked Mrs. Randall about Karen's hypersensitivity, and she'd said the girl was O.K., that Whiting would have been free and clear. The girl would still have died, of course, but Whiting would be clear. His mistake was not killing Karen Randall; it was not asking permission first.

I thought about saying this, but I didn't.

"Any indication in the chart of psychiatric problems?" I asked.

"No."

"Nothing unusual at all?"

"No." Then he frowned. "Wait a minute. There was one strange thing. A complete set of skull films were ordered about six months ago."

"Did you see the films?"

"No. I just read the radiologist's dx."

"And what was that?"

"Normal. No pathology."

"Why were the films taken?"

"It didn't say."

"Was she in an accident of some kind? A fall, or an auto accident?"

"Not that I know of."

"Who ordered the films?"

"Probably Dr. Randall. Peter Randall, that is. He was her doctor."

"And you don't know why the X rays were taken?"

"No."

"But there must be a reason," I said.

"Yes," he said, but he didn't seem very interested. He stared moodily at his coffee, then sipped it. Finally he said, "I hope they take that abortionist and screw him to the wall. Whatever he gets, he deserves worse."

I stood. The boy was under stress and almost on the verge of tears. All he could see was a promising medical career jeopardized because he had made a mistake with the daughter of a prominent physician. In his anger and frustration and self-pity, he, too, was looking for a goat. And he needed one worse than most.

"Are you planning to settle in Boston?" I asked.

"I was," he said with a wry look.

WHEN I LEFT THE INTERN I called Lewis Carr. I wanted to see Karen Randall's chart more than ever. I had to find out about those X rays.

"Lew," I said, "I'm going to need your help again."

"Oh?" He sounded thrilled by the prospect.

"Yes. I've got to get her chart. It's imperative."

"I thought we went over that."

"Yes, but something new has come up. This thing is getting crazier by the minute. Why were X rays ordered——"

"I'm sorry," Carr said. "I can't help you."

"Lew, even if Randall does have the chart, he can't keep——"

"I'm sorry, John. I'm going to be tied up here for the rest of the day and most of tomorrow. I'm just not going to have time."

He was speaking formally, a man counting his words, repeating the sentences over to himself before speaking them aloud.

"What happened? Randall get to you and button your mouth?"

"I feel," Carr said, "that the case should be left in the hands of those best equipped to deal with it. I'm not, and I don't think other doctors are, either."

I knew what he was saying and what he meant. Art Lee used to laugh about the elaborate way doctors back out of things, leaving behind a spoor of double-talk. Art called it The Pilate Maneuver.

"O.K.," I said, "if that's the way you feel."

I hung up.

In a way, I should have expected it. Lewis Carr always played the game, following all the rules just like a good boy. That was the way he always had been, and the way he always would be.

TEN

MY ROUTE FROM WHITING to the medical school took me past the Lincoln Hospital. Standing out in front near the taxi stand was Frank Conway, hunched over, his hands in his pockets, looking down at the pavement. Something about his stance conveyed sadness and a deep, dulling fatigue. I pulled over to the curb.

"Need a ride?"

"I'm going to Children's," he said. He seemed surprised that I had stopped. Conway and I aren't close friends. He is a fine doctor but not pleasant as a man. His first two wives had divorced him, the second after only six months.

"Children's is on the way," I said.

It wasn't, but I'd take him anyway. I wanted to talk to him. He got in and I pulled out into traffic.

"What takes you to Children's?" I said.

"Conference. They have a congenital CPC once a week. You?"

"Just a visit," I said. "Lunch with a friend."

He nodded and sat back. Conway was young, only thirty-five. He had breezed through his residencies, working under the best men in the country. Now he was better than any of them, or so it was said. You couldn't be sure about a man like Conway: he was one of the few doctors who become so famous so fast that they take on some aspects of politicians and movie stars; they acquire blindly loyal fans and blindly antagonistic critics; one either loves them or loathes them. Physically, Conway was a commanding presence, a stocky, powerful man with gray-flecked hair and deep, piercing blue eyes.

"I wanted to apologize," Conway said, "about this morning. I didn't mean to blow up that way."

"It's O.K."

"I have to apologize to Herbie. I said some things . . ."

"He'll understand."

"I feel like hell," Conway said. "But when you watch a patient just collapse under you, just fall apart before your very eyes. . . . You don't know how it is."

"I don't," I admitted.

We drove for a while in silence, then I said, "Can I ask you a favor?"

"Sure."

"Tell me about J. D. Randall."

He paused. "Why?"

"Just curious."

"Bullshit."

"All right," I said.

"They got Lee, didn't they?" Conway said.

"Yes."

"Did he do it?"

"No."

"Are you sure?"

"I believe what he tells me," I said.

Conway sighed. "John," he said, "you're not a fool. Suppose somebody hung this thing on you. Wouldn't you deny it?"

"That's not the question."

"Sure it is. Anybody'd deny it."

"Isn't it possible Art didn't do it?"

"It's not merely possible. It's likely."

"Well then?"

Conway shook his head. "You're forgetting the way it works. J. D. is a big man. J. D. lost a daughter. There happens to be a convenient Chinaman in the neighborhood, who is known to do the nasty deed. A perfect situation."

"I've heard that theory before. I don't buy it."

"Then you don't know J. D. Randall."

"That's true."

"J. D. Randall," Conway said, "is the arch-prick of the universe. He has money and power and prestige. He can have whatever he wants—even a little Chinaman's head."

I said, "But why should he want it?"

Conway laughed. "Brother, where have you been?"

I must have looked puzzled.

"Don't you know about . . ." He paused, seeing that I did not. Then he very deliberately folded his arms across his chest and said nothing. He stared straight ahead.

"Well?" I said.

"Better ask Art."

"I'm asking you," I said.

"Ask Lew Carr," Conway said. "Maybe he'll tell you. I won't."

"Well then," I said, "tell me about Randall."

"As a surgeon."

"All right, as a surgeon."

Conway nodded. "As a surgeon," he said, "he isn't worth shit. He's mediocre. He loses people he shouldn't lose. Young people. Strong people."

I nodded.

"And he's mean as hell. He chews out his residents, puts them through all sorts of crap, keeps them miserable. He has a lot of good young men working under him, and that's how he controls them. I know; I did two years of thoracic under Randall before I did my cardiac at Houston. I was twenty-nine when I first met Randall, and he was forty-nine. He comes on very strong with his busy manner and his Bond Street suits and his friends with châteaux in France. None of it means he's a good surgeon, of course, but it carries over. It throws a halo around him. It makes him look good."

I said nothing. Conway was warming to his subject, raising his voice, moving his strong hands. I didn't want him to stop.

"The trouble," Conway said, "is that J. D. is in the old line. He started surgery in the forties and fifties, with Gross and Chartriss and Shackleford and the boys. Surgery was different then; manual skill was important and science didn't really count. Nobody knew about electrolytes or chemistry, and Randall's never felt comfortable with it. The new boys are; they've been weaned on enzymes and serum sodium. But it's all a troublesome puzzle to Randall."

"He has a good reputation," I said.

"So did John Wilkes Booth," Conway said. "For a while."

"Do I sense a professional jealousy?"

"I can cut circles around him with my left hand," Conway said. "Blindfolded."

I smiled.

"And hung over," he added. "On a Sunday."

"What's he like personally?"

"A prick. Just a prick. The residents say he walks around with a hammer in his pocket and a half-dozen nails, just in case he sees the opportunity to crucify somebody."

"He can't be that unpleasant."

"No," Conway admitted. "Not unless he's in especially good form. Like all of us, he has his off days."

"You make him sound very grim."

"No worse than the average bastard," he said. "You know, the residents say something else, too."

"Oh?"

"Yes. They say J. D. Randall likes cutting hearts because he never had one of his own."

ELEVEN

NO ENGLISHMAN IN HIS RIGHT MIND would ever go to Boston, particularly in 1630. To embark on a long sea journey to a hostile wilderness took more than courage, more than fortitude—it required desperation and fanaticism. Above all it required a deep and irreconcilable break with English society.

Fortunately, history judges men by their actions, not their motivations. It is for that reason that Bostonians can comfortably think of their ancestors as proponents of democracy and freedom, Revolutionary heroes, liberal artists and writers. It is the city of Adams and Revere, a city that still cherishes the Old North Church and Bunker Hill.

But there is another face to Boston, a darker face, which lies hidden in the pillory, the stocks, the dunking stool, and the witch hunts. Hardly a man now alive can look at these devices of torture for what they are: evidences of obsession, neurosis, and perverse cruelty. They are proofs of a society encircled by fear of sin, damnation, hellfire, disease, and Indians—in roughly that order. A tense, fearful, suspicious society. In short, a society of reactionary religious fanatics.

There is also a geographical factor, for Boston

was once a swamp. Some say this accounts for its outstandingly bad weather and uniformly humid climate; others say it is unimportant.

Bostonians are inclined to overlook much of the past. Like a slum kid who makes good, the city has swung far from its origins, and attempted to conceal them. As a colony of common men, it has established an untitled aristocracy to rival the most ancient and rigid of Europe. As a city of religion, it has developed a scientific community unrivaled in the East. It is also strongly narcissistic—a trait it shares with another city of questionable origin, San Francisco.

Unfortunately for both these cities, they can never quite escape their past. San Francisco cannot quite shake off its booming, crude, gold-rush spirit to become a genteel Eastern town. And Boston, no matter how hard it tries, cannot quite elude Puritanism and become English again.

We are all tied to the past, individually and collectively. The past shows through in the very structure of our bones, the distribution of our hair, and the coloring of our skin, as well as the way we walk, stand, eat, dress—and think.

I was reminded of this as I went to meet William Harvey Shattuck Randall, student of medicine.

ANYONE NAMED AFTER WILLIAM HARVEY[1] to say nothing of William Shattuck, must feel like a damned

---

[1] The English court physician who, in 1628, discovered that blood circulated in a closed loop.

fool. Like being named after Napoleon or Cary Grant, it places too great a burden on a child, too much of a challenge. Many things in life are difficult to live down, but nothing is more difficult than a name.

George Gall is a perfect example. After medical school, where he suffered through countless jokes and puns, he became a surgeon, specializing in liver and gallbladder disease. It was the worst possible thing he could do with a name like that, but he went into it with a strange, quiet certainty, as if it had all been foreordained. In a sense perhaps it had. Years later, when the jokes began to wear very thin, he wished he could change his name, but that was impossible.[2]

I doubted that William Harvey Shattuck Randall would ever change his own name. Though a liability, it was also an asset, particularly if he remained in Boston; besides, he seemed to be bearing up well. He was husky and blond and open-faced in a pleasant way. There was an All-American wholesomeness about him which made his room incongruous and faintly ridiculous.

William Harvey Shattuck Randall lived on the first floor of Sheraton Hall, the medical-school dormitory. Like most rooms in the dorm, his was a single, though rather more spacious than most. Cer-

[2] A doctor cannot change his name after receiving his M.D. degree without invalidating that degree. This means that there is a great rush in the final weeks of med school among doctors flocking into court to change their names before they receive their diplomas.

tainly more spacious than the fourth-floor pigeonhole I had occupied when I was a student. The top-floor rooms are cheaper.

They'd changed the paint color since my day. It was dinosaur-egg gray, then; now it was vomit green. But it was still the same old dorm—the same bleak corridors, the same dirty stairs, the same stale odor of sweat socks, textbooks, and hexachlorophene.

Randall had fixed his room up nicely. The decor was antique; the furniture looked as if it had been bought at a Versailles auction. There was a faded, nostalgic splendor about it, with its tattered red velvet and chipped gilded wood.

Randall stood back from the door. "Come in," he said. He didn't ask who I was. He had taken one look and smelled doctor. You get so you can do it, when you've been around them long enough.

I came into the room and sat down.

"Is it about Karen?" He seemed more preoccupied than sad, as if he had just returned from something important or were about to leave.

"Yes," I said. "I know this is a bad time . . ."

"No, go ahead."

I lit a cigarette and dropped the match into a gilded Venetian-glass ashtray. It was ugly but expensive.

"I wanted to talk to you about her."

"Sure."

I kept waiting for him to ask who I was, but he didn't really seem to care. He sat down in an armchair across from me, crossed his legs, and said, "What do you want to know?"

"When did you see her last?"

"Saturday. She came in from Northampton on the bus, and I picked her up at the terminal after lunch. I had a couple of hours free. I drove her out to the house."

"How did she seem?"

He shrugged. "Fine. There was nothing wrong with her, she seemed very happy. Talked all about Smith and her roommate. Apparently she had this wild roommate. And she talked about clothes, that sort of thing."

"Was she depressed? Nervous?"

"No. Not at all. She acted the same as always. Maybe a little excited about coming home after being away. I think she was a little worried about Smith. My parents treat her as the baby of the family, and she thought they didn't have confidence in her ability to make it. She was a little . . . defiant, I guess you'd say."

"When did you see her before last Saturday?"

"I don't know. Not since late August, I guess."

"So this was a reunion."

"Yes," he said. "I was always glad to see her. She was very bubbly, with a lot of energy, and she was a good mimic. She could give you an imitation of a professor or a boyfriend and she was hysterical. In fact, that was how she got the car."

"The car?"

"Saturday night," he said. "We were all at dinner. Karen, myself, Ev, and Uncle Peter."

"Ev?"

"My stepmother," he said. "We all call her Ev."

"So there were five of you?"

"No, four."

"What about your father?"

"He was busy at the hospital."

He said it very matter-of-factly, and I let it drop.

"Anyway," William said, "Karen wanted a car for the weekend and Ev refused, saying she didn't want her to be out all night. So Karen turned to Uncle Peter, who is a softer touch, and asked if she could borrow his car. He was reluctant, so she threatened to imitate him, and he immediately loaned her the car."

"What did Peter do for transportation?"

"I dropped him off at his place that night, on my way back here."

"So you spent several hours with Karen on Saturday."

"Yes. From around one o'clock to nine or ten."

"Then you left with your uncle?"

"Yes."

"And Karen?"

"She stayed with Ev."

"Did she go out that night?"

"I imagine so. That was why she wanted the car."

"Did she say where she was going?"

"Over to Harvard. She had some friends in the college."

"Did you see her Sunday?"

"No. Just Saturday."

"Tell me," I said, "when you were with her—did she look any different to you?"

He shook his head. "No. Just the same. Of course, she'd put on a little weight, but I guess all girls do that when they go to college. She was very active in the summer, playing tennis and swimming. She stopped that when she got to school, and I guess she put on a few pounds." He smiled slowly. "We kidded her about it. She complained about the lousy food, and we kidded her about eating so much of it that she still gained weight."

"Had she always had a weight problem?"

"Karen? No. She was always a skinny little kid, a real tomboy. Then she filled out in a real hurry. It was like a caterpillar, you know, and the cocoon."

"Then this was the first time she'd ever been overweight?"

He shrugged. "I don't know. To tell you the truth, I never paid that much attention."

"Was there anything else you noticed?"

"No, nothing else."

I looked around the room. On his desk, next to copies of Robbins' *Pathology and Surgical Anatomy,* was a photograph of the two of them. They both looked tanned and healthy. He saw me looking and said, "That was last spring, in the Bahamas. For once the whole family managed to get a week off together. We had a great time."

I got up and took a closer look. It was a flattering

picture of her. Her skin was darkly tanned, contrasting nicely with her blue eyes and blonde hair.

"I know it's a peculiar question," I said, "but has your sister always had dark hair on her lips and arms?"

"That was funny," he said, in a slow voice. "Now that you mention it. She had just a little bit there, on Saturday, Peter told her she'd better bleach it or wax it. She got mad for a couple of minutes, and then she laughed."

"So it was new?"

"I guess so. She might have had it all along, but I never noticed it until then. Why?"

"I don't know," I said.

He stood and came over to the picture. "You'd never think she would be the type for an abortion," he said. "She was such a great girl, funny and happy and full of energy. She had a real heart of gold. I know that sounds stupid, but she did. She was kind of the family mascot, being the youngest. Everybody loved her."

I said, "Where was she this summer?"

He shook his head. "I don't know."

"You don't know?"

"Well, not exactly. In theory, Karen was on the Cape, working in an art gallery in Provincetown." He paused. "But I don't think she was there much. I think she spent most of her time on the Hill. She had some kooky friends there; she collected oddball types."

"Men friends? Women friends?"

"Both." He shrugged. "But I don't really know. She only mentioned it to me once or twice, in casual references. Whenever I tried to ask her about it, she'd laugh and change the subject. She was very clever about discussing only what she wanted to."

"Did she mention any names?"

"Probably, but I don't remember. She could be maddening about names, talking about people casually as if you knew them intimately. Using just their first names. It was no good reminding her that you'd never heard of Herbie and Su-su and Allie before." He laughed. "I do remember she once did an imitation of a girl who blew bubbles."

"But you can't remember any names?"

He shook his head. "Sorry."

I stood to go. "Well," I said, "you must be very tired. What are you on these days?"

"Surgery. We just finished OB-GYN."

"Like it?"

"It's O.K.," he said blandly.

As I was leaving, I said, "Where did you do your OB?"

"At the BLI." He looked at me for a moment and frowned. "And to answer your question, I assisted on several. I know how to do one. But I was on duty at the hospital Sunday night. All night long. So there it is."

"Thanks for your time," I said.

"Sure," he said.

* * *

AS I LEFT THE DORMITORY, I saw a tall, lean, silver-haired man walking toward me. Of course I recognized him, even from a distance.

J. D. Randall was, if nothing else, distinctive.

TWELVE

THE SUN WAS SETTING, and the light on the quadrangle was turning yellow-gold. I lit a cigarette and walked up to Randall. His eyes widened slightly as he saw me, and then he smiled.

"Dr. Berry."

Very friendly. He held out his hand. I shook it: dry, clean, scrubbed to two inches above the elbow for ten minutes. A surgeon's hand.

"How do you do, Dr. Randall."

He said, "You wanted to see me?"

I frowned.

"My secretary," he said, "told me you had stopped by my office. About the chart."

"Oh, yes," I said, "the chart."

He smiled benignly. He was half a head taller than I. "I think we had better clear up a few things."

"All right."

"Come with me."

He didn't intend it as a command, but it came out that way. I was reminded that surgeons were the last autocrats in society, the last class of men who were given total control over a situation. Surgeons assumed the responsibility for the welfare of the patient, the staff, everything.

We walked back toward the parking lot. I had the feeling that he had come especially to see me. I had no idea how he knew I was there, but the feeling was very strong. As he walked, he swung his arms loosely at his sides. For some reason, I watched them; I remembered the neurologist's law of swinging arms.[1] I saw his hands, which were huge, all out of proportion to the rest of his body, huge hands, thick and hairy and red. His nails were trimmed to the required one-millimeter surgical length. His hair was cut short and his eyes were cold, gray, and businesslike.

"Several people have mentioned your name to me lately," he said.

"Oh?"

"Yes."

We came into the parking lot. His car was a silver Porsche; he stopped beside it and leaned casually against the polished fender. Something about his manner told me I was not invited to do the same. He looked at me for a moment in silence, his eyes flicking over my face, and then he said, "They speak highly of you."

"I'm glad to hear that."

"A man of good judgment and good sense."

---

[1] A paralyzed man will swing a paralyzed arm less than a good arm.

I shrugged. He smiled at me again, then said, "Busy day?"

"Busier than some days."

"You're at the Lincoln, is that right?"

"Yes."

"You're well thought of there."

"I try to do a good job."

"I'm told your work is excellent."

"Thank you." His approach was throwing me off; I didn't see where he was going. I didn't have to wait long.

"Did you ever think of changing hospitals?"

"What do you mean?"

"There may be other . . . possibilities. Openings."

"Oh?"

"Indeed."

"I'm quite happy where I am."

"For the present," he said.

"Yes, for the present."

"Do you know William Sewall?"

William Sewall was chief pathologist of the Mem. He was sixty-one and would shortly retire. I found myself disappointed in J. D. Randall. The last thing I had expected him to be was obvious.

"Yes, I know Sewall," I said. "Slightly."

"He will soon retire—"

"Timothy Stone is second man there, and he's excellent."

"I suppose," Randall said. He stared up at the sky. "I suppose. But many of us are not happy with him."

"I hadn't heard that."

He smiled thinly. "It isn't widely known."

"And many of you would be happier with me?"

"Many of us," Randall said carefully, "are looking for a new man. Perhaps someone from the outside, to bring a new viewpoint to the hospital. Change things around a bit; shake things up."

"Oh?"

"That is our thinking," Randall said.

"Timothy Stone is a close friend," I said.

"I don't see the relevance of that."

"The relevance," I said, "is that I wouldn't screw him."

"I would never suggest that you do."

"Really?"

"No," Randall said.

"Then maybe I'm missing the point," I said.

He gave his pleasant smile. "Maybe you are."

"Why don't you explain?"

He scratched the back of his head reflectively. I could see he was about to change tactics, to try a different approach. He frowned.

"I'm not a pathologist, Dr. Berry," he said, "but I have some friends who are."

"Not Tim Stone, I'll bet."

"Sometimes I think pathologists work harder than surgeons, harder than anyone. Being a pathologist seems to be a full-time job."

"That may be right," I said.

"I'm surprised you have so much free time," he said.

"Well, you know how it is," I said. I was beginning to be angry. First the bribe, then the threat. Buy him off or scare him off. But along with my anger, I had a strange curiosity: Randall was not a fool, and I knew he wouldn't be talking this way to me unless he was afraid of something. I wondered for a moment whether he had done the abortion himself, and then he said, "You have a family?"

"Yes," I said.

"Been in Boston some time?"

"I can always leave," I said, "if I find the pathological specimens too distasteful."

He took that very well. He didn't move, didn't shift his weight on the fender of the car. He just looked at me with those gray eyes and said, "I see."

"Maybe you'd better come right out and tell me what's on your mind."

"It's quite simple," he said. "I'm concerned about your motives. I can understand the ties of friendship, and I can even see how personal affection can be blinding. I admire your loyalty to Dr. Lee, though I would admire it more if you chose a less reprehensible subject. However, your actions seem to extend beyond loyalty. What *are* your motives, Dr. Berry?"

"Curiosity, Dr. Randall. Pure curiosity. I want to know why everybody's out to screw an innocent guy. I want to know why a profession dedicated to the objective examination of facts has chosen to be biased and uninterested."

He reached into his suit pocket and took out a

cigar case. He opened it and withdrew a single slim
cigar, clipped off the end, and lit it.

"Let's be sure," he said, "that we know what we're
talking about. Dr. Lee is an abortionist. Is that correct?"

"You're talking," I said. "I'm listening."

"Abortion is illegal. Furthermore, like every surgical procedure, it carries with it a finite risk to the
patient—even if practiced by a competent person,
and not a drunken . . ."

"Foreigner?" I suggested.

He smiled. "Dr. Lee," he said, "is an abortionist,
operating illegally, and his personal habits are questionable. As a doctor, his ethics are questionable.
As a citizen of the state, his actions are punishable
in a court of law. That's what's on my mind, Dr.
Berry. I want to know why you are snooping around,
molesting members of my family—"

"I hardly think that's the word for it."

"—and making a general nuisance of yourself in
this matter when you have better things to do,
things for which the Lincoln Hospital pays you a
salary. Like every other doctor, you have duties and
responsibilities. You are not fulfilling those duties.
Instead you are interfering in a family matter, creat-
ing a disturbance, and attempting to throw a smoke
screen around a reprehensible individual, a man
who has violated all the codes of medicine, a
man who has chosen to live beyond the limits of
the law, to thumb his nose at the dictates of the
framework of society—"

"Doctor," I said. "Looking at this as purely a family matter: What would you have done if your daughter had come to you with the news that she was pregnant? What if she had consulted you instead of going directly to an abortionist? What would you have done?"

"There is no point in mindless conjecture," he said.

"Surely you have an answer."

He was turning a bright crimson. The veins in his neck stood out above his starched collar. He pursed his lips, then said, "Is this your intention? To slander my family in the wild hope of helping your so-called friend?"

I shrugged. "It strikes me as a legitimate question," I said, "and there are several possibilities." I ticked them off on my fingers. "Tokyo, Switzerland, Los Angeles, San Juan. Or perhaps you have a good friend in New York or Washington. That would be much more convenient. And cheaper."

He turned on his heel and unlocked the door to his car.

"Think about it," I said. "Think hard about what you would have done for that family name."

He started the engine and glared at me.

"While you're at it," I said, "think about why she didn't come to you for help."

"My daughter," he said, his voice trembling with rage, "my daughter is a wonderful girl. She is sweet and beautiful. She doesn't have a malicious or dirty thought in her head. How dare you drag her down to your—"

"If she was so sweet and pure," I said, "how did she get pregnant?"

He slammed the door shut, put the car in gear, and roared off in a cloud of angry blue exhaust.

THIRTEEN

WHEN I RETURNED HOME, the house was dark and empty. A note in the kitchen told me that Judith was still over at the Lees with the kids. I walked around the kitchen and looked into the refrigerator; I was hungry but restless, unwilling to sit down and make a sandwich. Finally I settled for a glass of milk and some leftover cole slaw, but the silence of the house depressed me. I finished and went over to the Lees; they live just a block away.

From the outside, the Lee house is brick, massive, New England, and old, like all the other houses on the street. It had absolutely no distinguishing characteristics. I had always wondered about the house; it didn't seem suited to Art.

Inside, things were grim. In the kitchen, Betty sat with a rigid smile on her face as she fed the year-old baby; she looked tired and ragged; normally she was immaculately dressed with an unwilting, indefatigable manner. Judith was with her and Jane, our youngest, was holding on to Judith's skirt. She had begun that just a few weeks earlier.

From the living room, I heard the sound of the boys playing cops and robbers with cap pistols. With every bang, Betty shuddered. "I wish they'd stop," she said, "but I haven't the heart. . . ."

I went into the living room. All the furniture was overturned. From behind an easy chair Johnny, our four-year-old, saw me and waved, then fired his gun. Across the room the two Lee boys were huddled behind the couch. The air was acrid with smoke and the floor littered with rolls of paper caps.

Johnny fired, then called, "I got you."

"Did not," said Andy Lee, who was six.

"I did too. You're dead."

"I'm not dead," Andy said and fanned his gun. He was out of caps, though, and made only a clicking noise. He ducked down and said to Henry Lee, "Cover me while I reload."

"O.K., partner."

Andy reloaded, but his fingers were slow, and he grew impatient. Halfway through he stopped, aimed his gun, and shouted "Bang! Bang!" Then he continued.

"No fair," Johnny called, from behind the chair. "You're dead."

"So are you," Henry said. "I just got you."

"Oh, yeah?" Johnny said and fired three more caps. "You only winged me."

"Oh, yeah?" Henry said. "Take that."

The shooting continued. I walked back to the kitchen, where Judith was standing with Betty. Betty said, "How is it?"

I smiled. "They're arguing over who got whom."

"What did you find out today?"

"Everything's going to be all right," I said. "Don't worry."

She gave me a wry smile. Art's smile. "Yes, Doctor."

"I'm serious."

"I hope you're right," she said, putting a spoon of apple sauce into the baby's mouth. It dribbled out over her chin; Betty scooped it up and tried again.

"We just had some bad news," Judith said.

"Oh?"

"Bradford called. Art's lawyer. He won't take the case."

"Bradford?"

"Yes," Betty said. "He called half an hour ago."

"What did he say?"

"Nothing. Just that he couldn't take it at this time."

I lit a cigarette and tried to be calm. "I'd better call him," I said.

Judith looked at her watch. "It's five-thirty. He probably won't be—"

"I'll try anyway," I said. I went into Art's study. Judith came with me. I shut the door, closing off the sounds of gunfire.

Judith said, "What's really happening?"

I shook my head.

"Bad?"

"It's too early to say," I said. I sat down behind Art's desk and started to call Bradford.

"Are you hungry? Did you get anything to eat?"

"I stopped for a bite," I said, "on my way over."

"You look tired."

"I'm O.K.," I said. She leaned over the desk and I kissed her cheek.

"By the way," she said, "Fritz Werner has been calling. He wants to talk to you."

I might have expected that. Count on Fritz to know everything. Still, he might have something important; he might be very helpful. "I'll call him later."

"And before I forget," she said, "there's that party tomorrow."

"I don't want to go."

"We have to," she said. "It's George Morris."

I had forgotten. "All right," I said. "What time?"

"Six. We can leave early."

"All right," I said.

She went back to the kitchen as the secretary answered the phone and said, "Bradford, Wilson and Sturges."

"Mr. Bradford, please."

"I'm sorry," the secretary said. "Mr. Bradford has gone for the day."

"How can I reach him?"

"Mr. Bradford will be in the office at nine tomorrow morning."

"I can't wait that long."

"I'm sorry, sir."

"Don't be sorry," I said. "Just find him for me. This is Dr. Berry calling." I didn't know if the name would mean anything, but I suspected it might.

Her tone changed immediately. "Hold the line please, Doctor."

There was a pause of several seconds while I waited in the mechanical humming silence of the "Hold" button. Being on the "Hold" button is the technological equivalent of purgatory. That was what Art used to say. He hates telephones and never uses them unless he has to.

The secretary came back on. "Mr. Bradford is just leaving, but he will speak to you now."

"Thank you."

A mechanical click.

"George Bradford speaking."

"Mr. Bradford, this is John Berry."

"Yes, Dr. Berry. What can I do for you?"

"I'd like to speak to you about Art Lee."

"Dr. Berry, I'm just leaving—"

"Your secretary told me. Perhaps we could meet somewhere."

He hesitated and sighed into the phone. It sounded like a hissing, impatient serpent. "That won't serve any purpose. I'm afraid my decision is quite firm. The matter is out of my hands."

"Just a short meeting."

He paused again. "All right. I'll meet you at my

club in twenty minutes. The Trafalgar. See you then."

I hung up. The bastard: his club was downtown. I would have to run like hell to make it in time. I straightened my tie and hurried off to my car.

THE TRAFALGAR CLUB is located in a small, dilapidated house on Beacon Street, just down from the Hill. Unlike the professional clubs of larger cities, the Trafalgar is so quiet that few Bostonians even know of its existence.

I had never been there before, but I could have predicted the decor. The rooms were paneled in mahogany; the ceilings were high and dusty; the chairs heavy, padded tan leather, comfortable and wrinkled; the carpets were worn Orientals. In atmosphere, it reflected its members—stiff, aging, and masculine. As I checked my coat, I saw a sign which stated crisply, FEMALE GUESTS MAY BE ENTERTAINED BETWEEN THE HOURS OF 4 AND 5:30 O'CLOCK ON THURSDAYS ONLY. Bradford met me in the lobby.

He was a short, compact man, impeccably dressed. His black chalk-stripe suit was unwrinkled after a day of work, his shoes gleamed, and his cuffs protruded the proper length beyond his jacket sleeves. He wore a pocket watch on a silver chain, and his Phi Beta Kappa key contrasted nicely with the dark material of his vest. I didn't have to look him up in *Who's Who* to know that he lived someplace like Beverly Farms, that he had attended Harvard College and Harvard Law School, that his wife had gone to Vassar and still wore pleated skirts, cashmere sweaters, and pearls, or that his children attended Groton and Concord. Bradford wore it all, quietly and confidently.

"I'm ready for a drink," he said as we shook hands. "How about you?"

"Fine."

The bar was on the second floor, a large room with high windows looking out on Beacon Street and the Commons. It was a subdued room, smelling faintly of cigar smoke. Men spoke in low voices and talked in small groups. The bartender knew what everyone drank without being told: everyone, that is, except me. We sat in two comfortable chairs by the window and I ordered a vodka Gibson. Bradford just nodded to the bartender. While we waited for the drinks, he said, "I am sure you must be disappointed in my decision, but frankly——"

"I'm not disappointed," I said, "because I'm not on trial."

Bradford reached into his pocket, looked at his watch, and put it back.

"No one," he said crisply, "is on trial at this moment."

"I disagree. I think a great many people are on trial."

He rapped the table irritably and frowned across the room at the bartender. The psychiatrists call that displacement.

"And what," he said, "is that supposed to mean?"

"Everybody in this town is dropping Art Lee as if he had bubonic plague."

"And you suspect a dark conspiracy?"

"No," I said. "I'm just surprised."

"I have a friend," Bradford said, "who claims that all doctors are essentially naïve. You don't strike me as naïve."

"Is that a compliment?"

"That's an observation."

"I try," I said.

"Well, there's really no mystery and no conspiracy here. In my case, you must realize that I have many clients, of whom Mr. Lee is just one."

"Dr. Lee."

"Quite right. Dr. Lee. He is just one of my clients, and I have obligations to all of them which I discharge as I am best able. It happens that I spoke with the district attorney's office this afternoon, to determine when Dr. Lee's case would come up for hearing. It seems that Dr. Lee's case will conflict with another I have previously accepted. I cannot be in two courtrooms at once. I explained this to Dr. Lee."

The drinks came. Bradford raised his glass. "Cheers."

"Cheers."

He sipped his drink and looked at the glass. "When I explained my position to him, Dr. Lee accepted it. I also told him that my firm would make every effort to see that he had excellent legal counsel. We have four senior partners, and it is quite likely that one of them will be able to——"

"But not certain?"

He shrugged. "Nothing is certain in this world."

I sipped the drink. It was lousy, mostly vermouth with a touch of vodka.

"Are you a good friend of the Randalls?" I asked.

"I know them, yes."

"Does that have anything to do with your decision?"

"Certainly not." He sat up quite stiffly. "A lawyer learns very early to separate clients and friends. It's frequently necessary."

"Especially in a small town."

He smiled. "Objection, Your Honor."

He sipped his drink again. "Off the record, Dr. Berry, you should know that I am in complete sympathy with Lee. We both recognize that abortion is a fact of life. It happens all the time. The last figures I saw listed American abortions at a million yearly; it's very common. Speaking practically, it is necessary. Our laws relating to abortion are hazy, ill-defined, and absurdly strict. But I must remind you that the doctors are much more strict than the law itself. The abortion committees in hospitals are overcautious. They refuse to perform abortions under circumstances where the law would never intervene. In my opinion, before you can change the abortion laws, you must change the prevailing climate of medical opinion."

I said nothing. The Passing of the Buck is a time-honored ceremony, to be observed in silence. Bradford looked at me and said, "You don't agree?"

"Of course," I said. "But it strikes me as an interesting defense for an accused man."

"I wasn't proposing it as a defense."

"Then perhaps I misunderstood you."

"I wouldn't be surprised," he said dryly.

"Neither would I," I said, "because you haven't been making much sense. I always thought lawyers got right to the problem, instead of running circles around it."

"I am trying to clarify my position."

"Your position is quite clear," I said. "I'm worried about Dr. Lee."

"Very well. Let's talk about Dr. Lee. He has been indicted under a seventy-eight-year-old Massachusetts law which makes any abortion a felony punishable by fines and imprisonment up to five years. If the abortion results in death, the sentence may be from seven to twenty years."

"Is it second-degree murder or manslaughter?"

"Neither, technically. In terms of——"

"Then the charge is bailable?"

"Conceivably so. But in this case not, because the prosecution will attempt a murder charge under a common law act which says any death resulting from a felony is murder."

"I see."

"In terms of the progress of the case, the prosecution will bring forth evidence—good evidence, I'm sure—that Dr. Lee is an abortionist. They will show that the girl, Karen Randall, previously visited Dr. Lee and that he inexplicably kept no records of her visit. They will show that he cannot account for several crucial hours during Sunday evening. And they will present Mrs. Randall's testimony that the girl told her Lee performed the abortion.

"In the end, it will come down to a conflict of testimony. Lee, a proven abortionist, will say he didn't do it; Mrs. Randall will say he did. If you were the jury, whom would you believe?"

"There is no proof that Dr. Lee aborted that girl. The evidence is wholly circumstantial."

"The trail will be held in Boston."

"Then hold it elsewhere," I said.

"On what grounds? That the moral climate here is unfavorable?"

"You're talking technicalities. I'm talking about saving a man."

"In the technicalities lies the strength of the law."

"And the weaknesses."

He gave me a thoughtful look. "The only way to 'save' Dr. Lee, as you say, is to demonstrate that he did not perform the operation. That means the real abortionist must be found. I think the chances of doing so are slim."

"Why?"

"Because, when I talked to Lee today, I came away convinced he was lying through his teeth. I think he did it, Berry. I think he killed her."

FOURTEEN

WHEN I RETURNED TO THE HOUSE, I found that Judith and the kids were still at Betty's. I made myself another drinks—a strong one, this time—and sat in the living room, dead tired but unable to relax.

I have a bad temper. I know that, and I try to control it, but the truth is I am clumsy and abrupt with people. I guess I don't like people much; maybe that's why I became a pathologist in the first place. Looking back over the day, I realized I had lost my temper too often. That was stupid; there was no percentage in it; no gain, and potentially a great deal of loss.

The telephone rang. It was Sanderson, head of the path labs at the Lincoln. The first thing he said was, "I'm calling from the hospital phone."

"O.K.," I said.

The hospital phone had at least six extensions. In the evening, anyone could listen in.

"How was your day?" Sanderson said.

"Interesting," I said. "How was yours?"

"It had its moments," Sanderson said.

I could imagine. Anyone who wanted me out of his hair would put the squeeze on Sanderson. It was the most logical thing to do, and it could be managed quite subtly. A few jokes: "Say, I hear you're shorthanded these days." A few earnest inquiries: "What's this I hear about Berry being sick? Oh? I heard that he was. But he hasn't been in, has he?" Then a few choice words from the chiefs of service: "Sanderson, how the hell do you expect me to keep my medical staff in line when you're letting your path people take off all the time?" And finally someone from the administration: "We run a ship-shape hospital here, everybody has his job and everybody does it, no deadwood on board."

The net effect would be an intense pressure to get me back in the lab or find a new man.

"Tell them I've got tertiary syphilis," I said. "That should hold them."

Sanderson laughed. "There's no problem," he said. "Yet. I've got a pretty tough old neck. I can keep it stuck out a while longer."

Then he paused, and said, "How much longer do you think it will be?"

"I don't know," I said. "It's complicated."

"Come by and see me tomorrow," he said. "We can discuss it."

"Good," I said. "Maybe by then I'll know more. Right now, it's just as bad as the Peru case."

"I see," Sanderson said. "Tomorrow, then."

"Right."

I hung up, certain he knew what I was talking about. I had meant that there was something wrong with the Karen Randall business, something out of place. It was like a case we had three months ago, a rare thing called agranulocytosis, the complete absence of white cells in the blood. It's a serious condition because without white cells, you can't fight infection. Most people are carrying disease organisms around in their mouth or body normally—staph or strep, sometimes diphtheria and pneumococcus—and if your bodily defenses go down, you infect yourself.

Anyhow, the patient was American, a doctor working for the Public Health Service in Peru. He was taking a Peruvian drug for asthma, and one day he began to get sick. He had sores in his mouth and a temperature, and he felt lousy. He went to a doctor in Lima and had a blood test. His white count was 600.[1] The next day it was down to 100, and the next day it was zero. He got a plane to Boston and checked into our hospital.

They did a bone-marrow biopsy, sticking a hollow needle into his sternum[2] and drawing out some marrow. I looked at it microscopically and was puzzled. He had lots of immature cells of the granulocyte series in his marrow, and while it was abnormal, it was not terribly bad. I thought, "Hell, something is wrong here," so I went to see his doctor.

His doctor had been tracing the Peruvian drug the patient was taking. It turned out to contain a substance removed from the American market in 1942 because it suppressed white-cell formation.

[1] Normal white count is 4–9,000 cells/cubic centimeter. With infection, this may double or triple.
[2] Breastbone.

The doctor figured this was what was wrong with his patient—he had suppressed his own white cells, and now he was infecting himself. The treatment was simple: take him off the drug, do nothing, and wait for his marrow to recover.

I told the doctor that the marrow didn't look so bad on the slide. We went to see the patient and found he was still sick. He had ulcers in his mouth, and staph infections on his legs and back. He had a high fever, was lethargic, and answered questions slowly.

We couldn't understand why his marrow should seem so basically normal when he was so damned sick; we puzzled over this for most of the afternoon. Finally, about four, I asked the doctor if there had been any infection at the site of biopsy, where they had made the puncture to draw marrow. The doctor said he hadn't checked. We went to the patient and examined his chest.

Surprise: unpunctured. The marrow biopsy hadn't been taken from this patient. One of the nurses or residents had screwed up the tags, mislabeling a marrow sample from a man with suspected leukemia. We immediately drew a sample from our patient and found a very suppressed marrow indeed.

The patient later recovered, but I would never forget our puzzling over the lab results.

I HAD THE SAME FEELING NOW—something was wrong, something was out of place. I couldn't put my finger on it, but I had the suspicion that people were working at cross-purposes, almost as if we were talking about different things. My own position was clear: Art was innocent until proven guilty, and that wasn't proven yet.

Nobody else seemed to care whether Art was guilty or not. The issue that was crucial to me was irrelevant to them.

Now why was that?

TUESDAY
OCTOBER 11

ONE

WHEN I AWOKE IT FELT LIKE A NORMAL DAY. I was exhausted and it was drizzling outside, cold, gray, and uninviting. I pulled off my pajamas and took a hot shower. While I was shaving, Judith came in and kissed me, then went to the kitchen to make breakfast. I smiled into the mirror and caught myself wondering what the surgical schedule would be like.

Then I remembered: I wasn't going to the hospital today. The whole business came back to me.

It was not a normal day.

I went to the window and stared at the drizzle on the glass. I wondered then for the first time whether I ought to drop everything and go back to work. The prospect of driving to the lab, parking in the lot, hanging up my coat, and putting on my apron and gloves—all the familiar details of routine—seemed suddenly very appealing, almost enticing. It was my job; I was comfortable at it;

there were no stresses or strains; it was what I was trained to do. I had no business playing amateur detective. In the cold morning light, the idea seemed ludicrous.

Then I began to remember the faces I had seen. Art's face, and the face of J. D. Randall, and Bradford's smug confidence. And I knew that if I didn't help Art, nobody would.

In one sense, it was a frightening, almost terrifying thought.

JUDITH SAT WITH ME AT BREAKFAST. The kids were still asleep; we were alone.

"What are you planning today?" she said.

"I'm not sure."

I had been asking myself that very question. I had to find out more, lots more. About Karen, and Mrs. Randall particularly. I still didn't know very much about either of them.

"I'll start with the girl," I said.

"Why?"

"From what I've been told, she was all sweetness and light. Everybody loved her; she was a wonderful girl."

"Maybe she was."

"Yes," I said, "but it might be good to get the opinion of someone besides her brother and her father."

"How?"

"I'll begin," I said, "with Smith College."

* * *

SMITH COLLEGE, Northampton, Massachusetts, 2,200 girls getting an exclusive education in the middle of nowhere. It was two hours on the turnpike to the Holyoke exit; another half-hour on small roads until I passed under the train tracks and came into the town. I've never liked Northampton. It has a peculiarly repressed atmosphere for a college town; you can almost smell irritation and frustration in the air, the heavy combined frustration of 2,200 pretty girls consigned to the wilderness for four years, and the combined irritation of the natives who are forced to put up with them for that time.

The campus is beautiful, particularly in autumn, when the leaves are turning. Even in the rain, it's beautiful. I went directly to the college information office and looked up Karen Randall in the paperback directory of students and faculty. I was given a map of the campus and set out for her dorm, Henley Hall.

It turned out to be a white frame house on Wilbur Street. There were forty girls living inside. On the ground floor was a living room done in bright, small-print fabric, rather foolishly feminine. Girls wandered around in dungarees and long, ironed hair. There was a bell desk by the door.

"I'd like to see Karen Randall," I said to the girl.

She gave me a startled look, as if she thought I might be a middle-aged rapist.

"I'm her uncle," I said. "Dr. Berry."

"I've been away all weekend," the girl said. "I

haven't seen Karen since I got back. She went to Boston this weekend."

I was in luck: this girl apparently didn't know. I wondered whether the other girls did; it was impossible to tell. It seemed likely that her housemother would know, or would find out soon. I wanted to avoid the housemother.

"Oh," said the girl behind the desk. "There's Ginnie. Ginnie's her roommate."

A dark-haired girl was walking out the door. She wore tight dungarees and a tight poor-boy sweater, but the overall effect remained oddly prim. Something about her face disowned the rest of her body.

The desk girl waved Ginnie over and said, "This is Dr. Berry. He's looking for Karen."

Ginnie gave me a shocked look. She knew. I quickly took her and steered her to the living room, and sat her down.

"But Karen's—"

"I know," I said. "But I want to talk to you."

"I think I'd better check with Miss Peters," Ginnie said. She started to get up. I pushed her gently back down.

"Before you do," I said, "I'd better tell you that I attended Karen's autopsy yesterday."

Her hand went to her mouth.

"I'm sorry to be so blunt, but there are serious questions that only you can answer. We both know what Miss Peters would say."

"She'd say I can't talk to you," Ginnie said. She

was looking at me suspiciously, but I could see I
had caught her curiosity.

"Let's go someplace private," I said.

"I don't know . . ."

"I'll only keep you a few minutes."

She got up and nodded toward the hall. "Men
aren't normally allowed in our rooms," she said,
"but you're a relative, aren't you?"

"Yes," I said.

Ginnie and Karen shared a room on the ground
floor, at the back of the building. It was small and
cramped, cluttered with feminine mementos—
pictures of boys, letters, joke birthday cards, pro-
grams from Ivy football games, bits of ribbon,
schedules of classes, bottles of perfume, stuffed toy
animals. Ginnie sat on one bed and waved me to a
desk chair.

"Miss Peters told me last night," Ginnie said,
"that Karen had . . . died in an accident. She asked
me not to mention it to anyone for a while. It's
funny. I never knew anybody who died—I mean,
my age, that kind of thing—and it's funny. I mean
peculiar, I didn't feel anything, I couldn't get very
worked up. I guess I don't really believe it yet."

"Did you know Karen before you were roommates?"

"No. The college assigned us."

"Did you get along?"

She shrugged. Somehow, she had learned to
make every bodily gesture a wiggle. But it was un-

real, like a practiced gesture perfected before the mirror.

"I guess we got along. Karen wasn't your typical freshman. She wasn't scared of the place, and she was always going away for a day or the weekend. She practically never went to class, and she always talked about how she hated it here. That's the thing to say, you know, but she meant it, she really did. I think she really *did* hate it."

"Why do you think so?"

"Because of the way she acted. Not going to class, always leaving campus. She'd sign out for weekends, saying she was going to visit her parents. But she never did, she told me. She hated her parents."

Ginnie got up and opened a closet door. Inside, tacked to the door, was a large glossy photograph of J. D. Randall. The picture was covered with minute punctures.

"You know what she used to do? She used to throw darts at this picture. That's her father, he's a surgeon or something; she threw darts at him every night, before going to sleep."

Ginnie closed the door.

"What about her mother?"

"Oh, she liked her mother. Her real mother; she died. There's a stepmother now. Karen never liked her very much."

"What else did Karen talk about?"

"Boys," Ginnie said, sitting on the bed again. "That's all any of us talk about. Boys. Karen went to private school around here someplace, and she knew a lot of boys. Yalies were always coming to see her."

"Did she date anyone in particular?"

"I don't think so. She had lots of guys. They were all chasing her."

"Popular?"

"Or something," Ginnie said, wrinkling her nose. "Listen, it isn't nice to say things about her now, you know? And I have no reason to think it's true. Maybe it's all a big story."

"What's that?"

"Well, you get here as a freshman and nobody knows you, nobody's ever *heard* of you before, and you can tell people anything you like and get away with it. I used to tell people I was a high-school cheerleader, just for the fun of it. Actually I went to private school, but I always wanted to be a high-school cheerleader."

"I see."

"They're so wholesome, you know?"

"What kind of stories did Karen tell you?"

"I don't know. They weren't exactly stories. Just sort of implications. She liked people to believe that she was wild, and all her friends were wild. Actually, that was her favorite word: *wild*. And she knew how to make something sound real. She never just told you straight out, in a whole long thing. It was little comments here and there. About her abortions and all."

"Her abortions?"

"She said she had had two before she ever got to college. Now that's pretty incredible, don't you think? Two abortions? She was only seventeen, after all. I told her I didn't believe it, so she went into this explanation of how it was done, the complete explanation. Then I wasn't so sure."

A girl from a medical family could easily acquire a knowledge of the mechanics of a D & C. That didn't prove she'd had an abortion herself.

"Did she tell you anything specific about them? Where they were done?"

"No. She just said she'd had them. And she kept saying things like that. She wanted to shock me, I know that, but she could be pretty crude when she wanted. I remember the first—no, the second weekend we were here, she went out Saturday night, and she got back late. I went to a mixer. Karen came in all a mess, crawled into bed with the lights out, and said, 'Jesus, I love black meat.' Just like that. I didn't know what to say, I mean, I didn't know her well then, so I didn't say anything. I just thought she was trying to shock me."

"What else did she say to you?"

Ginnie shrugged. "I can't remember. It was always little things. One night, as she's getting ready to go out for the weekend, and she's whistling in front of the mirror, she says to me, 'I'm really going to get it this weekend.' Or something like that, I don't remember the exact words."

"And what did you say?"

"I said, 'Enjoy yourself.' What *can* you say when

you get out of the shower and somebody says that to you? So she said, 'I will, I will.' She was always coming up with shocking little comments."

"Did you ever believe her?"

"After a couple of months, I was beginning to."

"Did you ever have reason to think she was pregnant?"

"While she was here? At school? No."

"You're sure?"

"She never said anything. Besides, she was on the pill."

"Are you certain of that?"

"Yeah, I think so. At least, she made this big ceremony of it every morning. The pills are right there."

"Where?"

Ginnie pointed. "Right there on her desk. In that little bottle."

I got up and went to the desk, and picked up the plastic bottle. The label was from Beacon Pharmacy; there were no typed directions. I took out my notebook and wrote down the prescription number and the name of the doctor. Then I opened the bottle and shook out a pill. There were four left.

"She took these every day?"

"Every single day," Ginnie said.

I was no gynecologist and no pharmacologist, but I knew several things. First, that most birth-control pills were now sold in a dispenser to help a woman keep track of the days. Second, that the initial hormone dosage had been cut from ten milligrams a day to two milligrams. That meant the pills were small.

These pills were huge in comparison. There were no surface markings of any kind; they were chalky white and rather crumbly to the touch. I slipped one into my pocket and replaced the others in the bottle. Even without checking, I had a pretty good idea what the pills were.

"Did you ever meet any of Karen's boyfriends?" I asked.

Ginnie shook her head.

"Did Karen ever talk about them? Talk about her dates?"

"Not really. Not personally, if you know what I mean. She'd talk about how they'd been in bed, but it was usually just gross stuff. She was always trying to gross you out. You know, the earthy bit. Wait a minute."

She got up and went to Karen's dresser. There was a mirror over the dresser; stuck into the frame were several pictures of boys. She plucked out two and handed them to me.

"This guy was one she talked about, but I don't think she was seeing him anymore. She used to date him over the summer or something. He goes to Harvard."

The picture was a standard publicity pose of a boy in a football uniform. He had the number 71, and was crouched down in a three-point stance, snarling into the camera.

"What's his name?"

"I don't know."

I picked up a Harvard-Columbia football program and looked up the roster. Number 71 was a right guard, Alan Zenner. I wrote the name in my notebook and gave the picture back to Ginnie.

"This other one," she said, handing me the second picture, "is a newer guy. I think she was seeing him. Some nights, she'd come back and kiss the picture before she went to bed. His name was Ralph, I think. Ralph or Roger."

The picture showed a young Negro standing in a tight, shiny suit with an electric guitar in one hand. He was smiling rather stiffly.

"You think she was seeing him?"

"Yes, I think so. He's part of a group that plays in Boston."

"And you think his name is Ralph?"

"Something like that."

"You know the name of the group?"

Ginnie frowned. "She told me once. Probably more than once, but I don't remember. Karen sort of liked to keep her boys a mystery. It wasn't like some girl sitting down and telling you every little thing about her boyfriend. Karen never did that, it was always bits and snatches."

"You think she was meeting this fellow when she went away for weekends?"

Ginnie nodded.

"Where did she go on weekends? Boston?"

"I imagine. Boston or New Haven."

I turned the picture over in my hands. On the back it said, "Photo by Curzin, Washington Street."

"Can I take this picture with me?"

"Sure," she said. "I don't care."

I slipped it into my pocket, then sat down again.

"Did you ever meet any of these people? Any of the boys?"

"No. I never met any of her friends. Oh—wait a minute. I did, once. A girl."

"A girl?"

"Yes. Karen told me one day that this good friend of hers was coming up for a day. She told me all about how cool this girl was, how wild. This big build-up. I was really waiting for something spectacular. Then when she showed up . . ."

"Yes?"

"Really strange," Ginnie said. "Very tall, with real long legs, and all the time Karen kept saying how she wished she had long legs like that, and the girl just sort of sat there and didn't say anything. She was pretty, I guess. But really strange. She acted like she was asleep. Maybe she was up on something; I don't know. Finally she began to talk, after about an hour of just sitting there, and she said these weird things."

"Like what?"

"I don't know. Weird things. 'The rain in Spain is mainly down the drain.' And she made up poetry about people running in spaghetti fields. It was pretty dull, I mean, not what you'd call good."

"What was this girl's name?"

"I don't remember. Angie, I think."

"Was she in college?"

"No. She was young, but she wasn't in college. She worked. I think Karen said she was a nurse."

"Try to remember her name," I said.

Ginnie frowned and stared at the floor, then shook her head. "I can't," she said. "I didn't pay that much attention."

I didn't want to let it go, but it was getting late. I said, "What else can you tell me about Karen? Was she nervous? Jittery?"

"No. She was always very calm. Everybody else in the house was nervous, especially around hourly time, when we have our exams, but she didn't seem to care."

"Did she have a lot of energy? Was she bouncy and talkative?"

"Karen? Are you kidding? Listen, she was always half dead, except for her dates, when she'd perk up, but otherwise she was always tired and always complaining about how tired she was."

"She slept a lot?"

"Yes. She slept through most of her classes."

"Did she eat a lot?"

"Not particularly. She slept through most of her meals, too."

"She must have lost weight, then."

"Actually, it went up," Ginnie said. "Not too much, but enough. She couldn't get into most of her dresses, after six weeks. She had to buy some more."

"Did you notice any other changes?"

"Well, only one, but I'm not sure it really matters. I mean, it mattered to Karen, but nobody else cared."

"What was that?"

"Well, she had the idea that she was getting hairy. You know, arms and legs and on her lip. She complained that she was shaving her legs all the time."

I looked at my watch and saw that it was nearly noon. "Well, I don't want to keep you from your classes."

"Doesn't matter," Ginnie said. "This is interesting."

"How do you mean?"

"Watching you work, and all."

"You must have talked with a doctor before."

She sighed. "You must think I'm stupid," she said, in a petulant voice "I wasn't born yesterday."

"I think you're very intelligent," I said.

"Will you want me to testify?"

"Testify? Why?"

"In court, at the trial."

Looking at her, I had the feeling she was practicing before the mirror once again. Her face had a secretly wise expression, like a movie heroine.

"I'm not sure I follow you."

"You can admit it to me," she said. "I know you're a lawyer."

"Oh."

"I figured it out ten minutes after you arrived. You want to know how?"

"How?"

"When you picked up those pills and looked at them. You did it very carefully, not like a doctor at all. Frankly, I think you'd make a terrible doctor."

"You're probably right," I said.

"Good luck with your case," she said as I was leaving.

"Thanks."

Then she winked at me.

TWO

THE X-RAY ROOM on the second floor of the Mem had a fancy name: Radiological Diagnosis. It didn't matter what they called it, it was the same inside as every other X-ray room anywhere. The walls were sheets of white frosted glass, and there were little jam-clips for the films. It was quite a large room, with sufficient space for a half-dozen radiologists to work at once.

I came in with Hughes. He was a radiologist at the Mem that I'd known for a long time; he and his wife sometimes played bridge with Judith and me. They were good players, blood players, but I didn't mind. Sometimes I get that way myself.

I hadn't called Lewis Carr because I knew he wouldn't help me. Hughes was low on the General totem pole and didn't give a damn whether I wanted to look at films from Karen Randall or the Aga Khan, who had come here for a kidney operation some years ago. He took me right up to the X-ray room.

On the way I said, "How's your sex life?"

That's a standard rib for a radiologist. It's well known that radiologists have the shortest lifespan of any medical specialist. The exact reasons are unknown, but the natural assumption is that the X rays get to them. In the old days, radiologists used to stand in the same room as the patient when the films were taken. A few years of that, and they'd soak up enough gamma to finish them. Then, too, in the old days the film was less sensitive, and it took a whopping big dose to get a decent contrast exposure.

But even now, with modern techniques and better knowledge, a ribald tradition remains, and radiologists are condemned to suffer through a lifetime of jokes about their lead-lined jockstraps and their shriveled gonads. The jokes, like the X rays, are an occupational hazard. Hughes took it well.

"My sex life," he said, "is a damn sight better than my bridge game."

As we came into the room, three or four radiologists were at work. They were each seated in front of an envelope full of films and a tape recorder; they took out films individually and read off the patient's name and unit number, and the kind of film it was—AP or LAO, IVP, or thorax, and so forth— and then they slapped it up against the frosted glass and dictated their diagnosis.[1]

One wall of the room was given over to the intensive care patients. These were seriously ill people, and their films were not stored in manila envelopes. Instead they were hung on revolving racks. You pressed a button and waited until the rack came around to the films of the patient you wanted to see. It meant you could get to a critically ill patient's films rapidly.

The film storeroom was adjacent to the X-ray room. Hughes went in and pulled Karen Randall's films, and brought them back. We sat down in front of a sheet of glass, and Hughes clipped up the first picture.

"Lateral skull film," he said, peering at it. "Know why it was ordered?"

"No," I said.

I, too, looked at the plate, but I could make little of it. Skull films—X rays of the head—are difficult to interpret. The cranium is a complex piece of bone, producing a confusing interlocking pattern of light and dark. Hughes examined it for some time, occasionally tracing lines with the cap of his fountain pen.

---

[1] AP is anteroposterior, indicating that the X rays penetrated from front to back, where they struck the plate. LAO is left anterior oblique and IVP is contrast media in the genitourinary tract, a film showing kidneys, ureters, and bladder.

"Seems normal," he said at last. "No fractures, no abnormal calcification, no evidence of air or hematoma. Of course, it'd be nice to have an arteriogram or a PEG."[2]

"Let's have a look at the other views," he said. He pulled down the lateral view and put up the face-on, AP film. "This looks normal, too," he said. "I wonder why they were taken—was she in an auto accident?"

"Not that I know of."

He rummaged in the file. "No," he said. "Obviously. They didn't do face films. Only skull films."

Face films were a separate series of angles, utilized to check for fractures of the facial bones.

Hughes continued to examine the AP film, then put the lateral back up. He still could find nothing abnormal.

"Damned if I can figure it," he said, tapping the plate. "Nothing. Not a goddamned thing there, for my money."

"All right," I said, standing up. "Thanks for your help."

As I left I wondered whether the X rays had helped clear things up or just made everything worse.

[2] These are ways of making skull films easier to interpret. An arteriogram is an X ray taken after the cerebral arteries have been filled with radio opaque liquid. A PEG, or pneumoencephalogram, consists of draining all the cerebrospinal fluid and pumping in air to increase contrast in the ventricles. It is a painful procedure which cannot be done under anesthesia. Both techniques are considered minor surgery, and are not done unless there is good evidence for their necessity.

THREE

I STEPPED INTO A PHONE BOOTH near the hospital lobby. I got out my notebook and found the pharmacy number and the prescription number. I also found the pill I had taken from Karen's room.

I chipped off a flake with my thumbnail and ground it into the palm of my hand. It crushed easily into a soft powder. I was pretty sure what it was, but to be certain I touched the tip of my tongue to the powder.

There was no mistaking the taste. Crushed aspirin on your tongue tastes terrible.

I dialed the pharmacy.

"Beacon Pharmacy."

"This is Dr. Berry at the Lincoln. I'd like to know a drug as follows—"

"Just a minute while I get a pencil."

A short pause.

"Go ahead, Doctor."

"The name is Karen Randall. The number is one-four-seven-six-six-seven-three. Prescribing doctor Peter Randall."

"I'll check that for you."

The phone was put down. I heard whistling and pages flipping, then: "Yes, here it is. Darvon, twenty capsules, 75 milligram. Orders—'Once every four hours as needed for pain.' It was refilled twice. Do you want the dates?"

"No," I said. "That's fine."

"Is there anything else?"

"No, thanks. You've been very helpful."

"Any time."

I replaced the receiver slowly. Things were getting more and more screwy. What kind of girl pretended to take birth-control pills but actually took aspirin, which she stored in an empty bottle that once contained pills for menstrual cramps?

FOUR

DEATH FROM ABORTION is a relatively rare event. This basic fact tends to be obscured in all the fanfare and statistics. The statistics, like the fanfare, are emotional and imprecise. Estimates vary widely, but most people agree that about a million illegal abortions are performed each year, and about 5,000 women die as a result of them. This means that the operative mortality is about 500/100,000.

This is a very high figure, especially in the light of mortality in hospital abortions. Death in hospital abortions ranges from 0–18/100,000, which makes it, at worst, about as dangerous as a tonsillectomy (17/100,000).

All this means is that illegal abortions are about twenty-five times as deadly as they have to be. Most people are horrified by this. But Art, who thought clearly and carefully about such things, was impressed by the statistic. And he said something very interesting: that one reason abortion remained illegal was because it was so safe.

"You have to look at the volume of business," he once said. "A million women is a meaningless number. What it comes down to is one illegal abortion every thirty seconds, day in, day out, year after year. That makes it a very common operation, and for better or worse, it's safe."

In his cynical way, he talked about the Death Threshold, as he called it. He defined the Death Threshold as the number of people who must die each year of needless, accidental causes before anyone gets excited about it. In numerical terms, the Death Threshold was set at about 30,000 a year— the number of Americans who died of automobile accidents.

"There they are," Art said, "dying on the highways at the rate of about eighty a day. Everybody accepts it as a fact of life. So who's going to care about the fourteen women who die every day of abortions?"

He argued that in order to force doctors and lawyers into action, the abortion death figures would have to approach 50,000 a year, and perhaps more.

At the current mortality rates, that meant ten million abortions a year.

"In a way, you see," he said, "I'm doing a disservice to society. I haven't lost anybody in abortion, so I'm keeping those death figures down. That's good for my patients, of course, but bad for society as a whole. Society will only act out of fear and gross guilt. We are attuned to large figures; small statistics don't impress us. Who'd give a damn if Hitler had only killed ten thousand Jews?"

He went on to argue that by doing safe abortions he was preserving the status quo, keeping the pressure off legislators to change the laws. And then he said something else.

"The trouble with this country," he said, "is that the women have no guts. They'd rather slink off and have a dangerous, illegal operation performed than change the laws. The legislators are all men, and men don't bear the babies; they can afford to be moralistic. So can the priests: if you had women priests, you'd see a hell of a quick change in religion. But politics and religion are dominated by the men, and the women are reluctant to push too hard. Which is bad, because abortion is their business—their infants, their bodies, their risk. If a million women a year wrote letters to their congressmen, you might see a little action. Probably not, but you might. Only the women won't do it."

I think that thought depressed him more than anything else. It came back to me as I drove to meet a woman who, from all reports, had plenty of guts: Mrs. Randall.

NORTH OF COHASSET, about half an hour from downtown Boston, is an exclusive residential community built along a stretch of rocky coast. It is rather reminiscent of Newport—old frame houses with elegant lawns, looking out at the sea.

The Randall house was enormous, a four-story Gothic white frame building with elaborate balconies and turrets. The lawn sloped down to the water; altogether there were probably five acres of land surrounding the house. I drove up the long gravel drive and parked in the turnabout next to two Porsches, one black, the other canary-yellow. Apparently the whole family drove Porsches. There was a garage tucked back to the left of the house with a gray Mercedes sedan. That was probably for the servants.

I got out and was wondering how I would ever get past the butler when a woman came out of the front door and walked down the steps. She was pulling on her gloves as she went, and seemed in a great hurry. She stopped when she saw me.

"Mrs. Randall?"

"Yes," she said.

I don't know what I was expecting, but certainly nothing like her. She was tall, and dressed in a beige Chanel suit. Her hair was jet black and glossy, her legs long, her eyes very large and dark. She couldn't have been older than thirty. You could have cracked ice-cubes on her cheekbones, she was so hard.

I stared at her in dumb silence for several moments, feeling like a fool but unable to help myself. She frowned at me impatiently. "What do you want? I haven't got all day."

Her voice was husky and her lips were sensual. She had the proper accent, too: flattened inflection and the slightly British intonation.

"Come on, come on," she said. "Speak up."

"I'd like to talk to you," I said, "about your daughter."

"My stepdaughter," she said quickly. She was sweeping past me, moving toward the black Porsche.

"Yes, your stepdaughter."

"I've told everything to the police," she said. "And I happen to be late for an appointment, so if you will excuse me . . ." She unlocked the door to her car and opened it.

I said, "My name is—"

"I know who you are," she said. "Joshua was talking about you last night. He told me you might try to see me."

"And?"

"And he told me, Dr. Berry, to suggest that you go to hell."

She was doing her best to be angry, but I could see she was not. There was something else showing in her face, something that might have been curiosity or might have been fear. It struck me as odd.

She started the engine. "Good day, Doctor."

I leaned over toward her. "Following your husband's orders?"

"I usually do."

"But not always," I said.

She was about to put the car in gear, but she stopped, her hand resting on the shift. "I beg your pardon," she said.

"What I mean is that your husband doesn't quite understand everything," I said.

"I think he does."

"You know he doesn't, Mrs. Randall."

She turned off the engine and looked at me. "I'll give you thirty seconds to get off this property," she said, "before I call the police." But her voice was trembling, and her face was pale.

"Call the police? I don't think that's wise."

She was faltering; her self-confidence draining away from her.

"Why did you come here?"

"I want you to tell me about the night you took Karen to the hospital. Sunday night."

"If you want to know about that night," she said, "go look at the car." She pointed to the yellow Porsche.

I went over and looked inside.

It was like a bad dream.

The upholstery had once been tan, but now it was red. Everything was red. The driver's seat was red. The passenger seat was deep red. The dashboard knobs were red. The steering wheel was red in places. The floor carpet was crusty and red.

Quarts of blood had been lost in that car.

"Open the door," Mrs. Randall said. "Feel the seat."

I did. The seat was damp.

"Three days later," she said. "It still hasn't dried out. That's how much blood Karen lost. That's what he did to her."

I shut the door. "Is this her car?"

"No. Karen didn't have a car. Joshua wouldn't let her have one until she was twenty-one."

"Then whose car is it?"

"It's mine," Mrs. Randall said.

I nodded to the black car she was sitting in. "And this?"

"It's new. We just bought it yesterday."

"We?"

"I did. Joshua agreed."

"And the yellow car?"

"We have been advised by the police to keep it, in case it is needed as evidence. But as soon as we can . . ."

I said, "What exactly happened Sunday night?"

"I don't have to tell you anything," she said, tightening her lips.

"Of course not." I smiled politely. I knew I had her; the fear was still in her eyes.

She looked away from me, staring straight forward through the glass of the windshield.

"I was alone in the house," she said. "Joshua was

at the hospital with an emergency. William was at medical school. It was about three-thirty at night and Karen was out on a date. I heard the horn blowing on the car. It kept blowing. I got out of bed and put on a bathrobe and went downstairs. My car was there, the motor running and the lights on. The horn was still blowing. I went outside . . . and saw her. She had fainted and fallen forward onto the horn button. There was blood everywhere."

She took a deep breath and fumbled in her purse for cigarettes. She brought out a pack of French ones. I lit one for her.

"Go on."

"There isn't any more to tell. I got her into the other seat and drove to the hospital." She smoked the cigarette with a swift, nervous movement. "On the way, I tried to find out what had happened. I knew where she was bleeding from, because her skirt was all wet but her other clothes weren't. And she said, 'Lee did it.' She said it three times. I'll never forget it. That pathetic, weak little voice . . ."

"She was awake? Able to talk to you?"

"Yes," Mrs. Randall said. "She passed out again just as we got to the hospital."

"How do you know it was an abortion?" I said. "How do you know it wasn't a miscarriage?"

"I'll tell you," Mrs. Randall said. "Because when I looked at Karen's purse, I found her checkbook. The last check she had made out was to 'cash.' And it was for three hundred dollars. Dated Sunday. *That's* how I know it was an abortion."

"Was the check ever cashed? Have you inquired?"

"Of course it wasn't cashed," she said. "The man who has that check is now in jail."

"I see," I said thoughtfully.

"That's good," she said. "And now you must excuse me."

She got out of the car and hurried back up the steps to the house.

"I thought you were late for an appointment," I said.

She paused and looked back at me. "Go to hell," she said, and then slammed the door behind her.

I walked back to my car, considering her performance. It was very convincing. There were only two flaws that I could spot. One was the amount of blood in the yellow car. I was bothered that there was more blood on the passenger seat.

Then too, apparently Mrs. Randall didn't know that Art's fee for an abortion was $25—just enough to cover the lab costs. Art never charged more. It was a way, in his own mind, of keeping himself honest.

FIVE

THE SIGN WAS BATTERED: CURZIN PHOTOS. Underneath, in small, yellowing print, "Photos for all Purposes. Passports, Publicity, Friends. One-Hour Service."

The shop stood on a corner at the north end of Washington Street, away from the lights of the movie houses and the big department stores. I went inside and found a little old man and a little old woman, standing side by side.

"Yes?" said the man. He had a gentle manner, almost timid.

"I have a peculiar problem," I said.

"Passport? No problem at all. We can have the pictures for you in an hour. Less, if you're in a rush. We've done it thousands of times."

"That's right," said the woman, nodding primly. "More than thousands."

"My problem is different," I said. "You see, my daughter is having her sweet-sixteen party, and—"

"We don't do engagements," said the man. "Sorry."

"No indeed," the woman said.

"It's not an engagement, it's a sweet-sixteen party."

"We don't do them," the man said. "Out of the question."

"We used to," explained the woman. "In the old days. But they were such a fright."

I took a deep breath. "What I need," I said, "is some information. My daughter is mad about a rock-'n-'roll group, and you took their picture. I want this to be a surprise, so I thought that I'd—"

"Your daughter is sixteen?" He seemed suspicious.

"That's right. Next week."

"And we took a picture of a group?"

"Yes," I said. I handed him the photograph.

He looked at it for a long time.

"This isn't a group, this is one man," he said finally.

"I know, but he's part of a group."

"It's just one man."

"You took the picture, so I thought that perhaps—"

By now the man had turned the picture over in his hand.

"We took this picture," he announced to me. "Here, you can see our stamp on the back. Curzin Photos, that's us. Been here since 1931. My father had it before I did, God rest his soul."

"Yes," said the woman.

"You say this is a group?" the man asked, waving the picture at me.

"One member of a group."

"Possibly," he said. He handed the picture to the woman. "Did we do any groups like that?"

"Possibly," she said. "I can never keep them clear."

"I think it was a publicity picture," I offered.

"What's the name of this group?"

"I don't know. That's why I came to you. The picture had your stamp—"

"I saw it, I'm not blind," the man snapped. He bent over and looked under the counter. "Have to check the files," he said. "We keep everything on file."

He began producing sheafs of pictures. I was surprised; he really had photographed dozens of groups.

He shuffled through them very fast. "My wife can never remember them, but I can. If I can see them all, I remember them. You know? That's Jimmy and the Do-Dahs." He flipped through rapidly. "The Warblers. The Coffins. The Cliques. The Skunks. The names stick with you. Funny thing. The Lice. The Switchblades. Willy and the Willies. The Jaguars."

I tried to glance at the faces as he went, but he was going very fast.

"Wait a minute," I said, pointing to one picture. "I think that's it."

The man frowned. "The Zephyrs," he said, his tone disapproving. "That's what they are, the Zephyrs."

I looked at the five men, all Negro. They were

dressed in the same shiny suits that I'd seen in the single photo. They were all smiling uneasily, as if they disliked having their picture taken.

"You know the names?" I said.

He turned the picture over. The names were scrawled there. "Zeke, Zach, Roman, George, and Happy. That's them."

"O.K.," I said. I took out my notebook and wrote the names down. "Do you know how I can reach them?"

"Listen, you sure you want them for your girl's party?"

"Why not?"

The man shrugged. "They're a little tough."

"Well, I think they'll be O.K. for one night."

"I don't know," he said doubtfully. "They're pretty tough."

"Know where I can find them?"

"Sure," the man said. He jerked his thumb down the street. "They work nights at the Electric Grape. All the niggers hang out there."

"O.K.," I said. I went to the door.

"You be careful," the woman advised me.

"I will."

"Have a nice party," the man said.

I nodded and shut the door.

ALAN ZENNER WAS A HUGE MOUNTAIN OF A KID. He wasn't as big as a Big Ten tackle, but he was plenty large. I guessed he was about six-one and two-twenty.

Give or take.

I found him as he was leaving the Dillon Field House at the end of practice. It was late afternoon; the sun was low, casting a golden glow over Soldiers' Field stadium and the buildings nearby—the Field House, the Hockey Rink, the indoor tennis courts. On a side field, the freshman squad was still scrimmaging, raising a cloud of yellow-brown dust in the fading light.

Zenner had just finished showering; his short black hair was still damp and he was rubbing it, as if remembering the coach's admonition not to go out with wet hair.

He said he was in a hurry to eat dinner and start studying, so we talked as we crossed over the Lars Anderson bridge toward the Harvard houses. For a while I made small talk. He was a senior in Leverett House, the Towers, and he was majoring in history. He didn't like his thesis topic. He was worried about getting into law school; the law school didn't give athletes a break. All they cared about were grades. Maybe he would go to Yale law instead. That was supposed to be more fun.

We cut through Winthrop House and walked up toward the Varsity Club. Alan said he was eating two meals a day there, lunch and dinner, during the season. The food was O.K. Better than the regular crap anyway.

Finally, I shifted the conversation to Karen.

"What, you, too?"

"I don't understand."

"You're the second one today. Foggy was here earlier."

"Foggy?"

"The old man. That's what she used to call him."

"Why?"

"I don't know. It was her name for him, that's all. She had lots of names for him."

"You talked with him?"

Zenner said carefully, "He came to see me."

"And?"

Zenner shrugged. "I told him to go away."

"Why is that?"

We came to Massachusetts Avenue. The traffic was heavy. "Because," he said, "I didn't want to get involved."

"But you already are involved."

"Like hell I am." He started across the street, deftly maneuvering among the cars.

I said, "Do you know what happened to her?"

"Listen," he said, "I know more about it than anybody. Even her parents. Anybody."

"But you don't want to get involved."

"That's the picture."

I said, "This is very serious. A man has been charged with murdering her. You have to tell me what you know."

"Look," he said. "She was a nice girl, but she had problems. We had problems together. For a while it was O.K., and then the problems got too big, and it was over. That's all. Now get off my back."

I shrugged. "During the trial," I said, "the defense

will call you. They can make you testify under
oath."

"I'm not testifying in any trial."

"You won't have a choice," I said. "Unless, perhaps, there never is a trial."

"Meaning what?"

"Meaning we'd better have a talk."

Two blocks down Massachusetts Avenue toward
Central Square was a dirty little tavern with an out-
of-focus color TV over the bar. We ordered two
beers and watched the weather report while we
waited. The forecaster was a cheerful little pudgy
fellow who smiled as he predicted rain tomorrow,
and the next day.

Zenner said, "What's your interest in all this?"

"I think Lee is innocent."

He laughed. "You're the only one who does."

The beers came. I paid. He sipped his and licked
the foam off his lips.

"O.K.," he said, settling back in the booth. "I'll
tell you how it was. I met her at a party last spring,
around April. We got along well, right off. It
seemed just great. I didn't know anything about her
when I met her, she was just a good-looking girl. I
knew she was young. I didn't know how young until
the next morning when I practically flipped. I
mean, Christ, sixteen. . . . But I liked her. She
wasn't cheap."

He drank half the glass in a single gulp.

"So, we started seeing each other. And little by
little, I found out about her. She had a way of ex-

plaining things in bits and snatches. It was very tantalizing, like the old movie serials. Come back next Saturday for the next installment, that kind of thing. She was good at it."

"When did you stop seeing her?"

"June, early June. She was graduating from Concord, and I said I'd come out to see the graduation. She didn't want that. I said why. And then the whole thing came out about her parents and how I wouldn't get along. You see," he said, "my name was Zemnick before, and I grew up in Brooklyn. It's that way. She made her point, and I kissed her off. I was really pissed at the time. Now, I don't care anymore."

"You never saw her again?"

"Once. It must have been late July. I had a construction job on the Cape, a real soft one, and a lot of my friends were out there. I'd heard some things about her, things I hadn't heard when I was dating her. And how she collects jocks. About her problems with her parents and how she hated her old man. Things began to make sense when they hadn't made sense before. And I heard that she'd had an abortion and was telling people it was my kid."

He finished his beer and motioned to the bartender. I had another with him.

"One day I run into her out by Scusset. She's in a gas station getting her car filled and I happen to pull in. So we have a little talk. I ask her if it was true about the abortion, and she says yes. I ask her if it was my kid, and she says in a real steady voice that she doesn't know who the father is. So I tell her to go to hell and walk off. Then she comes running up and says she's sorry, can't we be friends again and see each other. I say no we can't. So she starts to cry. Well, hell, that's awful to have a girl crying in a gas station. So I said I'd take her out that night."

"Did you?"

"Yeah. It was terrible. Alan, do this; Alan, do that; faster, Alan, now slower. Alan, you sweat so much. She never shut up."

"Was she living on the Cape last summer?"

"She said she was. Working in an art gallery or something. But I heard she spent most of her time in Beacon Hill. She had some crazy friends."

"What friends?"

"I don't know. Friends."

"Did you ever meet any of them?"

"Only one. At a party one time on the Cape. Somebody introduced me to a girl named Angela who was supposed to be a friend of Karen's. Angela Harley or Hardy, something like that. Damned good-looking girl, but strange."

"How do you mean?"

"Just strange. Far out. When I met her, she was high on something. She kept saying strange things like 'The nose of God has the power of sour.' You couldn't talk to her; she was out of it. Too bad, she was damned good-looking."

"Did you ever meet her parents?"

"Yeah," he said. "Once. Quite a pair. Old stiff upper lip and warm lower lips. No wonder she hated them."

"How do you know she hated them?"

"What do you think she talked about? Her parents. Hour after hour. She hated Foggy. She sometimes called him Good Old Dad, because of the initials. She had names for her stepmother, too, but you wouldn't believe them. The funny thing is, though, that she was very close to her mother. Her real mother. She died when Karen was about fourteen or fifteen. I think that was when it all started."

"What started?"

"The wild stuff. All the drugs and the action. She wanted people to think she was wild. She wanted to be shocking. As if she had to prove it. She was very big on drugs and always took them in public. Some people said she was addicted to amphetamines, but I don't know if that was true. A lot of people on the Cape had been stung by her, and there were lots of nasty stories. They used to say that Karen Randall would go up on anything, and down on everything." He grimaced slightly as he said it.

"You liked her," I said.

"Yeah," he said, "as long as I could."

"That time on the Cape, was it the last time you saw her?"

"Yeah."

The next beer came. He looked at his glass and twisted it around in his hands for a few seconds.

"No," he said, "that's not true."

"You saw her again?"

He hesitated. "Yes."

"When?"

"Sunday," he said, "last Sunday."

SIX

"IT WAS ALMOST LUNCHTIME," Zenner said. "I was hung over from a party after the game. Really hung. Too hung. I was worried about looking good at practice Monday, because I had missed a few plays on Saturday. The same play: an end sweep. I wasn't pulling fast enough, it kept happening. So I was a little worried.

"Anyway, I was in my room trying to get dressed for lunch. Tying my tie. I had to do it three times, because I kept getting it crooked. I was really hung. And I had a bad headache; and in she walks, right into the room, just like I was expecting her."

"Were you?"

"I never wanted to see anyone less in my life. I had finally gotten over her, you know, worked it all out of my system. Then she shows up again, looking better than ever. A little heavy, but still good. My roommates had all gone to lunch, so I was the only one there. She asked me if I would take her to lunch."

"What did you say?"

"I said no."

"Why?"

"Because I didn't want to see her. She was like the plague, she infected you. I didn't want her around. So I asked her to please leave, but she didn't. She sat down and lit a cigarette and said she knew it was all over with us, but she needed somebody to talk to. Well, I'd heard that one before, and I wasn't having any. But she wouldn't leave. She sat there on the couch and wouldn't leave. She said I was the only person she could talk to.

"So finally I just gave up. I sat down and said, 'O.K., talk.' And I kept telling myself that I was a fool and that I'd regret it, just the way I regretted the last time. There are some people you just can't be around."

"What did you talk about?"

"Her. That was all she ever talked about. Herself, her parents, her brother—"

"Was she close to her brother?"

"In a way. But he's kind of straight arrow, like Foggy. Fired for the medical bit. So Karen never told him a lot of things. Like the drugs and stuff. She just never mentioned it to him."

"Go on."

"So I sat there and listened to her talk. She talked about school for a while, and then about some mystical thing she was starting where you meditated twice a day for half an hour. It was supposed to be like washing out your mind, or dipping a cloth in ink, or something. She had just started it but she thought it was great."

"How did she act during this time?"

"Nervous," Zenner said. "She smoked a pack just while she sat there, and she kept fiddling with her hands. She had a Concord Academy ring. She kept pulling it off, and putting it on, and twisting it. The whole damned time."

"Did she say why she had come down from Smith for the weekend?"

"I asked her," Zenner said. "And she told me."

"Told you what?"

"That she was going to have an abortion."

I sat back and lit a cigarette. "What was your reaction?"

He shook his head. "I didn't believe her." He glanced quickly at me, then sipped the beer. "I didn't believe anything about her anymore. That was the trouble. I was just turned off, I wasn't paying attention. I couldn't let myself, because she still . . . had an effect on me."

"Was she aware of that?"

"She was aware of everything," he said. "She didn't miss anything. She was like a cat; she worked by her instincts and they were always right. She could walk into a room and just look around, and she immediately knew everything about everyone. She had this sense for emotions."

"Did you talk to her about the abortion?"

"No. Because I didn't believe her. I just let it drop. Only she came back to it, about an hour later.

She said she was scared, that she wanted to be with me. She kept saying she was scared."

"Did you believe that?"

"I didn't know what to believe. No. No, I didn't believe her." He finished his beer in a gulp and put the mug down. "But look," he said, "what the hell was I supposed to do? She was nuts, that girl. Everybody knew it and it was true. She had this thing with her parents and with everybody else, and it pushed her over the brink. She was crazy."

"How long did you talk with her?"

"About an hour and a half. Then I said I had to eat lunch and study and that she'd better go. So she left."

"You don't know where she was going?"

"No. I asked her, and she just laughed. She said she never knew where she was going."

SEVEN

IT WAS LATE IN THE DAY when I left Zenner, but I called Peter Randall's office anyway. He wasn't there. I said it was urgent so his nurse suggested I try his lab. He often worked late in his lab on Tuesday and Thursday nights.

I didn't call. I went right over.

Peter Randall was the only member of the Randall family I had ever met before. I'd run into him once or twice at medical parties. It was impossible to miss him—first, because he was so physically outstanding, and second, because he like parties and attended every one he heard about.

He was a titanic fat man, jowled and jovial, with a hearty laugh and a flushed face. He smoked continuously, drank exorbitantly, talked amusingly, and was in general the treasure of every hostess. Peter could make a party. He could revive one instantly. Betty Gayle, whose husband was chief of medicine at the Lincoln, had once said, "Isn't he a marvelous social animal?" She was always saying things like that, but for once she was right. Peter Randall was a social animal—gregarious, extroverted, relaxed, good-humored. His wit and his manner gave him a remarkable kind of freedom.

For instance, Peter could successfully tell the most foul and revolting dirty joke, and you would laugh. Inside, you would be thinking, "That's a pretty dirty joke," but you would be laughing despite yourself, and all the wives would be laughing, too. He could also flirt with your wife, spill his drink, insult the hostess, complain, or do anything else. You never minded, never frowned.

I wondered what he would have to say about Karen.

HIS LAB WAS ON THE FIFTH FLOOR of the biochem wing of the medical school. I walked down the corridor, smelling the smell of laboratories—a combination of acetone, Bunsen burners, pipette soap, and reagents. A clean, sharp smell. His office was small. A girl behind the desk was typing a letter, wearing a white lab coat. She was strikingly attractive, but I suppose I should have expected that.

"Yes? May I help you?" She had a slight accent.

"I'm looking for Dr. Randall."

"Is he expecting you?"

"I'm not sure," I said. "I called earlier, but he may not have gotten my message."

She looked at me and sized me up for a clinician. There was that slightly supercilious look in her eyes that all researchers get when they are around clinicians. Clinicians don't use their minds, you see. They fool with dirty, unscientific things like patients. A researcher, on the other hand, inhabits a world of pure, satisfying intellectualism.

"Come with me," she said. She got up and walked down the hall. She wore wooden shoes without heels—that explained her accent. Following behind her, I watched her bottom and wished she was not wearing a lab coat.

"He's about to start a new incubation run," she said over her shoulder. "He'll be very busy."

"I can wait."

We entered the lab. It was bare, at a corner of the wing, looking down over the parking lot. So late in the day, most of the cars were gone.

Randall was bent over a white rat. As the girl came in, he said, "Ah, Brigit. You're just in time." Then he saw me. "Well now, what have we here?"

"My name is Berry," I said. "I——"

"Of course, of course. I remember you well." He dropped the rat and shook hands with me. The rat scampered across the table but stopped at the edge, looking down at the floor and sniffing.

"John, isn't it?" Randall said. "Yes, we've met several times." He picked up the rat again and chuckled. "In fact, my brother just called me about you. You've got him quite ruffled—a snot-nosed snoop, I believe his words were."

He seemed to find this very amusing. He laughed again and said, "It's what you get for pestering his dearly beloved. Apparently you upset her."

"I'm sorry about that."

"Don't be," Peter said cheerfully. He turned to Brigit and said, "Call the others, will you? We have to get this thing going."

Brigit wrinkled her nose, and Peter winked at her. When she was gone, he said, "Adorable creature, Brigit. She keeps me in shape."

"In shape?"

"Indeed," he said, patting his stomach. "One of the great pitfalls to modern, easy living is weak eye muscles. Television's to blame; we sit there and don't exercise our eyes. The result is flabby eyes, a terrible tragedy. But Brigit prevents all that. Preventive medicine of the finest sort." He sighed happily. "But what can I do for you? I can't imagine why you'd want to see me. Brigit, yes, but not me."

I said, "You were Karen's physician."

"So I was, so I was."

He took the rat and placed it in a small cage. Then he looked among a row of larger cages for another.

"Those damned girls. I keep telling them dye is cheap, but they never put enough on. There!" His hand darted in and brought out a second rat. "We're taking all the ones with dye on the tail," he explained. He held the rat so I could see the spot of purple color. "They were injected with parathyroid hormone yesterday morning. Now," he said, "I regret to say they are going to meet their Maker. Know anything about killing rats?"

"A little."

"You wouldn't care to dispatch them for me, would you? I hate to sacrifice them."

"No, thanks."

He sighed. "I thought so. Now, about Karen: yes, I was her physician. What can I tell you?"

He seemed apparently friendly and open.

"Did you treat her in the middle of the summer for an accident?"

"An accident? No."

The girls came in. There were three, including Brigit. They were all attractive, and whether by chance or design, one was blonde, one brunette, and one redhead. They stood in a line in front of him, and Peter smiled benignly at each of them, as if he were about to bestow presents.

"We have six tonight," he said, "and then we can all go home. Is the dissecting equipment set out?"

"Yes," Brigit said. She pointed to a long table with three chairs. In front of each chair was a cork pad, some pins, a pair of forceps, a scalpel, and an ice bath.

"What about the agitation bath? All ready?"

"Yes," said another girl.

"Good," Peter said. "Then let's get started."

The girls took their places at the table. Randall looked at me and said, "I guess I'll have to go through with it. I really hate this. Someday I'll get so worried about the little beasts' last moments that I'll chop off my fingers as well as their heads."

"What do you use?"

"Well, that's a long story." He grinned. "You see before you the squeamish connoisseur of rat-dispatching. I have tried everything—chloroform, neck breaking, squeezing. Even a little guillotine that the British are so fond of. I have a friend in London who sent me one—he swears by it—but it was always getting clogged with fur. So," he said, picking up one rat and examining it thoughtfully, "I went back to basics. I use a meat cleaver."

"You're kidding."

"Oh, I know it sounds bad. It looks bad, too, but it's the best way. You see, we have to get the dissection done quickly. The experimental design demands that."

He took the rat over to the sink. A heavy butcher's block was there, by the rim of the basin. He set the rat on the block and put a wax bag in the sink. Then he went over to the cabinet and brought out a meat cleaver, a heavy, stubby thing with a solid wooden handle.

"They sell these things," he said, "in the chemical supply houses. But they're too delicate and they never stay sharp. I bought this one secondhand from a butcher. It's superb."

He sharpened the edge on a stone briefly, then tested it on a piece of paper. It cut through cleanly.

The telephone rang at that moment, and Brigit jumped up to answer it. The other girls relaxed, obviously glad for a delay. Peter also seemed relieved.

Brigit spoke for a moment, then said, "It's the rental agency. They are going to deliver the car."

"Good," Peter said. "Tell them to leave it in the parking lot and leave the keys over the sun visor."

While Brigit was relaying the instructions, Peter said to me, "Damned nuisance. My car's been stolen."

"Stolen?"

"Yes. Quite annoying. It happened yesterday."

"What kind of a car was it?"

"A little Mercedes sedan. Battered, but I was fond of it. If I had my way," he said with a grin, "I'd see the thieves arrested for kidnapping, not car theft. I was very fond of that car."

"Have you reported it to the police?"

"Yes." He shrugged. "For whatever it's worth."

Brigit hung up and returned to her seat. Peter sighed, picked up the cleaver, and said, "Well, better get on with it."

He held the rat by the tail. The rat tried to pull

away, spread-eagling its body on the block. In a swift motion, Peter lifted the cleaver over his head and brought it down. There was a loud *thump!* as the blade struck the block. The girls stared away. I looked back and saw Peter holding the wriggling decapitated body over the sink. The blood drained out for a few moments. Then he carried it over to Brigit and placed it on the cork pad.

"Number one," he said briskly. He returned to the block, pushed the head into the paper bag, and selected a second rat.

I watched Brigit work. With swift, practiced moves she pinned the body on its back to the cork. Then she cut into the legs, clearing away the flesh and muscle around the bones. Next she clipped the bones free of the body and dropped them into the ice bath.

"A minor triumph," Peter said, preparing the next rat on the block. "In this lab, we perfected the first *in vitro* bone cultures. We are able to keep isolated bone tissue alive for as long as three days. The real problem is getting the bone out of the animal and into the bath before the cells die. We've got it down to a fine art now."

"What exactly is your field?"

"Calcium metabolism, particularly as it relates to parathyroid hormone and thyrocalcitonin. I want to know how those hormones work to release calcium from bone."

Parathyroid hormone was a little-understood substance secreted by four small glands attached to the thyroid. Nobody knew much about it, except that the parathyroids seemed to control calcium levels in the blood, and that these levels were strictly regulated—much more so than, say, blood sugar or free fatty acid. Blood calcium was necessary for normal nerve transmission and normal muscle contraction, and it was theorized that calcium was shunted to and from the bone, as occasion demanded. If you had too much calcium in your blood, you deposited it in bone. If you had too little, you drew it out of bone. But nobody knew quite how this was accomplished.

"The time course is crucial," Peter continued. "I once performed an interesting experiment. I took a dog and put in an arterial bypass. I was able to take his blood, treat it with chemicals to remove all calcium, and put it back again. I ran this thing for hours, taking out literally pounds of calcium. Yet the blood levels remained normal, readjusting instantly. That dog was draining large quantities of calcium out of his bone and into his blood at a very rapid rate."

The cleaver swung down again with a heavy sound. The rat wriggled and was still. It was given to the second girl.

"I got interested in all this," Peter said. "The whole problem of calcium storage and release. It's fine to say you can put your calcium into bone, or take it out; but bone is a crystal, it's hard and rigidly structured. We can apparently build it up or tear it down in fractions of a second. I wanted to know how."

He reached into a cage and produced another rat with a purple tail.

"So I decided to set up an *in vitro* system to study bone. Nobody thought I could do it. Bone metabolism was too slow, they said. Impossible to measure. But I succeeded, several hundred rats later." He sighed. "If the rats ever take over the world, I'll be tried for my war crimes."

He positioned the rat on the block.

"You know, I've always wanted to find a girl to do this work for me. I kept looking for a cold-blooded German girl, or a sadist of some sort. Never found one. All of those"—he nodded to the three at the table—"came to work only after I agreed that they would never have to kill the animals."

"How long have you been doing this work?"

"Seven years now. I started very slowly, half a day a week. Then it got to be every Tuesday. Pretty soon it was Tuesdays and Thursdays. Then it was all weekend as well. I've cut down my practice as much as I can. This work is really addicting."

"You like it?"

"I adore it. It's a game, a big wonderful game. A puzzle where nobody knows the answer. If you're not careful, though, you can become obsessed with the answer. Some people in the biochem department work longer hours than any practicing doctor. They drive themselves. But I won't let that happen to me."

"How do you know?"

"Because whenever I feel the symptoms coming on—the urge to work round the clock, to keep going until midnight, or to come in at five in the morning—I say to myself, it's just a game. I repeat that over and over. And it works: I settle down."

The cleaver finished the third rat.

"Ah," Peter said, "halfway there." He scratched his stomach reflectively. "But enough about me. What about you?"

"I'm just interested in Karen."

"Ummm. And you wanted to know about an accident? There was none, that I recall."

"Why were skull films taken last summer?"

"Oh *that*." He stroked the fourth victim soothingly and set it on the block. "That was typical Karen."

"What do you mean?"

"She came into my office and said, 'I'm going blind.' She was very concerned, in her own breathless way. You know how sixteen-year-old girls can be: she was losing her vision, and her tennis game was suffering. She wanted me to do something. So I drew some blood and ordered a few tests. Drawing blood always impresses them. And I checked her blood pressure and listened to her and generally gave the impression I was being very thorough."

"And you ordered skull films."

"Yes. That was part of the cure."

"I don't follow you."

"Karen's problems were purely psychosomatic,"

he said. "She's like ninety percent of the women I see. Some little thing goes wrong—like your tennis game—and bang! you have a medical problem. You go to see your doctor. He can find nothing physically wrong with you. But does this satisfy you? No: on to another doctor, and still another, until you find one who will pat your hand and say, 'Yes, you're a very sick woman.' " He laughed.

"So you ordered all these tests as a diversion?"

"Largely," he said. "Not entirely. I believe in caution, and when one hears a complaint as serious as vision loss, one must investigate. I checked her fundi. Normal. I did a visual fields. Normal, but she said it came and went. So I took a blood sample and ordered tests of thyroid function and hormone levels. Normal. And the skull films. They were normal, too, or have you already seen them?"

"I saw them," I said. I lit a cigarette as the next rat died. "But I'm still not sure why—"

"Well, put it together. She's young, but it's still possible—vision and headache, slight weight gain, lethargy. That could be pan hypopituitarism with optic nerve involvement."

"You mean a pituitary tumor?"

"It's possible, just possible. I figured the tests would show if she was pan hypopit. The skull films might show something if she was really badly off. But everything came back negative. It was all in her mind."

"Are you sure?"

"Yes."

"The labs might have made a mistake."

"That's true. I would have run a second test, just to be sure."

"Why didn't you?"

"Because she never came back," Peter said. "That's the key to it all. One day she comes in near hysteria because she's going blind. I say come back in a week, and my nurse makes the appointment. A week later, no show. She's out playing tennis, having a fine time. It was all in her mind."

"Was she menstruating when you saw her?"

"She said her periods were normal," he said. "Of course, if she were four months' pregnant at the time of her death, she would just have conceived when I saw her."

"But she never came back to you?"

"No. She was rather scatterbrained, actually."

He killed the last rat. All the girls were now busily working. Peter collected the carcasses and put them into the paper bag, then dropped the bag into a wastebasket. "Ah," he said, "at last." He washed his hands vigorously.

"Well," I said, "thanks for your time."

"Not at all." He dried his hands on a paper towel, then stopped. "I suppose I ought to make some sort of official statement," he said, "since I'm the uncle and so forth."

I waited.

"J. D. would never speak to me again if he knew I'd had this conversation with you. Try to keep that in mind if you talk to anybody else."

"O.K.," I said.

"I don't know what you're doing," Peter said, "and I don't want to know. You've always struck me as pretty level and sensible, and I assume you're not wasting your time."

I didn't know what to say. I couldn't see what he was leading up to, but I knew he was leading up to something.

"My brother, at this moment, is neither level nor sensible. He's paranoid; you can't get anything out of him. But I understand that you were present at the autopsy."

"That's right."

"What's the dx[1] there?"

"It's uncertain on the basis of the gross," I said. "Nothing clear at all."

"And the slides?"

"I haven't seen them yet."

"What was your impression at autopsy?"

I hesitated, then made my decision. He had been honest with me; I'd be honest with him.

"Not pregnant," I said.

"Hmmm," he said. "Hmmmm."

He scratched his stomach again, then held out his hand.

"That's very interesting," he said.

We shook hands.

---

[1] See Appendix IV: Abbreviations.

EIGHT

WHEN I GOT HOME, a big squad car with a flashing light was waiting at the curb. Captain Peterson, still crew-cut and tough-looking, leaned against the fender and stared at me as I pulled into my drive-way.

I got out of my car and looked at the nearby houses. People had noticed the flasher and were staring out of their windows.

"I hope," I said, "that I didn't keep you waiting."

"No," Peterson said with a little smile. "Just arrived. I knocked at the door and your wife said you weren't back yet, so I waited out here."

I could see his bland, smug expression in the alternating flashes of red from the light. I knew he had kept the light on to irritate me.

"Something on your mind?"

He shifted his position on the car. "Well, yes, actually. We've had a complaint about you, Dr. Berry."

"Oh?"

"Yes."

"From whom?"

"Dr. Randall."

I said innocently, "What kind of complaint?"

"Apparently you have been harassing members of

his family. His son, his wife, even his daughter's college friends."

"Harassing?"

"That," said Peterson carefully, "was what he said."

"And what did you say?"

"I said I'd see what could be done."

"So here you are."

He nodded and smiled slowly.

The flasher was beginning to get on my nerves. Down the block, one or two kids were standing in the street, watching in silence.

I said, "Have I broken any law?"

"That hasn't been determined yet."

"If I have broken a law," I said, "then Dr. Randall may go to court about it. Or he may go to court if he feels he can show material damage as a result of my alleged actions. He knows that, and so do you." I smiled at him, giving him some of his own. "And so do I."

"Maybe we should go down to the station and talk about it."

I shook my head. "Haven't got time."

"I can take you in for questioning, you know."

"Yes," I said, "but it wouldn't be prudent."

"It might be quite prudent."

"I doubt it," I said. "I am a private citizen acting within my rights as a private citizen. I did not force myself upon anyone, did not threaten anyone. Any person who did not wish to speak with me did not have to."

"You trespassed on private property. The Randall home."

"That was quite inadvertent. I was lost, and I wanted to ask directions. I passed a large building, so large it never occurred to me it might be a private dwelling. I thought it was some kind of institution."

"Institution?"

"Yes. Like an orphanage, you know. Or a nursing home. So I drove in to ask questions. Imagine my surprise when I discovered that by purest chance—"

"Chance?"

"Can you prove otherwise?"

Peterson gave a fair imitation of a good-natured chuckle. "You're being very clever."

"Not really," I said. "Now why don't you turn off that flasher and stop drawing attention? Because otherwise I will file a complaint of harassment by the police. And I'll file it with the Chief of Police, the District Attorney's office, and the Mayor's office."

He reached indolently through the window and flicked a switch. The light stopped.

"Someday," he said, "all this may catch up with you."

"Yes," I said. "Me, or somebody else."

He scratched the back of his hand, as he had done in his office. "There are times," he said, "when I think you're either an honest man or a complete fool."

"Maybe both."

He nodded slowly. "Maybe both." He opened the door and swung into the driver's seat.

I went up to the front door and let myself in. As I closed the door, I heard him pull away from the curb.

NINE

I DIDN'T FEEL MUCH LIKE ATTENDING A COCKTAIL party, but Judith insisted. As we drove to Cambridge, she said, "What was it all about?"

"What?"

"The business with the police?"

"It was an attempt to call me off."

"On what grounds?"

"Randall filed a complaint. Harassment."

"Justified?"

"I think so."

I told her quickly about the people I had seen that day. When I was finished, she said, "It sounds complicated."

"I'm sure I've barely scratched the surface."

"Do you think Mrs. Randall was lying about the check for three hundred dollars?"

"She might have been," I admitted.

Her question stopped me. I realized then that

things had been happening so fast, I hadn't had time to consider everything I had learned, to sift it out and put it together. I knew there were inconsistencies and trouble spots—several of them—but I hadn't worked on them in any logical way.

"How's Betty?"

"Not good. There was an article in the paper today. . . ."

"Was there? I didn't see it."

"Just a small article. Arrest of physician for abortion. Not many details, except his name. She's gotten a couple of crank calls."

"Bad?"

"Pretty bad. I try to answer the phone, now."

"Good girl."

"She's trying to be very brave about it, trying to go on as if everything was normal. I don't know if that's worse or better. Because she can't. Things aren't normal, and that's all there is to it."

"Going over there tomorrow?"

"Yes."

I parked on a quiet residential block in Cambridge not far from the Cambridge City Hospital. It was a pleasant area of old frame houses and maple trees along the road. Brick-paved sidewalks; the whole Cambridge bit. As I parked Hammond pulled up on his motorcycle.

Norton Francis Hammond III represents the hope of the medical profession. He doesn't know it, and it's just as well; if he did, he'd be insufferable. Hammond comes from San Francisco, from what he calls "a long line of shipping." He looks like a walking advertisement for the California life—tall, blond, tanned, and handsome. He is an excellent doctor, a second-year resident in medicine at the Mem, where he is considered so good that the staff overlooks things like his hair, which reaches almost to his shoulders, and his moustache, which is long, curling and flamboyant.

What is important about Hammond, and the few other young doctors like him, is that they are breaking old patterns without rebelling against the Establishment. Hammond is not trying to antagonize anyone with his hair, his habits, or his motorcycle; he simply doesn't give a damn what the other doctors think of him. Because he takes this attitude, the other doctors cannot object—he does, after all, know his medicine. Though they find his appearance irritating, they have no ground for complaint.

So Hammond goes his way unmolested. And because he is a resident, he has a teaching function. He influences the younger men. And therein lies the hope of future medicine.

Since World War II, medicine has undergone great change, in two successive waves. The first was an outpouring of knowledge, techniques, and methods, beginning in the immediate postwar period. It was initiated by the introduction of antibiotics, continued with understanding of electrolyte balances, protein structure, and gene function. For the most part, these advances were scientific and technical, but they changed the face of medical practice drastically, until by 1965 three of the four most commonly prescribed drug classes—antibiotics, hormones (mostly The Pill), and tranquilizers—were all postwar innovations.[1]

The second wave was more recent and involved social, not technical, change. Social medicine, and socialized medicine, became real problems to be solved, like cancer and heart disease. Some of the older physicians regarded socialized medicine as a cancer in its own right, and some of the younger ones agreed. But it has become clear that, like it or not, doctors are going to have to produce better medical care for more people than they ever have before.

It is natural to expect innovation from the young, but in medicine this has not been easy, for the old doctors train the young ones, and too often the students become carbon copies of their teachers. Then, too, there is a kind of antagonism between generations in medicine, particularly now. The young men are better prepared than the old guard; they know more science, ask deeper questions, demand more complex answers. They are also, like young men everywhere, hustling for the older men's jobs.

That was why Norton Hammond was so remark-

---

[1] The fourth class, analgesics, was mostly that old standby, aspirin, synthesized in 1853. Aspirin is as much a wonder drug as any other. It is a painkiller, a swelling-reducer, a fever-breaker, and an antiallergic drug. None of its actions can be explained.

able. He was effecting a revolution without a rebellion.

He parked his motorcycle, locked it, patted it fondly, and dusted off his whites.[2] Then he saw us.

"Hiya, kids." As nearly as I could tell, Hammond called everyone kid.

"How are you, Norton?"

"Hanging in." He grinned. "Against all obstacles." He punched my shoulder. "Hey, I hear you've gone to war, John."

"Not exactly."

"Any scars yet?"

"A few bruises," I said.

"Lucky," he said, "taking on old A. R."

Judith said, "A. R.?"

"Anal Retentive: that's what the boys on the third floor call him."

"Randall?"

"None other." He smiled at Judith. "The kid's bitten off quite a chunk."

"I know."

"They say A. R. prowls the third floor like a wounded vulture. Can't believe anybody'd oppose his majestic self."

"I can imagine," I said.

"He's been in a terrible state," Hammond said. "He even chewed out Sam Carlson. You know Sam? He's a resident up there, working under A. R., rooting about in the nether regions of surgical politics.

Sam is A.R.'s golden boy. A.R. loves him, and nobody can figure out why. Some say it's because he
is stupid, Sam is, blindingly stupid. Crushingly,
awesomely stupid."

"Is he?" I said.

"Beyond description," Hammond said. "But Sam
got chewed out yesterday. He was in the cafeteria,
eating a chicken-salad sandwich—no doubt after
asking the serving ladies what a chicken was—
when Randall came in, and said, 'What are you
doing here?' And Sam said, 'Eating a chicken-salad
sandwich.' And A. R. said, 'What the hell for?' "

"What did Sam say?"

Hammond grinned broadly. "I have it on good authority, that Sam said, 'I don't know, sir.' And he put
aside the sandwich and walked out of the cafeteria."

"Hungry," I said.

Hammond laughed. "Probably." He shook his
head. "But you can't really blame A. R. He's lived in
the Mem for a hundred years or so, and never had
a problem. Now, with the headhunt, and then his
daughter . . ."

"Headhunt?" Judith said.

"My, my, the grapevine is collapsing. The wives
are usually the first to know. All hell's broken out at
the Mem over the Clinic pharmacy."

I said, "They lose something?"

"You bet."

"What?"

"A gross of morphine ampoules. Hydromorphine

hydrochloride. That's three to five times more powerful on a weight basis than morphine sulfate."

"When?"

"Last week. The pharmacist nearly got the ax—he was off hustling a nurse when it happened. It was lunchtime."

"They haven't found the stuff?"

"No. Turned the hospital upside down, but nothing."

"Has this ever happened before?" I said.

"Apparently it has, a few years back. But only a couple of ampoules were taken then. This was a major haul."

I said, "Paramedical?"

Hammond shrugged. "Could be anybody. Personally, I think it must have been a commercial move. They took too much. The risk was too great: can you imagine yourself waltzing into the Mem outpatient clinic and waltzing out with a box of morphine bottles under your arm?"

"Not really."

"Guts."

"But surely that's too much for one person," I said.

"Of course. That's why I think it was commercial. I think it was a robbery, carefully planned."

"By somebody outside?"

"Ah," he said. "Now you get down to the question."

"Well?"

"The thinking is that somebody did it from the inside."

"Any evidence?"

"No. Nothing."

We walked up the stairs to the wooden frame house. I said, "That's very interesting, Norton."

"You bet your ass it's interesting."

"Know anybody who's up?"

"On the staff? No. The word is that one of the girls in cardiac cath used to shoot speeds,[3] but she kicked it a year ago. Anyhow, they went over her pretty hard. Stripped her down, checked for needle marks. She was clean."

I said, "How about—"

"Doctors?"

I nodded. Doctors and drugs are a taboo subject. A reasonable number of doctors are addicts; that's no secret, any more than it's a secret that doctors have a high suicide rate.[4] Less widely known is a classic psychiatric syndrome involving a doctor and his son, in which the son becomes an addict and the doctor supplies his needs, to the mutual satisfaction of both. But nobody talks about these things.

"The doctors are clean," Hammond said, "as far as I know."

"Anybody quit their job? Nurse, secretary, anybody?"

---

[3] Injected amphetamines, such as methedrene, intravenously.
[4] Psychiatrists have the highest suicide rate of all, more than ten times that of the GP.

He smiled. "You're really hot on this, aren't you?"

I shrugged.

"Why? Think it's related to the girl?"

"I don't know."

"There's no reason to connect the two," Hammond said. "But it would be interesting."

"Yes."

"Purely speculative."

"Of course."

"I'll call you," Hammond said, "if anything turns up."

"Do that," I said.

We came to the door. Inside, we could hear party sounds: tinkling glasses, talk, laughter.

"Good luck with your war," Hammond said. "I hope to hell you win."

"So do I."

"You will," Hammond said. "Just don't take any prisoners."

I smiled. "That's against Geneva Conventions."

"This," Hammond said, "is a very limited war."

THE PARTY WAS HELD BY GEORGE MORRIS, chief resident in medicine at the Lincoln. Morris was about to finish his residency and begin private practice, so it was a kind of coming-out party, given for himself.

It was done very well, with an understated comfortability that must have cost him more than he could afford. I was reminded of those lavish parties given by manufacturers to launch a new product, or a new line. In a sense, that was what it was.

George Morris, twenty-eight, with a wife and two children, was deeply in debt: any doctor in his position would be. Now he was about to start burrowing out from under, and to do that he needed patients. Referrals. Consults. In short, he needed the good will and help of established physicians in the area, and that was why he had invited 200 of them to his home and filled them to the neck with the best booze he could buy and the best canapés the caterers could provide.

As a pathologist, I was flattered to have received an invitation. I couldn't do anything for Morris; pathologists deal with corpses and corpses don't need referrals. Morris had invited Judith and me because we were friends.

I think we were his only friends at the party that night.

I looked around the room: the chiefs of service from most of the big hospitals were there. So were the residents, and so were the wives. The wives had clustered in a corner, talking babies; the doctors were clustered into smaller groups, by hospital or by specialty. It was a kind of occupational division, very striking to see.

In one corner, Emery was arguing the therapeutic advantage of lower I^{131} doses in hyperthyroidism; in another, Johnston was talking about hepatic pressures in porto caval shunts; in still another, Lewiston could be heard muttering his usual line about the inhumanity of electroshock therapy for depressives. From the wives, occasional words like "IUD" and "chickenpox" drifted out.

Judith stood next to me, looking sweet and rather young in a blue A-line. She was drinking her Scotch quickly—she's a gulper—and obviously preparing to plunge into the group of wives.

"I sometimes wish," she said, "that they'd talk about politics or something. Anything but medicine."

I smiled, remembering Art's line about doctors being illpolitical. He meant it the way you used words like illiterate. Art always said doctors not only held no real political views, but also were incapable of them. "It's like the military," he had once said. "Political views are considered unprofessional." As usual, Art was exaggerating, but there was something to what he said.

I think Art likes to overstate his case, to shock and irritate and goad people. It is a characteristic of his. But I think he is also fascinated by the thin line that separates truth from untruth, statement from overstatement. It is a characteristic of his to constantly throw out his comments and see who picks them up and how they react to them. He does this particularly when he is drunk.

Art is the only doctor I know who will get drunk. The others can apparently pour back fantastic quantities of alcohol without really showing it; they get talkative for a while, and then sleepy. Art gets drunk, and when he is drunk he is particularly angry and outrageous.

I have never understood this about him. For a while I thought he was a case of pathological intoxication,[5] but later I decided it was a sort of personal indulgence, a willingness to let himself go when others kept themselves rigidly in control. Perhaps he needs this indulgence; perhaps he can't help it; perhaps he actively seeks it as an excuse to blow off steam.

Certainly he is bitter toward his profession. Many doctors are, for various reasons: Jones because he is hooked on research and can't make as much money as he'd like; Andrews because urology cost him his wife and a happy family life; Telser because he is surrounded in dermatology by patients whom he considers neurotic, not sick. If you talk to any of these men, the resentment shows itself sooner or later. But they are not like Art. Art is resentful against the medical profession itself.

I suppose in any profession you meet men who despise themselves and their colleagues. But Art is an extreme example. It is almost as if he went into medicine to spite himself, to make himself unhappy and angry and sad.

In my blackest moments, I think he does abortions only to jar and irritate his colleagues. That is unfair, I think, but I can never be sure. When he is sober, he talks intellectually, unreeling arguments

[5] Defined as a person who becomes more inebriated than his blood alcohol levels would explain. In the most extreme cases, a single drink may make a man a raving, destructive lunatic.

for abortion. When he is drunk, he talks emotions, attitudes, stances, complacency.

I think he feels hostility toward medicine and gets drunk so that he can release his hostility with an excuse—he's drunk. Certainly he has gotten into bitter, almost vicious fights with other doctors when he was drunk; he once told Janis that he'd aborted his wife and Janis, who didn't know, looked as if he'd been kicked in the balls. Janis is Catholic but his wife isn't. Art managed to end a perfectly happy dinner party right on the spot.

I attended that party, and I was annoyed with Art afterward. He apologized to me a few days later, and I told him to apologize to Janis, which he did. For some strange reason, Janis and Art subsequently became close friends, and Janis became a convert to abortion. I don't know what Art said to him or how he convinced him, but whatever it was, it worked.

Because I know Art better than most people, I attach a great importance to his being Chinese. I think his origin and his physical appearance have been a great influence on him. There are a lot of Chinese and Japanese men in medicine, and there are a lot of jokes about them—half-nervous jokes about their energy and their cleverness, their drive to success. It is precisely the kind of jokes one hears about Jews. I think Art, as a Chinese-American, has fought this tradition, and he has also fought his upbringing, which was essentially conservative. He swung the other way, became radical and leftist. One proof of this is his willingness to

accept all things new. He has the most modern office equipment of any OB man in Boston. Whenever a new product comes out, he buys it. There
are jokes about this, too—the gadget-oriented
Orientals—but the motivation is different. Art is
fighting tradition, routine, the accepted way.

When you talk to him, he seems bursting with
ideas. He has a new method for doing the Papp
smear.[6] He wants to abandon the routine, digital
pelvic exam as a waste of time. He thinks that basal
temperature as an indicator of ovulation is more effective than reported. He thinks forceps should be
eliminated from all deliveries, no matter how complicated. He thinks that general anesthesia in deliveries should be abandoned in favor of heavy doses
of tranquilizers.

When you first hear these ideas and theories, you
are impressed. Only later do you realize that he is
compulsively attacking tradition, finding fault
whenever and wherever he can.

I suppose it is only natural that he should begin
performing abortions. And I suppose that I should
question his motives. But I don't usually, because I
feel that a man's reasons for doing something are
less important than the ultimate value of what he
does. It is a historical truth that a man may do the
wrong thing for the right reasons. In that case
he loses. Or he may do the right thing for the
wrong reasons. In that case, he is a hero.

---

[6] The Papp smear is the most accurate diagnostic test in all of medicine.

Of all the people at the party, one might be able to help me. That was Fritz Werner, but I didn't see him; I kept looking.

Instead I ran into Blake. Blake is a senior pathologist at the General, but he is principally known for his head, which is enormous, round, and smooth. The features of his face are small and childlike, a tiny jaw and wide-set eyes, so that Blake looks like everybody's vision of future man. He is coldly, sometimes maddeningly intellectual man, and he is fond of games. He and I have played one game, off and on, for years.

He greeted me with a wave of his martini glass and, "Ready?"

"Sure."

"Moans to Rocky," he said.

It sounded easy. I took out my notebook and pencil and tried it out. At the top of the page I wrote MOANS and at the bottom, ROCKY. Then I tried to fit things together.

MOANS
   LOANS
      LOINS
         LOONS
            BOONS
               BOOKS
                  ROOKS
                     ROCKS
                        ROCKY

It took only a few moments.

"How many?" Blake said.

"Nine."

He smiled. "I'm told it can be done in five. I have seven." He took the pad from me and wrote:

MOANS
LOANS
LOONS
LOOKS
ROOKS
ROCKS
ROCKY

I reached into my pocket and gave him a quarter. He had won the last three in a row, and over the years, he had beaten me consistently. But then Blake beat everybody.

"By the way," he said, "I heard another argument. Do you know the DNA template one?"[7]

"Yes," I said.

He shook his head. "Pity. I enjoy it. Springing it on people, I mean."

I smiled at him, barely able to conceal my pleasure.

"You know the latest on Youth in Asia? The one about the right to refuse medication? You can fit it into the fluoride arguments, very neatly."[8]

[7] See Appendix VI: Arguments on Abortion.
[8] See Appendix VII: Medical Morals.

I'd heard that one, too, and I told him so. This seemed to depress him. He wandered off to try his luck with someone else.

Blake collects arguments on medical philosophy. He is never happier than when he is logically demonstrating to a surgeon that he has no right to operate, or to an internist that he is ethically bound to kill every patient he can. Blake likes words and tosses around ideas the way small children play softball in the street. It is easy for him, effortless and amusing. He and Art get along well together. Last year the two of them had a four-hour argument over whether an obstetrician was morally responsible for all children born under his direction, from the time they were born until they died.

In retrospect, all of Blake's arguments seem no more useful or important than watching an athlete exercise in a gym, but at the time they can be fascinating. Blake has a keen sense of the arbitrary, and it stands him in good stead when working with members of the most arbitrary profession on earth.

Wandering around the party, I heard snatches of jokes and conversations; it was, I thought, a typical medical party.

"Did you hear about the French biochemist who had twins. He baptized one and kept the other as a control."

"They all get bacteremia sooner or later, anyway. . . ."

"And he was walking around—*walking around,*

mind you, with a blood pH of seven-point-six and a potassium of one. . . ."

"Well, what the hell do you expect of a Hopkins man?"

"So he said, 'I gave up smoking, but I'll be damned if I'll give up drinking.' "

"Sure, you can correct the blood gases, but it doesn't help the vasculature. . . ."

"She was always a nice girl. Very well dressed. They must have spent a fortune on her clothes. . . ."

". . . course he's pissed. Anybody'd be pissed. . . ."

". . . oliguric my ass. He was *an*uric for five days, and he still survived. . . ."

". . . in a seventy-four-year-old man, we just excised it locally and sent him home. It's slow growing, anyhow. . . ."

". . . liver reached down to his knees, practically. But no hepatic failure. . . ."

"She said she'd sign herself out if we didn't operate, so naturally, we . . ."

". . . but the students are always bitching; it's a nonspecific response. . . ."

"Well, apparently this girl had bitten it off of him. . . ."

"Really? Harry, with that little nurse in Seven? The blonde?"

". . . don't believe it. He publishes more journal articles than most people can read in a lifetime. . . ."

". . . metastases to the *heart* . . ."

"Anyway, it goes like this: there's this desert

prison, see, with an old prisoner, resigned to his life, and a young one just arrived. The young one talks constantly of escape, and, after a few months, he makes a break. He's gone a week, and then he's brought back by the guards. He's half dead, crazy with hunger and thirst. He describes how awful it was to the old prisoner. The endless stretches of sand, no oasis, no signs of life anywhere. The old prisoner listens for a while, then says, 'Yep. I know. I tried to escape myself, twenty years ago.' The young prisoner says, 'You did? Why didn't you tell me, all these months I was planning my escape? Why didn't you let me know it was impossible?' And the old prisoner shrugs, and says, 'So who publishes negative results?' "

AT EIGHT, I was beginning to get tired. I saw Fritz Werner come in, waving to everyone and talking gaily. I started over toward him, but Charlie Frank caught me on the way.

Charlie stood half hunched over, with a twisted, painful expression on his face as if he'd just been stabbed in the stomach. His eyes were wide and sad. Altogether, it was quite a dramatic effect, but Charlie always looked that way. He wore an air of impending crisis and imminent tragedy on his shoulders, and it burdened him, crushing him to the floor. I had never seen him smile.

In a tense, half whisper, he said, "How is he?"

"Who?"

"Art Lee."

"He's all right." I didn't want to talk about Lee with Charlie Frank.

"Is it true he's been arrested?"

"Yes."

"Oh, my God." He gave a little gasp.

"I think it will turn out all right in the end," I said.

"Do you?"

"Yes," I said, "I do."

"Oh, my God." He bit his lip. "Is there anything I can do?"

"I don't think so."

He was still holding on to my arm. I looked across the room at Fritz, hoping Charlie'd notice and let go. He didn't.

"Say, John . . ."

"Yes?"

"What's this I heard about you, ah, getting involved?"

"Let's say I'm interested."

"I ought to tell you," Charlie said, leaning close, "that there's talk in the hospitals. People are saying that you're concerned because you're mixed up in it yourself."

"Talk is cheap."

"John, you could make a lot of enemies."

In my mind, I was thinking over Charlie Frank's friends. He was a pediatrician, and very successful: he worried over his young patients more than their mothers and that comforted them.

"Why do you say that?"

"It's just a feeling I get," he said with a sad look. "What do you suggest I do?"

"Stay away from it, John. It's ugly. Really ugly."

"I'll remember that."

"A lot of people feel very strongly—"

"So do I."

"—that this is something to be left to the courts."

"Thanks for the advice."

His grip on my arm hardened. "I'm saying this as a friend, John."

"O.K., Charlie. I'll remember."

"It's really ugly, John."

"I'll remember."

"These people won't stop at anything," he said.

"What people?"

Quite abruptly, he let go of my arm. He gave an embarrassed little shrug. "Well, you have to do what you think is best, in any case."

And he turned away.

FRITZ WERNER WAS STANDING, as usual, by the bar. He was a tall, painfully thin, almost emaciated man. He kept his hair trimmed short, and this emphasized his large, dark, brooding eyes. He had a birdlike manner, a gawky walk, and a habit of craning his thin neck forward when he was addressed, as if he could not hear well. There was an intensity about him, which might have stemmed from his Austrian ancestry or from his artistic nature. Fritz painted and sketched as a hobby, and his office always had a cluttered, studiolike appearance. But he made his money as a psychiatrist, listening patiently to bored, middle-aged matrons who had decided at a late date that there was something wrong with their minds.

He smiled as we shook hands. "Well, well, if it isn't poison ivy."

"I'm beginning to think so myself."

He looked around the room. "How many lectures so far?"

"Just one. Charlie Frank."

"Yes," Fritz said, "you can always count on him for bad advice."

"And what about you?"

He said, "Your wife is looking very charming tonight. Blue is her color."

"I'll tell her."

"Very charming. How is your family?"

"Good, thanks. Fritz—"

"And your work?"

"Listen, Fritz. I need help."

He laughed softly. "You need more than help. You need rescue."

"Fritz—"

"You've been seeing people," he said. "I imagine you've met them all by now. What did you think of Bubbles?"

"Bubbles?"

"Yes."

I frowned. I had never heard of anyone named Bubbles. "You mean, Bubbles the stripper?"

"No. I mean Bubbles the roommate."

"*Her* roommate?"

"Yes."

"The one at Smith?"

"God, no. The one from last summer, on the Hill. Three of them shared an apartment. Karen, and Bubbles, and a third girl who had some kind of medical connections—nurse, or technician, or something. They made quite a group."

"What's the real name of this girl Bubbles? What does she do?"

Someone came up to the bar for another drink. Fritz looked out at the room and said in a professional voice, "This sounds quite serious. I suggest you send him to see me. As it happens, I have a free hour tomorrow at two-thirty."

"I'll arrange it," I said.

"Good," he said. "Nice to see you again, John."

We shook hands.

JUDITH WAS TALKING TO NORTON HAMMOND, who was leaning against the wall. As I walked up, I thought to myself that Fritz was right: she was looking good. And then I noticed that Hammond was smoking a cigarette. There was nothing wrong with that, of course, except that Hammond didn't smoke.

He didn't have a drink in his hand, and he was smoking rather slowly and deeply.

"Say," I said, "you want to watch that."

He laughed. "My social protest for the night."

Judith said, "I tried to tell him somebody would smell it."

"Nobody here can smell anything," Hammond said. It was probably true; the room was thick with blue smoke. "Besides, remember Goodman and Gilman."[9]

"Still. Be Careful."

"Think of it," he said, taking a deep drag. "No bronchogenic carcinoma, no oat-cell carcinoma, no chronic bronchitis and emphysema, no arteriosclerotic heart disease, no cirrhosis, no Wernicke-Korsakoff. It's beautiful."

"It's illegal."

He smiled and pulled at his moustache. "You're up for abortion but not maryjane, is that it?"

"I can only take one crusade at a time."

A thought came to me as I watched him suck in a mouthful of smoke and exhale clear air. "Norton, you live on the Hill, don't you?"

"Yes."

"Do you know anybody named Bubbles?"

He laughed. "Everybody knows Bubbles. Bubbles and Superhead. They're always together."

"Superhead?"

"Yeah. That's her bag at the moment. He's an electronic musician. A composer. He likes things

---

[9] Goodman and Gilman, *The Pharmacological Basis of Therapeutics*, the definitive text of pharmacology used by doctors. There is a discussion of the effects of marijuana on page 300 which has been widely quoted in recent legal proceedings.

that sound like ten dogs howling. They're living together."

"Didn't she live with Karen Randall?"

"I don't know. Maybe. Why?"

"What's her real name? Bubbles."

He shrugged. "I never heard her called anything else. But the guy: his name is Samuel Archer."

"Where does he live?"

"Over behind the State House somewhere. In a basement. They have it fixed up like a womb."

"A womb?"

"You have to see it to believe it," Norton said, and he gave a relaxed, satisfied sigh.

TEN

JUDITH SEEMED TENSE ON THE DRIVE BACK. She sat with her knees together and her hands clasped around them. She was squeezing her hands hard; the knuckles were white.

"Something wrong?"

"No," she said. "Just tired."

I said, "Was it the wives?"

She smiled slightly. "You've become very famous. Mrs. Wheatstone was so upset that she missed a bid at this afternoon's game, I understand."

"What else did you hear?"

"They all asked me why you were doing it, help-ing Art. They thought it was a marvelous example of a man sticking by his friend. They thought it was heartwarming and humane and wonderful."

"Uh-huh."

"And they kept asking why."

"Well, I hope you told them it's because I'm a nice guy."

She smiled in the darkness. "I wish I'd thought of that."

Her voice was sad, though, and her face in the reflected light of the headlights was drawn. I knew it wasn't easy for her to be with Betty all the time. But somebody had to do it.

For some reason, I remembered my student days and Purple Nell. Purple Nell was a seventy-eight-year-old former alcoholic who had been dead a year before she became our cadaver. We called her Nell, and a lot of other things, small grim jokes to help us get through our work. I remembered my desire to quit, to stop cutting the cold, damp, stinking flesh, to stop peeling away the layers. I dreamed of the day I would be finished with Nell, when I could forget her, and the smells, and the feel of greasy, long-dead flesh. Everyone said it got easier. I wanted to stop, to be finished and done. But I never quit until all the dissections had been com-pleted, all the nerves and arteries traced out and learned.

After my initial harsh experience with cadavers, I was surprised to find I was interested in pathology.

I like the work and have learned to push from my mind the smells and the sight of each new corpse, each new postmortem. But somehow autopsies are different, in some strange sense more hopeful. At autopsy you are dealing with a man, newly dead, and you know his story. He is not a faceless, anonymous cadaver but a person who had recently waged a very private battle, the only private battle in life, and lost. Your job is to find out how, and why, he lost, in order to help others who will soon do battle—and yourself. It is a far cry from the dissection cadavers, which exist in a kind of sickening, professional death, as if their only purpose in their twilight, embalmed afterlife is to be thoroughly, inspectably dead.

WHEN WE GOT HOME, Judith went in to check on the kids and call Betty. I took the sitter home. She was a short, pert girl named Sally, a cheerleader at Brookline High. Normally, when I drove her home we talked about neutral, safe things: how she liked school, where she wanted to go to college, things like that. But tonight I was feeling inquisitive, and old, and out of touch, like a man returning to his country after an extended time abroad. Everything was different, even the kids, even youth. They weren't doing what we had done. They had different challenges and different problems. At least, they had different drugs. Perhaps the problems were still the same. At least, that was what you wanted to think.

Finally I decided I had had too much to drink at the party, and had better keep my mouth shut. So I let Sally talk about passing her driver's test, and nothing more. As she talked, I felt both cowardly and relieved. And then I thought that it was foolish, that there was no reason for me to be curious about my babysitter, no reason to get to know her, and that if I tried it might be interpreted wrongly. It was safer to talk about drivers' licenses; solid, respectable, reasonable ground.

Then, for some reason, I thought of Alan Zenner. And something Art had said. "If you want to know about this world, turn on your television to an interview program, and turn off the sound." I did, a few days later. It was bizarre: the faces moving, the tongues going, the expressions and the hands. But no sound. Nothing at all. You had no idea what they were saying.

I FOUND THE ADDRESS in the phone book: Samuel F. Archer, 1334 Langdon Street. I dialed the number. A recorded voice came on.

"I am sorry, sir, the number you have dialed is not in service at this time. If you hold the line, an operator will give you further information."

I waited. There was a series of rhythmic clicks, like the beat of a telephone heart, and then the operator. "Information. What number are you calling?"

"Seven-four-two-one-four-four-seven."

"That number has been disconnected."

"Do you have another listing?"

"No, sir."

Probably Samuel F. Archer had moved, but perhaps he hadn't. I drove there directly. The apartment was located on a steep hill on the east slope of Beacon Hill, in a battered apartment building. The hallway smelled of cabbage and baby formula. I went down a flight of creaking wooden stairs to the basement, where a green light flashed, illuminating a door painted flat black.

A sign said, GOD GROWS HIS OWN.

I knocked.

From inside, I could hear screeches, whines, warbles, and something that sounded like groans. The door opened and I faced a young man in his twenties with a full beard and long, damp black hair. He wore dungarees, sandals, and a purple polka-dot shirt. He looked at me blandly, showing neither surprise nor interest. "Yes?"

"I am Dr. Berry. Are you Samuel Archer?"

"No."

"Is Mr. Archer in?"

"He's busy right now."

"I'd like to see him."

"You a friend of his?"

He was staring at me with open suspicion. I heard more sounds—a grating, a rumble, and a long, drawnout whistle.

"I need his help," I said.

He seemed to relax slightly. "This is a bad time."

"It's urgent."

"You're a doctor?"

"Yes."

"You have a car?"

"Yes."

"What kind?"

"Chevrolet. Nineteen-sixty-five."

"What's the license?"

"Two-one-one-five-sixteen."

He nodded. "O.K.," he said. "Sorry, but you know how it is these days. You can't trust anyone.[1] Come in." He stepped back from the door. "But don't say anything, all right? I'll tell him first. He's composing, and he gets pretty wrapped up. It's the seventh hour and it should be O.K. But he does flip out easy. Even late."

We walked through what seemed to be a living room. There were studio couches and a few cheap lamps. The walls were white, and painted in weird, flowing designs in fluorescent colors. An ultraviolet lamp heightened the effect.

"Wild," I said, hoping that was the right thing.

"Yeah, man."

We went into the next room. The lighting was low. A pale, short boy with an immense head of curly blond hair squatted on the floor surrounded by electronic equipment. Two speakers stood by the far wall. A tape recorder was running. The pale boy was working with his equipment, twirling knobs, producing the sounds. He did not look up at us as

[1] The Federal narcotics agents, or "narcs," are known in Boston to favor Chevrolets with licenses beginning with 412 or 414.

we entered. He seemed to be concentrating hard, but his movements were slow.

"Stay here," said the bearded boy. "I'll tell him."

I stood by the door. The bearded boy approached the other and said gently, "Sam. Sam."

Sam looked up at him. "Hi," he said.

"Sam, you have a visitor."

Sam seemed puzzled. "I do?" He still had not noticed me.

"Yes. He is a very nice man. A very nice man. Do you understand that? He is very friendly."

"Good," Sam said slowly.

"He needs your help. Will you help him?"

"Sure," Sam said.

The bearded boy beckoned to me. I came over and said to him, "What is it?"

"Acid," he said. "Seventh hour. He should be coming down now. But go easy, right?"

"O.K.," I said.

I squatted down so I was on Sam's level. Sam looked at me with blank eyes.

"I don't know you," he said finally.

"I'm John Berry."

Sam did not move. "You're old, man," he said. "Really *old*."

"In a way," I said.

"Yeah, man, wow. Hey, Marvin," he said, looking up at his friend, "did you see this guy? He's really *old*."

"Yes," Marvin said.

"Hey, wow, old."

"Sam," I said, "I'm your friend."

I held out my hand, slowly, so as not to frighten him. He did not shake it; he took it by the fingers and held it to the light. He turned it slowly, looking at the palm, then the back. Then he moved the fingers.

"Hey, man," he said, "you're a doctor."

"Yes," I said.

"You have doctor's hands. I can feel it."

"Yes."

"Hey, man. Wow. Beautiful hands."

He was silent for a time, examining my hands, squeezing them, stroking them, feeling the hairs on the back, the fingernails, the tips of the fingers.

"They shine," he said. "I wish I had hands like that."

"Maybe you do," I said.

He dropped my hands and looked at his own. Finally he said, "No. They're different."

"Is that bad?"

He gave me a puzzled look. "Why did you come here?"

"I need your help."

"Yeah. Hey. O.K."

"I need some information."

I did not realize this was a mistake until Marvin started forward. Sam became agitated; I pushed Marvin back.

"It's O.K., Sam. It's O.K."

"You're a cop," Sam said.

"No. No cop. I'm not a cop, Sam."

"You are, you're lying."

"He often gets paranoid," Marvin said. "It's his bag. He's worried about freaking out."

"You're a cop, a lousy cop."

"No, Sam. I'm not a cop. If you don't want to help me, I'll leave."

"You're a rock, a cop, a sock, a lock."

"No, Sam. No. No."

He settled down then, his body relaxing, his muscles softening.

I took a deep breath. "Sam, you have a friend. Bubbles."

"Yes."

"Sam, she has a friend named Karen."

He was staring off into space. It was a long time before he answered. "Yes. Karen."

"Bubbles lived with Karen. Last summer."

"Yes."

"Did you know Karen?"

"Yes."

He began to breathe rapidly, his chest heaving, and his eyes got wide.

I put my hand on his shoulder, gently. "Easy, Sam. Easy. Easy. Is something wrong?"

"Karen," he said, staring across the room. "She was . . . terrible."

"Sam—"

"She was the worst, man. The worst."

"Sam, where is Bubbles now?"

"Out. She went to visit Angela. Angela . . ."

"Angela Harding," Marvin said. "She and Karen and Bubbles all roomed together in the summer."

"Where is Angela now?" I asked Marvin.

At that moment, Sam jumped up and began to shout "Cop! Cop!" at the top of his lungs. He swung at me, missed, and tried to kick me. I caught his foot, and he fell, striking some of the electronic equipment. A loud, high-pitched whee-whee-whee filled the room.

Marvin said, "I'll get the thorazine."[2]

"Screw the thorazine," I said. "Help me." I grabbed Sam and held him down. He screamed over the howl of the electronic sound.

"Cop! Cop! Cop!"

He kicked and thrashed. Marvin tried to help, but he was ineffectual. Sam was banging his head against the floor.

"Get your foot under his head."

He didn't understand.

"Move!" I said.

He got his foot under, so Sam would not hurt his head. Sam continued to thrash and twist in my grip. Abruptly, I released him. He stopped writhing, looked at his hands, then looked at me.

"Hey, man. What's the matter?"

"You can relax now," I said.

---

[2] Thorazine is a tranquilizer, universally used as an antidote to LSD and employed to end bad trips. However, when other psychedelic compounds such as STP are used, thorazine heightens the drug effect instead of abolishing it. Thus physicians who see LSD psychosis in the EW no longer automatically administer thorazine.

"Hey, man. You let me go."

I nodded to Marvin, who went and unplugged the electronic equipment. The howls stopped. The room became strangely silent.

Sam sat up, staring at me. "Hey, you let me go. You really let me go."

He looked at my face.

"Man," he said, touching my cheek, "you're beautiful."

And then he kissed me.

WHEN I GOT HOME, Judith was lying awake in bed.

"What happened?"

As I undressed, I said, "I got kissed."

"By Sally?" She sounded amused.

"No. By Sam Archer."

"The composer?"

"That's right."

"Why?"

"It's a long story," I said.

"I'm not sleepy," she said.

I told her about it, then got into bed and kissed her. "Funny," I said, "I've never been kissed by a man before."

She rubbed my neck. "Like it?"

"Not much."

"That's strange," she said, "I like it fine," and she pulled me down to her.

"I bet you've been kissed by men all your life," I said.

"Some are better than others."

"Who's better than others?"

"You're better than others."

"Is that a promise?"

She licked the tip of my nose with her tongue. "No," she said, "that's a come-on."

WEDNESDAY
OCTOBER 12

ONE

ONCE A MONTH, the Lord takes pity on the Cradle of Liberty and lets the sun shine on Boston. Today was that day: cool, bright and clear, with an autumn crispness in the air. I awoke feeling good, with the sharp expectation that things would happen.

I had a large breakfast, including two eggs, which I ate with guilty relish, savoring their cholesterol. Then I went into my study to plan the day. I began by drawing up a list of everyone I had seen and trying to determine if any of them were suspects. Nobody really was.

The first person to suspect in any abortion question is the woman herself, since so many are self-induced. The autopsy showed that Karen must have had anesthetic for the operation; therefore she didn't do it.

Her brother knew how to do the procedure, but he was on duty at the time. I could check that, and

227

might, later on, but for the moment, there was no reason to disbelieve him.

Peter Randall and J. D. were both possibilities, technically speaking. But somehow I couldn't imagine either of them doing it.

That left Art, or one of Karen's Beacon Hill friends, or somebody I hadn't met yet and didn't even know existed.

I stared at the list for a while, and then called the Mallory Building at the City. Alice wasn't there; I talked with another secretary.

"Have you got the path diagnosis on Karen Randall?"

"What's the case number?"

"I don't know the case number."

Very irritably, she said, "It would help if you did."

"Please check it anyway," I said.

I knew perfectly well that the secretary had a filecard system right in front of her, with all the finished posts for a month arranged alphabetically and by number. It would be no trouble for her.

After a long pause, she said, "Here it is. Vaginal hemorrhage secondary to uterine perforation and lacerations, following attempted dilation and curettage for three-month pregnancy. The secondary diagnosis is systemic anaphylaxis."

"I see," I said, frowning. "Are you sure?"

"I'm just reading what it says," she said.

"Thanks," I said.

I hung up, feeling odd. Judith gave me a cup of coffee and said, "What happened?"

"The autopsy report says Karen Randall was pregnant."

"Oh?"

"Yes."

"Wasn't she?"

"I never thought so," I said.

I knew I could be wrong. It might have been proven in the micro exam, where the gross had shown nothing. But somehow it didn't seem likely.

I called Murph's lab to see if he had finished with the blood-hormone assay, but he hadn't; it wouldn't be finished until after noon. I said I'd call him back.

Then I opened the phone book and looked up the address of Angela Harding. She was living on Chestnut Street, a very good address.

I went over to see her.

CHESTNUT STREET IS OFF CHARLES, near the bottom of the Hill. It's a very quiet area of town houses, antique shops, quaint restaurants, and small grocery stores; most of the people who live here are young professionals—doctors and lawyers and bankers—who want a good address but can't yet afford to move out to Newton or Wellesley. The other people who live here are old professionals, men in their fifties and sixties whose children are grown and married, permitting them to move back to the city. If you are going to live anywhere in Boston, you have to live on Beacon Hill.

There were, of course, some students living here,

but usually they were stacked three or four deep in small apartments; it was the only way they could afford the rents. Older residents seemed to like the students; they added a little color and youth to the neighborhood. That is, they liked the students so long as the students looked clean and behaved themselves.

Angela Harding lived on the second floor of a walk-up; I knocked on the door. It was answered by a slim, dark-haired girl wearing a miniskirt and a sweater. She had a flower painted on her cheek, and large, blue-tinted granny glasses.

"Angela Harding?"

"No," said the girl. "You're too late. She's already gone. But maybe she'll call back."

I said, "My name is Dr. Berry. I'm a pathologist."

"Oh."

The girl bit her lip and stared at me uncertainly.

"Are you Bubbles?"

"Yes," she said. "How did you know?" And then she snapped her fingers. "Of course. You were the one with Superhead last night."

"Yes."

"I heard you'd been around."

"Yes."

She stepped back from the door. "Come in."

The apartment had almost no furniture at all. A single couch in the living room, and a couple of pillows on the floor; through an open door, I saw an unmade bed.

"I'm trying to find out about Karen Randall," I said.

"I heard."

"Is this where you all lived last summer?"

"Yeah."

"When did you last see Karen?"

"I haven't seen her for months. Neither has Angela," she said.

"Did Angela tell you that?"

"Yes. Of course."

"When did she say that to you?"

"Last night. We were talking about Karen last night. You see, we'd just found out about her, uh, accident."

"Who told you?"

She shrugged. "The word got around."

"What word?"

"That she got a bad scrape."

"Do you know who did it?"

She said, "They've picked up some doctor. But you know that."

"Yes," I said.

"He probably did it," she said, with a shrug. She brushed her long black hair away from her face. She had very pale skin. "But I don't know."

"How do you mean?"

"Well, Karen was no fool. She knew the score. Like, she'd been through the routine before. Including last summer."

"An abortion?"

"Yeah. That's right. And afterward she was real

depressed. She took a couple of down-trips, real freaks, and it shook her up. She had this thing about babies, and she knew it was rotten because it gave her freak trips. We didn't want her to fly for a while after the abortion, but she insisted, and it was bad. Real bad."

I said, "How do you mean?"

"One time she became the knife. She was scraping out the room and screaming the whole time that it was bloody, that all the walls were covered with blood. And she thought the windows were babies and that they were turning black and dying. Really bad news."

"What did you do?"

"We took care of her." Bubbles shrugged. "What else could we do?"

She reached over to a table and picked up a jar and a small wire loop. She swung the loop in the air and a stream of bubbles floated out and drifted gently downward. She watched them. One after another, they fell to the floor and popped.

"Real bad."

"Last summer," I said, "who did the abortion?"

Bubbles laughed. "I don't know."

"What happened?"

"Well, she got knocked up. So she announces that she's going to get rid of it, and she takes off for a day, and then comes back all smiling and happy."

"No problems?"

"None." She swung out another stream of bubbles and watched them. "None at all. Excuse me a minute."

She went into the kitchen, poured a glass of water, and swallowed it with a pill.

"I was coming down," she said, "you know?"

"What was it?"

"Bombs."

"Bombs?"

"Sure. You know." She waved her hand impatiently. "Speed. Lifts. Jets. Bennies."

"Amphetamine?"

"Methedrene."

"You on it all the time?"

"Just like a doctor." She brushed her hair back again. "Always asking questions."

"Where do you get the stuff?"

I had seen the capsule. It was at least five milligrams. Most of the black-market material is one milligram.

"Forget it," she said. "All right? Just forget it."

"If you wanted me to forget it," I said, "why did you let me see you take it?"

"A shrink, too."

"Just curious."

"I was showing off," she said.

"Maybe you were."

"Maybe I was." She laughed.

"Was Karen on speed, too?"

"Karen was on everything." Bubbles sighed. "She used to shoot speed."

I must have looked puzzled, because she made

jabbing motions at her elbow with her finger, imitating intravenous injection.

"Nobody else shoots it," Bubbles said. "But Karen went all out."

I said, "Her trips . . ."

"Acid. Once, DMT."

"How did she feel afterward?"

"Like hell. She was really turned off. Wired out. Down, you know, they were really down-trips."

"Did she stayed turned off?"

"Yeah. The rest of the summer. Never made it once with a guy for the rest of the summer. Like she was afraid."

"Are you sure about that?"

"Yeah," she said. "Sure."

I looked around the apartment. "Where is Angela?"

"Out."

"Where did she go? I'd like to talk to her."

"She really needs to talk to you, right now."

I said, "Is she in some kind of trouble?"

"No."

"I'd like to talk to her."

Bubbles shrugged. "If you can find her, talk to her."

"Where did she go?"

"I told you. Out."

"I understand she's a nurse," I said.

"That's right," Bubbles said. "You got the—"

At this point, the door opened and a tall girl

burst into the room. She said, "That bastard isn't anywhere, he's hiding, the rotten—"

She stopped when she saw me.

" 'Lo, Ang," Bubbles said. She nodded to me. "You got an oldie but goodie here to see you."

Angela Harding swept into the room and slumped on the couch, and lit a cigarette. She wore a very short black dress, black-net stockings, and patent-leather black boots. She had long dark hair and a hard, classically beautiful face with bones that looked chiseled; the face of a model. I had trouble picturing her as a nurse.

"You're the one who wants to know about Karen?"

I nodded.

"Sit down," she said. "Take a load off."

Bubbles said, "Ang, I didn't tell him—"

"Get me a Coke, would you, Bubbles?" Angela said. Bubbles nodded quietly and went into the kitchen. "You want a Coke?"

"No, thanks."

She shrugged. "Suit yourself." She sucked on the cigarette and stubbed it out. Her movements were quick but she kept her composure, a calm in her face. She lowered her voice. "I didn't want to talk about Karen in front of Bubbles. She's pretty upset about it."

"Karen?"

"Yes. They were close."

"And you?"

"Not so close."

"How's that?"

"She came on strong, in the beginning. Nice girl, a little wild, but fun. Very strong in the beginning. So we decided to share a room, the three of us. Then later Bubbles moves in with Superhead, and I'm stuck with Karen. It wasn't so easy."

"Why?"

"She was a crazy kid. She was nuts."

Bubbles came back with the Coke. "She wasn't."

"Not around you. She had an act for you."

"You're just mad because of—"

"Yeah. Right. Sure." Angela tossed her head and shifted her long legs. She turned to me and said, "She's talking about Jimmy. Jimmy was a resident I knew, in OB."

"That was the service you were on?"

"Yes," she said. "Jimmy and I had a thing, and I thought it was good. It *was* good. Then Karen stepped in."

Angela lit another cigarette and avoided my eyes. I could not really tell whether she was talking to me or to Bubbles. Obviously the two girls did not agree.

"I never thought she'd do it," Angela said. "Not your own roommate. I mean, there are rules . . ."

"She liked him," Bubbles said.

"She *liked* him. Yeah, I suppose so. For a quick seventy-two hours."

Angela stood up and paced up and down the room. Her dress barely reached to mid thigh. She was a strikingly beautiful girl, much more beautiful than Karen.

"You're not fair," Bubbles said.

"I don't *feel* fair."

"You know what you're saying is a lie. You know that Jimmy—"

"I don't know anything," Angela said. "All I know is that Jimmy's in Chicago now finishing his residency, and I am not with him. Maybe if I was—" She stopped.

"Maybe," Bubbles said.

"Maybe what?" I said.

"Skip it," Angela said.

I said, "When did you last see Karen?"

"I don't know. It must have been August sometime. Before she started school."

"You didn't see her last Sunday?"

"No," she said, still pacing. She didn't even break step. "No."

"That's funny. Alan Zenner saw her last Sunday."

"Who?"

"Alan Zenner. He was a friend of hers."

"Uh-huh."

"He saw her, and she told him she was coming over here."

Angela and Bubbles exchanged looks. Bubbles said, "The dirty little—"

"It's not true?" I asked.

"No," Angela said tightly. "We didn't see her."

"But he was positive—"

"She must have changed her mind. She usually

did, you know. Karen changed her mind so often you wondered if she had one."

Bubbles said, "Ang, listen . . ."

"Get me another Coke, will you?"

There was no mistaking the command in the voice. Bubbles got up meekly for another Coke.

"Bubbles is nice," Angela said, "but a little naïve. She likes everything to be sweet and nice in the end. That's why what happened to Karen bothers her so much."

"I see."

She stopped pacing and stood in front of me. Her body took on a rigidity that melted slowly into an icy calm. "Was there anything in particular you wanted to ask me?"

"Just if you'd seen Karen."

"No. The answer is no."

I stood. "Well then, thank you for your time."

Angela nodded. I went to the door. As I left I heard Bubbles say, "Is he leaving?"

And Angela said, "Shut up."

TWO

SHORTLY BEFORE NOON I called Bradford's office and was told that one of the staff was taking Dr. Lee's case. The man was named George Wilson. My call was put through to him. Over the phone he sounded smooth and self-confident; he agreed to meet me for drinks at five, but not at the Trafalgar Club. We would meet at Crusher Thompson's, a bar downtown.

After that, I had lunch in a drive-in and read the morning papers. The story about Art's arrest had finally broken, big, hitting all the front pages, though there was still no link to Karen Randall's death. Along with the story was a picture of Art. There were dark, sadistic circles under his eyes. His mouth drooped in a sinister way and his hair was disheveled. He could have been any cheap hood.

The stories didn't say much, just a bare outline of the facts of his arrest. They didn't have to say much: the picture said it all. In a way it was clever. You couldn't move for a prejudicial pretrial publicity on the basis of an unflattering picture.

After lunch I smoked a cigarette and tried to put it all together. I didn't have much success. The·descriptions I had heard of Karen were too conflicting, too uncertain. I had no clear picture of her, or what she might have done. Particularly what she might have done if she arrived in Boston for a weekend, pregnant, and needing an abortion.

At one I called Murphy's lab again. Murph answered the phone.

"Hormones Unlimited."

"Hello, Murph. What's the word?"

"On Karen Randall?"

"Murph, you've been doing homework."

"Not exactly," he said. "The City just called. Weston was on the phone. Wanted to know if you'd brought in a blood sample."

"And what did you say?"

"Yes."

"And what did he say?"

"Wanted to know the results. I told him."

"What are the results?"

"All the hormone and excretion metabolite levels are flat low. She wasn't pregnant. Absolutely impossible."

"O.K.," I said. "Thanks."

Murph had just put some life back into my theory. Not much, but some.

"You going to explain all this, John?"

"Not now," I said.

"You promised."

"I know," I said. "But not now."

"I knew you'd do this to me," Murph said. "Sarah will hate me." Sarah was his wife. She thrived on gossip.

"Sorry, but I just can't."

"Hell of a thing to do to an old friend."

"Sorry."

"If she divorces me," Murph said, "I'm naming you as co-defendant."

THREE

I ARRIVED AT THE MALLORY PATH LABS AT THREE. The first man I ran into was Weston, who was looking tired. He gave me a lopsided smile of greeting.

"What did you find out?" I said.

"The findings are negative," he said, "for pregnancy."

"Oh?"

"Yes." He picked up the folder containing the path protocol and thumbed through it. "No question."

"I called here earlier and was told the report was three months' pregnancy."

Weston said carefully, "Whom did you talk with?"

"A secretary."

"There must have been some kind of mistake."

"I guess," I said.

He handed me the folder. "Want to see the slides, too?"

"Yes. I'd like to."

We walked to the pathologists' reading room, a long room divided into individual cubicles, where the pathologists kept their microscopes and slides, and wrote up their autopsies.

We stopped at one booth.

"There it is," Weston said, pointing to a box of slides. "I'll be curious to have your opinion on them when you're through."

He left me, and I sat down in front of the scope, switched on the light, and began work. There were thirty slides in the box, made from all the major organs. Six had been made from different parts of the uterus: I began with them.

It was immediately clear that the girl was not pregnant. The endometrium was not hyperplastic. If anything, it appeared dormant and atrophic, with a thin proliferative layer, few glands, and decreased vascularity. I checked several other slides to be sure. They were all the same. Some contained thromboses from the scraping, but that was the only difference.

As I looked at the slides I considered their meaning. The girl had not been pregnant, yet she had been convinced she was. Therefore her periods must have stopped. That could account for the dormant appearance of the endometrium. But what had caused the periods to stop? I ran through the differential in my mind.

In a girl of this age, neurogenic factors came immediately to mind. The pressures and excitement of beginning school and moving to a new environment might have temporarily suppressed menstruation—but not for three months, and not with the associated signs: obesity, change in hair distribution, and so on.

Then there were hormonal disorders. Adrenal virilizing syndromes, Stein-Leventhal, irradiation. All of them seemed unlikely for one reason or another, but there was one quick way to find out.

I put the adrenal slide under the stage. There was good evidence of cortical atrophy, particularly in the cells of the zona fascicularis. The zona glomerulosa appeared normal.

Rule out virilizing syndromes and adrenal tumor.

Next I looked at the ovaries. Here the changes were striking. The follicles were small, immature, withered-looking. The whole organ, like the uterine endometrium, had a dormant appearance.

Rule out Stein-Levanthal and ovarian tumor.

Finally, I put the thyroid slide under the stage. Even under the lowest power, the atrophy of the gland was apparent. The follicles were shrunken and the lining cells were low. Clear hypothyroidism.

That meant that the thyroid, adrenals, and ovaries were all atrophic. The diagnosis was clear, though the etiology was not. I opened the folder and read through the official report. Weston had done it; the style was brisk and direct. I came to the micro write-ups. He had noted the endometrium was low and aberrant-looking, but he had considered the other glands to be "of normal appearance, question mark early atrophic changes."

I shut the folder and went to see him.

HIS OFFICE WAS LARGE, lined with books, and very neat. He sat behind an old, heavy desk smoking a briar pipe, looking scholarly and venerable.

"Something wrong?" he asked.

I hesitated. I had been wondering whether he had covered up, whether he had joined the others who were out to frame Art. But that was ridiculous; Weston couldn't be bought, not at his age, not with his reputation. Nor was he particularly close to the Randall family. He would have no reason to falsify the report.

"Yes," I said. "I wondered about your micro diagnosis."

He puffed the pipe calmly. "Oh?"

"Yes. I've just reviewed the slides, and they seem pretty atrophic to me. I thought perhaps—"

"Well, John," Weston said, chuckling, "I know what you're going to say. You thought perhaps I'd want to review them." He smiled at me. "I *have* reviewed them. Twice. This is an important postmortem and I did it as carefully as I know how. The first time I examined the slides, I felt as you did, that they seemed to show pan hypopituitarism affecting all three target organs—thyroid, adrenals, gonads. I felt that very strongly, so I went back to the gross organs. As you yourself say, the gross organs were not strikingly abnormal."

"It might have been recently acquired," I said.

"Yes," he said, "it might. That's what makes it so difficult. Then, too, we'd like a look at the brain, to check for evidence of neoplasm or infarction. But that's not possible; the body was cremated this morning."

"I see."

He smiled up at me. "Sit down, John. It makes me nervous to have you standing like that." When I was sitting, he said, "Anyway I looked at the gross, and then went back to the slides. This time I was less certain. I wasn't fully convinced. So I checked some old cases of pan hypopit, reviewed the old slides, and finally looked at the Randall slides a third time. By then I felt I could not be certain of a diagnosis of pituitary dysfunction. The more I looked, the less certain I felt. I wanted some kind of corroboratory evidence—brain pathology, or X rays, or blood hormones. That was why I called Jim Murphy."

"Oh?"

"Yes." His pipe went out; he relit it again. "I suspected you'd taken the blood sample to do estradiol tests, and that you'd get Murphy to do it. I wanted to know if you'd also decided to have other hormone levels checked—TSH, ACTH, T_4, anything that might help."

"Why didn't you just call me?"

"I did, but your lab didn't know where you were."

I nodded. Everything he had said made perfect sense. I felt my body slowly relaxing.

"By the way," Weston said, "I understand some skull films of Karen Randall were taken a while back. Any idea what they showed?"

"Nothing," I said. "They were negative."

Weston sighed. "Pity."

"I'll tell you something interesting though," I said.

"What's that?"

"They were ordered because she complained of blurring vision."

Weston sighed. "John, do you know the most common cause of blurring vision?"

"No."

"Lack of sleep," Weston said. He pushed the pipe to the side of his mouth and held it in his teeth. "What would you do if you were in my position? Make a diagnosis on the basis of a complaint which led to negative X rays?"

"The slides *are* suggestive," I reminded him.

"But only suggestive." He shook his head slowly. "This is already a confused case, John. I'm not going to make it more confused by throwing in a diagnosis I'm not sure about. After all, I may be called into court to defend it. I'd rather not stick my neck out. If the prosecution or the defense wants to find a pathologist to review the material and stick *his* neck out, that's fine. The material is here for anyone to see. But I'm not going to do it. My years in the courtroom have taught me one thing, at least."

"What's that?"

"Never take a position unless you are certain it can be defended against any onslaught. That may sound like good advice to a general," he said, smiling, "but then, a courtroom is nothing more than a very civilized war."

FOUR

I HAD TO SEE SANDERSON. I had promised to see him, and now I needed his advice badly. But as I entered the lobby of the Lincoln Hospital, the first person I saw was Harry Fallon.

He was slinking down a corridor, wearing a raincoat and hat pulled down over his forehead. Harry is an internist with a large suburban practice in Newton; he is also a former actor and something of a clown. I greeted him and he raised the brim of his hat slowly. His eyes were bloodshot and his face sallow.

"I hab a code," Harry said.

"Who are you seeing?"

"Gordon. The cheeb residend." He took out a Kleenex and blew his nose loudly. "Aboud my bat code."

I laughed. "You sound like you've swallowed cotton."

"Thang you bery mugh." He sniffled. "This is no labbing madder."

He was right, of course. All practicing doctors feared getting sick. Even small colds were considered bad for your image, for what is loosely called "patient rapport," and any serious illness became a matter for the utmost secrecy. When old Henley finally developed chronic glomerulonephritis, he went to elaborate lengths to be sure his patients never found out; he would visit his doctor in the middle of the night, sneaking about like a thief.

"It doesn't sound like a bad cold," I told Harry.

"Hah. You thingh so? Listen to me." He blew his nose again, a long, honking sound, somewhere between a foghorn and the death rattle of a hippopotamus.

"How long have you had it?"

"Du days. Du miberable, miberable days. My padends are nodicing."

"What are you taking for it?"

"Hod toddies," he said. "Besd thing for a virus. Bud the world is againsd me, John. Today, on tob ov my code, I got a tickud."

"A thickud?"

"Yes. For double-barking."

I laughed, but at the back of my mind, something was bothering me, something I knew I should be remembering and thinking about, something I had forgotten and ignored.

It was a strange and irritating feeling.

I MET SANDERSON IN THE PATH LIBRARY. It's a square room with lots of chairs, the folding kind, and a projector and screen. Path conferences are held here, in which autopsies are reviewed, and they are so frequent you can practically never get in to use the library books.

On the shelves, in boxes, were autopsy reports for every person done in the Lincoln since 1923, the year we began to keep good records. Prior to that time, nobody had a very good idea of how many people were dying from what diseases, but as knowledge of medicine and the human body increased that information became vitally important. One proof of increased interest was the number of autopsies performed in 1923 all the reports filled one slim box—but by 1965 it required half a shelf for all the records. At present, more than seventy percent of all patients who died in the hospital were autopsied, and there was talk of microfilming the reports for the library.

In one corner of the room was a portable electric coffeepot, a bowl of sugar, a stack of paper cups, and a sign that said, "5 cents a cup. Scout's honor." Sanderson was fussing with the pot, trying to get it to work. The pot represented an ancient challenge: it was said nobody was permitted to finish his path residency at the Lincoln until he had mastered its workings.

"Someday," Sanderson muttered, "I'm going to electrocute myself on this damned thing." He plugged it in; crackling sounds were heard. "Me, or some other poor bastard. Cream and sugar?"

"Please," I said.

Sanderson filled two cups, holding the pot at arm's length. Sanderson was notoriously bad with anything mechanical. He had a superb, almost instinctive understanding of the human body and its functions of flesh and bone, but mechanical, steel, and electrical objects were beyond him. He lived in constant fear that his car, or his TV, or his stereo would break down; he regarded them all as potential traitors and deserters.

He was a tall, powerfully built man who had once rowed stroke for the Harvard heavyweights. His forearms and wrists were as thick as most men's calves. He had a solemn, thoughtful face: he might have been a judge, or an excellent poker player.

"Did Weston say anything else?" he asked.

"No."

"You sound unhappy."

"Let's say I'm worried."

Sanderson shook his head. "I think you're barking up the wrong tree here," he said. "Weston wouldn't fake a report for anybody. If he says he was unsure, then he was."

"Maybe you should examine the slides yourself."

"I'd like to," Sanderson said, "but you know that's impossible."

He was right. If he showed up at Mallory and asked to see the slides, it would be taken as a personal insult by Weston. That kind of thing just wasn't done.

I said, "Maybe if he asked you . . ."

"Why should he?"

"I don't know."

"Weston has made his diagnosis and signed his

name to it. The matter closes there, unless it comes up again during the trial."

I felt a sinking feeling. Over the past days, I had come to believe very strongly that there must not be a trial. Any trial, even an acquittal, would seriously damage Art's reputation, his standing, and his practice. A trial had to be prevented.

"But you think she was hypopit," Sanderson said.

"Yes."

"Etiology?"

"Neoplasm, I think."

"Adenoma?"[1]

"I imagine. Maybe craniopharyngioma."

"How long?"

"It couldn't be very long," I said. "X rays four months ago were normal. No enlargement or erosion of the sella turcica. But she did complain of vision trouble."

"What about pseudotumor?"

Pseudotumor cerebri is a disorder of women and young children. Patients get all the symptoms of a tumor, but don't actually have one. It is related to withdrawal of steroid therapy; women sometimes get it when taking birth-control pills. But as far as I knew, Karen wasn't taking pills. I told Sanderson.

"Too bad we don't have slides of the brain," he said.

I nodded.

---

[1] A chromophobe adenoma is the most common tumor of the pituitary. It is slow-growing and relatively benign, but it presses on the optic nerve, causing visual symptoms, and it may create endocrine dysfunction.

"On the other hand," Sanderson said, "an abortion was performed. We can't forget that."

"I know," I said. "But it's just another indicator that Art didn't do it. He wouldn't have aborted her without doing a bunny test first, and such a test would have been negative."

"That's only circumstantial evidence, at best."

"I know," I said, "but it's something. A start."

"There is another possibility," Sanderson said. "Supposing the abortionist was willing to take Karen's word that she was pregnant."

I frowned. "I don't understand. Art didn't know the girl; he had never seen her before. He would never—"

"I'm not thinking of Art," Sanderson said. He was staring at his feet, as if he had something embarrassing on his mind.

"What do you mean?"

"Well, this is all highly speculative. . . ."

I waited for him.

"A lot of muck has been thrown already. I hate to add to it," he said.

I said nothing.

"I never knew it before," Sanderson continued. "I thought I was pretty well informed about these things, but I never knew it until today. As you can imagine, the whole medical community is buzzing. J. D. Randall's girl dies from an abortion—you can't keep other doctors from talking about *that*." He sighed. "Anyway, it was something one of the wives told my wife. I don't even know if it's true."

I wasn't going to push Sanderson. He could take his time in telling me; I lit a cigarette and waited patiently.

"Oh hell," Sanderson said, "it's probably just a rumor. I can't imagine I'd never heard of it before."

"What?" I said finally.

"Peter Randall. Peter does abortions. Very quiet and exclusive, but he does them."

"Jesus," I said, sitting down in a chair.

"It's hard to believe," Sanderson said.

I smoked a cigarette and thought it over. If Peter did abortions, did J. D. know? Did he think Peter had done it, and was covering up for him? Was that what he meant by "a family matter"? If so, why had Art been dragged into this?

And why would Peter abort the girl in the first place? Peter had evidence that there might be something wrong with the girl. He was a good enough doctor to think of a pit tumor. If the girl came to him saying she was pregnant, he'd certainly think back to her vision trouble. And he'd run tests.

"Peter didn't do it," I said.

"Maybe she put pressure on him. Maybe she was in a hurry. She only had one weekend."

"No. He wouldn't respond to pressure from her."

"She was family."

"She was a young and hysterical girl," I said, remembering Peter's description.

Sanderson said, "Can you be sure Peter didn't do it?"

"No," I admitted.

"Let's suppose he did. And let's suppose Mrs. Randall knew about the abortion. Or that the girl told her, as she was bleeding to death, that Peter had done it. What would Mrs. Randall do? Turn in her brother-in-law?"

I could see where he was leading me. It certainly provided an explanation for one of the puzzles of the case—why Mrs. Randall had called in the police. But I didn't like it, and I told Sanderson so.

"The reason you don't like it is you're fond of Peter."

"That may be."

"You can't afford to exclude him or anyone else. Do you know where Peter was last Sunday night?"

"No."

"Neither do I," Wes Sanderson said, "but I think it's worth checking."

"No," I said, "it's not. Peter wouldn't do it. And even if he did, he wouldn't have botched it so badly. No professional would have."

"You're prejudging the case," Sanderson said.

"Look, if Peter could have done it—without tests, without anything—then so could Art."

"Yes," Sanderson said mildly. "That has occurred to me."

FIVE

I WAS FEELING IRRITABLE when I left Sanderson. I couldn't decide exactly why. Perhaps he was right; perhaps I was unreasonably and illogically searching for fixed points, for things and people to believe in.

But there was something else. In any court action, there was always the chance that Sanderson and I could be implicated, and our role in fooling the tissue committee brought out. Both Sanderson and I had a large stake in this business, a stake as large as Art's. We hadn't talked about that, but it was there in the back of my mind, and I was sure in the back of his as well. And that put a different interpretation on things.

Sanderson was perfectly correct: we could put the squeeze on Peter Randall. But if we did, we'd never know why we did. We could always say it was because we believed Peter was guilty. Or because it was expedient, to save a falsely accused man.

But we would always wonder whether we did it simply to protect ourselves.

Before I did anything, I would have to get more information. Sanderson's argument made no distinction between Mrs. Randall knowing that Peter had done the abortion and merely suspecting that he had.

And there was another question. If Mrs. Randall suspected that Peter had done the abortion and wished to keep him from being arrested, why had she named Art? What did she know about Art?

Art Lee was a circumspect and cautious man. He was hardly a household word among the pregnant women of Boston. He was known to a few physicians and a relatively small number of patients. His clientele was carefully chosen.

How had Mrs. Randall known he performed abortions? There was one man who might know the answer: Fritz Werner.

FRITZ WERNER lived in a town house on Beacon Street. The ground floor was given over to his office—an anteroom and a large, comfortable room with desk, chair, and couch—and to his library. The upper two floors comprised his living quarters. I went directly to the second floor and entered the living room to find it the same as always: a large desk by the window, covered with pens, brushes, sketchbooks, pastels; drawings by Picasso and Miró on the walls; a photograph of T. S. Eliot glowering into the camera; an informal, signed portrait of Marianne Moore talking with her friend Floyd Patterson.

Fritz was sitting in a heavy armchair, wearing slacks and an enormous bulky sweater. He had stereophonic earphones on his head, was smoking a thick cigar, and crying. The tears rolled down his flat, pale cheeks. He wiped his eyes when he saw me, and took off the earphones.

"Ah, John. Do you know any Albinoni?"

"No," I said.

"Then you don't know the adagio."

"I'm afraid not."

"It always makes me sad," he said, dabbing his eyes. "Infernally, infernally sad. So sweet. Do sit down."

I sat. He turned off his record player and took off the record. He dusted it carefully and replaced it in the jacket.

"It was good of you to come. How was your day?"

"Interesting."

"You've looked up Bubbles?"

"Yes, I did."

"How did you find her?"

"Confusing."

"Why do you say that?"

I smiled. "Don't analyze me, Fritz. I never pay my doctor bills."

"No?"

"Tell me about Karen Randall," I said.

"This is very nasty, John."

"Now you sound like Charlie Frank."

"Charlie Frank is not a *complete* fool," Fritz said. "By the way, did I tell you I have a new friend?"

"No," I said.

"I do, a marvelous creature, most amusing. We must talk about him sometime."

"Karen Randall," I said, bringing him back to the point.

"Yes, indeed." Fritz took a deep breath. "You didn't know the girl, John," he said. "She was not a nice child. Not at all. She was a mean, lying, unpleasant little child with severe neuroses. Bordering on psychosis, if you ask me."

He walked into the bedroom, stripping off his sweater. I followed him in and watched as he put on a clean shirt and a tie.

"Her problems," Fritz said, "were sexual in nature, stemming from a repressed childhood with her parents. Her father is not the most well-adjusted man I know. Marrying that woman is a perfect example. Have you met her?"

"The present Mrs. Randall?"

"Yes. Ghastly, *ghastly* woman."

He shuddered as he knotted his tie and straightened it in the mirror.

"Did you know Karen?" I asked.

"It was my misfortune to do so. I knew her parents as well. We first met at that marvelous, glorious party given by the Baroness de—"

"Just tell me," I said.

Fritz sighed. "This girl, this Karen Randall," he said, "she presented her parents with their own neuroses. In a sense she acted out their fantasies."

"What do you mean?"

"Breaking the mold—being sexually free, not caring what people said, dating the wrong kinds of people, and always with sexual undertones. Athletes. Negroes. That sort of thing."

"Was she ever your patient?"

He sighed. "No, thank God. At one point it was suggested that I take her, but I refused. I had three other adolescent girls at the time, and they were quite enough. Quite enough."

"Who asked you to take her?"

"Peter, of course. He's the only one with any sense in the family."

"What about Karen's abortions?"

"Abortions?"

"Come on, Fritz."

He went to a closet and found a sports coat, pulled it on, and tugged at the lapels. "People never understand," he said. "There is a cycle here, a pattern which is as easily recognizable, as familiar, as an MI.[1] You learn the pattern, the symptoms, the trouble. You see it acted out before you again and again. A rebellious child chooses the weak point of its parent—with unfailing, uncanny accuracy—and proceeds to exploit it. But then when punishment comes, it must be in terms of the same weak point. It must all fit together: if someone asks you a question in French, you must answer in French."

"I don't understand."

"For a girl like Karen, punishment was important. She wanted to be punished, but her punishment, like her rebellion, had to be sexual in nature. She

---

[1] Myocardial infarction, a heart attack.

wanted to suffer the pain of childbirth, so she could compensate for breaking with her family, her society, her morality. . . . Dylan put it beautifully; I have the poem here somewhere." He began rummaging through a bookshelf.

"It's all right," I said.

"No, no, a lovely quotation. You'd enjoy it." He searched for a few more moments, then straightened. "Can't find it. Well, never mind. The point is that she needed suffering, but never experienced it. That was why she kept getting pregnant."

"You talk like a psychiatrist."

"We all do, these days."

"How many times did she get pregnant?"

"Twice, that I know of. But that is just what I hear from my other patients. A great many women felt threatened by Karen. She impinged upon their system of values, their framework of right and wrong. She challenged them, she implied that they were old and sexless and timid and foolish. A middle-aged woman can't stand such a challenge; it is terrifying. She must respond, must react, must form an opinion which vindicates herself—and therefore condemns Karen."

"So you heard a lot of gossip."

"I heard a lot of fear."

He smoked his cigar. The room was filled with sunlight and blue smoke. He sat on the bed and began pulling on his shoes.

"Frankly," he said, "after a while I began to resent

Karen myself. She went overboard, she did too much, she went too far."

"Perhaps she couldn't help it."

"Perhaps," Fritz said, "she needed a good spanking."

"Is that a professional opinion?"

He smiled. "That is just my human irritation showing through. If I could count the number of women who have run out and had affairs— disastrous affairs—just because of Karen. . . ."

"I don't care about the women," I said, "I care about Karen."

"She's dead now," Fritz said.

"That pleases you?"

"Don't be silly. Why do you say that?"

"Fritz . . ."

"Just a question."

"Fritz," I said, "how many abortions did Karen have before last weekend?"

"Two."

"One last summer," I said, "in June. And one before that?"

"Yes."

"And who aborted her?"

"I haven't the slightest," he said, puffing on his cigar.

"It was somebody good," I said, "because Bubbles said that Karen was only gone for an afternoon. It must have been very skillful and nontraumatic."

"Very likely. She was a rich girl, after all."

I looked at him, sitting there on the bed, tying

his shoes and smoking the cigar. Somehow, I was convinced he knew.

"Fritz, was it Peter Randall?"

Fritz grunted. "If you know, why ask?"

"I need confirmation."

"You need a strong noose around your neck, if you ask me. But yes: it was Peter."

"Did J. D. know?"

"Heaven help us! Never!"

"Did Mrs. Randall know?"

"Hmmm. There I am not certain. It is possible but somehow I doubt it."

"Did J. D. know that Peter did abortions?"

"Yes. Everyone knows that Peter does abortions. He is *the* abortionist, believe me."

"But J.D. never knew Karen had been aborted."

"That's correct."

"What's the connection between Mrs. Randall and Art Lee?"

"You are very acute today," Fritz said.

I waited for an answer. Fritz puffed twice on his cigar, producing a dramatic cloud around his face, and looked away from me.

"Oh," I said. "When?"

"Last year. Around Christmas, if I recall."

"J. D. never knew?"

"If you will remember," Fritz said, "J. D. spent the months of November and December in India last year working for the State Department. Some kind of goodwill tour, or public health thing."

"Then who was the father?"

"Well, there is some speculation about that. But nobody knows for sure—perhaps not even Mrs. Randall."

Once again, I had the feeling that he was lying.

"Come on, Fritz. Are you going to help me or not?"

"Dear boy, you are immensely clever." He stood, walked to the mirror, and straightened his jacket. He ran his hands over his shirt. It was something you always noticed about Fritz: he was continually touching his body, as if to assure himself that he had not disappeared.

"I have often thought," Fritz said, "that the present Mrs. Randall might as well have been Karen's mother, since they are both such bitches in heat."

I lit a cigarette. "Why did J. D. marry her?"

Fritz gave a helpless shrug and fluffed a handkerchief in his pocket. He tugged his shirt cuffs down his jacket sleeves. "God only knows. There was great talk at the time. She comes from a good family, you know—a Rhode Island family—but they sent her to a Swiss school. Those Swiss schools will destroy a girl. In any event, she was a poor choice for a man in his sixties, and a busy surgeon. She grew rapidly bored sitting around her cavernous home. The Swiss schools teach you to be bored in any case."

He buttoned his jacket and turned away from the mirror, with a final glance over his shoulder at himself. "So," he said, "she amused herself."

"How long has this been going on?"

"More than a year."

"Did she arrange Karen's abortion?"

"I doubt it. One can't be sure, but I doubt it. More likely it would be Signe."

"Signe?"

"Yes. J. D.'s mistress."

I took a deep breath and wondered if Fritz was kidding me. I decided he wasn't.

"J. D. had a mistress?"

"Oh, yes. A Finnish girl. She worked in the cardiology lab of the Mem. Quite a stunner, I'm told."

"You never met her?"

"Alas."

"Then how do you know?"

He smiled enigmatically.

"Karen liked this Signe?"

"Yes. They were good friends. Rather close in ages, actually."

I ignored the implications in that.

"You see," Fritz continued, "Karen was very close to her mother, the first Mrs. Randall. She died two years ago of cancer—rectum, I think—and it was a great blow for Karen. She never liked her father much, but had always confided in her mother. The loss of a confidante at the age of sixteen was a great blow to her. Much of her subsequent . . . activity can be attributed to bad advice."

"From Signe?"

"No. Signe was quite a proper girl, from what I'm told."

"I don't get it."

"One of the reasons Karen disliked her father was that she knew about his propensities. You see, he has always had women friends. Young ones. The first was Mrs. Jewett, and then there was—"

"Never mind," I said. I had already gotten the picture. "He cheated on his first wife, too?"

"Wandered," Fritz said. "Let us say wandered."

"And Karen knew?"

"She was quite a perceptive child."

"There's one thing I don't understand," I said. "If Randall likes variety, why did he remarry?"

"Oh, that's quite clear. One look at the present Mrs. Randall and you'd know. She is a fixture in his life, a decoration, an ornament to his existence. Rather like an exotic potted plant—which is not far from the truth, considering how much she drinks."

"It doesn't make sense," I said.

He gave me an amused, askance look. "What about that nurse you have lunch with twice a week?"

"Sandra is a friend. She's a nice girl." As I said it, it occurred to me that he was astonishingly well informed.

"Nothing further?"

"Of course not," I said, a little stiffly.

"You just happen to run into her at the cafeteria on Thursdays and Fridays?"

"Yes. Our schedules—"

"What do you think this girl feels about you?"

"She's just a girl. She's ten years younger than I am."

"Aren't you flattered?"

"What do you mean?" I said, knowing exactly what he meant.

"Don't you derive satisfaction from talking with her?"

Sandra was a nurse on the eighth-floor medical service. She was very pretty, with very large eyes and a very small waist, and a way of walking. . . .

"Nothing has happened," I said.

"And nothing will. Yet you meet her twice a week."

"She happens to be a welcome change from my work," I said. "Twice a week. A rendezvous in the intimate, sexually charged atmosphere of the Lincoln Hospital cafeteria."

"There's no need to raise your voice."

"I'm not raising my voice," I said, lowering it.

"You see," Fritz said, "men handle things differently. You feel no compulsion to do more than talk to this girl. It is enough that she be there, hanging on your every word, mildly in love with you—"

"Fritz—"

"Look," Fritz said. "Let's take a case from my experience. I had a patient who felt a desire to kill people. It was a very strong desire, difficult to control. It bothered the patient; he was in constant fear of actually killing someone. But this man finally got a job in the Midwest, working as an executioner. He electrocuted people as his livelihood. And he did it very well; he was the best electrocutioner in the history of the state. He holds several patents, little techniques he has developed to do the job faster, more painlessly. He is a student of death. He likes his work. He is dedicated. He sees his methods and his advances much as a doctor does: a relief of suffering, an improvement, a bettering."

"So?"

"So I am saying that normal desires can take many forms, some legitimate, some not. Everyone must find a way to deal with them."

"We're a long way from Karen," I said.

"Not really. Have you ever wondered why she was so close to her mother and so estranged from her father? Have you ever wondered why, when her mother died, she chose the particular mode of behavior she did? Sex, drugs, self-humiliation? Even to the point of befriending her father's mistress?"

I sat back. Fritz was being rhetorical again.

"The girl," he said, "had certain stresses and strains. She had certain reactions, some defensive, some offensive, to what she knew was going on with her parents. She reacted to what she knew. She had to. In a sense, she stablized her world."

"Some stability."

"True," Fritz said. "Unpleasant, nasty, perverse. But perhaps it was all she could manage."

I said, "I'd like to talk with this Signe."

"Impossible. Signe returned to Helsinki six months ago."

"And Karen?"

"Karen," Fritz said, "became a lost soul. She had

no one to turn to, no friends, no aid. Or so she felt."

"What about Bubbles and Angela Harding?"

Fritz looked at me steadily. "What about them?"

"They could have helped her."

"Can the drowning save the drowning?"

We walked downstairs.

SIX

CRUSHER THOMPSON used to be a wrestler in the fifties. He was distinguished by a flat, spatulalike head, which he used to press down on his opponent's chest once the man was down, and thus crush him. For a few years, it was good for some laughs—and enough money to buy a bar which had become a hangout for young professional men. It was a well-run bar; Thompson, despite the shape of his head, was no fool. He had some corny touches—you wiped your feet on a wrestling mat as you entered—and the inevitable pictures of himself on the walls, but the overall effect was pleasing.

There was only one person in the bar when I arrived, a heavyset, well-dressed Negro sitting at the far end, hunched over a martini. I sat down and ordered a Scotch. Thompson himself was bartending, his sleeves rolled up to expose massive, hairy fore-arms.

I said, "You know a fellow named George Wil-son?"

"Sure," Thompson said, with a crooked grin.

"Tell me when he comes in, will you?"

Thompson nodded to the man at the far end of the bar. "That's him, right there."

The Negro looked up and smiled at me. It was a half-amused, half-embarrassed look. I went over and shook his hand.

"Sorry," I said. "I'm John Berry."

"It's all right," he said, "this is new for me, too."

He was young, in his late twenties. There was a pale scar running down his neck from his right ear, disappearing below his shirt collar. But his eyes were steady and calm as he tugged at his red striped tie and said, "Shall we go to a booth?"

"All right."

As we walked to a booth, Wilson turned over his shoulder and said, "Two more of the same, Crusher."

The man behind the bar winked.

I said, "You're with Bradford's firm, is that it?"

"Yes. I was hired a little over a year ago."

I nodded.

"It was the usual thing," Wilson said. "They gave me a good office with a view out to the reception desk, so that people coming in and out could see me. That kind of thing."

I knew what he was saying, but I still felt a twist

of irritation. I had several friends who were young lawyers, and none of them had gotten an office of any kind for several years after joining a firm. By any objective standard, this young man was lucky, but it was no good telling him that, because we both knew why he was lucky—he was a kind of freak, a product which society had suddenly deemed valuable, an educated Negro. His horizons were now open and his future was good. But he was still a freak.

"What kind of work have you been doing?"

"Tax, mostly. A few estates. One or two civil proceedings. The firm doesn't have many criminal cases, as you might expect. But when I joined them, I expressed an interest in trial work. I never expected they'd drop this one on me."

"I see."

"I just want you to understand."

"I think I do. They've stuck you with a dead horse, is that it?"

"Maybe." He smiled. "At least, that's what they think."

"And what do you think?"

"I think," he said, "that a case is decided in the courtroom, not before."

"You have an approach?"

"I'm working on one," Wilson said. "It's going to take a lot of work, because it will have to be good. Because that jury's going to see an uppity Negro defending a Chinese abortionist, and they won't like it."

I sipped my drink. The second round was brought and set at one side of the table.

"On the other hand," Wilson said, "this is a big break for me."

"If you win."

"That," he said evenly, "is my intention."

I suddenly thought that Bradford, whatever his reasons for giving Wilson the case, had made a very wise decision. Because this kid was going to want to win. Badly.

"Have you talked with Art?"

"This morning."

"What was your impression?"

"Innocent. I'm sure of it."

"Why?"

"I understand him," Wilson said.

OVER THE SECOND DRINK, I outlined what I had done for the last few days. Wilson listened in silence, not interrupting me, though he occasionally made notes. When I was through, he said, "You've saved me a lot of work."

"In what way?"

"From what you've already told me, we can close the case. We can get Dr. Lee off easily."

"You mean because the girl wasn't pregnant?"

He shook his head. "In several cases, among them *Commonwealth versus Taylor*, it was concluded that pregnancy is not an essential element. Nor does it matter if the fetus was already dead prior to the abortion."

"In other words, it makes no difference that Karen Randall wasn't pregnant?"

"None."

"But isn't it evidence that the job was done by an amateur, a person who did not first run a pregnancy test? Art would never perform an abortion without checking first."

"Is that going to be your case? That Dr. Lee is too skilled an abortionist to make so simple a mistake?"

I was chagrined. "No, I guess not."

"Look," Wilson said, "you can't conduct a defense based on the character of the accused. It won't work, no matter how you try it." He flipped through his notebook. "Let me give you a rundown on the legal situation. In 1845, a Massachusetts General Law stated that it was an offense to procure an abortion, by any means. If the patient did not die, the sentence was not more than seven years; if the patient did die, it was five to twenty. Since then the law has been enlarged upon. Some years later, it was decided that an abortion, if necessary to save the life of the mother, was not an unlawful abortion. That doesn't apply in this case."

"No."

"Later revisions include *Commonwealth versus Viera*, which decided that use of an instrument with intent constituted a crime, even without proof that miscarriage or death resulted. This might be very important. If the prosecution attempts, as I am sure they will, to show that Dr. Lee is an abortionist of many years' standing, they will then imply that an absence of direct evidence is not sufficient to get Lee off the hook."

"Can they do that?"

"No. But they can try, and it would be immensely damaging to our case."

"Go on."

"There are two other rulings that are important, because they show how the laws are slanted against the abortionist, with no interest in the women involved. *Commonwealth versus Wood* ruled that the consent of the patient was immaterial and did not constitute a justification of abortion. The same court also concluded that the ensuing death of a woman is only an aggravation of the offense. In effect, this means that your investigation of Karen Randall is, from a legal standpoint, a waste of time."

"But I thought—"

"Yes," he said, "I said that the case is closed. And it is."

"How?"

"There are two alternatives. The first is to present the Randall family with the material at hand, before the trial. Point out the fact that Peter Randall, the deceased's personal physician, is an abortionist. The fact that he aborted her previously. The fact that Mrs. Randall, the wife, had had an abortion from Dr. Lee, and hence might be bearing a grudge against him, causing her to lie about what Karen had said. The fact that Karen was an unstable and unsavory young lady, whose dying words in any case were open to question. We could present all this to the family, in the hope of persuading them to drop charges before the trial."

I took a deep breath. This kid played rough. "And the second alternative?"

"The second is an extension, within the courtroom. Clearly, the crucial questions concern the relationships of Karen, Mrs. Randall, and Dr. Lee. The prosecution's case now stands on Mrs. Randall's testimony. We must discredit it, and her. We must destroy her until no juror dares believe a word she says. Then we must examine Karen's personality and behavior. We must demonstrate that she was an habitual drug-user, a promiscuous person, and a pathological liar. We must convince the jury that anything Karen said, whether to her stepmother or anyone else, is of doubtful veracity. We can also demonstrate that she was twice aborted by Peter Randall and that in all likelihood he performed the third abortion."

"I'm certain Peter Randall didn't do it," I said.

"That may be," Wilson said, "but it is immaterial."

"Why?"

"Because Peter Randall is not on trial. Dr. Lee is, and we must use anything we can to free him."

I looked at him. "I'd hate to meet you in a dark alley."

"You don't like my methods?" He smiled slightly.

"No, frankly."

"Neither do I," Wilson said. "But we are forced into this by the nature of the laws. In many instances, laws are slanted against a doctor in the doctor-patient relationship. We had a case only last year of an intern at the Gorly Clinic who performed a pelvic and rectal exam on a woman. At least, that was what he said. The woman claimed he raped her. There was no nurse present at the examination; no witnesses. The woman had been treated three times in mental institutions for paranoia and schizophrenia. But she won the case, and the intern was out of luck—and out of a profession."

"I still don't like it."

"View it rationally," Wilson said. "The law is clear. Right or wrong, it is clear. It offers both the prosecution and the defense certain patterns, certain approaches, certain tactics in regard to the present statutes. Unfortunately, for both prosecution and defense, these approaches will come down to character assassinations. The prosecution will attempt to discredit Dr. Lee as thoroughly as they know how. We, the defense, will attempt to discredit the deceased, Mrs. Randall, and Peter Randall. The prosecution will have, as an advantage, the innate hostility of a Boston jury to anyone accused of abortion. We will have as an advantage the desire of any random jury from Boston to witness the defilement of an old family."

"Dirty."

He nodded. "Very dirty."

"Isn't there another way to handle it?"

"Yes," he said. "Of course. Find the real abortionist."

"When will the trial be?"

"A preliminary hearing next week."

"And the trial itself?"

"Perhaps two weeks later. It's gotten some kind of priority. I don't know how, but I can guess."

"Randall pushing his weight around."

Wilson nodded.

"And if an abortionist isn't found by the trial?" I asked.

Wilson smiled sadly. "My father," he said, "was a preacher. In Raleigh, North Carolina. He was the only educated man in the community. He liked to read. I remember once asking him if all the people he read, like Keats and Shelley, were white. He said yes. I asked him if there were any coloreds that he read. He said no." Wilson scratched his forehead, hiding his eyes with his hands. "But anyway, he was a preacher, and he was a Baptist, and he was strict. He believed in a wrathful god. He believed in thunderbolts from heaven striking a sinner to the ground. He believed in hellfire and damnation for eternity. He believed in right and wrong."

"Do you?"

"I believe," Wilson said, "in fighting fire with fire."

"Is the fire always right?"

"No," he said. "But it is always hot and compelling."

"And you believe in winning."

He touched the scar along his neck. "Yes."

"Even without honor?"

"The honor," he said, "is in winning."

"Is it?"

He stared at me for a moment. "Why are you so eager to protect the Randalls?"

"I'm not."

"You sound like you are."

"I'm doing what Art would want."

"Art," Wilson said, "wants to get out of jail. I'm telling you I can get him out. Nobody else in Boston will touch him; he's a hot potato. And I'm telling you I can get him out."

"It's dirty."

"Yes, Christ, it's dirty. What did you expect—a croquet game?" He finished his drink and said, "Look, Berry. If you were me, what would you do?"

"Wait," I said.

"For what?"

"The real abortionist."

"And if he doesn't turn up?"

I shook my head. "I don't know," I said.

"Then think about it," he said and left the bar.

SEVEN

WILSON HAD IRRITATED ME, but he had also left me with plenty to think about. I drove home, poured myself a vodka on the rocks, and sat down to put it together. I thought about everyone I talked to, and I realized that there were significant questions I had never asked. There were gaps, big gaps. Like what Karen had done Saturday night, when she went out in Peter's car. What she had said to Mrs. Randall the next day. Whether she had returned Peter's car—it was now stolen; when had Peter gotten it back?

I drank the vodka and felt a calm settle over me. I had been too hasty; I had lost my temper too often; I had reacted more to people than to information, more to personalities than to facts.

I would be more careful in the future.

The telephone rang. It was Judith. She was over at the Lees.

"What's going on?"

In a very steady voice, she said, "You'd better come over here. There's some kind of demonstration outside."

"Oh?"

"There's a mob," Judith said, "on the lawn."

"I'll be right over," I said and hung up. I grabbed my coat and started for the car, then stopped.

It was time to be more careful.

I went back and quickly dialed the city desk of the *Globe*. I reported a demonstration at the Lees' address. I made it a breathless and melodramatic call; I was sure they'd act on it.

Then I got in my car and drove over.

When I got to the Lees', the wooden cross was still smoldering on the front lawn. A police car was there and a large crowd had gathered, mostly neighborhood kids and their stunned parents. It was still early evening; the sky was deepening blue and the smoke from the cross curled straight upward.

I pushed through the crowd toward the house. Every window that I could see had been smashed. Someone was crying inside. A cop stopped me at the door.

"Who're you?"

"Dr. Berry. My wife and children are inside."

He stepped aside and I went in.

They were all in the living room. Betty Lee was crying; Judith was taking care of the children. There was broken glass all around. Two of the children had been cut deeply but not seriously. A policeman was questioning Mrs. Lee. He wasn't getting anywhere. All she said was, "We asked for protection. We asked for it. We pleaded with you, but you never came. . . ."

"Jesus, lady," said the cop.

"We asked. Don't we have any rights?"

"Jesus, lady," he said again.

I helped Judith bandage the kids.

"What happened?"

Suddenly the cop turned on me. "Who're you?"

"I'm a doctor."

"Yeah, well, high time," he said and turned back to Mrs. Lee.

Judith was subdued and pale. "It stated twenty minutes ago," she said. "We've been getting threats all day, and letters. Then it finally happened: four cars pulled up and a bunch of kids got out. They set up the cross and poured gasoline over it and lighted it. There must have been about twenty of them. They all stood there and sang 'Onward Christian Soldiers.' Then they started to throw rocks when they saw us looking at them through the window. It was like a nightmare."

"What did the kids look like? Were they well-dressed? What were the cars like?"

She shook her head. "That was the worst part. They were young, nice-looking kids. If they had been old bigots, I could understand, but they were just teen-agers. You should have seen their faces."

We finished bandaging the children and got them out of the room.

"I'd like to see the letters you've received," I said.

Just then the Lees' year-old baby crawled into the living room. He was smiling and making little gurgling, drooling noises. The glinting glass on the carpet obviously intrigued him.

"Hey!" I said to the cop at the door. "Get him!"

The cop looked down. He had been watching the baby all along.

Now he bent over and stopped the baby by holding on to his pudgy ankle.

"Pick him up," I said to the cop. "He can't hurt you."

Reluctantly, the cop picked him up. He handled the baby as if he might be diseased. You could see the distaste on his face: abortionist's baby.

Judith walked over, her shoes crunching on the glass. She took the baby from the cop. The baby didn't know how the cop felt. He had been happily playing with the cop's shiny buttons and drooling on his blue uniform. He didn't like it when Judith took him away from those buttons.

I heard the other cop say to Mrs. Lee, "Well, look, we get threats all the time. We can't respond to them all."

"But we called when they burned that . . . that *thing* on the lawn."

"That's a cross."

"I know what it is," she said. She was no longer crying. She was mad.

"We came as fast as we could," the cop said. "That's the truth, lady. As fast as we could."

Judith said to me, "It took them fifteen minutes. By that time, all the windows were broken and the teenagers were gone."

I went over to the table and looked at the letters. They had been carefully opened and stacked in a neat pile. Most were handscrawled; a few were typewritten. They were all short, some just a sentence, and they all had the breathless hiss of a curse.

Dirty comminist Jewlover Nigger lover killer. You and youre kind will get what you deserve, baby killers. You are the scum of the earth. You may think you are in Germany but you are not.
    Unsigned.

Our Lord and Saviour spake this 'Suffer the little children to come to me.' You have sinned against the Lord Jesus Our God and you will suffer the retrobution at his Almighty Hands. Praise God in his infinite wisdom and mercy.
    Unsigned.

The decent Godfearing people of the Commonwealth will not sit idly by. We shall fight you wherever the fight is to be. We shall drive you from your homes, we shall drive you from this country. We shall drive all of you out, until our Commonwealth is a decent place for all to live.
    Unsigned.

We caught you. We'll catch all your friends. Doctors think they can do anything, a) Driving those big Cadillacs. b) charging high costs. c) making patients wait that's why they call them patients because they wait patiently. d) But you are all evil. You will be stopped.
    Unsigned.

You like to kill kids? See how it feels to have yours killed.

Unsigned.

Abortion is a crime against God and man and society and the newborn yet to be. You will pay on this earth. But the Lord in his infinite way will burn you in hell forever.

Unsigned.

Abortion is worse than murder. What did they ever do to you? Answer that and you will see I am right. May you rot in jail and your family die.

Unsigned.

There was a final letter, written in a neat feminine hand.

I am sorry to hear of your misfortune. I know this must be a trying time for all of you. I only wanted to say that I am very grateful for what you did for me last year, and that I believe in you and what you are doing. You are the most wonderful doctor I have ever known, and the most honest. You have made my life much better than it would be otherwise, and my husband and I are eternally grateful. I shall pray for you every night.

Mrs. Allison Banks

I slipped it into my pocket. It wouldn't do to have that one lying around.

I heard voices behind me.

"Well, well, well. Fancy that."

I turned. It was Peterson.

"My wife called me."

"Fancy that." He looked around the room. With all the broken windows, it was getting chilly as night fell. "Quite a mess, isn't it?"

"You might say so."

"Yes, indeed." He walked around the room. "Quite a mess."

Watching him, I had a sudden horrifying vision of a uniformed man in heavy boots struggling among ruins. It was a generalized vision, nonspecific, attached to no particular time or place or era.

Another man pushed into the room. He wore a raincoat and had a pad in his hand.

"Who're you?" Peterson said.

"Curtis. From the *Globe*, sir."

"Now who called you, fella?"

Peterson looked around the room. His eyes rested on me.

"Not nice," Peterson said. "Not nice at all."

"It's a reputable newspaper. This boy will report the facts accurately. You surely can't object to that."

"Listen," Peterson said. "This is a city of two and a half million and the police department is understaffed. We can't investigate every crackpot complaint and lunatic threat that comes along. We can't do that if we want to do the regular things, like direct traffic."

"Family of an accused," I said. I was aware that

the reporter was watching me closely. "Family of an accused receives threats by telephone and letter. Wife and young family. She's afraid. You ignore her."

"That's not fair and you know it."

"Then something big happens. They start to burn a cross and tear the place apart. The wife calls for help. It takes your boys fifteen minutes to get here. How far away is the nearest station?"

"That's not the point."

The reporter was writing.

"You'll look bad," I said. "Lots of citizens in this town are opposed to abortion, but still more are against the wanton, lawless destruction of private property by a band of young hoodlums—"

"They weren't hoodlums."

I turned to the reporter. "Captain Peterson expresses the opinion that the kids who burned the cross and broke every window in the house were not young hoodlums."

"That's not what I meant," Peterson said quickly.

"It's what he said," I told the reporter. "Furthermore, you may be interested to know that two children were seriously lacerated by flying glass. Children ages three and five, seriously lacerated."

"That's not what I was told," Peterson said. "The cuts were only—"

"I believe," I said, "that I am the only doctor present at this time. Or did the police bring a doctor when they finally answered the call for help?"

He was silent.

"Did the police bring a doctor?" the reporter asked.

"No."

"Did they summon a doctor?"

"No."

The reporter wrote swiftly.

"I'll get you, Berry," Peterson said. "I'll get you for this."

"Careful. You're in front of a reporter."

His eyes shot daggers. He turned on his heel.

"By the way," I said, "what steps will the police now take to prevent a recurrence?"

He stopped. "That hasn't been decided yet."

"Be sure," I said, "to explain to this reporter how unfortunate it all is and how you'll post a twenty-four-hour guard. Be sure to make that clear."

He curled his lips, but I knew he would do it. That's all I wanted—protection for Betty, and a little pressure on the police.

EIGHT

JUDITH TOOK THE KIDS HOME; I stayed with Betty and helped her board up the windows. It took nearly an hour, and with each one I did, I got angrier.

Betty's kids were subdued, but would not go to

sleep. They kept coming downstairs to complain that their cuts hurt or that they wanted a glass of water. Young Henry in particular complained about his foot, so I removed the bandage to be certain I had not missed any glass. I found a small sliver still lodged in the wound.

Sitting there, with his small foot in my hand, and Betty telling him not to cry as I cleaned the wound again, I suddenly felt tired. The house smelled of burning wood, from the cross. It was chilly and drafty from the broken windows. Everything was a shambles; it would take days to clean it up.

All so unnecessary.

When I finished with Henry's foot, I went back to the letters Betty had received. Reading them made me feel more tired. I kept wondering how people could do it, what they must have been thinking. The obvious answer was that they were thinking nothing. They were simply reacting, as I had been reacting, as everyone had been reacting.

I suddenly wanted it finished. I wanted the letters to stop, the windows to be fixed, the wounds to heal, and life to return to normal. I wanted it very badly.

So I called George Wilson.

"I thought you might call," Wilson said.

"How'd you like to take a trip?"

"Where?"

"J. D. Randall's."

"Why?"

"To call off the dogs," I said.

"Meet me in twenty minutes," he said and hung up.

AS WE DROVE TOWARD THE SOUTH SHORE and the Randall house, Wilson said, "What made you change your mind?"

"A lot of things."

"The kids?"

"A lot of things," I repeated.

We drove for a while in silence, then he said, "You know what this means, don't you? It means we put the squeeze on Mrs. Randall and on Peter."

"That's all right," I said.

"I thought he was your buddy."

"I'm tired."

"I thought doctors never got tired."

"Lay off, will you?"

It was late, approaching nine. The sky was black.

"When we get to the house," Wilson said, "I'll do the talking, right?"

"O.K.," I said.

"It's no good if we both talk. It has to be just one."

"You can have your moment," I said.

He smiled. "You don't like me much, do you?"

"No. Not much."

"But you need me."

"That's right," I said.

"Just so we understand each other," he said.

"Just so you do the job," I said.

I did not remember exactly where the house was,

so I slowed the car as I approached. Finally I found it and was about to turn into the drive when I stopped. Up ahead, in the gravel turnabout in front of the house, were two cars. One was J. D. Randall's silver Porsche. The other was a gray Mercedes sedan.

"What's the matter?"

I doused my lights and backed away.

"What's going on?" Wilson said.

"I'm not sure," I said.

"Well are we going in, or not?"

"No," I said. I backed across the road and parked on the opposite side, near the shrubs. I had a good view up the drive to the house and could see both cars clearly.

"Why not?"

"Because," I said, "there's a Mercedes parked there."

"So?"

"Peter Randall owns a Mercedes."

"All the better," Wilson said. "We can confront them together."

"No," I said. "Because Peter Randall told me his car was stolen."

"Oh?"

"That's what he said."

"When?"

"Yesterday."

I thought back. Something was beginning to bother me, to pick at my mind. Then I remembered: the car I had seen in the Randall garage when I had visited Mrs. Randall.

I opened my door. "Come on."

"Where are we going?"

"I want to see that car," I said.

We stepped out into the night, which was damp and unpleasant. Walking up the drive, I reached into my pocket and felt my little penlight. I always carried it; a throwback to my days as an intern. I was glad to have it now.

"You realize," Wilson whispered, "that we're trespassing on private property."

"I realize."

We moved from the crunching gravel to the soft grass and climbed the hill toward the house. There were lights burning on the ground floor, but the shades were drawn, and we could not see inside.

We came to the cars and stepped onto the gravel again. The sounds of our footsteps seemed loud. I reached the Mercedes and flicked on my penlight. The car was empty; there was nothing in the back seat.

I stopped.

The driver's seat was soaked in blood.

"Well, well," Wilson said.

I was about to speak when we heard voices and a door opening. We hurried back to the grass and slipped behind a bush near the drive.

J. D. Randall came out of the house. Peter was with him. They were arguing about something in low voices; I heard Peter say, "All ridiculous," and

J. D. said, "Too careful"; but otherwise their voices were inaudible. They came down the steps to the cars. Peter got into the Mercedes and started the engine. J. D. said, "Follow me," and Peter nodded. Then J. D. got into the silver Porsche and started down the drive.

At the road, they turned right, heading south.

"Come on," I said.

We sprinted down the drive to my car, parked on the opposite side of the road. The other two cars were already far away; we could barely hear their engines, but we could see their lights moving down the coast.

I started the car and followed them.

Wilson had reached into his pocket and was fiddling with something.

"What have you got there?"

He held it over so I could see. A small, silver tube.

"Minox."

"You always carry a camera?"

"Always," he said.

I stayed back a good distance, so the other cars would not suspect. Peter was following J. D. closely.

After a five-minute drive, the two cars entered the ramp for the southeast expressway. I came on a moment later.

"I don't get it," Wilson said. "One minute you're defending the guy, and the next minute you're tracking him like a bloodhound."

"I want to know," I said. "That's all. I just want to know."

I followed them for half an hour. The road narrowed at Marshfield, becoming two lanes instead of three. Traffic was light; I dropped even farther back.

"This could be completely innocent," Wilson said. "The whole thing could be a——"

"No," I said. I had been putting things together in my own mind. "Peter loaned this car to Karen for the weekend. The son, William, told me that. Karen used that car. There was blood on it. Then the car was garaged in the Randall house, and Peter reported it as stolen. Now . . ."

"Now they're getting rid of it," Wilson said.

"Apparently."

"Hot damn," he said. "This one's in the bag."

The cars continue south, past Plymouth, down toward the Cape. The air here was chilly and tangy with salt. There was almost no traffic.

"Doing fine," Wilson said, looking at the taillights ahead. "Give them plenty of room."

"As the road became more deserted, the two cars gained speed. They were going very fast now, near eighty. We passed Plymouth, then Hyannis, and out toward Provincetown. Suddenly, I saw their brake lights go on, and they turned off the road to the right, toward the coast.

We followed, on a dirt road. Around us were scrubby pine trees. I doused my lights. The wind was gusty and cold off the ocean.

"Deserted around here," Wilson said.

I nodded.

Soon I could hear the roar of the breakers. I pulled off the road and parked. We walked on foot toward the ocean and saw the two cars parked, side by side.

I recognized the place. It was the east side of the Cape, where there was a long, one-hundred-foot sandy drop to the sea. The two cars were at the ledge, overlooking the water. Randall had gotten out of his Porsche and was talking with Peter. They argued for a moment, and then Peter got back in the car and drove it until the front wheels were inches from the edge. Then he got out and walked back.

J. D. had meanwhile opened the trunk to the Porsche and taken out a portable can of gasoline. Together the two men emptied the can of gasoline inside Peter's car.

I heard a click near me. Wilson, with the little camera pressed to his eye, was taking pictures.

"You don't have enough light."

"Tri-X," he said, still taking pictures. "You can force it to 2400, if you have the right lab. And I have the right lab."

I looked back at the cars. J. D. was returning the tank to his trunk. Then he started the Porsche engine and backed the car around, so it was facing the road, away from the ocean.

"Ready for the getaway," Wilson said. "Beautiful."

J. D. called to Peter and got out of the car. He stood by Peter, then I saw the brief flare of a match. Suddenly the interior of the Mercedes burst into flames.

The two men immediately ran to the rear of the car and leaned their weight against the car. It moved slowly, then faster, and finally began the slide down the sandy slope. They stepped back and watched its descent. At the bottom, it apparently exploded, because there was a loud sound and a bright red flash of light.

They sprinted for the car, got in, and drove past us.

"Come on," Wilson said. He ran forward to the edge with his camera. Down below, at the edge of the water, was the burning, smashed hulk of the Mercedes.

Wilson took several pictures, then put his camera away and looked at me.

He was grinning broadly. "Baby," he said, "have we got a case."

NINE

ON THE WAY BACK, I turned off the expressway at the Cohasset exit.

"Hey," Wilson said, "what're you doing?"

"Going to see Randall."

"*Now?*"

"Yes."

"Are you crazy? After what we saw?"

I said, "I came out tonight to get Art Lee off the hook. I still intend to do it."

"Uh-uh," Wilson said. "Not now. Not after what we saw." He patted the little camera in his hand. "Now we can go to court."

"But there's no need. We have an iron case. Unbeatable. Unshakable."

I shook my head.

"Listen," Wilson said, "you can rattle a witness. You can discredit him, making him look like a fool. But you can't discredit a picture. You can't beat a photograph. We have them by the balls."

"No," I said.

He sighed. "Before, it was going to be a bluff. I was going to walk in there and bullshit my way through it. I was going to scare them, to frighten them, to make them think we had evidence when we didn't. But now, it's all different. We have the evidence. We have everything we need."

"If you don't want to talk to them, I will."

"Berry," Wilson said, "if you talk to them, you'll blow our whole case."

"I'll make them quit."

"Berry, you'll blow it. Because they've just done something very incriminating. They'll know it. They'll be taking a hard line."

"Then we'll tell them what we know."

"And if it comes to trial? What then? We'll have blown our cool."

"I'm not worried about that. It won't come to trial."

Wilson scratched his scar again, running his finger down his neck. "Listen," he said, "don't you want to win?"

"Yes," I said, "but without a fight."

"There's going to be a fight. Any way you cut it, there'll be a fight. I'm telling you."

I pulled up in front of the Randall house and drove up the drive. "Don't tell me," I said. "Tell them."

"You're making a mistake," he said.

"Maybe," I said, "but I doubt it."

We climbed the steps and rang the doorbell.

RELUCTANTLY, the butler led us into the living room. It was no larger than the average-size basketball court, an immense room with a huge fireplace. Seated around the roaring fire were Mrs. Randall, in lounging pajamas, and Peter and J. D., both with large snifters of brandy in their hands.

The butler stood erectly by the door and said, "Dr. Berry and Mr. Wilson, sir. They said they were expected."

J. D. frowned when he saw us. Peter sat back and allowed a small smile to cross his face. Mrs. Randall seemed genuinely amused.

J. D. said, "What do you want?"

I let Wilson do the talking. He gave a slight bow and said, "I believe you know Dr. Berry, Dr. Randall. I am George Wilson. I am Dr. Lee's defense attorney."

"That's lovely," J. D. said. He glanced at his watch. "But it's nearly midnight, and I am relaxing with my family. I have nothing to say to either of you until we meet in court. So if you will—"

"If you will pardon me, sir," Wilson said, "we have come a long way to see you. All the way from the Cape, in fact."

J. D. blinked once and set his face rigidly. Peter coughed back a laugh. Mrs. Randall said, "What were you doing on the Cape?"

"Watching a bonfire," Wilson said.

"A bonfire?"

"Yes," Wilson said. He turned to J. D. "We'd like some brandies, please, and then a little chat."

Peter could not suppress a laugh this time. J. D. looked at him sternly, then rang for the butler. He ordered two more brandies, and as the butler was leaving, he said, "Small ones, Herbert. They won't be staying long."

Then he turned to his wife. "If you will, my dear."

She nodded and left the room.

"Sit down, gentlemen."

"We prefer to stand," Wilson said. The butler brought two small crystal snifters. Wilson raised his glass. "Your health, gentlemen."

"Thank you," J. D. said. His voice was cold. "Now what's on your minds?"

"A small legal matter," Wilson said. "We believe

that you may wish to reconsider charges against Dr. Lee."

"Reconsider?"

"Yes. That was the word I used."

"There is nothing to reconsider," J. D. said.

Wilson sipped the brandy. "Oh?"

"That's right," J. D. said.

"We believe," Wilson said, "that your wife may have been mistaken in hearing that Dr. Lee aborted Karen Randall. Just as we believe that Peter Randall was mistaken when he reported his automobile stolen to the police. Or hasn't he reported it yet?"

"Neither my wife, nor my brother, were mistaken," J. D. said.

Peter coughed again and lit a cigar.

"Something wrong, Peter?" J.D. asked.

"No, nothing."

He puffed the cigar and sipped his brandy.

"Gentlemen," J. D. said, turning to us. "You are wasting your time. There has been no mistake, and there is nothing to reconsider."

Wilson said softly, "In that case, it must go to court."

"Indeed it must," Randall said, nodding.

"And you will be called to account for your actions tonight," Wilson said.

"Indeed we may. But we will have Mrs. Randall's firm testimony that we spent the evening playing chess." He pointed to a chessboard in the corner.

"Who won?" Wilson asked, with a faint smile.

"I did, by God," Peter said, speaking for the first time. And he chuckled.

"How did you do it?" Wilson said.

"Bishop to knight's twelve," Peter said and chuckled again. "He is a terrible chess player. If I've told him once, I've told him a thousand times."

"Peter, this is no laughing matter."

"You're a sore loser," Peter said.

"Shut up, Peter."

Quite abruptly, Peter stopped laughing. He folded his arms across his massive belly and said nothing more.

J. D. Randall savored a moment of silence, then said, "Was there anything else, gentlemen?"

"YOU SON OF A BITCH," I said to Wilson. "You blew it."

"I did my best."

"You got him angry. You were forcing him into court."

"I did my best."

"That was the lousiest, rottenest—"

"Easy," Wilson said, rubbing his scar.

"You could have scared him. You could have told them how it would go—the way you explained it to me in the bar. You could have told them about the pictures. . . ."

"It wouldn't have done any good," Wilson said.

"It might."

"No. They are determined to take the case to court. They—"

"Yes," I said, "thanks to you. Strutting around like a self-satisfied bastard. Making cheap threats like a penny tough. Demanding a brandy—that was beautiful, that was."

"I attempted to persuade them," Wilson said.

"Crap."

He shrugged.

"I'll tell you what you did, Wilson. You pushed them into a trial, because you want one. You want an arena, a chance to show your stuff, a chance to make a name for yourself, to prove that you're a ruthless hotshot. You know, and I know, that if the case ever comes to trial, Art Lee—no matter what the outcome—will lose. He'll lose his prestige, his patients, maybe even his license. And if it comes to trial, the Randalls will also lose. They'll be smeared, shot through with half-truths and implications, destroyed. Only one person will come out on top."

"Yes?"

"You, Wilson. Only you can win in a trial."

"That's your opinion," he said. He was getting angry. I was getting him.

"That's a fact."

"You heard J. D. You heard how unreasonable he was."

"You could have made him listen."

"No," Wilson said. "But he'll listen in court." He sat back in the car and stared forward for a moment, thinking over the evening. "You know, I'm surprised at you, Berry. You're supposed to be a scientist. You're supposed to be objective about evidence. You've had a bellyful of evidence tonight that Peter Randall is guilty, and you're still unhappy."

"Did he strike you," I said, "as a guilty man?"

"He can act."

"Answer the question."

"I did," Wilson said.

"So you believe he's guilty?"

"That's right," Wilson said. "And I can make a jury believe it, too."

"What if you're wrong?"

"Then it's too bad. Just the way it's too bad that Mrs. Randall was wrong about Art Lee."

"You're making excuses."

"Am I?" He shook his head. "No, man. You are. You're playing the loyal doctor, right down the line. You're sucking up to the tradition, to the conspiracy of silence. You'd like to see it handled nice and quietly, very diplomatic, with no hard feelings at the end."

"Isn't that the best way? The business of a lawyer," I said, "is to do whatever is best for his client."

"The business of a lawyer is to win his cases."

"Art Lee is a man. He has a family, he has goals, he has personal desires and wishes. Your job is to implement them. Not to stage a big trial for your own glory."

"The trouble with you, Berry, is that you're like all doctors. You can't believe that one of your own is rotten. What you'd really like to see is an ex-army medical orderly or a nurse on trial. Or a nice little old midwife. That's who you'd like to stick with this rap. Not a doctor."

"I'd like to stick the guilty person," I said, "nobody else."

"You know who's guilty," Wilson said. "You know damned well."

I DROPPED WILSON OFF, then drove home and poured myself a very stiff vodka. The house was silent; it was after midnight.

I drank the vodka and thought about what I had seen. As Wilson had said, everything pointed to Peter Randall. There had been blood on his car, and he had destroyed the car. I had no doubt that a gallon of gasoline on the front seat would eliminate all evidence. He was clean, now—or would be, if we hadn't seen him burning the car.

Then, too, as Wilson had said, everything made sense. Angela and Bubbles were right in claiming that they hadn't seen Karen; she had gone to Peter that Sunday night. And Peter had made a mistake; Karen had gone home and begun to bleed. She had told Mrs. Randall, who had taken her to the hospital in her own car. At the hospital, she hadn't known that the EW diagnosis would not call in the police; to avert a family scandal she had blamed the abortion on the only other abortionist she knew: Art Lee. She had jumped the gun, and all hell had broken loose.

Everything made sense.

Except, I thought, for the original premise. Peter

Randall had been Karen's physician for years. He knew she was a hysterical girl. Therefore he would have been certain to perform a rabbit test on her. Also, he knew that she had had a prior complaint of vision trouble, which suggested a pituitary tumor which could mimic pregnancy. So he would certainly have tested.

Then again, he had apparently sent her to Art Lee. Why? If he had been willing to see her aborted, he would have done it himself.

And still again, he had aborted her twice without complications. Why should he make a mistake—a major and serious mistake—the third time?

No, I thought, it didn't make sense.

And then I remembered something Peterson had said: "You doctors certainly stick together." I realized he, and Wilson, were right. I wanted to believe that Peter was innocent. Partly because he was a doctor, partly because I liked him. Even in the face of serious evidence, I wanted to believe he was innocent.

I sighed and sipped my drink. The fact was I had seen something very serious that night, something clandestine and incriminating. I could not overlook it. I could not pass it off as accident or coincidence. I had to explain it.

And the most logical explanation was that Peter Randall was the abortionist.

THURSDAY
OCTOBER 13

ONE

I AWOKE FEELING MEAN. Like a caged animal, trapped, enclosed. I didn't like what was happening and didn't see any way to stop it. Worst of all, I didn't see any way to beat Wilson. It was hard enough to prove Art Lee was innocent; to prove Peter Randall was innocent as well was impossible.

Judith took one look at me and said, "Grumpy."

I snorted and showered.

She said, "Find out anything?"

"Yeah. Wilson wants to pin it on Peter Randall."

She laughed. "Jolly old Peter?"

"Jolly old Peter," I said.

"Has he got a case?"

"Yes."

"That's good," she said.

"No," I said, "it's not."

I turned off the shower and stepped out, reaching for a towel. "I can't believe Peter would do it," I said.

"Charitable of you."

I shook my head. "No," I said, "it's just that getting another innocent man for it solves nothing."

"It serves them right," Judith said.

"Who?"

"The Randalls."

"It isn't just," I said.

"That's fine for you to say. You can immerse yourself in the technicalities. I've been with Betty Lee for three days."

"I know it's been hard—"

"I'm not talking about me," she said. "I'm talking about her. Or have you forgotten last night?"

"No," I said, thinking to myself that last night had started it all, the whole mess. My decision to call in Wilson.

"Betty has been through hell," Judith said. "There's no excuse for it, and the Randalls are to blame. So let them boil in their own oil for a while. Let them see how it feels."

"But Judith, if Peter is innocent—"

"Peter is very amusing," she said. "That doesn't make him innocent."

"It doesn't make him guilty."

"I don't care who's guilty anymore. I just want it finished and Art set free."

"Yes," I said. "I know how you feel."

While I shaved, I stared at my face. A rather ordinary face, too heavy in the jowls, eyes too small, hair thinning. But all in all, nothing unusual about me. It gave me a strange feeling to know that I had been at the center of things, at the center of a crisis affecting a half-dozen people, for three days. I wasn't the sort of person for that.

As I dressed and wondered what I would do that morning, I also wondered if I had ever been at the center of things. It was an odd thought. Suppose I had been circling at the periphery, digging up unimportant facts? Suppose the real heart of the matter was still unexplored?

Trying to save Peter again.

Well, why not? He was as much worth saving as anyone else.

It occurred to me then that Peter Randall was as much worth saving as Art. They were both men, both doctors, both established, both interesting, both a little noncomformist. When you came down to it, there was nothing really to choose between them. Peter was humorous, Art was sarcastic. Peter was fat and Art was thin.

But essentially the same.

I pulled on my jacket and tried to forget the whole thing. I wasn't the judge; thank God for that. It wouldn't be my job to unsnarl things at the trial.

The telephone rang. I didn't answer it. A moment later, Judith called, "It's for you."

I picked up the receiver.

"Hello?"

A familiar, booming voice said, "John, this is Peter. I'd like you to come by for lunch."

"Why?" I said.

"I want you to meet the alibi I haven't got," he said.

"What does that mean?"

"Twelve-thirty?" he asked.

"See you then," I said.

TWO

PETER RANDALL LIVED WEST OF NEWTON, in a modern house. It was small but beautifully furnished: Breuer chairs, a Jacobsen couch, a Rachmann coffee table. The style was sleekly modern. He met me at the door with a drink in his hand.

"John. Come in." He led the way into the living room. "What will you drink?"

"Nothing, thanks."

"I think you'd better," he said. "Scotch?"

"On the rocks."

"Have a seat," he said. He went into the kitchen; I heard ice cubes in a glass. "What did you do this morning?"

"Nothing," I said. "I sat around and thought."

"About what?"

"Everything."

"You don't have to tell me, if you don't want to," he said, coming back with a glass of Scotch.

"Did you know Wilson took pictures?"

"I had a suspicion. That boy is ambitious."

"Yes," I said.

"And I'm in hot water?"

"It looks that way," I said.

He stared at me for a moment, then said, "What do you think?"

"I don't know what to think anymore."

"Do you know, for example, that I do abortions?"

"Yes," I said.

"And Karen?"

"Twice," I said.

He sat back in a Breuer chair, his rounded bulk contrasting with the sharp, linear angles of the chair. "Three times," he said, "to be precise."

"Then you—"

"No, no," he said. "The last was in June."

"And the first?"

"When she was fifteen." He sighed. "You see, I've made some mistakes. One of them was trying to look after Karen. Her father was ignoring her, and I was . . . fond of her. She was a sweet girl. Lost and confused, but sweet. So I did her first abortion, as I have done abortions for other patients from time to time. Does that shock you?"

"No."

"Good. But the trouble was that Karen kept getting pregnant. Three times in three years; for a girl of that age, it wasn't wise. It was pathological. So I finally decided that she ought to bear the fourth child."

"Why?"

"Because she obviously wanted to be pregnant. She kept doing it. She obviously needed the shame and trouble of an illegitimate child. So I refused the fourth time."

"Are you sure she was pregnant?"

"No," he said. "And you know why I had my doubts. That vision business. One wonders about primary pituitary dysfunction. I wanted to do tests, but Karen refused. She was only interested in an abortion, and when I wouldn't give it to her, she became angry."

"So you sent her to Dr. Lee."

"Yes," he said.

"And he did it?"

Peter shook his head. "Art is far too clever for that. He would have insisted on tests. Besides, she was four months' pregnant, or so she claimed. So he wouldn't have done it."

"And you didn't, either," I said.

"No. Do you believe that?"

"I'd like to."

"But you aren't fully convinced?"

I shrugged. "You burned your car. It had blood in it."

"Yes," he said. "Karen's blood."

"How did it happen?"

"I lent Karen my car for the weekend. I did not know at the time that she planned an abortion."

"You mean she drove your car to the abortion, had it, and drove it back to her home, bleeding? Then she switched to the yellow Porsche?"

"Not exactly," Peter said. "But you can get a better explanation from someone else." He called, "Darling. Come on out."

He smiled at me. "Meet my alibi."

Mrs. Randall came into the room, looking taut and hard and sexy. She sat in a chair next to Peter.

"You see," Peter said, "what a bind I am in."

I said, "Sunday night?"

"I am afraid so."

"That's embarrassing," I said, "but also convenient."

"In a sense," Randall said. He patted her hand and lifted himself heavily out of the chair. "I don't call it either embarrassing or convenient."

"You were with her all night Sunday?"

He poured himself another Scotch. "Yes."

"Doing what?"

"Doing," Peter said, "what I would rather not explain under oath."

"With your brother's wife?" I said.

He winked at Mrs. Randall. "Are you my brother's wife?"

"I've heard a rumor," she said, "but I don't believe it."

"You see, I'm letting you into some quite private family affairs," Peter said.

"They are family affairs, if nothing else."

"You're indignant?"

"No," I said. "Fascinated."

"Joshua," Peter said, "is a fool. You know that, of course. So does Wilson. That is why he could be so confident. But unfortunately, Joshua married Evelyn."

"Unfortunately," Evelyn said.

"Now we are in a bind," Peter said. "She cannot divorce my brother to marry me. That would be impossible. So we are resigned to our life as it is."

"Difficult, I imagine."

"Not really," Peter said, sitting down again with a fresh drink. "Joshua is very dedicated. He often works long into the night. And Evelyn has many clubs and civil functions to attend."

"He'll find out sooner or later."

"He already knows," Peter said.

I must have reacted, because he said quickly, "Not consciously, of course. J. D. knows nothing consciously. But in the back of his mind, he realizes that he has a young wife whom he neglects and who is finding . . . satisfaction elsewhere."

I turned to Mrs. Randall, "Would you swear Peter was with you Sunday night?"

"If I had to," she said.

"Wilson will make you. He wants a trial."

"I know," she said.

"Why did you accuse Art Lee?"

She turned away from me and glanced at Peter. Peter said, "She was trying to protect me."

"Art was the only other abortionist she knew?"

"Yes," Evelyn said.

"He aborted you?"

"Yes. Last December."

"Was it a good abortion?"

She shifted in the chair. "It worked, if that's what you mean."

"That's what I mean," I said. "Do you know Art wouldn't implicate you?"

She hesitated, then said, "I was confused. I was frightened. I didn't know what I was doing."

"You were screwing Art."

"Yes," she said, "that was how it turned out."

"Well," I said, "you can clear him now."

"How?"

"Drop the charges."

Peter said, "It's not that easy."

"Why not?"

"You saw for yourself last night. J. D. is fixed on the battle, once the lines are drawn. He has a surgeon's view of right and wrong. He sees only black and white, day and night. No gray. No twilight."

"No cuckolds."

Peter laughed. "He may be a lot like you."

Evelyn got up and said, "Lunch will be ready in five minutes. Will you have another drink?"

"Yes," I said, looking at Peter, "I'd better."

When Evelyn had gone, Peter said, "You see me as a cruel and heartless beast. Actually I'm not. There has been a long chain of errors here, a long list of mistakes. I would like to see it cleaned up—"

"With no harm done."

"More or less. Unfortunately my brother is no help. Once his wife accused Dr. Lee, he took it as gospel truth. He pounced upon it as truth the way a man grasps a life preserver. He will never relent."

"Go on," I said.

"But the central fact remains. I insist—and you can believe it or not—that I did not do the abortion. You are equally certain that Dr. Lee did not do it. Who is left?"

"I don't know," I said.

"Can you find out?"

"You're asking me to help you?"

"Yes," he said.

OVER LUNCH, I said to Evelyn, "What did Karen really say to you in the car?"

"She said, 'That bastard.' Over and over again. Nothing else."

"She never explained?"

"No."

"Did you have any idea who she meant?"

"No," Evelyn said, "I didn't."

"Did she say anything else?'

"Yes," she said. "She talked about the needle. Something about how she didn't want the needle, didn't want it in her, didn't want it around her. The needle."

"Was it a drug?"

"I couldn't tell," Evelyn said.

"What did you think at the time?"

"I didn't think anything," Evelyn said. "I was driving her to the hospital and she was dying right before my eyes. I was worried that Peter might have done it, even though I didn't think he had. I was worried that Joshua would find out. I was worried about a lot of things."

"But not her?"

"Yes," she said, "her, too."

THREE

THE MEAL WAS GOOD. Toward the end, staring at the two of them, I found myself wishing I had not come and did not know about them. I didn't want to know, didn't want to think about it.

Afterward, I had coffee with Peter. From the kitchen I heard the sounds of Evelyn washing dishes. It was hard to imagine her washing dishes, but she acted differently around Peter; it was almost possible to like her.

"I suppose," Peter said, "that it was unfair to ask you here today."

"It was," I said.

He sighed and straightened his tie down his massive belly. "I've never been in this kind of situation before."

"How's that?"

"Caught," he said.

I thought to myself that he had done it to himself, going in with both eyes wide open. I tried to resent him for that but could not quite manage it.

"The terrible thing," he said, "is to think back and wonder what you'd do differently. I keep doing that. And I never find the point I'm looking for, that one crucial point in time where I made the wrong turn in the maze. Getting involved with Ev, I suppose. But I'd do that again. Getting involved with Karen. But I'd do that again, too. Each individual thing was all right. It was the combination. . . ."

I said, "Get J. D. to drop the charges."

He shook his head. "My brother and I," he said, "have never gotten along. For as long as I can remember. We are different in every way, even physically. We think differently, we act differently. When I was young I used to resent the fact that he was my brother, and I secretly suspected that he was not, that he had been adopted or something. I suppose he thought the same thing."

He finished his coffee and rested his chin on his chest. "Ev has tried to convince J. D. to drop charges," he said. "But he's firm, and she can't really—"

"Think of an excuse?"

"Yes."

"It's too bad she ever named Lee in the first place."

"Yes," he said. "But what's done is done."

He walked with me to the door. I stepped outside into a gray, pale sunlight. As I went down to my car, he said, "If you don't want to get involved, I'll understand."

I looked back at him. "You knew damned well I'd have no choice."

"I didn't," he said. "But I was hoping."

* * *

WHEN I GOT INTO MY CAR, I wondered what I would do next. I had no idea, no leads, nothing. Perhaps I could call Zenner again and see if he could remember more of his conversation. Perhaps I could visit Ginnie at Smith, or Angela and Bubbles, and see if they remembered more. But I doubted they would.

I reached into my pocket for the keys and felt something. I brought it out: a picture of a Negro in a shiny suit. Roman Jones.

I had forgotten all about Roman. Somewhere along the line he had disappeared in the rush, the stream of faces. I stared at the picture for a long time, trying to read the features, to measure the man. It was impossible; the pose was standard, the cocky look of a silver-suited stud, swaggering, half grinning, half leering. It was a pose for the crowds, and it told me nothing at all.

I am not good with words, and it has always been surprising to me that my son, Johnny, is. When he is alone, he plays with his toys and makes up word games; he rhymes or tells himself stories. He has very sharp ears and always comes to me for explanations. Once he asked me what an ecdysiast was, pronouncing the word perfectly but carefully, as if it were fragile.

So I was not really surprised when, as I was minding my own business, he came up and said, "Daddy, what's an abortionist mean?"

"Why?"

"One of the policemen said Uncle Art was an abortionist. Is that bad?"

"Sometimes," I said.

He leaned against my knee, propping his chin on it. He has large brown eyes; Judith's eyes.

"But what's it mean, Daddy?"

"It's complicated," I said, stalling for time.

"Does it mean a kind of doctor? Like neurologist?"

"Yes," I said. "But an abortionist does other things." I hoisted him up on my knee, feeling the weight of his body. He was getting heavy, growing up. Judith was saying it was time for another.

"It has to do with babies," I said.

"Like obsetrician?"

"Obstetrician," I said. "Yes."

"He takes the baby out of the mommy?"

"Yes," I said, "but it is different. Sometimes the baby isn't normal. Sometimes it is born so it can't talk—"

"Babies can't talk," he said, "until later."

"Yes," I said. "But sometimes it is born without arms or legs. Sometimes it is deformed. So a doctor stops the baby and takes it away early."

"Before it's grown up?"

"Yes, before it's grown up."

"Was I taken away early?"

"No," I said and hugged him.

"Why do some babies have no arms or legs?"

"It's an accident," I said. "A mistake."

He stretched out his hand and looked at it, flexing the fingers.

"Arms are nice," he said.

"Yes."

"But everybody has arms."

"Not everybody."

"Everybody *I* know."

"Yes," I said, "but sometimes people are born without them."

"How do they play catch without arms?"

"They can't."

"I don't like that," he said. He looked at his hand again, closing his fingers, watching them.

"Why do you have arms?" he asked.

"Because." It was too big a question for me.

"Because what?"

"Because inside your body there is a code."

"What's a code?"

"It's instructions. It tells the body how it is going to grow."

"A code?"

"It's like a set of instructions. A plan."

"Oh."

He thought about this.

"It's like your erector set. You look at the pictures and you make what you see. That's a plan."

"Oh."

I couldn't tell if he understood or not. He considered what I had said, then looked at me. "If you take the baby out of the mommy, what happens to it?"

"It goes away."

"Where?"

"Away," I said, not wanting to explain further.

"Oh," he said. He climbed down off my knee. "Is Uncle Art really an abortionist?"

"No," I said. I knew I had to tell him that, otherwise I would get a call from his kindergarten teacher about his uncle the abortionist. But I felt badly, all the same.

"Good," he said, "I'm glad."

And he walked off.

JUDITH SAID, "YOU'RE NOT EATING."

I pushed my food away. "I'm not very hungry."

Judith turned to Johnny and said, "Clean your plate, Johnny."

He held the fork in a small, tight fist. "I'm not hungry," he said and glanced at me.

"Sure you are," I said.

"No," he said, "I'm not."

Debby, who was barely big enough to see over the table, threw her knife and fork down. "I'm not hungry either," she said. "The food tastes icky."

"I think it tastes very good," I said and dutifully ate a mouthful. The kids looked at me suspiciously. Especially Debby: at three, she was a very level-headed little girl.

"You just want us to eat, Daddy."

"I like it," I said, eating more.

"You're pretending."

"No, I'm not."

"Then why aren't you smiling?" Debby said.

Fortunately, Johnny decided at that moment to eat more. He rubbed his stomach. "It's good," he said.

"It is?" Debby said.

"Yes," Johnny said, "very good."

Debby nibbled. She was very tentative. She took another forkful, and as she moved it to her mouth, she spilled it on her dress. Then, like a normal woman, she got mad at everyone around her. She announced that it was terrible and she didn't like it; she wouldn't eat any more. Judith began to call her "Young lady," a sure sign that Judith was getting mad. Debby backed off while Johnny continued to eat until he held up his plate and showed it to us proudly: clean.

It was another half-hour before the kids were in bed. I stayed in the kitchen; Judith came back and said, "Coffee?"

"Yes. I'd better."

"Sorry about the kids," she said. "They've had a wearying few days."

"We all have."

She poured the coffee and sat down across the table from me.

"I keep thinking," she said, "about the letters. The ones Betty got."

"What about them?"

"Just what they mean. There are thousands of people out there, all around you, waiting for their chance. Stupid, bigoted, small-minded—"

"This is a democracy," I said. "Those people run the country."

"Now you're making fun of me."

"No," I said. "I know what you mean."

"Well, it frightens me," Judith said. She pushed the sugar bowl across the table to me and said, "I think I want to leave Boston. And never come back."

"It's the same everywhere," I said. "You might as well get used to it."

I KILLED TWO HOURS IN MY STUDY, looking over old texts and journal articles. I also did a lot of thinking. I tried to put it together, to match up Karen Randall, and Superhead, and Alan Zenner, and Bubbles and Angela. I tried to make sense of Weston, but in the end nothing made sense.

Judith came in and said, "It's nine."

I got up and put on my suit jacket.

"Are you going out?"

"Yes."

"Where?"

I grinned at her. "To a bar," I said. "Downtown."

"Whatever for?"

"Damned if I know."

The Electric Grape was located just off Washington Street. From the outside it was unimpressive, an old brick building with large windows. The windows were covered with paper, making it impossible to see inside. On the paper was written: "The Zephyrs Nightly. Go-Go Girls." I could hear jarring rock-'n'-roll sounds as I approached.

It was ten P.M. Thursday night, a slow night. Very few sailors, a couple of hookers, down the block, standing with their weight on one hip, their pelvises thrust outward. One cruised by in a little sports car and batted her mascara at me. I entered the building.

It was hot, damp, smelly, animal heat, and the sound was deafening: vibrating the walls, filling the air, making it thick and liquid. My ears began to ring. I paused to allow my eyes to adjust to the darkness of the room. There were cheap wooden tables in the center booths along one wall, and a bar along another. A tiny dance floor near the bandstand; two sailors were dancing with two fat, dirty-looking girls. Otherwise the place was empty.

On stage, the Zephyrs were beating it out. Five of them—three steel guitars, a drummer, and a singer who caressed the microphone and wrapped his legs around it. They were making a lot of noise, but their faces were oddly bland, as if they were waiting for something, killing time by playing.

Two discothèque girls were stationed on either side of the band. They wore brief costumes, bikinis with fringes. One was chubby and one had a beautiful face on a graceless body. Their skins were chalky-white under the lights.

I stepped to the bar and ordered straight Scotch on the rocks. That way, I'd get Scotch and water, which was what I wanted.

I paid for my drink and turned to watch the group. Roman was one of the guitarists, a wiry muscular man in his late twenties, with a thick head of curly black hair. The grease shone in the pink stage lights. He stared down at his fingers as he played.

"They're pretty good," I said to the bartender.

He shrugged. "You like this kinda music?"

"Sure. Don't you?"

"Crap," the bartender said. "All crap."

"What kind of music do you like?"

"Opera," he said and moved down to another customer. I couldn't tell if he was kidding me or not.

I stood there with my drink. The Zephyrs finished their piece, and the sailors on the dance floor clapped. Nobody else did. The lead singer, still swaying from the song, leaned into the microphone and said, "Thank you, thank you," in a breathless voice, as if thousands were wildly applauding.

Then he said, "For our next song we want to do an old Chuck Berry piece."

It turned out to be "Long Tall Sally." Really old. Old enough for me to know it was a Little Richard song, not Chuck Berry. Old enough for me to remember from the days before my marriage, when I took girls to places like this for a wild evening, from the days when Negroes were sort of amusing, not people at all, just a musical sideshow. The days when white boys could go to the Apollo in Harlem.

The old days.

They played the song well, loud and fast. Judith

loathes rock 'n' roll, which is sad; I've always kept a taste for it. But it wasn't fashionable when our generation was growing up. It was crude and lower class. The deb set was still fixed on Lester Lanin and Eddie Davis, and Leonard Bernstein hadn't learned the twist yet.

Times change.

Finally the Zephyrs finished. They hooked a record player to their amplifiers and started the records going. Then they climbed down off the stage and headed for the bar. As Roman walked toward me, I came up to him and touched his arm.

"Buy you a drink?"

He gave me a surprised look. "Why?"

"I'm a fan of Little Richard."

His eyes swept up and down me. "Get off it," he said.

"No, seriously."

"Vodka," he said, sitting down next to me.

I ordered a vodka. It came, and he gulped it down quickly.

"We'll just have another," he said, "and then we can go talk about Little Richard, right?"

"O.K.," I said.

He got another vodka and carried it to a table across the room. I followed him. His silver suit shimmered in the near darkness. We sat down, and he looked at the drink and said, "Let's see the silver plate."

"What?"

He gave me a pained look. "The badge, baby. The

little pin. I don't do nothing unless you got the badge."

I must have looked puzzled.

"Christ," he said, "when they gonna get some bright fuzz?"

"I'm not fuzz," I said.

"Sure." He took his drink and stood up.

"Wait a minute," I said. "Let me show you something."

I took out my wallet and flipped to my M.D. card. It was dark; he bent down to look at it.

"No kidding," he said, his voice sarcastic. But he sat down again.

"It's the truth. I'm a doctor."

"O.K.," he said. "You're a doctor. You smell like a cop to me, but you're a doctor. So let's have the rules: you see those four guys over there?" He nodded toward his group. "If anything happens, they all testify you showed me a doctor's card and no badge. That's entrapment, baby. Don't hold in court. Clear?"

"I just want to talk."

"No kidding," he said and sipped the drink. He smiled slightly. "Word sure does get around."

"Does it?"

"Yeah," he said. He glanced at me. "Who told you about it?"

"I have ways."

"What ways?"

I shrugged. "Just . . . ways."

"Who wants it?"

"I do."

He laughed. "You? Get serious, man. You don't want nothing."

"All right," I said. I stood up and started to go. "Maybe I got the wrong man."

"Just a minute, baby."

I stopped. He was sitting at the table, looking at the drink, twisting the glass in his hands. "Sit down."

I sat down again. He continued to stare at the glass. "This is good stuff," he said. "We don't cut it with nothing. It's the finest quality and the price is high, see?"

"O.K.," I said.

He scratched his arms and his hands in a quick, nervous way. "How many bags?"

"Ten. Fifteen. Whatever you have."

"I got as much as you want."

"Then fifteen," I said. "But I want to see it first."

"Yeah, yeah, right. You can see it first, it's good."

He continued to scratch his arms through the silver material, then smiled. "But one thing first."

"What's that?"

"Who told you?"

I hesitated. "Angela Harding," I said.

He seemed puzzled by this. I could not decide whether I had said something wrong. He shifted in his chair, as if making up his mind, then said, "She a friend of yours?"

"Sort of."

"When did you see her last?"

"Yesterday," I said.

He nodded slowly. "The door," he said, "is over there. I'll give you thirty seconds to get out of here before I tear you to pieces. You hear me, cop? Thirty seconds."

I said, "All right, it wasn't Angela. It was a friend of hers."

"Who's that?"

"Karen Randall."

"Never heard of her."

"I understand you knew her quite well."

He shook his head: "Nope."

"That's what I was told."

"You was told wrong, baby. Dead wrong."

I reached into my pocket and brought out his picture. "This was in her room at college."

Before I knew what was happening, he had snatched the picture from my hand and torn it up.

"What picture?" he said evenly. "I don't know no picture. I never even seen the girl."

I sat back.

He regarded me with angry eyes. "Beat it," he said.

"I came here to buy something," I said. "I'll leave when I have it."

"You'll leave now, if you know what's good for you."

He was scratching his arms again. I looked at him and realized that I would learn nothing more. He wasn't going to talk, and I had no way to make him.

"All right," I said. I got up, leaving my glasses on the table. "By the way, do you know where I can get some thiopental?"

For a moment, his eyes widened. Then he said, "Some what?"

"Thiopental."

"Never heard of it. Now beat it," he said, "before one of those nice fellas at the bar picks a fight with you and beats your head in."

I walked out. It was cold; a light rain had started again. I looked toward Washington Street and the bright lights of the other rock-'n'-roll joints, strip joints, clip joints: I waited thirty seconds, then went back.

My glasses were still on the table. I picked them up and turned to leave, my eyes sweeping the room.

Roman was in the corner, talking on a pay phone.

That was all I wanted to know.

FOUR

AROUND THE CORNER at the end of the block was a stand-up, self-service greasy spoon. Hamburgers twenty cents. It had a large glass window in front. Inside I saw a few teen-age girls giggling as they ate, and one or two morose derelicts in tattered overcoats that reached almost to their shoes. At one side, three sailors were laughing and slapping each other on the back, reliving some conquest or planning the next. A telephone was in the back.

I called the Mem and asked for Dr. Hammond. I was told he was on the EW that night; the desk put the call through.

"Norton, this is John Berry."

"What's up?"

"I need more information," I said, "from the record room."

"You're lucky," he said. "It seems to be a slow night here. One or two lacerations and a couple of drunken fights. Nothing else. What do you need?"

"Take this down," I said. "Roman Jones, Negro, about twenty-four or -five. I want to know whether he's ever been admitted to the hospital and whether he's been followed in any of the clinics. And I want the dates."

"Right," Hammond said. "Roman Jones. Admissions and clinic visits. I'll check it out right away."

"Thanks," I said.

"You going to call back?"

"No. I'll drop by the EW later."

That, as it turned out, was the understatement of the year.

WHEN I FINISHED THE CALL I was feeling hungry, so I got a hot dog and coffee. Never a hamburger in a place like this. For one thing, they often use horsemeat or rabbit or entrails or anything else they can grind up. For another, there's usually enough pathogens to infect an army. Take trichinosis—Boston has six times the national rate of infection from that. You can't be too careful.

I have a friend who's a bacteriologist. He spends his whole time running a hospital lab where they culture out organisms that have infected the patients. By now this guy is so worked up that he practically never goes out to dinner, even to Joseph's or Locke-Ober. Never eats a steak unless it's well done. He really worries. I've been to dinner with him, and it's terrible—he sweats all through the main course. You can see him imagining a blood agar petri dish, with those little colonies streaked out. Every bite he takes, he sees those colonies. Staph. Strep. Gram negative bacilli. His life is ruined.

Anyway, hot dogs are safer—not much, but some—so I had one and took it over to the stand-up counter with my coffee. I ate looking out the window at the crowd passing by.

Roman came to mind. I didn't like what he'd told me. Clearly, he was selling stuff, probably strong stuff. Marijuana was too easy to get. LSD was no longer being made by Sandoz, but lysergic acid, the precursor, is produced by the ton in Italy, and any college kid can convert it if he steals a few reagents and flasks from his chem lab. Psilocybin and DMT are even easier to make.

Probably Roman was dealing in opiates, morphine or heroin. That complicated matters a great deal—particularly in view of his reaction to mention of Angela Harding and Karen Randall. I wasn't sure what the connection was but I felt, somehow, that I'd find out very soon.

I finished the hot dog and drank my coffee. As I looked out the window, I saw Roman hurry by. He did not see me. He was looking forward, his face intent and worried.

I gulped the rest of my coffee and followed him.

[Ed note: the three-step synthesis of lysergic acid diethylamine (LSD) from common precursors has been omitted from this manuscript.]

FIVE

I LET HIM GET HALF A BLOCK AHEAD OF ME. He was hurrying through the crowds, pushing and shoving. I kept him in sight as he walked toward Stuart Street. There he turned left and headed for the expressway. I followed him. This end of Stuart was deserted; I dropped back and lit a cigarette. I pulled my raincoat tighter and wished I had a hat. If he looked back over his shoulder, he would certainly recognize me.

Roman walked one block, then turned left again. He was doubling back. I didn't understand, but I played it more cautiously. He was walking in a quick, jerky way, the movements of a frightened man.

We were on Harvey Street now. There were a couple of Chinese restaurants here. I paused to look at the menu in one window. Roman was not looking back. He went another block, then turned right.

I followed.

South of the Boston Commons, the character of the town changes abruptly. Along the Commons, on Tremont Street, there are elegant shops and high-class theaters. Washington Street is one block over, and it's a little sleazier: there are bars and tarts and nude movie houses. A block over from that, things get even tougher. Then there's a block of Chinese restaurants, and that's it. From then on, you're in the wholesale district. Clothes mostly.

That's where we were now.

The stores were dark. Bolts of cloth stood upright in the windows. There were large corrugated doors where the trucks pulled up to load and unload. Several little dry-goods stores. A theatrical supply shop, with costumes in the window—chorus girl stockings, an old military uniform, several wigs. A basement pool hall, from which came the soft clicking of balls.

The streets were wet and dark. We were quite alone. Roman walked quickly for another block, then he stopped.

I pulled into a doorway and waited. He looked

back for a moment and kept going. I was right after him.

Several times, he doubled back on his own path, and he frequently stopped to check behind him. Once a car drove by, tires hissing on the wet pavement. Roman jumped into a shadow, then stepped out when the car had gone.

He was nervous, all right.

I followed him for perhaps fifteen minutes. I couldn't decide whether he was being cautious or just killing time. He stopped several times to look at something he held in his hand—perhaps a watch, perhaps something else. I couldn't be sure.

Eventually he headed north, skirting along side streets, working his way around the Commons and the State House. It took me awhile to realize that he was heading for Beacon Hill.

Another ten minutes passed, and I must have gotten careless, because I lost him. He darted around a corner, and when I turned it moments later, he was gone: the street was deserted. I stopped to listen for footsteps, but heard nothing. I began to worry and hurried forward.

Then it happened.

Something heavy and damp and cold struck my head, and I felt a cool, sharp pain over my forehead, and then a strong punch to my stomach. I fell to the pavement and the world began to spin sickeningly. I heard a shout, and footsteps, and then nothing.

SIX

IT WAS ONE OF THOSE PECULIAR VIEWS YOU HAVE, like a dream where everything is distorted. The buildings were black and very high, towering above me, threatening to collapse. They seemed to rise forever. I felt cold and soaked through, and rain spattered my face. I lifted my head up from the pavement and saw that it was all red.

I pulled up on one elbow. Blood dripped down onto my raincoat. I looked stupidly down at the red pavement. Hell of a lot of blood. Mine?

My stomach churned and I vomited on the sidewalk. I was dizzy and the world turned green for a while.

Finally, I forced myself to get to my knees.

In the distance, I heard sirens. Far off but getting closer. I stood shakily and leaned on an automobile parked by the curb. I didn't know where I was; the street was dark and silent. I looked at the bloody sidewalk and wondered what to do.

The sirens were coming closer.

Stumbling, I ran around the corner, then stopped to catch my breath. The sirens were very close now; a blue light flashed on the street I had just left.

I ran again. I don't know how far I went. I don't know where I was.

I just kept running until I saw a taxi. It was parked at a stand, the motor idling.

I said, "Take me to the nearest hospital."

He looked at my face.

"Not a chance," he said.

I started to get in.

"Forget it, buddy." He pulled the door shut and drove away, leaving me standing there.

In the distance, I heard the sirens again.

A wave of dizziness swept over me. I squatted and waited for it to pass. I was sick again. Blood was still dripping from somewhere on my face. Little red drops spattered into the vomit.

The rain continued. I was shivering cold, but it helped me to stay conscious. I got up and tried to get my bearings; I was somewhere south of Washington Street; the nearest signpost said Curley Place. It didn't mean anything to me. I started walking, unsteady, pausing frequently.

I hoped I was going in the right direction. I knew I was losing blood, but I didn't know how much. Every few steps, I had to stop to lean on a car and catch my breath.

The dizziness was getting worse.

I stumbled and fell. My knees cracked into the pavement and pain shot through me. For an instant, it cleared my head, and I was able to get back to my feet. The shoes, soaked through, squeaked. My clothes were damp with sweat and rain.

I concentrated on the sound of my shoes and forced myself to walk. One step at a time. Three blocks ahead, I saw lights. I knew I could make it.

One step at a time.

I leaned against a blue car for a moment, just a moment, to catch my breath.

"THAT'S IT. That's the boy." Somebody was lifting me up. I was in a car, being lifted out. My arm was thrown over a shoulder, and I was walking. Bright lights ahead. A sign: "Emergency Ward." Blue-lighted sign. Nurse at the door.

"Just go slow, boy. Just take it easy."

My head was loose on my neck. I tried to speak but my mouth was too dry. I was terribly thirsty and cold. I looked at the man helping me, an old man with a grizzled beard and a bald head. I tried to stand better so he wouldn't have to support me, but my knees were rubber, and I was shivering badly.

"Doing fine, boy. No problem at all."

His voice was gruffly encouraging. The nurse came forward, floating in the pool of light near the EW door, saw me, and ran back inside. Two interns came out and each took an arm. They were strong; I felt myself lifted up until my toes were scraping through the puddles. I felt rain on the back of my neck as my head drooped forward. The bald man was running ahead to open the door.

They helped me inside where it was warm. They

put me on a padded table and started pulling off my clothes, but the clothes were wet and blood-soaked; they clung to my body, and finally they had to cut them off with a scissors. It was all very difficult and it took hours. I kept my eyes closed because the lights overhead were painfully bright.

"Get a crit and cross-match him," said one of the interns. "And set up a four kit with sutures in room two."

People were fussing with my head; I vaguely felt hands and gauze pads being pressed against my skin. My forehead was numb and cold. By now they had me completely undressed. They dried me with a hard towel and wrapped me in a blanket, then transferred me to another padded table. It started to roll down the hall. I opened my eyes and saw the bald man looking down at me solicitously.

"Where'd you find him?" one of the interns asked.

"On a car. He was lying on a car. I saw him and thought he was a drunk passed out. He was half in the street, you know, so I figured he could get run over and stopped to move him. Then I saw he was nicely dressed and all bloody. I didn't know what happened, but he looked bad, so I brought him here."

"You have any idea what happened?" the intern asked.

"Looks beat up, if you ask me," the man said.

"He didn't have a wallet," the intern said. "He owe you money for the fare?"

"That's all right," the bald man said.

"I'm sure he'll want to pay you."

"That's all right," the cabby said. "I'll just go now."

"Better leave your name at the desk," the intern said.

But the man was already gone.

They wheeled me into a room tiled in blue. The surgical light over my head switched on. Faces peered down at me. Rubber gloves pulled on, gauze masks in place.

"We'll stop the bleeding," the intern said. "Then get some X rays." He looked at me. "You awake, sir?"

I nodded and tried to speak.

"Don't talk. Your jaw may be broken. I'm just going to close this wound on your forehead, and then we'll see."

The nurse bathed my face, first with warm soap. The sponges came away bloody.

"Alcohol now," she said. "It may sting a little."

The interns were talking to each other, looking at the wound. "Better mark that as a six-centimeter superficial on the right temple."

I barely felt the alcohol. It felt cool and tingled slightly, nothing more.

The intern held the curved suture needle in a needle holder. The nurse stepped back and he moved over my head. I expected pain, but it was nothing more than a slight pricking on my forehead.

The intern who was sewing said, "Damned sharp incision here. Looks almost surgical."

"Knife?"

"Maybe, but I doubt it."

The nurse put a tourniquet on my arm and drew blood. "Better give him tetanus toxoid as well," the intern said, still sewing. "And a shot of penicillin." He said to me, "Blink your eyes once for yes, twice for no. Are you allergic to penicillin?"

I blinked twice.

"Are you sure?"

I blinked once.

"O.K.," said the intern. He returned to his sewing. The nurse gave me two injections. The other intern was examining my body, saying nothing.

I must have passed out again. When I opened my eyes, I saw a huge X-ray machine poised by my head. Someone was saying, "Gently, gently," in an irritated voice.

I passed out again.

I awoke in another room. This was painted light green. The interns were holding the dripping-wet X rays up to the light, talking about them. Then one left and the other came over to me.

"You seem all right," he said. "You may have a few loose teeth, but no fractures anywhere that we can see."

My head was clearing; I was awake enough to ask, "Has the radiologist looked at those films?"

That stopped them cold. They froze, thinking what I was thinking, that skull films were so hard to interpret and required a trained eye. They also didn't understand how I knew to ask such a question.

"No, the radiologist is not here right now."

"Well, where is he?"

"He just stepped out for coffee."

"Get him back," I said. My mouth was dry and stiff; my jaw hurt. I touched my cheek and felt a large swelling, very painful. No wonder they had been worried about a fracture.

"What's my crit?" I said.

"Pardon, sir?"

It was hard for them to hear me, my tongue was thick and my speech unclear.

"I said, what's my hematocrit?"

They glanced at each other, then one said, "Forty, sir."

"Get me some water."

One of them went off to get water. The other looked at me oddly, as if he had just discovered I was a human being. "Are you a doctor, sir?"

"No," I said, "I'm a well-informed Pygmy."

He was confused. He took out his notebook and said, "Have you ever been admitted to this hospital before, sir?"

"No," I said. "And I'm not being admitted now."

"Sir, you came in with a laceration—"

"Screw the laceration. Get me a mirror."

"A mirror?"

I sighed. "I want to see how good your sewing is," I said.

"Sir, if you're a doctor—"

"Get the mirror."

With remarkable speed, a mirror and a glass of water were produced. I drank the water first, quickly; it tasted marvelous.

"Better go easy on that, sir."

"A crit of forty isn't bad," I said. "And you know it." I held up the mirror and examined the cut on my forehead. I was angry with the interns, and it helped me forget the pain and soreness in my body. I looked at the cut, which was clean and curved, sloping down from above one eyebrow toward my ear.

They had put about twenty stitches in.

"How long since I came in?" I said.

"An hour, sir."

"Stop calling me sir," I said, "and do another hematocrit. I want to know if I'm bleeding internally."

"Your pulse is only seventy-five, sir, and your skin color—"

"Do it," I said.

They took another sample. The intern drew five cc's into a syringe. "Jesus," I said, "it's only a hematocrit."

He gave me a funny apologetic look and quickly left. Guys on the EW get sloppy. They need only a fraction of a cc to do a crit; they could get it from a drop of blood on a finger.

I said to the other intern, "My name is John Berry. I am a pathologist at the Lincoln."

"Yes, sir."

"Stop writing it down."

"Yes, sir." He put his notebook aside.

"This isn't an admission and it isn't going to be officially recorded."

"Sir, if you were attacked and robbed—"

"I wasn't," I said. "I stumbled and fell. Nothing else. It was just a stupid mistake."

"Sir, the pattern of contusions on your body would indicate—"

"I don't care if I'm not a textbook case. I'm telling you what happened and that's it."

"Sir—"

"No," I said. "No arguments."

I looked at him. He was dressed in whites and he had some spatterings of blood on him; I guessed it was my blood.

"You're not wearing your name tag," I said.

"No."

"Well, wear it. We patients like to know who we're talking to."

He took a deep breath, then said, "Sir, I'm a fourth-year student."

"Jesus Christ."

"Sir—"

"Look, son. You'd better get some things straight." I was grateful for the anger, the fury, which gave me energy. "This may be a kick for you to spend one month of your rotation in the EW, but it's no kicks at all for me. Call Dr. Hammond."

"Who, sir?"

"Dr. Hammond. The resident in charge."

"Yes, sir."

He started to go, and I decided I had been too hard on him. He was, after all, just a student, and he seemed a nice enough kid.

"By the way," I said, "did you do the suturing?"

There was a long, guilty pause. "Yes, I did."

"You did a good job," I said.

He grinned. "Thanks, sir."

"Stop calling me sir. Did you examine the incision before you sutured it up?"

"Yes, s——. Yes."

"What was your impression?"

"It was a remarkably clean incision. It looked like a razor cut to me."

I smiled. "Or a scalpel?"

"I don't understand."

"I think you're in for an interesting night," I said. "Call Hammond."

ALONE, I had nothing to think about but the pain. My stomach was the worst; it ached as if I had swallowed a bowling ball. I rolled over onto my side, and it was better. After a while, Hammond showed up, with the fourth-year student trailing along behind.

Hammond said, "Hi, John."

"Hello, Norton. How's business?"

"I didn't see you come in," Norton said, "otherwise——"

"Doesn't matter. Your boys did a good job."

"What happened to you?"

"I had an accident."

"You were lucky," Norton said, bending over the wound and looking at it. "Cut your superficial temporal. You were spurting like hell. But your crit doesn't show it."

"I have a big spleen," I said.

"Maybe so. How do you feel?"

"Like a piece of shit."

"Headache?"

"A little. Getting better."

"Feel sleepy? Nauseated?"

"Come on, Norton—"

"Just lie there," Hammond said. He took out his penlight and checked my pupils, then looked into the fundi with an ophthalmoscope. Then he checked my reflexes, arms and legs, both sides.

"You see?" I said. "Nothing."

"You still might have a hematoma."

"Nope."

"We want you to stay under observation for twenty-four hours," Hammond said.

"Not a chance." I sat up in bed, wincing. My stomach was sore. "Help me get up."

"I'm afraid your clothes—"

"Have been cut to shreds. I know. Get me some whites, will you?"

"Whites? Why?"

"I want to be around when they bring the others in," I said.

"What others?"

"Wait and see," I said.

The fourth-year student asked me what size

whites I wore, and I told him. He started to get them when Hammond caught his arm.

"Just a minute." He turned to me. "You can have them on one condition."

"Norton, for Christ's sake, I don't have a hematoma. If it's subdural, it may not show up for weeks or months anyway. You know that."

"It might be epidural," he said.

"No fractures on the skull films," I said. An epidural hematoma was a collection of blood inside the skull from a torn artery, secondary to skull fracture. The blood collected in the skull and could kill you from the compression of the brain.

"You said yourself, they haven't been read by a radiologist yet."

"Norton, for Christ's sake. You're not talking to an eighty-year old lady. I—"

"You can have the whites," he said calmly, "if you agree to stay here overnight."

"I won't be admitted."

"O.K. Just so you stay here in the EW."

I frowned. "All right," I said finally, "I'll stay."

The fourth-year student left to get me the clothes. Hammond stood there and shook his head at me.

"Who beat you up?"

"Wait and see."

"You scared hell out of the intern and that student."

"I didn't mean to. But they were being kind of casual about things."

"The radiologist for the night is Harrison. He's a fuck-off."

"You think that matters to me?"

"You know how it is," he said.

"Yes," I said, "I do."

The whites came, and I climbed into them. It was an odd feeling; I hadn't worn whites for years. I'd been proud of it then. Now the fabric seemed stiff and uncomfortable.

They found my shoes, wet and bloody; I wiped them off and put them on. I felt weak and tired, but I had to keep going. It was all going to be finished tonight. I was certain of it.

I got some coffee and a sandwich. I couldn't taste it, it was like eating newspaper, but I thought the food was necessary. Hammond stayed with me.

"By the way," he said, "I checked on Roman Jones for you."

"And?"

"He was only seen once. In the GU[1] clinic. Came in with what sounded like renal colic, so they did a urinalysis."

"Yes?"

"He had hematuria, all right. Nucleated red cells."

"I see."

It was a classic story. Patients often showed up in clinic complaining of severe pain in the lower abdomen and decreased urine output. The most likely diagnosis was a kidney stone, one of the five most

[1] Genitourinary.

painful conditions there are; morphine is given almost immediately when the diagnosis is made. But in order to prove it, one asks for a urine sample and examines it for slight blood. Kidney stones are usually irritating and cause a little bleeding in the urinary tract.

Morphine addicts, knowing the relative ease of getting morphine for kidney stones, often try to mimic renal colic. Some of them are very good at it; they know the symptoms and can reproduce them exactly. Then when they're asked for a urine sample, they go into the bathroom, collect the sample, prick their fingers, and allow a small drop of blood to fall in.

But some of them are squeamish. Instead of using their own blood, they use the blood of an animal, like a chicken. The only trouble is that chicken red cells have nuclei, while those of humans do not. So nucleated red cells in a patient with renal colic almost always meant someone faking the symptoms, and that usually meant an addict.

"Was he examined for needle marks?"

"No. When the doctor confronted him, he left the clinic. He's never been seen again."

"Interesting. Then he probably is an addict."

"Yes. Probably."

After the food, I felt better. I got to my feet, feeling the exhaustion and the pain. I called Judith and told her I was at the Mem OPD and that I was fine, not to worry. I didn't mention the beating or the cut. I knew she would have a fit when I got home, but I wasn't going to excite her now.

I walked down the corridor with Hammond, trying not to wince from the pain. He kept asking me how I felt, and I kept telling him I felt fine. In fact, I didn't. The food was beginning to make me nauseated, and my headache was worse standing up. But the worst thing was the fatigue. I was terribly, terribly tired.

We went to the emergency entrance of the EW. It was a kind of stall, an open-ended garage where the ambulances backed up and unloaded their cargoes. Swinging, automatic doors, operated by foot-pressure pads, led into the hospital. We walked out and breathed the cool night air. It was a rainy, misty night, but the cool air felt good to me.

Hammond said, "You're pale."

"I'm O.K."

"We haven't even begun to evaluate you for internal hemorrhage."

"I'm O.K.," I said.

"Tell me if you're not," Hammond said. "Don't be a hero."

"I'm not a hero," I said.

We waited there. An occasional automobile drove past us, tires hissing on the wet streets; otherwise it was silent.

"What's going to happen?" Hammond said.

"I'm not sure. But I think they're going to bring in a Negro and a girl."

"Roman Jones? Is he involved in all this?"

"I think so."

In fact, I was almost certain that it had been Roman Jones who had beaten me up. I didn't remember exactly any more; the events right before the accident were hazy. I might have expected that. I didn't have true retrograde amnesia, which is common with concussions and extends back for fifteen minutes before the accident. But I was a little confused.

It must have been Roman, I thought. He was the only logical one. Roman had been heading for Beacon Hill. And there was only one logical reason for that, too.

We would have to wait.

"How do you feel?"

"You keep asking," I said. "And I keep telling you I'm fine."

"You looked tired."

"I am tired. I've been tired all week."

"No. I mean you look drowsy."

"Don't jump the gun," I said. I glanced at my watch. Nearly two hours had passed since I had been beaten up. That was plenty of time. More than enough time.

I began to wonder if something had gone wrong.

At that moment, a police car came around the corner, tires squealing, siren going, blue light flashing. Immediately afterward an ambulance pulled up, followed by a third car. As the ambulance backed in, two men in business suits jumped out of the third car: reporters. You could tell by their eager little faces. One had a camera.

"No pictures," I said.

The ambulance doors were opened and a body on a stretcher was brought out. The first thing I saw was the clothes—slashed and ripped across the trunk and upper limbs, as if the body had been caught in some kind of monstrous machine. Then, in the cold fluorescent light of the EW entrance, I saw the face: Roman Jones. His skull was caved in on the right side like a deflated football, and his lips were purple-black.

The flashbulbs popped.

Right there in the alleyway, Hammond went to work. He was quick: in a single movement, he picked up the wrist with his left hand, put his ear over the chest, and felt the carotids in the neck with his right hand. Then he straightened and without a word began to pound the chest. He did it with one hand flat and the heel of the other thumping against the flat hand in sharp, hard, rhythmic beats.

"Call anesthesia," he said, "and get the surgical resident. Get an arrest cart here. I want aramine, one-in-a-thousand solution. Oxygen by mask. Positive pressure. Let's go."

We moved him inside the EW and down to one of the little treatment rooms. Hammond continued the cardiac massage all the time, not breaking his rhythm. When we got to the room the surgical resident was there.

"Arrested?"

"Yes," Hammond said. "Apneic, no pulses anywhere."

The surgeon picked up a paper packet of size-eight gloves. He didn't wait for the nurse to open them for him; he took them out of the paper himself and yanked them over his fingers. He never took his eyes off the motionless figure of Roman Jones.

"We'll open him up," the surgeon said, flexing his fingers in the gloves.

Hammond nodded, continuing his pounding of the chest. It didn't seem to be doing much good: Roman's lips and tongue were blacker. His skin, especially in the face and ears, was blotchy and dark.

An oxygen mask was slapped on.

"How much, sir?" said the nurse.

"Seven liters," said the surgeon. He was given a scalpel. Roman's already shredded clothes were torn away from his chest; nobody bothered to strip him down completely. The surgeon stepped forward, his face blank, the scalpel held tightly in his right hand with his index finger over the blade.

"All right," he said and made the incision, sloping, across the ribs on the left side. It was a deep incision and there was bleeding, which he ignored. He exposed the whitish glistening ribs, cut between them, and then applied retractors. The retractors were pulled wide and there was a crunching, snapping sound as the ribs snapped. Through the gaping incision, we could see Roman's lungs, collapsed and wrinkled-looking, and his heart, large, bluish, not beating, but wriggling like a bag of worms.

The surgeon reached into the chest and began to massage. He did it smoothly, contracting his little finger first, then all the others in his hand up to the index finger, expelling blood from the heart. He squeezed very hard and grunted rhythmically.

Someone had slapped on a blood-pressure cuff and Hammond pumped it up to take a reading. He watched the needle for a moment, then said, "Nothing."

"He's fibrillating," the resident said, holding the heart. "No epinephrine. Let's wait."

The massage continued for one minute, then two. Roman's color turned darker still.

"Getting weaker. Give me five cc's in one to a thousand."

A syringe was prepared. The surgeon injected it directly into the heart, then continued squeezing.

Several more minutes passed. I watched the squeezing heart, and the rhythmic inflation of the lungs from the respirator. But the patient was declining. Finally, they stopped.

"That's it," the surgeon said. He removed his hand from the chest, looked at Roman Jones, and stripped off his gloves. He examined the lacerations across the chest and arms and the dent in the skull.

"Probably primary respiratory arrest," he said. "He was hit pretty hard over the head." To Hammond: "You going to do the death certificate?"

"Yeah," Hammond said, "I'll do it."

At that moment, a nurse burst into the room. "Dr. Hammond," she said, "Dr. Jorgensen needs you. They've got a girl in hemorrhagic shock."

OUT IN THE HALL, the first one I saw was Peterson. He was standing there in a suit, looking both confused and annoyed. When he saw me he did a double take and plucked at my sleeve.

"Say, Berry—"

"Later," I said.

I was following Hammond and the nurse down to another treatment room. A girl was there, lying flat, very pale. Her wrists were bandaged. She was conscious, but just barely—her head rolled back and forth, and she made moaning sounds.

Jorgensen, the intern, was bent over her. "Got a suicide here," he said to Hammond. "Slashed wrists. We've stopped the bleeding and we're getting whole blood in."

He was finding a vein for the IV feeder. Working on the leg.

"She's cross-matched," he said, slipping the needle in. "We're getting more blood from the bank. She'll take at least two units. Hematocrit's O.K., but that doesn't mean anything."

"Why the legs?" Hammond said, nodding to the IV.

"Had to bandage her wrists. Don't want to fool with upper extremities."

I stepped forward. The girl was Angela Harding. She did not look so pretty now; her face was the color of chalk, with a grayish tinge around the mouth.

"What do you think?" Hammond said to Jorgensen.

"We'll keep her," he said. "Unless something goes wrong."

Hammond examined the wrists, which were bandaged.

"Is this the lesion?"

"Yes. Both sides. We've sutured it."

He looked at the hands. The fingers were stained dark brown. He looked at me. "Is this the girl you were talking about?"

"Yes," I said, "Angela Harding."

"Heavy smoker," Hammond said.

"Try again."

Hammond picked up one hand and smelled the stained fingers.

"These aren't tobacco," he said.

"That's right."

"Then . . ."

I nodded. "That's right."

". . . she's a nurse."

"Yes."

The stains were from tincture of iodine, used as a disinfectant. It was a brownish-yellowish liquid, and it stained tissues it came in contact with. It was employed for scrubbing a surgical incision before cutting, and for such other practices as introduction of an IV feeder.

"I don't get it," Hammond said.

I held up her hands. The balls of the thumb and the backs of the hands were covered with minute slashes which were not deep enough to draw blood.

"What do you make of this?"

"Testing." A classic finding in suicides by wrist-slashing is one or more preliminary cuts on the hand as if the suicide victim wishes to test the sharpness of the blade or the intensity of the pain that would result.

"No," I said.

"Then what?"

"Ever seen a fellow who's been in a knife fight?"

Hammond shook his head. Undoubtedly, he never had. It was the kind of experience one had only as a pathologist: small cuts on the hands were the hall-mark of a knife fight. The victim held up his hands to ward off the knife; he ended up with small cuts.

"Is this the pattern?"

"Yes."

"You mean she was in a knife fight?"

"Yes."

"But why?"

"Tell you later," I said.

I went back to Roman Jones. He was still in the same room, along with Peterson and another man in a suit, examining the eyes of the body.

"Berry," Peterson said, "you show up at the damnedest times."

"So do you."

"Yeah," Peterson said, "but it's my job."

He nodded toward the other man in the room.

"Since you were so worried the last time, I brought a doctor along. A police doctor. This is a coroner's case now, you know."

"I know."

"Fellow by the name of Roman Jones. We got that from the wallet."

"Where'd you find him?"

"Lying on the street. A nice quiet street in Beacon Hill. With his skull bashed in. Must have fallen on his head. There was a broken window two floors up, in an apartment owned by a girl named Angela Harding. She's here, too."

"I know."

"You know a lot tonight, don't you?"

I ignored him. My headache was worse; it was throbbing badly, and I felt terribly tired. I was ready to lie down and go to sleep for a long, long time. But I wasn't relaxed; my stomach was churning.

I bent over the body of Roman Jones. Someone had stripped off the clothing to expose multiple, deep lacerations of the trunk and upper arms. The legs were untouched. That, I thought, was characteristic.

The doctor straightened and looked at Peterson. "Hard to tell now what the cause of death was," he said. He nodded to the gaping chest wound. "They've mess it up pretty bad. But I'd say crush injury to the cranium. You said he fell from a window?"

"That's the way we figure it," Peterson said, glancing at me.

"I'll handle the forms," the doctor said. "Give me the wallet."

Peterson gave him Roman Jones' wallet. The doctor began to write on a clipboard at one side of the room. I continued to look at the body. I was particularly interested in the skull. I touched the indentation, and Peterson said, "What're you doing?"

"Examining the body."

"On whose authority?"

I sighed. "Whose authority do I need?"

He looked confused then.

I said, "I'd like your permission to conduct a superficial examination of the body."

As I said it, I glanced over at the doctor. He was making notes from the wallet, but I was sure he was listening.

"There'll be an autopsy," Peterson said.

"I'd like your permission," I said.

"You can't have it."

At that point, the doctor said, "Oh, for shit's sake, Jack."

Peterson looked from the police doctor, to me, and back again. Finally he said, "Okay, Berry. Examine. But don't disturb anything."

I looked at the skull lesion. It was a cup-shaped indentation roughly the size of a man's fist, but it hadn't been made by any fist. It had been made by the end of a stick, or a pipe, swung with considerable force. I looked more closely and saw small brown slivers of wood sticking to the bloody scalp. I didn't touch them.

"You say this skull fracture was caused by a fall?"

"Yes," Peterson said. "Why?"

"Just asking."

"Why?"

"What about the lacerations of the body?" I said.

"We figure he got those in the apartment. Apparently he had a fight with this girl, Angela Harding. There was a bloody kitchen knife in the apartment. She must have gone after him. Anyway, he fell out of the window or was pushed out. And he got this fracture, which killed him."

He paused and looked at me.

"Go on," I said.

"That's all there is to tell," he said.

I nodded, left the room, and returned with a needle and syringe. I bent over the body and jabbed the needle into the neck, hoping for the jugular vein. There was no point in fooling with arm veins, not now.

"What're you doing?"

"Drawing blood," I said, pulling back the syringe and drawing out several milliliters of bluish blood.

"What for?"

"I want to know whether he was poisoned," I said. It was the first thought, the first answer, that came into my head.

"Poisoned?"

"Yes."

"Why do you think he was poisoned?"

"Just a hunch," I said.

I dropped the syringe into my pocket and started

to leave. Peterson watched me, then said, "Just wait a minute."

I paused.

"I have one or two questions for you."

"Oh?"

"The way we figure it," Peterson said, "this fellow and Angela Harding had a fight. Then Jones fell, and the girl attempted suicide."

"You already told me that."

"There's only one problem," Peterson said. "Jones is a big fellow. He must have gone one-ninety, two hundred. You think a little girl like Angela Harding could have shoved him out?"

"Maybe he fell."

"Maybe she had help."

"Maybe she did."

He looked at my face, at the bandage covering my cut. "Have some trouble tonight?"

"Yes."

"What happened?"

"I fell on the wet streets."

"Then you have an abrasion?"

"No. I fell against one of the city's excellent parking meters. I have a laceration."

"A jagged laceration."

"No, quite fine."

"Like Roman Jones'?"

"I don't know."

"Ever met Jones before?"

"Yes."

"Oh? When?"

"Tonight. About three hours ago."

"That's interesting," Peterson said.

"Do your best with it," I said. "I wish you luck."

"I could take you in for questioning."

"Sure you could," I said. "But on what charge?"

He shrugged. "Accessory. Anything."

"And I'd have a lawsuit on you so fast your head would swim. I'd have two million dollars out of your hide before you knew what hit you."

"Just for questioning?"

"That's right," I said. "Compromising a doctor's reputation. A doctor's reputation is his life, you know. Anything, even the slightest shadow of suspicion, is potentially damaging—financially damaging. I could very easily prove damages in court."

"Art Lee doesn't take that attitude."

I smiled. "Want to bet?"

I continued on. Peterson said, "How much do you weigh, Doctor?"

"One hundred and eighty-five pounds," I said. "The same as I weighed eight years ago."

"Eight years ago?"

"Yes," I said, "when I was a cop."

MY HEAD FELT AS IF IT WERE IN A VISE. The pain was throbbing, aching, agonizing. On my way down the corridor, I felt sudden and severe nausea. I stopped in the men's room and vomited up the sandwich and coffee I had eaten. I felt weak, with cold sweat afterward, but that passed and I was better. I went back and returned to Hammond.

"How do you feel?"

"You're getting monotonous," I said.

"You look like hell," he said. "Like you're about to be sick."

"I'm not," I said.

I took the syringe with Jones' blood from my pocket and set it on the bedside table. I picked up a fresh syringe and went.

"Can you find me a mouse?" I said.

"A mouse?"

"Yes."

He frowned. "There are some rats in Cochran's lab; it may be open now."

"I need mice."

"I can try," he said.

We headed for the basement. On the way, a nurse stopped Hammond to say that Angela Harding's parents had been called. Hammond said to let him know when they arrived or when the girl recovered consciousness.

We went down to the basement and moved through a maze of corridors, crouching beneath pipes. Eventually we came to the animal-storage area. Like most large hospitals connected with a university, the Mem had a research wing, and many animals were used in experiments. We heard barking dogs and the soft flutter of birds' wings as we passed room after room. Finally we came to one which said MINOR SUB-JECTS. Hammond pushed it open.

It was lined, floor to ceiling, with row after row of rats and mice. The smell was strong and distinctive. Every young doctor knew that smell, and it was just as well, because it had clinical significance. The breath of patients in hepatic failure from liver disease had a peculiar odor known as *fetor hepaticus*; it was very similar to the smell of a room full of mice.

We found one mouse and Hammond plucked it from the cage in the accepted manner, by the tail. The mouse squirmed and tried to bite Hammond's hand, but had no success. Hammond set it down on the table and held the animal by a fold of loose flesh just behind the head.

"Now what?"

I picked up the syringe and injected some of the blood from Roman Jones' body. Then Hammond dropped the mouse in a glass jar.

For a long time, the mouse did nothing but run around the jar in circles.

"Well?" Hammond said.

"It's your failing," I said. "You aren't a pathologist. Have you ever heard of the mouse test?"

"No."

"It's an old test. It used to be the only bioassay available."

"Bioassay? For what?"

"Morphine," I said.

The mouse continued to run in circles. Then it seemed to slow, its muscles becoming tense, and the tail stuck straight up in the air.

"Positive," I said.

"For morphine?"

"Right."

There were better tests now, such as nalorphine, but for a dead person, the mouse test remained as good as any.

"He's an addict?" Hammond said.

"Yes."

"And the girl?"

"We're about to find out," I said.

She was conscious when we returned, tired and sad-eyed after taking three units[2] of blood. But she was no more tired than I was. I felt a deep, over-powering fatigue, a kind of general weakness, a great desire to sleep.

There was a nurse in the room who said, "Her pressure's up to one hundred over sixty-five."

"Good," I said. I fought back the fatigue and went up to her, patted her hand. "How are you feel-ing, Angela?"

Her voice was flat. "Like hell."

"You're going to be all right."

"I failed," she said in a dull monotone.

"How do you mean?"

A tear ran down her cheek. "I failed, that's all. I tried it and I failed."

"You're all right now."

"Yes," she said. "I failed."

"We'd like to talk to you," I said.

She turned her head away. "Leave me alone."

"Angela, this is very important."

[2] A liter and a half.

"Damn all doctors," she said. "Why couldn't you leave me alone? I wanted to be left alone. That's why I did it, to be left alone."

"The police found you."

She gave a choking laugh. "Doctors and cops."

"Angela, we need your help."

"No." She raised her bandaged wrists and looked at them. "No. Never."

"I'm sorry, then." I turned to Hammond and said, "Get me some nalorphine."

I was certain the girl had heard me, but she did not react.

"How much?"

"Ten milligrams," I said. "A good dose."

Angela gave a slight shiver, but said nothing.

"Is that all right with you, Angela?"

She looked up at me and her eyes were filled with anger and something else, almost hope. She knew what it meant, all right.

"What did you say?" she asked.

"I said, is it all right if we give you ten milligrams of nalorphine."

"Sure," she said. "Anything. I don't care."

Nalorphine was an antagonist of morphine.[3] If this girl was an addict, it would bring her down with brutal swiftness—possibly fatal swiftness, if we used enough.

A nurse came in. She blinked when she did not

---

[3] Actually a partial agonist, meaning that in low doses it has a morphinelike effect, but in high doses in an addict, it induces withdrawal symptoms.

recognize me, but recovered quickly. "Doctor, Mrs. Harding is here. The police called her."

"All right. I'll see her."

I went out into the corridor. A woman and man were standing there nervously. The man was tall, wearing clothes he had obviously put on hurriedly—his socks didn't match. The woman was handsome and concerned. Looking at her face, I had the strange feeling I had met her before, though I was certain I had not. There was something very, almost hauntingly, familiar about her features.

"I'm Dr. Berry."

"Tom Harding." The man held out his hand and shook mine quickly, as if he were wringing it. "And Mrs. Harding."

"How do you do."

I looked at them both. They seemed like nice fifty-year-old people, very surprised to find themselves in a hospital EW at four in the morning with a daughter who'd just slashed her wrists.

Mr. Harding cleared his throat and said, "The, uh, nurse told us what happened. To Angela."

"She's going to be all right," I said.

"Can we see her?" Mrs. Harding said.

"Not right now. We're still conducting some tests."

"Then it isn't—"

"No," I said, "these are routine tests."

Tom Harding nodded. "I told my wife it'd be all right. Angela's a nurse in this hospital, and I told her they'd take good care of her."

"Yes," I said. "We're doing our best."

"Is she really all right?" Mrs. Harding said.

"Yes, she's going to be fine."

Mrs. Harding said to Tom, "Better call Leland and tell him he doesn't have to come over."

"He's probably already on his way."

"Well, try," Mrs. Harding said.

"There's a phone at the admitting desk," I said.

Tom Harding left to call. I said to Mrs. Harding, "Are you calling your family doctor?"

"No," she said, "my brother. He's a doctor, and he was always very fond of Angela, ever since she was a little girl. He—"

"Leland Weston," I said, recognizing her face.

"Yes," she said. "Do you know him?"

"He's an old friend."

Before she could answer, Hammond returned with the nalorphine and syringe. He said, "Do you really think we should—"

"Dr. Hammond, this is Mrs. Harding," I said quickly. "This is Dr. Hammond, the chief medical resident."

"Doctor." Mrs. Harding nodded slightly, but her eyes were suddenly watchful.

"Your daughter's going to be fine," Hammond said.

"I'm glad to hear that," she said. But her tone was cool.

We excused ourselves and went back to Angela.

* * *

"I HOPE TO HELL you know what you're doing," Hammond said as we walked down the hall.

"I do." I paused at a water fountain and filled a cup with water. I drank it down, then filled it again. My headache was now very bad, and my sleepiness was terrible. I wanted to lie down, to forget everything, to sleep. . . .

But I didn't say anything. I knew what Hammond would do if he found out.

"I know what I'm doing," I said.

"I hope so," he said, "because if anything goes wrong, I'm responsible. I'm the resident in charge."

"I know. Don't worry."

"Worry, hell. Ten milligrams of this stuff will shove her into cold turkey so fast—"

"Don't worry."

"It could kill her. We ought to be doing graded doses. Start with two, and if there's no effect in twenty minutes, go to five, and so on."

"Yes," I said. "But graded doses won't kill her."

Hammond looked at me and said, "John, are you out of your mind?"

"No," I said.

We entered Angela's room. She was turned away from us, rolled over on her side. I took the ampoule of nalorphine from Hammond and set it with the syringe on the table just alongside her bed; I wanted to be sure she read the label.

Then I walked around to the other side of the bed, so her back was to me.

I reached across her and picked up the ampoule

and syringe. Then I quickly filled the syringe with water from the cup.

"Would you turn around, Angela, please?"

She rolled onto her back and held out her arm. Hammond was too astonished to move; I put the tourniquet on her arm and rubbed the veins in the crook of her elbow until they stood out. Then I slipped the needle in and squeezed out the contents. She watched me in silence.

When it was done, I stood back and said, "There now."

She looked at me, then at Hammond, then back to me.

"It won't be long," I said.

"How much did you give me?"

"Enough."

"Was it ten? Did you give me ten?".

She was becoming agitated. I patted her arm reassuringly. "There's nothing to worry about."

"Was it twenty?"

"Well, no," I said. "It was only two. Two milligrams."

"Two!"

"It won't kill you," I said mildly.

She groaned and rolled away from us.

"Disappointed?" I said.

"What are you trying to prove?" she said.

"You know the answer to that, Angela."

"But two milligrams. That's—"

"Just enough to give you symptoms. Just the cold

sweats and the cramps and the pain. Just the begin-
nings of withdrawal."

"Jesus."

"It won't kill you," I said again. "And you know it."

"You bastards. I didn't ask to come here, I didn't
ask to be—"

"But you are here, Angela. And you have nalorphine in your veins. Not much, but enough."

She began to break out into a sweat. "Stop it,"
she said.

"We can use morphine."

"Stop it. Please. I don't want it."

"Tell us," I said. "About Karen."

"First stop it."

"No."

Hammond was bothered by all this. He started
forward toward the bed. I pushed him back.

"Tell us, Angela."

"I don't know anything."

"Then we'll wait until the symptoms start. And
you'll have to tell us while you scream from the
pain."

Her pillow was soaked with sweat. "I don't know,
I don't know."

"Tell us."

"I don't know anything."

She began to shiver, slightly at first, and then
more uncontrollably, until her whole body shook.

"It's starting, Angela."

She gritted her teeth. "I don't care."

"It will get worse, Angela."

"No ... no ... no. ..."

I produced an ampoule of morphine and set it on the table in front of her.

"Tell us."

Her shivering got worse, until her whole body was wracked with spasms. The bed shook violently. I would have felt pity if I had not known that she was causing the reaction herself, that I had not injected any nalorphine at all.

"Angela."

"All right," she said, gasping. "I did it. I had to."

"Why?"

"Because of the heat. The heat. The clinic and the heat."

"You'd been stealing from the surgery?"

"Yes ... not much, just a little ... but enough ..."

"How long?"

"Three years ... maybe four ..."

"And what happened?"

"Roman robbed the clinic ... Roman Jones."

"When?"

"Last week."

"And?"

"The heat was on. They were checking everybody ..."

"So you had to stop stealing?"

"Yes ..."

"What did you do?"

"I tried to buy from Roman."

"And?"

"He wanted money. A lot."

"Who suggested the abortion?"

"Roman."

"To get money?"

"Yes."

"How much did he want?"

I already knew the answer. She said, "Three hundred dollars."

"So you did the abortion?"

"Yes . . . yes . . . yes. . . ."

"And who acted as anesthetist?"

"Roman. It was easy. Thiopental."

"And Karen died?"

"She was all right when she left. . . . We did it on my bed . . . the whole thing. . . . It was all right, everything . . . on my bed. . . ."

"But later she died."

"Yes . . . Oh God, give me some stuff. . . ."

"We will," I said.

I filled a syringe with more water, squeezed out the air until a fine stream shot into the air, and injected it intravenously. Immediately she calmed. Her breathing became slower, more relaxed.

"Angela," I said, "did you perform the abortion?"

"Yes."

"And it resulted in Karen's death?"

A dull voice. "Yes."

"All right." I patted her arm. "Just relax now."

* * *

WE WALKED DOWN THE CORRIDOR. Tom Harding was waiting there with his wife, smoking a cigarette and pacing up and down.

"Is she all right, Doctor? Did the tests—"

"Fine," I said. "She'll recover beautifully."

"That's a relief," he said, his shoulders sagging.

"Yes," I said.

Norton Hammond gave me a quick glance, and I avoided his eyes. I felt like hell; my headache was much worse and I was beginning to have moments when my vision blurred. It seemed much worse in my right eye than my left.

But someone had to tell them. I said, "Mr. Harding, I am afraid your daughter has been implicated in business that involves the police."

He looked at me, stunned, disbelieving. Then I saw his face melt into a peculiar acceptance. Almost as if he had known it all along. "Drugs," he said, in a low voice.

"Yes," I said and felt worse than ever.

"We didn't know," he said quickly. "I mean, if we had . . ."

"But we suspected," Mrs. Harding said. "We never could control Angela. She was a headstrong girl, very independent. Very self-reliant and sure of herself. Even as a child, she was sure of herself."

HAMMOND wiped the sweat from his face with his sleeve. "Well," he said, "that's that."

"Yes."

Even though he was close to me, he seemed far

away. His voice was suddenly faint and insignificant. Everything around me was insignificant. The
people seemed small and faded. My headache now
came in bursts of severe pain. Once, I had to stop
for a moment and rest.

"What's the matter?"

"Nothing. Just tired."

He nodded. "Well," he said, "it's all over. You
should be pleased."

"Are you?"

We went into the doctors' conference room, a
small cubbyhole with two chairs and a table. There
were charts on the walls, detailing procedure for
acute emergencies: hemorrhagic shock, pulmonary
edema, MI, burns, crush injuries. We sat down and
I lit a cigarette. My left hand felt weak as I flicked
the lighter.

Hammond stared at the charts for a while; neither of us said anything. Finally, Hammond said,
"Want a drink?"

"Yes," I said. I was feeling sick to my stomach, dis-
gusted, and annoyed. A drink would do me good,
snap me out of it. Or else it would make me sicker.

He opened a locker and reached into the back,
producing a flask. "Vodka," he said. "No smell. For
acute medical emergencies." He opened it and took
a swallow, then passed it to me.

As I drank, he said, "Jesus. Tune in, turn on,
drop dead. Jesus."

"Something like that."

I gave the flask back to him.

"She was a nice girl, too."

"Yes."

"And that placebo effect. You got her into with-drawal on water, and you snapped her out of it with water."

"You know why," I said.

"Yeah," he said, "she believed you."

"That's right," I said. "She believed me."

I looked up at a chart illustrating the pathological lesion and emergency steps for diagnosis and treat-ment of ectopic pregnancy. I got down to the place where they talked about menstrual irregularity and cramping right-lower-quadrant pain when the words began to blur.

"John?"

It took me a long time to answer. It seemed as if it took me a long time to hear the words. I was sleepy, slow-thinking, slow-acting.

"John?"

"Yes," I said. My voice was hollow, a voice in a tomb. It echoed.

"You O.K.?"

"Yes, fine."

I kept hearing the words repeated in a kind of dream: fine, fine, fine. . . .

"You look terrible."

"I'm fine. . . ." Fine, fine, fine . . .

"John, don't get mad—"

"I'm not mad," I said and shut my eyes. The lids were hard to keep open. They stuck down, were heavy, sticking to the lower lids. "I'm happy."

"Happy?"

"What?"

"Are you happy?"

"No," I said. He was talking nonsense. It meant nothing. His voice was squeaky and high like a baby, a chattering, childish voice. "No," I said, "I'm not mad at all."

"John—"

"Stop calling me John."

"That's your name," Norton said. He stood up, slowly, moving in dreamy slowness, and I felt very tired as I watched him move. He reached into his pocket and produced his light and shined it into my face. I looked away; the light was bright and hurt my eyes. Especially my right eye.

"Look at me."

The voice was loud and commanding. Drill sergeant's voice. Snappish and irritable.

"Fuck off," I said.

Strong fingers on my head, holding me, and the light shining into my eyes.

"Cut it out, Norton."

"John, hold still."

"Cut it out." I closed my eyes. I was tired. Very tired. I wanted to sleep for a million years. Sleep was beautiful, like the ocean washing the sand, lapping up with a slow, beautiful, hissing sound, cleaning everything.

"I'm O.K., Norton. I'm just mad."

"John, hold still."

John, hold still.

John, hold still.

John, hold still.

"Norton, for Christ's sake—"

"Shut up," he said.

Shut up, shut up.

He had his little rubber hammer out. He was tapping my legs. Making my legs bounce up and down. It tingled and irritated me. I wanted to sleep. I wanted to go fast, fast asleep.

"Norton, you son of a bitch."

"Shut up. You're as bad as any of them."

As any of them, as any of them. The words echoed in my head. As any of what? I wondered. Then the sleep, creeping up on me, fingers stretching out, plastic, rubbery fingers, closing over my eyes, holding them shut. . . .

"I'm tired."

"I know you are. I can see."

"I can't. I can't see anything."

Anything.

Can't see.

I tried to open my eyes. "Coffee. Need coffee."

"No," he said.

"Give me a fetus," I said and wondered why I said it. It made no sense. Did it? Didn't it? So confusing. Everything was confused. My right eye hurt. The headache was right behind my right eye. Like a little man with a hammer, pounding the back of my eyeball.

"A little man," I said.

"What?"

"A little man," I explained. It was obvious. He was stupid not to understand. It was perfectly obvious, a reasonable statement from a reasonable man. Norton was just playing games, pretending he didn't understand.

"John," he said, "I want you to count backward from one hundred. Subtract seven from one hundred. Can you do that?"

I paused. It wasn't easy. In my mind, I saw a piece of paper, a shining white piece of paper, with pencil on it. One hundred minus seven. And a line, for the subtraction.

"Ninety-three."

"Good. Continue."

That was harder. It needed a new piece of paper. I had to tear the old one off the pad before I could begin with a new piece. And when I had torn the old one off, I had forgotten what was on it. Complicated. Confusing.

"Go on, John. Ninety-three."

"Ninety-three minus seven." I paused. "Eighty-five. No. Eighty-six."

"Go on."

"Seventy-nine."

"Yes."

"Seventy-three. No. Seventy-four. No, no. Wait a minute."

I was tearing off pieces of paper. So hard. And so very confusing. It was so much *work* to concentrate.

"Eighty-seven."

"No."

"Eighty-five."

"John, what day is this?"

"Day?"

What a silly question. Norton was full of silly questions today. What day is this?

"Today," I said.

"What is the date?"

"The date?"

"Yes, the date."

"May," I said. It was the date of May.

"John, where are you?"

"I am in the hospital," I said, looking down at my whites. I opened my eyes a fraction, because they were heavy and I was groggy and the light hurt my eyes. I wished he would keep quiet and let me sleep. I wanted to sleep. I needed the sleep. I was very, very tired.

"What hospital?"

"The hospital."

"What hospital?"

"The—" I started to say something, but couldn't remember what I intended to say. My headache was fierce now, pounding on the right eye, on the front of my head on the right side, a terrible pounding headache.

"Raise your left hand, John."

"What?"

"Raise your left hand, John."

I heard him, heard the words, but they were foolish. No one would pay attention to those words. No one would bother.

"What?"

The next thing I felt was a vibration, on the right side of my head. A funny rumbling vibration. I opened my eyes and saw a girl. She was pretty, but she was doing strange things to me. Brown fluffy things were falling off my head. Drifting down. Norton was watching and calling for something, but I did not understand the words. I was nearly asleep, it was all very strange. After the fluff came a lather.

And the razor. I looked at it, and the lather, and I was suddenly sick, no warning, no nothing, but vomit all over and Norton was saying, "Hurry it up, let's go."

And then they brought in the drill. I could barely see it, my eyes kept closing, and I was sick again.

The last thing I said was "No holes in my head."

I said it very clearly and slowly and distinctly.

I think.

FRIDAY, SATURDAY
& SUNDAY
OCTOBER 14, 15 & 16

ONE

IT FELT LIKE SOMEBODY had tried to cut off my head and hadn't done a very good job. When I woke up I buzzed for the nurse and demanded more morphine. She said I couldn't have it in a smiling, difficult-patient way and I suggested she go to hell. She didn't much like that but I didn't much like her. I reached up and felt the bandages on the side of my skull and made a few comments. She didn't like those any better so she left. Pretty soon Norton Hammond came in.

"You're a hell of a barber," I said, touching my head.

"I thought we did pretty well."

"How many holes?"

"Three. Right parietal. We took out quite a bit of blood. You remember any of that?"

"No," I said.

"You were sleepy, vomiting, and one pupil was dilated. We didn't wait for the X rays; we put the burr holes right in."

"Oh," I said. " When do I get out of here?"

"Three or four days, at most."

"Are you kidding? Three or four days?"

"An epidural," he said, "is a rugged thing. We want to be sure you rest."

"Do I have any choice?"

"They always say," he said, "that doctors make the worst patients."

"More morphine," I said.

"No," he said.

"Darvon."

"No."

"Aspirin?"

"All right," he said. "You can have some aspirin."

"Real aspirin? Not sugar pills?"

"Watch it," he said, "or we'll call a psychiatric consult."

"You wouldn't dare."

He just laughed and left the room.

I slept for a while, and then Judith came in to see me. She acted annoyed with me for a while, but not too long. I explained to her that it wasn't my fault and she said I was a damned fool and kissed me.

Then the police came, and I pretended to be asleep until they left.

In the evening, the nurse got me some newspapers and I searched for news about Art. There wasn't any. Some lurid stories about Angela Hard-

ing and Roman Jones, but nothing else. Judith
came again during evening visiting hours and told
me that Betty and the kids were fine and that Art
would be released the next day.

I said that was great news and she just smiled.

THERE IS NO SENSE OF TIME IN A HOSPITAL. One day
blends into the next; the routine—temperatures,
meals, doctors' rounds, more temperatures, more
meals—was everything. Sanderson came to see me,
and Fritz, and some other people. And the police,
only this time I couldn't fake sleep. I told them everything I knew and they listened and made notes.
Toward the end of the second day I felt better. I
was stronger, my head was clearer, and I was sleeping less.

I told Hammond and he just grunted and said to
wait another day.

Art Lee came to see me in the afternoon. He had
the old, wry grin on his face but he looked tired.
And older.

"Hi," I said. "How's it feel to be out?"

"Good," he said.

He looked at me from the foot of the bed and
shook his head. "Hurt much?"

"Not anymore."

"Sorry it happened," he said.

"It's all right. It was interesting, in a way. My first
epidural hematoma."

I paused. There was a question I wanted to ask
him. I had been thinking about a lot of things and

kicking myself for my foolish mistakes. The worst
had been calling that reporter into the Lees' house
that night. That had been very bad. But there were
other bad things. So I wanted to ask him.

Instead, I said, "The police have things wrapped
up now, I imagine."

He nodded. "Roman Jones was supplying Angela.
He made her do the abortion. When it failed—and
you got curious—he went over to Angela's house,
probably to kill her. He decided he was being followed and caught you. Then he went to her place
and went after her with a razor. That was what happened to your forehead."

"Nice."

"Angela fought him with a kitchen knife. Slashed
him up a little. It must have been a pleasant scene,
him with the razor and her with the knife. Finally
she managed to hit him with a chair and knock him
out the window."

"She said that?"

"Yes, apparently."

I nodded.

We looked at each other for a while.

"I appreciate your help," he said, "in all this."

"Any time. You sure it was help?"

He smiled. "I'm a free man."

"That's not what I mean," I said.

He shrugged and sat down on the edge of the
bed.

"The publicity wasn't your fault," he said. "Besides, I was getting tired of this town. Ready for a change."

"Where will you go?"

"Back to California, I guess. I'd like to live in Los Angeles. Maybe I'll deliver babies for movie stars."

"Movie stars don't have babies. They have agents."

He laughed. For a moment, it was the old laugh, the momentary self-pleasure that came when he had just heard something that amused him and had hit upon an amusing response. He was about to speak, then closed his mouth and stared at the floor. He stopped laughing.

I said, "Have you been back to the office?"

"Just to close it up. I'm making arrangements for the movers."

"When will you go?"

"Next week."

"So soon?"

He shrugged. "I'm not eager to stay."

"No," I said, "I imagine you're not."

I SUPPOSE EVERYTHING THAT HAPPENED afterward was the result of my anger. It was already a rotten business, stinking rotten, and I should have left it alone. There was no need to continue anything. I could let it go and forget about it. Judith wanted to have a farewell party for Art; I told her no, that he wouldn't like it, not really.

That made me angry, too.

On the third hospital day I bitched to Hammond until he finally agreed to discharge me. I guess the nurses had been complaining to him as well. So they let me go at 3:10 in the afternoon, and Judith brought me clothes and drove me home. On the way, I said, "Turn right at the next corner."

"Why?"

"I have to make a stop."

"John—"

"Come on, Judith. A quick stop."

She frowned, but turned right at the corner. I directed her across Beacon Hill, to Angela Harding's street. A police car was parked in front of her apartment. I got out and went up to the second floor. A cop stood outside the door.

"Dr. Berry, Mallory Lab," I said in an official tone. "Have the blood samples been taken yet?"

The cop looked confused. "Blood samples?"

"Yes. The scrapings from the room. Dried samples. For twenty-six factor determinations. You know."

He shook his head. He didn't know.

"Dr. Lazare is worried about them," I said. "Wanted me to check."

"I don't know anything about it," the cop said. "There were some medical guys here yesterday. Those the ones?"

"No," I said, "they were the dermatology people."

"Uh. Oh. Well, you better check for yourself." He opened the door for me. "Just don't touch anything. They're dusting."

I entered the apartment. It was a shambles, furniture overturned, blood spattered on couches and tables. Three men were working on a glass, dusting powder onto it and blowing it off, then photographing the fingerprints. One looked up, "Help you?"

"Yes," I said. "The chair—"

"Over there," he said, jerking his thumb toward the chair in the corner. "But don't touch it."

I went over and stared at the chair. It was not very heavy, a cheap wood kitchen chair, rather nondescript. But it was sturdily made. There was some blood on one leg.

I looked back at the three men. "You dusted this one yet?"

"Yeah. Funny thing. There's hundreds of prints in this room. Dozens of people. It's going to take us years to unravel it all. But there were two things we couldn't get prints from. That chair and the doorknob to the outside door."

"How's that?"

The man shrugged. "Been wiped."

"Wiped?"

"Yeah. Somebody cleaned up the chair and the doorknob. Anyhow, that's the way it looks. Damned funny. Nothing else was wiped, not even the knife she used on her wrists."

I nodded. "The blood boys been here yet?"

"Yeah. Came and went."

"O.K.," I said. "Can I make a call? I want to check back with the lab."

He shrugged. "Sure."

I went to the phone, picked it up, and dialed the

weather bureau. When the voice came on, I said, "Give me Dr. Lazare."

"—sunny and cool, with a high in the mid-fifties. Partly cloudly in late afternoon—"

"Fred? John Berry. I'm over at the room now."

"—with fifty-percent chance of showers—"

"Yeah, they say the samples were taken. You sure you haven't gotten them yet?"

"—tomorrow, fair and colder with a high in the forties—"

"Oh. I see. O.K. Good. Right. See you."

—"wind from the east at fifteen miles per hour—"

I hung up and turned to the three men. "Thanks," I said.

"Sure."

Nobody paid any attention to me as I left. Nobody really cared. The men who were there were doing routine duty. They'd done things like this before, dozens of times. It was just routine.

POSTSCRIPT:
MONDAY
OCTOBER 17

I WAS IN A BAD MOOD MONDAY. I sat around for most of the morning drinking coffee and smoking cigarettes and tasting a lousy sour taste in my mouth. I kept telling myself that I could drop it and nobody would care. It was over. I couldn't help Art and I couldn't undo anything. I could only make things worse.

Besides, none of this was Weston's fault, not really. Even though I wanted to blame somebody, I couldn't blame him. And he was an old man.

It as a waste of time. I drank coffee and told myself that, over and over. A waste of time.

I did it anyway.

Shortly before noon I drove over to the Mallory and walked into Weston's office. He was going over some microscopic slides and dictating his findings into a small desk recorder. He stopped when I came in.

"Hello, John. What brings you over here?"

I said, "How do you feel?"

"Me?" He laughed. "I feel fine. How do you feel?" He nodded to the bandages on my head. "I heard what happened."

"I'm okay," I said.

I looked at his hands. They were under the table, in his lap. He had dropped them down as soon as I had come into the room.

I said, "Hurt much?"

"What?"

"Your hands."

He gave me a puzzled look or tried to. It didn't work. I nodded to his hands and he brought them out. Two fingers of his left hand were bandaged.

"Accident?"

"Yes. Clumsy of me. I was chopping an onion at home—helping out in the kitchen—and I cut myself. Just a superficial wound, but embarrassing. You'd think after all these years I'd know how to handle a knife."

"You bandaged it yourself?"

"Yes. It was just a small cut."

I sat down in the chair opposite his desk and lit a cigarette, aware that he was watching me carefully. I blew a stream of smoke out, toward the ceiling. He kept his face calm and blank; he was making it hard for me. But that was his right, I guess. I'd probably do the same.

"Was there something you wanted to see me about?" he asked.

"Yes," I said.

We stared at each other for a moment, and then

Weston pushed his microscope to one side and turned off the recorder.

"Was it about the path diagnosis on Karen Randall? I'd heard you were concerned."

"I was," I said.

"Would you feel better if someone else looked them over? Sanderson?"

"Not now," I said. "It doesn't really matter now. Not legally, anyway."

"I suppose you're right," he said.

We stared at each other again, a long silence falling. I didn't know how to bring it up, but the silence was killing me.

"The chair," I said, "was wiped. Did you know that?"

For a moment, he frowned, and I thought he was going to play dumb. But he didn't; instead, he nodded.

"Yes," he said. "She told me she'd wipe it."

"And the doorknob."

"Yes. And the doorknob."

"When did you show up?"

He sighed. "It was late," he said. "I had worked late at the labs and was on my way home. I stopped by Angela's apartment to see how she was. I often did. Just stopped in. Looked in on her."

"Were you treating her addiction?"

"You mean, was I supplying her?"

"I mean, were you treating her?"

"No," he said. "I knew it was beyond me. I considered it, of course, but I knew that I couldn't

handle it, and I might make things worse. I urged
her to go for treatment, but . . ."

He shrugged.

"So instead, you visited her frequently."

"Just to try and help her over the rough time. It
was the least I could do."

"And Thursday night?"

"He was already there when I arrived. I heard scuf-
fling and shouts, so I opened the door, and found him
chasing her with a razor. She had a kitchen knife—a
long one, the kind you use for bread—and she was
fighting back. He was trying to kill her because she
was a witness. He said that, over and over. 'You're a
witness, baby,' in a low voice. I don't remember exactly what happened next. I had always been fond of
Angela. He said something to me, some words, and
started at me with the razor. He looked terrible;
Angela had already cut him with the knife, or at least,
his clothes . . ."

"So you picked up the chair."

"No. I backed off. He went after Angela. He was
facing her, away from me. That was when . . . I
picked up the chair."

I pointed to his fingers. "And your cuts?"

"I don't remember. I guess he did it. There was
a little slash on the sleeve of my coat, too, when I
got home. But I don't remember."

"After the chair—"

"He fell down. Unconscious. Just fell."

"What did you do then?"

"Angela was afraid for me. She told me to leave

immediately, that she could take care of everything. She was terrified that I would be involved. And I . . ."

"You left," I said.

He looked at his hands. "Yes."

"Was Roman dead when you left?"

"I don't really know. He had fallen near the window. I guess she just pushed him out and then wiped up. But I don't know for sure. I don't know for sure."

I looked at his face, at the lines in the skin and the white of the hair, and remembered how he had been as a teacher, how he had prodded and pushed and cajoled, how I had respected him, how he had taken the residents every Thursday afternoon to a nearby bar for drinks and talk, how he used to bring a big birthday cake in every year on his birthday and share it with everyone on the floor. It all came back, the jokes, the good times, the bad times, the questions and explanations, the long hours in the dissecting room, the points of fact and the matters of uncertainty.

"Well," he said with a sad smile, "there it is."

I lit another cigarette, cupping my hands around it and ducking my head, though there was no breeze in the room. It was stifling and hot and airless, like a greenhouse for delicate plants.

Weston didn't ask the question. He didn't have to.

"You might get off," I said, "with self-defense."

"Yes," he said, very slowly. "I might."

OUTSIDE, cold autumnal sun splashed over the bare branches of the skeletal trees along Massachusetts

Avenue. As I came down the steps of Mallory, an ambulance drove past me toward the Boston City EW. As it passed I glimpsed a face propped up on a bed in the back, with an oxygen mask being held in place by an attendant. I could see no features to the face; I could not even tell if it was a man or a woman.

Several other people on the street had paused to watch the ambulance go by. Their expressions were fixed into attitudes of concern, or curiosity, or pity. But they all stopped for a moment, to look, and to think their private thoughts.

You could tell they were wondering who the person was, and what the disease was, and whether the person would ever leave the hospital again. They had no way of knowing the answers to those questions, but I did.

This particular ambulance had its light flashing, but the siren was off, and it moved with almost casual slowness. That meant the passenger was not very sick.

Or else he was already dead. It was impossible to tell which.

For a moment, I felt a strange, compelling curiosity, almost an obligation to go to the EW and find out who the patient was and what the prognosis was.

But I didn't. Instead I walked down the street, got into my car, and drove home. I tried to forget about the ambulance, because there were millions of ambulances, and millions of people, every day, at every hospital. Eventually, I did forget. Then I was all right.

APPENDIX I:
Delicatessen Pathologists

PART OF ANY PATHOLOGIST'S JOB is to describe what he sees quickly and precisely; a good path report will allow the reader to see in his mind exactly what the pathologist saw. In order to do this, many pathologists have taken to describing diseased organs as if they were food, earning themselves the name, delicatessen pathologists.

Other pathologists are revolted by the practice; they deplore path reports that read like restaurant menus. But the device is so convenient and useful that nearly all pathologists use it, at one time or another.

Thus there are currant jelly clots and postmortem chicken-fat clots. There is ripe raspberry mucosa or strawberry gallbladder mucosa, which indicates the presence of cholesterol. There are nutmeg livers of congestive heart failure and Swiss-cheese endometria of hyperplasia. Even something as unpleasant as cancer may be described as food, as in the case of oat-cell carcinoma of the lung.

APPENDIX II:
Cops and Doctors

DOCTORS ARE GENERALLY MISTRUSTFUL of the police and try to avoid police business. One reason:

A brilliant resident at the General was called out of bed one night to examine a drunk brought in by the police. The police may know that certain medical disorders—such as diabetic coma—may closely imitate inebriation, even including an "alcoholic" breath. So this was routine. The man was examined, pronounced medically sound, and carted off to jail.

He died during the night. At autopsy, he was found to have a ruptured spleen. The family sued the resident for negligence, and the police were extraordinarily helpful to the family in attempting to put the blame on the doctor. At the trial, it was decided that the doctor had indeed been negligent, but no damages were awarded.

This doctor later tried to obtain certification from the Virginia State Board to practice in that state, and succeeded only with the greatest difficulty. This incident will follow him for the rest of his life.

While it is possible that he missed the enlarged or ruptured spleen in his examination, it is highly unlikely considering the nature of the injury and extremely high caliber of doctor. The conclusion of the hospital staff was that probably the man had received a good kick in the stomach by the police, after he had been examined.

There is, of course, no proof either way. But enough incidents such as this have occurred that doctors mistrust police almost as a matter of general policy.

APPENDIX III:
Battlefields and Barberpoles

THROUGHOUT HISTORY, surgery and war have been intimately related. Even today, of all doctors, young surgeons are the ones who least object to being sent to the battlefield. For it is there that surgeons and surgery have traditionally developed, innovated, and matured.

The earliest surgeons were not doctors at all; they were barbers. Their surgery was primitive, consisting largely of amputations, blood-letting, and wound-dressing. Barbers accompanied the troops during major campaigns and gradually came to learn more of their restorative art. They were hampered, however, by a lack of anesthesia; until

1890, the only anesthetics available were a bullet clenched between the victim's teeth and a shot of whiskey in his stomach. The surgeons were always looked down on by the medical doctors, men who did not deign to treat patients with their hands, but took a more lofty and intellectual approach. The attitude, to some extent, persists to the present day.

Now, of course, surgeons are not barbers, or vice versa. But the barbers retain the symbol of their old trade—the red-and-white-striped pole which represents the bloody white dressings of the battlefield.

But if surgeons no longer give haircuts, they still accompany armies. Wars gives them vast experience in treating trauma, wounds, crush injuries, and burns. War also allows innovation; most of the techniques now common to plastic or reconstructive surgery were developed during World War II.

All this does not necessarily make surgeons either prowar or antipeace. But the historical background of their craft does give them a somewhat different outlook from other doctors.

APPENDIX IV:
Abbreviations

DOCTORS LOVE ABBREVIATIONS, and probably no other major profession has so many. Abbreviations serve an important time-saving function, but there seems to be an additional purpose. Abbreviations are a code, a secret and impenetrable language, the cabalistic symbols of medical society.

For instance: "The PMI, corresponding to the LBCD, was located in the 5th ICS two centimeters lateral to the MCL." Nothing could be more mysterious to an outsider than that sentence.

X is the most important letter of the alphabet in medicine, because of its common use in abbreviations. Use ranges from the straightforward "Polio x3" for three polio vaccinations, to "Discharged to Ward X," a common euphemism for the morgue. But there are many others: dx is diagnosis; px, prognosis; Rx, therapy; sx, symptoms; hx, history; mx, metastases; fx, fractures.

Letter abbreviations are particularly favored in cardiology, with its endless usage of LVH, RVF, AS, MR to describe heart conditions, but other specialties have their own.

On occasion, abbreviations are used to make comments which one would not want to write out in full. This is because any patient's hospital record is a legal document which may be called into court; doctors must therefore be careful what they say, and a whole vocabulary and series of abbreviations have sprung up. For instance, a patient is not demented, but "disoriented" or "severely confused"; a patient does not lie, but "confabulates"; a patient is not stupid, but "obtunded." Among surgeons, a favorite expression to discharge a patient who is malingering is SHA, meaning "Ship his ass out of here." And in pediatrics is perhaps the most unusual abbreviation of all, FLK, which means "Funny-looking kid."

APPENDIX V:
Whites

EVERYBODY KNOWS DOCTORS WEAR WHITE UNIFORMS, and nobody, not even the doctors, knows why. Certainly the "whites," as they are called, are distinctive, but they serve no real purpose. They are not even traditional.

In the court of Louis XIV, for example, all physicians wore black: long, black, imposing robes which were as striking and awe-inspiring in their day as shining whites are now.

Modern arguments for whites usually invoke sterility and cleanliness. Doctors wear white because it is a "clean" color. Hospitals are painted white for the same reason. This sounds quite reasonable until one sees a grubby intern who has been on duty for thirty-six consecutive hours, has slept twice in his clothes, and has ministered to dozens of patients. His whites are creased, wrinkled, dirty, and no doubt covered with bacteria.

Surgeons give it all away. The epitome of aseptic conditions, of germ-free living, is found in the operating room. Yet few OR's are white, and the surgeons themselves do not wear white clothing. They wear green, or blue, or sometimes gray.

So one must consider the medical "whites" as a uniform, with no more logic to the color than the designation of blue for a navy uniform or green for an army uniform. The analogy is closer than the casual observer might expect, for the medical uniform designates rank as well as service. A doctor can walk into a ward and can tell you the rank of everyone on the ward team. He can tell you who is the resident, who the intern, who the medical student, who the male orderly. He does this by reading small cues, just as a military man reads stripes and shoulder insignias. It comes down to questions like: Is the man carrying a stethoscope? Does he have one notebook in his pocket or two? File cards held by a metal clip? Is he carrying a black bag?

The process may even be extended to indicate the specialty of a doctor. Neurologists, for example, are readily identified by the three or four straight pins stuck through their left jacket lapels.

APPENDIX VI:
Arguments on Abortion

THERE ARE GENERALLY CONSIDERED to be six arguments for abortion, and six counterarguments.

The first argument considers the law and anthropology. It can be shown that many societies routinely practice abortion and infanticide without parental guilt or destruction of the moral fiber of the society. Usually examples are drawn from marginal societies, living in a harsh environment, such as the African Pygmies or Bushmen of the Kalahari. Or from societies which place a great premium on sons and kill off excess female infants. But the same argument has used the example of Japan, now the six-largest nation in the world and one of the most highly industrialized.

The reverse argument states that Western society has little in common with either Pygmies or the Japanese, and that what is right and acceptable for them is not necessarily so for us.

Legal arguments are related to this. It can be shown that modern abortion laws did not always exist; they evolved over many centuries, in response to a variety of factors. Proponents of abortion claim that modern laws are arbitrary, foolish, and irrelevant. They argue for a legal system which accurately reflects the mores and the technology of the present, not of the past.

The reverse argument points out that old laws are not necessarily bad laws and that to change them thoughtlessly invites uncertainty and flux in an already uncertain world. A less sophisticated form of the argument opposes abortion simply because it is illegal. Until recently, many otherwise thoughtful doctors felt comfortable taking this position. Now, however, abortion is being debated in many circles, and such a simplistic view is untenable.

The second argument concerns abortion as a form of birth control. Proponents regard abortion on demand as a highly effective form of birth control and point to its success in Japan, Hungary, Czechoslovakia, and elsewhere. Proponents see no essential difference between preventing a conception and halting a process which has not yet resulted in a fully viable infant. (These same people see no difference between the rhythm method and the pill, since the intention of both practices is identical.) In essence, the argument claims that "it's the thought that counts."

Those who disagree draw a line between prevention and correction. They believe that once conception has occurred, the fetus has rights and cannot be killed. This viewpoint is held by many who favor conventional birth-control measures, and for these people, the problem of what to do if birth control fails—as it does in a certain percentage of cases—is troublesome.

The third argument considers social and psychiatric factors. It has variants.

The first states that the physical and mental health of the mother always takes precedence over that of the unborn child. The mother, and her already existing family, may suffer emotionally and financially by the birth of another infant, and therefore, in such cases the birth should be prevented.

The second states that it is immoral and criminal to bring into the world an unwanted child. It states that, in our increasingly complex society, the proper rearing of a child is a time-consuming and expensive process demanding maternal attention and paternal financial support for education. If a family cannot provide this, they do a grave disservice to the child. The obvious extreme case is that of the unwed mother, who is frequently unprepared to rear an infant, either emotionally or financially.

The counterargument is vague here. There is talk of mothers who unconsciously wish to conceive; talk of the maternal urge to procreate; flat statements that "there never was a child born who wasn't wanted." Or an ex-post-facto approach: once the child is born, the family will adjust and love him.

The fourth argument states that a woman should never, under any circumstances, be required to bear a child if she does not wish to do so. Abortion on demand should be a right of every woman, like the right to vote. This is an interesting argument, but its usefulness has been diluted by many of its proponents, who often express a rather paranoid feeling that the world is dominated by men who cannot be expected to show any sympathy for the opposite sex.

Those who disagree with this argument usually point out that a modern, emancipated woman need not become pregnant if she does not wish it. A wide variety of birth-control methods and devices is available to her, and they believe that abortion is not a substitute for birth control. The case of birth-control failure and inadvertent pregnancy—such as rape—are difficult to handle within this framework, however.

The fifth argument states that abortion is safe, easy, simple, and cheap; thus there can be no practical objection to legalizing termination of pregnancy.

The counterargument states that abortion carries a finite risk of mortality, which, though small, nonetheless exists. Unfortunately for this viewpoint, it is now perfectly clear that a hospital abortion is one-sixth to one-tenth as dangerous as a hospital delivery. This means it is safer to abort a child than to carry it to term.

The sixth argument is the newest and the most ingenious. It was first proposed by Garrett Hardin, and it attacks the problem at a crucial question: Is abortion murder? Hardin says no. He argues that the embryo does not become human until after birth and a long period of training. He states that the embryo is nothing but a template, ultimately derived from DNA, the information-carrying genetic substance. Information in itself, he says, is of no value. It is like a blueprint. The blueprint of a building, he says, is worthless; only the building has value and significance. The blueprint may be destroyed with impunity, for another can easily be made, but a building cannot be destroyed without careful deliberation.

This is a swift and oversimplified summary of his argument. Hardin was trained both as an anthropologist and as a biologist, and his viewpoint is unique. It is interesting because it considers the question of *when* is a person human in terms of *what* is a human being? Returning to the analogy of blueprint and building, the blueprint specifies size, shape, and general structure, but it does not state whether the building will be erected in New York or Tokyo, whether in a slum or an affluent area, whether it will be used effectively or fall into disrepair. By implication, Hardin is defining a human being not only as an animal that walks on its hind legs, has a large brain, and an opposable thumb; he includes in the definition enough maternal care and education to make a person a well-adjusted and functioning unit of a social grouping.

The counterargument says that Hardin assumes DNA is a "non-unique" copy of information, when in fact it is quite unique. All children of a given mother and father are not identical; therefore the DNA cannot be "non-unique."

To this Hardin replies that we already, quite by chance, select only some of the potential DNA combinations of sperm and egg and allow these to reach maturation. He notes that an average woman has 30,000 eggs in her ovaries, yet will bring only a few to term. The others are destroyed just as surely as if they had been aborted. And, as he says, one of them might have been "a super Beethoven."

Hardin's argument is still new and strikes many as abstruse. But undoubtedly his is just the first of many new arguments, for and against abortion, which will be proposed on an increasingly subtle scientific basis. It is a commentary on modern man that he must justify his morality on the basis of the molecular mechanisms at work within a single cell of his body.

There are other arguments, but they are mostly evasive and petty. There are economic arguments concerning the cost of turning hospitals into abortion mills; there are vague and wild-eyed arguments of unleashed libertinism, similar to the arguments heard before the introduction of birth-control pills. There are also reflex liberal arguments that anything freer is by definition good and meritocratic arguments that the outpouring of children from the lower classes should be stemmed. There is no point in considering these viewpoints. They are advanced, for the most part, by thoughtless and irritable little men.

APPENDIX VII:
Medical Morals

IN MEDICINE TODAY, there are four great moral questions involving the conduct of medical practice. One is abortion. Another is euthanasia, the killing of a patient with a terminal and incurable illness. A third concerns the social responsibility of the doctors to administer care to as many people as possible. A fourth concerns the definition of death.

The interesting thing is that all these problems are new. They are products of our technology, moral and legal problems which have sprung up within the last decade or so.

Hospital abortion, for example, must now be regarded as a relatively inexpensive and safe procedure, carrying a mortality rate roughly similar to a tooth extraction. This was not always true, but in the modern context it is, and we must therefore deal with it.

Euthanasia was once much less serious a problem. When doctors had fewer "supportive" aids, artificial respirators, and knowledge of electrolyte balances, patients with terminal illnesses tended to die quickly. Now, medicine faces the fact that a person can be kept technically alive for an indefinite period, though he can never be cured. Thus the doctor must decide whether supportive therapy should be instituted and for how long. This is a problem because doctors have traditionally felt that they should keep their patients alive as long as possible, using every available technique. Now, the morality—and even the humanity—of such an approach must be questioned.

There is a corollary: whether the patient facing an incurable disease has the right to refuse supportive therapy; whether a patient facing weeks or months of terminal pain has a right to demand an easy and painless death; whether a patient who has put himself in a doctor's hands still retains ultimate life-and-death control over his own existence.

Social responsibility in its modern terms—responsibility to a community, not an individual—is something rather new to medicine. Formerly patients who were indigent were treated by kind doctors, or not at all; now, there is a growing feeling that medical care is a right, not a privilege. There is also a growing number of patients who were once charity cases but are now covered by health insurance or Medicare. The physician is today being forced to reconsider his role, not in terms of those patients who can afford to seek his help, but in terms of all the people in the community. Related to this is the increased medical emphasis on preventive care.

The definition of death is a problem with a single cause: organ transplants. As surgeons become more skilled in transplanting parts from the dead to the living, the question of when a man is dead becomes crucial, because transplantable organs should be removed as rapidly as possible from a dead man. The old, crude indicators—no pulse, no breathing—have been replaced by no EKG activity, or a flat EEG, but the question is still unresolved, and may not be for many years to come.

There is another problem involving medical ethics, and that concerns the doctor and the drug companies. This is currently being fought over in a four-way tug-of-war involving patient, doctor, government, and drug manufacturer. The issues, and the eventual outcome, are still unclear.

More bestselling fiction from Michael Crichton in Arrow . . .

DISCLOSURE

The thriller that opened a new chapter in the sex wars

Thomas Sanders' world collapses in just 24 hours – he is passed over for promotion, his new woman boss comes on to him during a drink after work, then, the next morning, he learns that she has accused him of sexually harassing her. She demands his transfer, thereby threatening to cut him off from the millions he would have made when his high-tech company was floated on the stock market.

What follows next made *Disclosure* the most talked about novel for decades.

'Sexual dynamite . . . Controversial and superbly written'
Daily Mail

'Throat-gripping'
Peter Hitchens, *Daily Express*

'Wonderfully entertaining'
Penny Perrick, *Sunday Times*

JURASSIC PARK

The No 1 International Bestseller

'The most frightening novel about dinosaurs . . . since *The Lost World*. Crichton's most compulsive novel yet'
Sunday Telegraph

On a remote jungle island, genetic engineers have created a dinosaur game park.

Drawing on all his bestselling talent and scientific brilliance Michael Crichton has, in *Jurassic Park*, written the most electrifying techo-thriller of our time.

'His best since *The Andromeda Strain*'
Time

'Breathtaking adventure . . . a book that is as hard to put down as it is to forget'
Time Out